Love Starts with Elle

Other Novels by Rachel Hauck

Love Starts with Elle
Sweet Caroline
Dining with Joy
Diva Nashvegas
Lost in Nashvegas

Novels Co-authored with Sara Evans

The Sweet By and By
Softly and Tenderly (available January 2011)

Love Starts with Elle

A Lowcountry Romance

Rachel Hauck

THOMAS NELSON
Since 1798

NASHVILLE DALLAS MEXICO CITY RIO DE JANEIRO

Published in Nashville, Tennessee by Thomas Nelson. Thomas Nelson is a registered trademark of Thomas Nelson, Inc.

Thomas Nelson, Inc. books may be purchased in bulk for educational, business, fund-raising, or sales promotional use. For information, please e-mail SpecialMarkets@ThomasNelson.com.

Publisher's Note: This novel is a work of fiction. Names, characters, places, and incidents are either products of the author's imagination or used fictitiously. All characters are fictional, and any similarity to people living or dead is purely coincidental.

ISBN 978-1-59554-897-9 (repak)

Library of Congress Cataloging-in-Publication Data

Hauck, Rachel, 1960–
 Love starts with Elle / Rachel Hauck.
   p. cm.
 ISBN 978-1-59554-338-7 (softcover)
 1. Women art dealers—Fiction. 2. Clergy—Fiction. 3. Art galleries—South Carolina—Beaufort—Fiction.
4. Beaufort (S.C.)—Fiction. I. Title.
 PS3608.A866L68 2008
 813'.6—dc22   2008020868

Printed in the United States of America

10 11 12 13 RRD 6 5 4 3 2 1

For my grandma, Grace Fausnaugh.

"I found I could say things with color and shapes that I couldn't say any other way—things I had no words for."

—Georgia O'Keefe (1887–1986)

One

BEAUFORT, SC
December 21

From the loft of her Bay Street art gallery, Elle Garvey leaned against the waist-high wall, admiring GG Galley's "Art in Christmas" show. Visitors and patrons—some Beaufort residence, others curious tourists—milled among the displays, speaking in low tones, sipping hot cider.

The mellow voice of Andy Williams serenaded them. "It's the most wonderful time of the year . . ."

"Elle, are you the queen, surveying her kingdom?" Arlene Coulter gazed up from the bottom of the loft stairs, her bright red Christmas suit its own fashion work of art.

"Yes, and are you my loyal servant?"

Arlene curtsied, her bottle-blonde hair falling forward like silky angel hair, the hem of her skirt sliding up her knee. "Yours and yours alone, O you of whom *Art News* wrote, 'One of the lowcountry's finest galleries.'"

"Best hundred-dollar bribe I ever spent." Elle descended the stairs, catching sight of her baby sister, Julianne, selling a bronze sculpture to a young woman wearing pearls.

"Darling"—Arlene linked arms with Elle and led her to the back wall—"your artist eye is truly God gifted. Tell me now . . . is this the work of the great Alyssa Porter?"

"It is." Elle surveyed the paintings. They spoke to her each time she viewed them. She envied Alyssa and artists like her—the ones who had the courage to chase *the* dream.

Elle had lost hers a long time ago.

"And what do you like about this artist?" Arlene squeezed Elle's arm tighter.

"Her paintings move me." Elle freed herself from Arlene and moved to Alyssa's *Rose Garden*, convinced it'd be a masterpiece one day.

"Move you?" Arlene studied one of the abstracts through a one-eyed slit, her short, red-tipped fingers squeezing the point of her chin. "I suppose they move me too. I'm just not sure where."

"You're looking for a definite image, Arlene. Don't be so concrete. Let your imagination run . . ." Elle hooked her arm around the woman's shoulders. "Follow my hand. See how you just moved out of the sunlight into the shade?"

"No, but, girl, I really love your bracelets. Where'd you get those?" Arlene grabbed Elle's wrist to study the tricolor bangles.

"You beat all, Arlene." Elle twisted her hand free.

"Well, a good set of bracelets is hard to find." Arlene gazed again at the painting. "So, what should I do about Miss Porter?"

"Buy her. The New York art scene has discovered Alyssa and if you don't purchase something before her first auction, you'll never be able to afford it. Here . . ." Elle walked to the other side of the display. "This one on the bottom right is only two thousand dollars."

Arlene stood an inch way from the bottom painting, tipping her head to one side. The track lighting haloed the back of her head.

"I'm afraid if I buy one of these I'll wake up one night with the dang thing hanging over my head whispering, 'I see dead people.'"

"If it does, call Pastor O'Neal, not me."

Arlene bent in half as if she hung upside down, then snapped upright. "What about this artist over here. Coco Nelson. Now this I get. Look—a woman's face, with eyes and hair."

"Coco's a wonderful artist," Elle said. "Very realistic work. This series is called 'Love and Romance.'"

"Very fitting for you, sugar." Arlene arched a brow at Elle. "This piece, *Proposal*, is stunning." Her voice rose and fell into a sing-song.

Elle ignore her subtle teasing. "Yes, there's something about it. An ordinary gentleman down on one knee proposing to an ordinary woman."

But the emotion Coco evoked in the scene was anything but ordinary. When she'd sent in the piece, Elle couldn't hang it at first. Too embarrassed after last year's Operation Wedding Day fiasco when she tried to date every available bachelor in Beaufort. She wanted no reminders of love and romance.

Until Jeremiah Franklin.

"Okay." Arlene spun around. "I'll take the Alyssa Porter and this Coco Nelson."

"You won't regret it."

"Says who?" Arlene passed Alyssa's abstract piece again, side-stepping the image as if it might spring to life and spar with her.

Elle laughed, leading the way to her desk across the old, former hardware store. She treasured the talented, sometimes whacky, interior designer who landed lowcountry clients like doctors, lawyers, and hotel developers. In the early days of GG Gallery, business from Coulter Designs had helped keep the gallery lights burning and Elle's hopes alive.

"What's the damage?" Arlene flashed her checkbook.

"Hold on, now, let me add a few more zeroes." Elle jammed her finger on the adding machine's Zero button.

"Add all you want. I'm only writing three." Arlene fanned her face with her opened checkbook. "So, how's it going with the good pastor?"

The mere hint of Dr. Jeremiah Franklin made Elle feel bubbly. "Good."

"If the glow on your cheeks is any indication, I'd say it's more than good. How long y'all been together now? Few months?"

"Two." Elle wrote up Arlene's order with a ten-percent discount.

"And it's love?" Arlene leaned to see Elle's eyes. "Don't tell me it ain't 'cause I can see it written all over your face."

"Here." Elle laughed low, passing over the order ticket with the total circled. "I appreciate your business—and nosiness—Arlene."

"Any time, sugar. Any time." Arlene peeked at the total, then started to write.

"Hey, babe."

Jeremiah.

He still took her breath away after two months. When he'd told her he loved her in the setting sunlight during a beach walk, Elle had handed him her heart on a silver—no, gold—platter. Key included.

"Jer, what are you doing here?" She met him on the other side of her desk and stepped into his arms. His fragrance awakened her yearnings.

"I'm on my way to rehearse tomorrow's sermon. Couldn't pass the gallery without stopping in for a minute." His kiss was soft and sweet, a pastorly display of public affection. But enough to make Elle glad to be a woman. His woman. "We're still on for dinner?"

"Absolutely. You still haven't said where you wanted to go."

Jeremiah's hazel wink teased her. "Patience, girl. Do you have to know everything?"

"Do you not know me after these few months?"

"Exactly . . ." He stooped for another soft kiss and backed away. "Good to see you, Arlene."

"You too, Dr. Franklin." Arlene watched Jeremiah exit the building with a wave. "Hmm-um, Elle, it must be breaking your heart." *Rippp*. She handed over her check.

"What? What are you talking about?" Elle brushed the check absently between her fingers.

Arlene gaped at Elle with an "Um, what now?" expression, then punched the air with a darn-it fist, chewing her bottom lip. "Me and my mouth. Shoot fire, my Dirk will kill me." She clutched her butter-colored Dooney & Burke to her chest. "Just forget I said anything, Elle. I am so sorry." She whirled around and hurried away with a swirling, swing-swing of her hips. "See you in church."

"Oh no you don't." Arlene's diverse network of informants was infamous—a mixture of truth and town lore, and eerily accurate. Elle scurried after her, blocking her before she reached the door. "You can't drop a bomb like that then wiggle out of here with a 'see you in church.' What were you talking about?"

"First of all, I have a very natural swing to my hips. It's what caught Dirk's eye in the first place, mind you. As for the other, well, Elle, Jeremiah can tell you himself. Don't worry. It's good, I think." She squared her red-jacketed shoulders. "Like I said, see you in church."

Elle watched her go, thoughts racing. Jeremiah had just been here. He'd acted perfect, like always. What was Arlene talking about? This time her information network must have supplied the wrong details. *What did you hear, Arlene Coulter?*

"Elle, Mrs. Beisner is curious about a discount for buying three pieces." Julianne held out an order pad, tapping the total. During art show openings and art fairs, Elle's baby sister worked part time for GG Gallery. "What do you think, fifteen percent?"

"Sure." Elle raked her hair with her fingers. "Whatever she wants."

Julianne observed her sister through narrowed eyes. "Whatever she wants? Elle, are you okay?"

"I don't know." Elle walked around Jules to her desk and opened the bottom drawer where her handbag lived. "Can you watch the gallery for me?"

"Where are you going?"

"To uncover a rumor." She didn't feel like waiting until dinner to hear his news—if there was any news.

"Now?" Julianne called after her.

"I won't be long." But the front door was blocked by Huckleberry

Johns and his fish tank of eco art. *Oh, please, not tonight.* "Huck, what are you doing? You're dripping muddy water all over my clean floor."

With a lopsided grin, he scanned the gallery, vying for attention. "I call it *Death at Coffin Creek.*" He raised his composition of reeking pluff mud and marsh grass. "Developers are ruining our ecosystem."

Elle dropped her shoulders in fake defeat. "Huckleberry, you are too good-looking and too young to be so weird." She grabbed his shoulders and turned him around. "Out. You're stinking up the place. Julianne, we need a mop up here."

Huck was an art school dropout—or, rather, they'd dropped him—and he hit the sidewalk, protesting, "I deserve to be heard."

"Not in my gallery." Elle stepped out after him. "Right message, wrong venue, Huck."

"Snob."

Elle's smile broke. "Slob. Talk about it later?"

"It may be too late."

"For who? You or Coffin Creek?" Elle backed up the sidewalk in the direction of her car.

"You." Huck hollered between his wide grin, spinning off in the opposite direction, disappearing around the corner.

Elle held the sanctuary door so it closed quietly without squeaking or thudding. She paused for her eyes to adjust to the dim light, then spotted Jeremiah up front, striding across the stage as he rehearsed his sermon, his lips moving in silent recitation.

His movement was graceful and controlled, an extension of his inner being.

"He can preach up a storm, that one." A slight, round-shouldered, snowy-haired Miss Anna Carlisle emerged from one of the sanctuary's dark pockets, jabbing her finger toward Jeremiah.

"Then we should bring our umbrellas tomorrow," Elle said, giving Miss Anna's shoulders a hug.

"Best to be prepared, I suppose." Miss Anna's pushed open the sanctuary door. "I'm praying for that boy," she said with a wag of her finger. "And you." Her words were intentional and steady.

"For me?" Elle asked.

"For you."

Elle regarded her for a moment. "Are you walking? Can I give you a ride?" Elle went with the older woman through the foyer to the outer doors.

"I do believe it's a fine, crisp evening for walking." She buttoned the top button of her blue sweater and buried her hands in the frayed pockets. Elle thought the garment's spacious weave would do little against the night's chill. "Good night, Elle."

"Are you sure you want to walk, Miss Anna?"

"I'm sure."

Elle watched her until she disappeared between the trees and night lights. Then, back inside, she slipped into the back pew and watched Jeremiah practice his message. She'd never met a man like him—one who breathed in confidence and exhaled all doubt.

Her emotions tugged between the man she knew and Arlene's slipup. *What's going on, Jeremiah? If anything?*

Even for a Saturday-night sermon rehearsal, Jeremiah wore gray slacks and a starched cotton button-down. For the hundredth time, Elle wondered how he'd survived three years in the National Football League, three years of Bible college, and seven years of full-time ministry single.

But she wasn't complaining. God had saved the best for her.

Under the low stage lights, Jeremiah paused as if waiting for a response. He acted out a laugh, making his way to center stage with an even gait. At the podium, he gripped the sides and leaned toward the empty sanctuary, bobbing his head to the beat of internal words. *Can I get an "Amen," somebody?*

Why not oblige? "Amen." Elle rose from the pew as Jeremiah squinted beyond the spotlights into the shadowy sanctuary.

"Elle, babe? Is that you?" He came off the stage with a touchdown power stride. "Is everything all right?"

"Yeah, fine, but"—she met him in the middle of the aisle—"I heard a rumor."

He growled, teasing her. "Is that ever good?" He touched his lips to hers with the passion that came when they were alone. "What kind of rumor?"

"Something about you and my breaking heart, Jeremiah."

"And who delivered such almost horrifying news?" He locked his arms around her waist, his hazel eyes searching hers.

"Arlene Coulter, though she stopped herself when she saw I didn't know what she was talking about."

"She heard from her husband, one of our trusty elders?"

"Who else?" Elle broke her gaze from Jeremiah's, smoothing her hand over the crisp surface of his shirt.

"You'd think the man would know better after twenty-five years of marriage."

"And what should I know after two months of dating?"

He brushed her hair away from her shoulder, letting his fingertips graze her skin. "Can it wait for dinner?"

His touch was fiery to her. "You tell me. Can it?"

"Are we answering questions with questions?"

"Are we?" Some time in the past week they'd started this new back-and-forth questions-with-questions dance.

"Did I start this, or you?"

"Does it matter?"

"Only if we want to get off this ride." He pressed his lips to hers again, breathing deep.

His kisses defied all bad news.

"Tell you what." He held up his wrist to see his watch in the stage light. "I'm almost done here. Another thirty minutes. What time does the gallery close?"

"Nine."

"Can Julianne close up for you? We'll slip off to dinner."

"If I pay her." Elle brushed her hand down the sleeve his oxford shirt. "That girl's all about *moh-ney*." She eyed him. "Monet. *Mo-net* . . . Get it?"

"Yes, I get it. Artist jokes. So, meet me here in thirty?" He walked backward to the stage. "Remember, I love you."

"What's up, Dr. Franklin? If I have to remember . . ." She caught the high and low contours of his face as he stood under the lights. "Not a good sign."

His smile dried up the beginnings of her self-pity. "Just remember, Elle."

Two

Elle followed Jeremiah's Honda down Hwy 21, surprised when he turned on Fripp Point Road toward her Coffin Creek cottage.

Coffin Creek. The environment Huckleberry claimed was dying. But as Elle parked alongside Jeremiah under the drooping branches of a live oak, she could hear the dissonant song of life thriving in and along the creek's murky water.

"This is where you're taking me to dinner?" she asked, approaching Jeremiah as he waited by the backyard gate in the silver light of the "starry, starry night."

"Yes, but"—he swung her into his arms—"you don't have to cook."

"Please tell me you're not cooking." She laughed against his chest. The first and last time Jeremiah cooked for Elle he served his house specialty, mac-n-cheese with cut-up hot dogs.

"Never fear." He fastened his arm around her waist and walked with her to the back porch. "Close your eyes."

"Close my eyes?"

"Yes, close your eyes."

Elle made a face. She didn't liked surprises. "Okay, but I'm counting to ten, then opening them."

"Give me twenty."

Standing with her eyes closed, she could hear Jeremiah fumbling around, running across the sun-washed boards muttering, "Hot, hot, hot." She heard the scrape of a match, followed by the kitchen door opening, then banging shut. The aroma of tomato sauce and garlic bread. Her stomach rumbled.

"What are you doing?" Twenty seconds had passed.

"Okay, open them."

When she did, Elle found her back porch warm and inviting with hundreds of white lights twinkling around a crystal-and-china-set table for two.

"Jeremiah, this is beautiful." She peeked under the foil-covered plates, her pulse racing. Arlene had one thing right: something was up.

"The lasagna is courtesy of Mrs. Marks." Jeremiah held out a chair draped with a blanket. "For you."

Elle sat though she floated. "If this is what Arlene is sad about, I'm most certainly not."

Jeremiah knelt next to her, eye to eye. When his lips met hers, Elle's heart throbbed in her throat, against her temples. Her senses were addicted to him.

"I hope I haven't overwhelmed you by moving too fast, too soon."

Too late. "What else would a former wide receiver do but run fast once he caught his girl?" She inhaled the air around him. "I just need a moment to catch my breath now and then."

Jeremiah cupped her neck with his hand, stroking her cheek with his thumb. "My first Sunday at Beaufort Community, Pastor O'Neal introduced me and asked me to say a few words. I sat on the first row during worship, focused but feeling at home in my new church. I'd practiced my two-minute greeting in front of the mirror a dozen times."

"How could I forget? You captured us all that morning."

"I wasn't prepared to look out over the congregation and see a gorgeous strawberry blonde with apple-green eyes."

She pressed her lips to his palm. "I certainly wasn't prepared for you."

"For a split second, I was caught in this Star Trek-like vortex. You were the only person in the room and I couldn't remember what I wanted to say or, oddly enough, where I was."

"You exaggerate." Elle exhaled the same moment the creek released its breeze.

"The next few times I preached, I found you in the congregation during worship and made sure I never looked your way."

"So, how does this answer Arlene Coulter's speculation?" Elle huddled close to Jeremiah, shivering with the night chill and anticipation.

"First things first." Raising his hand, Jeremiah dropped a small black-velvet box next to her plate, then looked into her eyes. "Elle Garvey, will you marry me?"

What? "Marry you?" She glanced from him to the ring box and back again. She'd expected a lot of things—but not this. After two months of dating, was he serious?

"Marry me. I love you. You are exceptional. I've waited a long time to ask a woman this question. Elle, please, say yes." Jeremiah opened the box, holding it up for Elle to see the diamond in the candlelight.

"Oh, Jeremiah." His proposal sent sparks all over her, but she had to snap the box shut. "Wait, wait. Tonight Arlene tried to console 'my breaking heart,' but it was really about you're asking me to marry you?"

Jeremiah laced his fingers through Elle's, still kneeling beside her chair. "Goes to show you Arlene doesn't know everything."

"Then tell me, what does she know, Jer?"

"Elle." Jeremiah took the platinum band from its velvet bed and slipped it onto Elle's finger. "Do you love me?"

The candles, the lights, the aroma of pasta, garlic, and sauce mingling with the cool dew of the night eased her anxiety. "Yes, I believe I do."

"Then marry me. This is right, I know it."

"I'll marry you, Jeremiah. Yes."

His arms shot over his head in victory. "She said yes!" He pulled her from her chair and locked her against him, sealing the deal with a hot, searching kiss. Finally, when he'd stolen her last bit of air, he pulled away. "Hungry?"

"Yes." Elle fell limply against him. When she opened her eyes, Jeremiah's smile looked a bit wicked.

"I meant for lasagna."

She flirted, tipping her chin to her raised shoulder. "So did I."

"Oh, I see how it's going to be." He grabbed her for another kiss, drawing her close, pressing his hands tightly against her spine.

Elle backed away when temptation bullied her senses. "Jer, let's eat before we do things we'll regret."

He sighed, his breath hot against her skin. "Sorry, Elle, but when I'm with you . . ."

Her passions cooled while Jeremiah dished up Mrs. Marks's excellent cooking and Elle drilled him about the details. *What did Daddy say? And Pastor O'Neal? Do you want to move into the cottage after the wedding? Do you want a spring wedding? Jeremiah, I've only met your parents once. Are they excited?*

He answered steadily, laughing as he recounted his meeting with Daddy. "He paused so long before giving his blessing he actually had me sweating."

"He tries to be a grumpy ole bear, but he's really a gentle Ben. Like he'd refuse the pastor anyway."

"He seemed pleased."

Elle thought tonight would always be a treasured memory, including Arlene's heartbreak scare. "Wait until Arlene hears, Jeremiah. She had it wrong this time."

Jeremiah reached for his tea. "Not entirely."

Elle studied him mid-chew. "What do you mean?"

"What Arlene does know is I've been offered a large church in Dallas, Elle."

"Dallas?" Absently, she wiped the corners of her mouth with a stiff linen napkin.

"Remember when I went home in October? We'd just started dating and I wasn't sure where our relationship was headed. Some friends invited me to interview at their church—a big metropolitan congregation, multicultural, growing beyond their ability to handle it."

"You never mentioned it." Her heart beat to a different rhythm now. Leaving Beaufort?

"Didn't think they'd come back with an offer. But they did. A few weeks ago. I would've told you, but I needed to work out a lot of details. Pray. Talk to Pastor O'Neal and the board."

"I see. So you accepted?"

"I did. Gave notice to the board this morning. I leave the day after Christmas, but I hope we are going together, you and me."

Sitting back in the Rubbermaid chair, Elle pondered Jeremiah's news. Moving? Texas? She'd moved back to Beaufort after college and studying in Florence because she wanted to be home, near her four sisters and their families, near Daddy and Mama, reconnecting with lifelong friends. Building her life upon their foundation.

"I never imagined moving from Beaufort again." Jeremiah's ring slipped around on her cold, trembling finger so the diamond was upside down.

Jer reached over, tucking the blanket in around her. "Babe, I need you with me. Please don't say this is a deal breaker."

Deal breaker? Good grief. Were they ending before they'd even started? "No, Jeremiah, I feel a little overwhelmed, that's all." Her laugh jittered. "A girl gets a proposal and a chance to move across country . . . all in one night."

"I'm sorry to spring it on you like this. I wasn't sure of the best approach." Jeremiah's countenance remained firm, confident. "You'll love this congregation. It's about six hundred members and growing, knee deep in a building project, desperate to add another Sunday service." He rubbed his palms together. "Rocking worship band, lots of ministries and activity going on."

"So, you really told them yes?" She twisted the ring around her finger until the diamond captured the candlelight.

He took his knife and slowly buttered his bread. "I tried to figure out if I should propose to you first or answer them. After thinking it over and praying, I decided to answer yes to the job, get it out of the way, not encumber our new relationship with such a huge decision. Besides, what if you said no?"

"You do realize our new engagement *is* encumbered with this decision?"

He nodded, biting off the tip of his bread. "I suppose so. No way around it."

The buttery aroma wafted past Elle. "Jeremiah, I love living here. I have a business. The art scene is robust and thriving."

"I see." Jeremiah dropped the remainder of his bread on top of the last bit of lasagna. "Then your answer is no?"

No, her answer was . . . uncertainty. Elle's pulse picked up. "I just need a second to process all of this." She untucked the blanket and walked to the edge of the porch. "Dallas, huh?"

All she knew of Dallas was an eighties nighttime soap opera her mama had watched after she and her sisters went to bed. If they came down for any unexpected reason, Daddy intercepted and dealt with them in the kitchen or living room, but always away from the TV and *Dallas*.

"It's a great city, Elle. They also have a very thriving, robust art scene." He came up from behind and embraced her. "I want you with me. I need you. You're the love of my life."

Well, if that confession didn't just warm a girl's cold feet. Elle turned in his arms. "And you're the love of mine. But see it from my point of view. I'm engaged for thirty minutes before I discover my future has been determined for me. In my mind, I've planned my life here. My gallery is here."

"I understand. But I have to go where the Lord is calling me, Elle. I hope you believe He's calling you to be with me."

She pressed her cheek to his chest, exhaling as he slipped his arms around her back. "Then you must go to Dallas, Jeremiah."

"And you?"

Elle roped her arms around his neck, kissing the base of his neck. "Since October, you've been a face, a voice, a touch on all my days. How can I walk away now? I love you. I want to marry you. I'm terrified, Jeremiah, but if you're going to be in Dallas, then so am I."

NEW YORK CITY

The knock on the door didn't inquire but demanded. "Tell me it's not true."

"Okay . . . it's not true." Heath dropped a copier-paper box on his desk and peeked from under his brow at Catherine Perry, who powered her way across his office in her blue, retro-eighties power suit.

"Heath, be serious."

Ah, her retro-eighties power voice. He'd miss her brilliant mind on a day-to-day basis, but not her I-am-woman-hear-me-roar inflections.

"You talked to Rock, I take it?" Heath gathered the pictures from the credenza without reminiscing over the images behind the glass. He'd been packing up little by little since last summer.

"If you leave the firm, even for a few months, it will kill your career." Catherine whacked the desk with her knuckles. "Rock's fought for you against the other partners, especially last summer when your life got complicated and they wanted to throw you over. Is this how you thank him? By resigning?"

"I'm not resigning. I'm taking a leave of absence—there's a difference." He regarded her with a hard glance. "I can't stay in Manhattan, Cate."

"Then move to White Plains, Poughkeepsie, or Connecticut, for crying out loud. Leaving a successful boutique firm like Calloway & Gardner is career insanity, Heath." She sounded like she did when key evidence wasn't going her way.

"Right now, I care about my personal sanity. Did you know I was late for the Glendale arraignment because I thought I saw Ava walking down Lexington Avenue?" He stared into the box. "I chased a scared, skinny teen boy with great hair for ten blocks."

Catherine covered her mouth. "Oh, Heath."

"Laugh. It's funny." Heath shoved the box with a fast pop of his palm. "But also very sad."

What he didn't confess to his prying co-counsel was how Ava's fragrance lingered in the apartment, no matter how many times it was cleaned. Or how he felt claustrophobic and chained up, how hope felt like a dirty little four-letter word.

He didn't confess to Catherine how he longed to be in a place that held no memories of *her*. Perhaps then he could draw a breath without a million pin-sized flames burning his lungs.

"Healing takes time, Heath. It's only been a few months." Catherine straightened the papers lying on the corner of the desk. "Rock said you weren't leaving right away?"

"Not until March."

"What about Tracey-Love?"

"I thought I'd take her with me." He put the lid on the box and walked it over to his closet, where dozen of other boxes waited. Some with case work, others with personal items and records. While Catherine watched, he emptied another drawer into another box and shoved on the lid, anchoring it with a crooked piece of tape. "This is for her as much as anyone."

"Really? Moving her to Hooterville, South Carolina?"

"It's Beaufort, and really, Cate, you should open your mind sometime and see what junk falls out."

As she clucked and fussed, trying to come up with one of her cunning replies, Rock Calloway entered without knocking and plopped into one of the matching leather club chair's opposite Heath's desk. "Cate, give us a minute."

Besides his father, Heath respected no man more than Rock Calloway. The sixty-four-year-old lawyer believed in the rule of law, in finding truth and dispensing justice. Behind his clear gray eyes, he still clung to the idea that right would always win.

"Just left Doc and Tom. They're concerned about the Glendale case, consider you leaving as a slap in the client's face and disloyalty to the firm."

"They can choose to believe what they want, but the truth is I haven't been an asset in months. Art Glendale would get life without parole if I tried his case."

Rock's rich white grin denied his years. "They'd hoped you'd kick in, fight this thing with Ava by throwing yourself into your work."

This thing? "Sorry to let them down, but until any of the partners have walked in my shoes . . ."

Rock surrendered with a flash of his palms. "I'm on your side, Heath."

"Tell them I'll do all I can on the case before I leave in March." Heath sat in his chair, facing Rock. His office matched his mood, barren and empty except for the basic necessities.

"I suppose you're going to tinker with novel writing again."

"Thought I might use the downtime to write, yes. Maybe come up with a novel that'll sell this time." Rock muffled his grin, but Heath caught the humor behind his eyes. "Go ahead, I know what you're thinking."

Rock chuckled. "Your first novel was . . . well, I'd read legal briefs more riveting."

Heath grinned, remembering how he'd passed his first novel, *Remove All Doubt*, around the office, convinced he'd bested Hemmingway. Made him the brunt of office jokes for months. But since then, he'd studied, improved, finished two more novels, and convinced Nate Collins, his old Yale classmate turned high-powered agent, to represent him.

"This thing"—now Rock had Heath saying it—"with Ava caused me to realize I can't always count on tomorrow. The sun may rise, but not for me."

Rock's soft laugh was one of speculative realization. "You make a point."

"I rented a cottage by a creek down near Beaufort, South Carolina. Little area called St. Helena."

Rock tightened his lips and nodded. "Sounds quaint."

"My grandfather owned a place on Edisto Island in the eighties and nineties. My brother Mark and I used to run the creeks and rivers, building forts, playing soldiers. Granddad's place is gone, but going back felt like a good place to start over."

"Heath, Doc and Tom won't let me hold your partnership for more than six months. Had to fight them for it. Best and worst thing I ever did was pair up with those two after Bill Gardner died. He was a great partner. Either way, I'm not calling the shots alone anymore."

"I understand, Rock, and appreciate you going to bat for me."

"I can't imagine the small-town South Carolina life will suit you for long. You're a New Yorker, a Yankee, and a lawyer." Rock arched his foot so the back of his chocolate-brown loafers dangled from his heel. "What about your daughter? Her education?"

"She's only four, Rock."

"Are you telling me her name wasn't put on a dozen elite pre-K lists five minutes after she was born? She should be enrolled by now, ready to start in the fall."

Heath ran his hand around his neck, stretching to relieve the steady tension. "Geneva and St. Luke's. But life changed, didn't it?

Took three people and ripped their lives apart. Right now, I just want to piece our lives back together. This move will be good, just the two of us in that cottage. No nanny, no sixty-hour work weeks."

Rock pinched his eyebrows together. "You've only been working sixty hours? Had I known you've been slacking . . ."

It felt good to laugh. "This from the man who leaves every afternoon at four with his tennis bag. Yeah, don't look surprised. I see you."

Rock owned up. Besides the law, tennis was his passion. "Tell me, though, does the pain get better?"

"The good days are rare, but the bad days are fewer, if that makes sense. I feel in limbo and . . . disoriented. I walk down to the law library and forget what I wanted in there. I pour a glass of milk and find it hours later, untouched. The other morning I woke up, panicked, convinced I'd overslept for a contract-law exam." Heath motioned to his packed closet. "Ten years I've been at this firm and all I've accumulated can be stored in boxes."

"Can't box all the cases you won. The people you've helped, your pro bono work."

"Nor can I get back all the hours I spent working instead of being with Ava and Tracey-Love."

"You're being too hard on yourself. Ava invested in her career as much as you, Heath. If not more."

Heath reached for a lone yellow pencil lying on his desk blotter. "Yeah, well, I can't confront her about it now, can I?"

"No, you can't." Rock exhaled through his nose and slapped his hands against his thighs as he stood. "If I mentored you right, you have more than enough to live on."

"Yes, there's money." Heath coughed, pressing his fist to his lips.

"Of course." Rock paused with his hand on the door knob. "Six months, Heath. Remember."

Heath tapped his forehead. "Got it right here."

Rock left, shutting the door as he went. Heath stared out his twentieth-floor window. Manhattan had been his promised land thirteen years ago when he and Ava arrived after three years of Yale Law. But today his promised land felt like a barren desert.

A light snow began to fall between the Manhattan skyscrapers. Heath watched the miniscule flakes swirl past his window, knowing they'd melt in the city's warmth before hitting the ground.

Catherine Perry, even Rock Calloway, had no concept of Heath's expanding wilderness. If he didn't leave this job, this city, and this place of memories behind, his heart would become a constant plain of winter.

Three

GG GALLERY
CLOSED
SOLD

BEAUFORT
March

The empty gallery felt cold and foreign, the bare walls echoing every word, bump, and scrape.

Elle purposefully ignored the big-hole in her chest as she boxed up Geoffrey Morley's February show, the last she'd ever have in Beaufort, in GG Gallery.

She'd seen the gallery empty once before. The day she bought it. Then her gallery days were beginning instead of ending.

Change was hard. Even chosen change.

Julianne descended the loft stairs with a box in her hands. "Your paints." She set them on the desk. She picked up a tube and twisted off the cap. "Are they still good?"

"Should be," Elle said, dragging the last box across the floor to line up with the rest of the packages for FedEx. "Oils last awhile."

Julianne replaced the cap and dropped the paint back into the box. "You should paint again, Elle. You do have a degree in fine arts, I believe. Studied in Florence."

"Running a gallery took all my time." Elle shrugged and walked around to the printer for a piece of paper.

"Are you going to open another gallery in Dallas?"

"Of course." With a big black marker, Elle wrote on the blank paper, "Desk for Sale. Best Offer. See Inside," then taped it to the front window.

"Are you sad?" Julianne leaned against the desk, crossing her arms. "About selling?"

"A little, but"—Elle smiled—"the things we do for love."

"Seems like you just opened this place, Elle."

"Yeah, I know."

Julianne walked the box of paints over to the front door and set it with the pile of stuff to be carted over to Elle's over-the-garage studio. "I can't see you in big ole Texas, living in the middle of a place with no trees or rivers or creek beds. You're the quintessential low-country girl. Parties at Bodean Good's place, spending summers on the sand bar, hosting oyster roasts and lowcountry boils in the fall."

"Guess I'll have to learn to barbeque and wear a cowboy hat." Elle picked up an empty box, not sure what she needed it for, then set it back on the floor. "Love isn't always easy, Jules. But if Jeremiah is going to be in Dallas, so am I."

"You don't think turning thirty isn't motivating you to jump into a serious commitment too fast?" Julianne kicked at the boxes, avoiding Elle's eye.

"You sound like Caroline when I e-mailed her the news. She asked the same question. No, I don't. I'd given up on engagement or marriage before thirty. Burned my Operation Wedding Day plan in the chimenea, remember?" The slight edge in Elle's voice came from irritation that both her best friend and her baby sister doubted her.

Julianne held up her hands. "Don't get snippy."

Elle started for the loft, trying to dig up some excitement about the days ahead, but only finding weariness. "Come on, help me finish clearing out upstairs."

She hadn't seen Jeremiah in over a month except on video chat. While they talked and e-mailed daily, he was harried and plagued with senior pastoritis while she was burdened with wedding planning, gallery selling, cottage renting, and all the pangs associated with uprooting a life.

Julianne ran up behind her. "You do love him, right?"

Elle kicked aside a pile of empty boxes sitting at the top of the stairs. "Good grief, Jules. No, I loath him and on our wedding night, he'll die mysteriously and I'll inherit all of his preacher's wealth. Of course I love him. And would you please remember all of this questioning the next time I drill you about something and you flash me your palm."

Jules tugged a thick black trash bag from the box. "I ask one, maybe two questions. You ask a hundred. So what do you want to do with all the papers in the filing cabinet."

"Toss them."

The sisters fell into a working silence, clearing away the last of Elle's gallery days. It was the culmination of a long list of duties.

Jeremiah's proposal had led to a manic Monday-before-Christmas with Mama, trying to nail down as many wedding details as possible before he left for Dallas. *Guest list. Tuxes. Groomsmen's gifts. Rehearsal dinner information. Limo to drive Elle to the church. Time, date, and location of the wedding. Reception ideas. Food choices.*

On Christmas evening, after the family dinner, while everyone dozed on couches and lounge chairs, Jeremiah drew Elle away for a long walk.

The night was clear, unusually cold, and Jeremiah cuddled her close as they walked, his hand low on the curve of her hip.

They talked about the upcoming months, the stress of being apart, planning a wedding, finding a home to buy in Dallas, the demand of being a senior pastor at 3:16 Metro Church.

It all seemed dreamy and unreal to Elle now, standing in the center of the loft.

"Elle, do you want to keep these?" Jules held up two canisters of brushes.

"Take them to the studio." She'd bought them the summer she lived in New York and attended classes at the Student Art League, the summer she came to a realization about her talent.

She came home and opened the gallery.

Dumping a pile of art magazines into the trash, Elle's thoughts drifted back to Jeremiah and Christmas.

She could still hear the rhythm of their heels scraping against the pavement until they arrived in front of the Baxters'. Jer stopped, eyes roaming their Christmas-light extravaganza.

"I understand."

"I've been thinking about your cottage and the gallery, Elle. You're going to have to sell the gallery. You can't run it from Dallas."

The directness of his summation startled her. But she knew he was right. "I thought I'd pretend I could."

He'd hugged her close and kissed her forehead. "On the other hand, why not keep the cottage? Rent it out. It'd be a nice investment."

On Christmas night, Elle realized how much everything was about to change. As much as she wanted to be with Jeremiah, leaving would be hard.

"I'm going to miss you," Julianne said now, without provocation.

Elle glanced around to see her sitting on a pile of art books. "I'm going to miss you too. And Rio. Daddy and Mama, and our three motley sisters."

"You've been my sanity at times." Julianne's eyes glistened when she looked at Elle. "I'll always be so grateful for the night you went with me to tell Mama and Daddy about Rio."

"It was a hard night, but a good one."

Twenty-two-year-old Julianne, sobbing, confessing she was pregnant, father unknown.

"Elle?" a male voice called from the ground floor, his voice echoing and bouncing. "Baby, you here?"

Elle stepped to the loft's low wall. "Jeremiah?"

His spread arms beckoned a "ta-da." "Surprise."

"What are you doing here?" *Why hadn't he called?* She was a mess, dirty and stinking from spending the past week packing up her life. Besides, she was to meet him in Dallas next week.

He ascended the loft one slow step at a time. "I thought you might need some support for the gallery closing tomorrow. Hey, Julianne, how are you?"

"Late to pick up Rio." Julianne thumped down the stairs, hugged Jeremiah, and waved at Elle. "The last time I was late the little booger chewed me out. Elle, I'll drop these boxes off at your house."

"Thanks, Julianne." Elle stepped down toward Jeremiah, her heart warming, her blood flowing. While she felt like a parking-lot penny, he looked like a million dollars. "I can't believe you're here."

"And it's ticked you off?"

She laughed softly at his gentle sarcasm. "Two months of phone conversations and e-mails with only one brief visit, wishing we could be together, and, *poof*, here you are . . . It feels strange."

Jeremiah kept his eyes steady on her face. "Keep coming toward me, I'll show you strange." He wiggled his eyebrows.

"Jeremiah." His implication tightened her belly.

"Can I kiss my wife-to-be?" he asked, taking her in his arms, his hot question flowing through her hair.

"Please." His kiss, the perfect reminder of why she'd said yes, why she'd agreed to sell the gallery and start life all over. "I'm glad you're here. Thank you for coming."

"Two months and five days, Elle, and we'll be together forever. For. Ever."

Elle liked the sound of that number.

Little doubts crept in at the oddest times.

Candace Harper, Elle's lawyer and the third of the five Garvey sisters, offered Elle the final sale document as she came from behind her polished oak desk.

"You sign where I've placed the sticky flags." She lowered her voice. "You did well, Elle. Nice profit."

"Thanks to you."

On the other side of the room, the gallery's new owner chatted with her lawyer. Angela Dooley was a black-haired beauty with bling on every finger, while her lawyer, Palmer Roth, epitomized the quiet southern gentleman, with gray temples and a sharp wit.

Elle sort of resented the affluent Angela, who not only was beautiful but had all the resources to open a newer and better gallery.

What did it matter? She'd be restarting in a new city with a vibrant art scene by the end of summer. Elle had spent a few hours on Google last night checking out the summer events and what part of the city she might select to set up shop.

"Where do I sign?" Elle's bracelets clattered against the desk as she flipped the pages.

"Here and here." Jeremiah pointed to the red sticky flags.

Yes, of course, the flags. A cold dew coated Elle's palms and the sliver of March sun spilling through Candace's windows didn't warm her. Nor did it emit enough light to overpower the doubt shadowing her heart.

"Elle?" Jeremiah nudged her pen hand, but she set it down instead of signing. "Candace, can we have a minute?"

Candace regarded her, eye to eye, as if trying to discern Elle's concern without asking. "Only a minute." She escorted Angela and Palmer to the conference room, asking if they'd like a cup of coffee.

"Talk to me, babe."

Elle stared out the window toward the Intracoastal Waterway. "Aren't you scared, Jeremiah?"

"To marry you?"

She glanced back at him. "Two people, in their thirties, trying to become one, bringing together their wants and desires, doesn't scare you a little?"

"No, it doesn't. We can do it."

She considered his posture, the confidence of his voice. He wasn't just saying what she wanted to hear, he voiced what he believed.

"Jeremiah, I'll be honest. I can't believe a man like you loves me and asked me to marry him. You're an amazing man, but moving is weirding me out. I wanted to raise my family here, playing with cousins, hanging off their uncles like monkeys, hearing all my growing-up stories from my parents and my sisters."

He ran his finger along the edge of her hair, grazing her face with his fingertip. "Babe, we'll visit. They'll visit. My parents are right there in Austin. Next week you'll come to Dallas and your fears will be abated. We'll find our house, get set to move in, and hey, I even know a great little coffee shop we can label 'our place.'"

"You make me want to be there with you." She kissed the back of his hand.

"Our relationship has moved fast, Elle." Kindness cushioned Jer's words. "But I know this is right. Don't you?"

Little doubts crept in at the oddest times.

"You're right." She smiled as a distant memory surfaced. "The first night I owned the gallery, Julianne and I dug out our old sleeping bags, left Rio with Mama, and slept on the cold, cement gallery floor. I never felt so right about anything."

"We can't compare owning a gallery to marriage, Elle." Jeremiah squeezed her hand. "But I'm going to hold on to you so you don't fall." He brought her hand to his lips.

"Besides, there will be other galleries, right? And the art scene in Dallas is excellent and exciting, a great place of opportunity."

"Do you trust me? Trust God?"

The posture of his questions denied her any chance to say no. Could she not trust God? Could she not trust the man she'd said yes to in marriage? Even if she truly didn't, she wanted to trust.

"Yes, but promise me a Dallas gallery is in my future."

He laughed. "I promise."

"Elle?" Candace entered the room. "Angela has another appointment. We need to get going."

Jeremiah kissed her. *You can do this.*

Elle stretched across the desk to pick up the pen. "Come in, Candace. I'm ready."

To: CSweeney
From: Elle Garvey
Subject: I sold the gallery

Hey Caroline,

It's done. Yesterday I signed the papers, selling GG Gallery to Angela Dooley. When Candace handed me the papers, I panicked. Thought my right arm was being cut off. But Jeremiah tenderly reminded me of our future and the life we'd have in Dallas.

He surprised me by flying in just to support me during the sale. Do I have a great man or what? When I asked him to promise me I could have a Dallas gallery, he did.

I don't know, Caroline. Were you nervous moving to Barcelona? Listen to me, all weak and scared. Wasn't I the one who said if you didn't go to Barcelona, I would go in your place? Now I'm chicken to leave my mama. Sad about selling my gallery. What a difference a year makes.

Hard to believe I was the one running around town luring Beaufort's single men into my Operation Wedding Day scheme. LOL. I kissed a lot of toads.

I liked my gallery life in little ole Beaufort. Do you know, C, we have fourteen galleries now? Fourteen. The Art Counsel is booming with ideas.

But I also love Jeremiah. He's the one. I'm sure I can't imagine all the great things God has for Jeremiah and me. I know you doubted my motives at first, but, Caroline, this is right. I know it.

Oh . . . did you get the picture of the bridesmaids' dresses? I love the full skirt. Yours will be the same style, but instead of the latte/champagne color, I ordered it in mocha. My sisters tried on the dresses with Sara Beth wearing your color. It looked stunning.

Well, it's late and I'm exhausted. I just arrived home from taking Jeremiah to the Savannah airport. He could only get away overnight. But I'm off to Dallas next week to house hunt. Jeremiah's leaving all the wedding details to me, but he's handling the honeymoon and insists we find a house before the wedding.

What's new with you? How's work with the European Donald Trump? Tell Carlos I said to treat you right. How are things with Mitch? Are y'all enduring the long-distance thing?

Okay, I've got to go to bed.
Love, Elle

In the few days between selling the gallery and flying to Dallas, Elle packed up her cottage, storing boxes in the garage and the over-the-garage studio.

Mama's Realtor friend, Marsha Downey, had rented the cottage starting mid-April and Elle wanted to be ready for the new tenant to move in.

Once she came home from Dallas, she had a feeling moving and wedding plans would consume her.

"When we get back from the honeymoon, babe," Jeremiah said to her on the phone last night before hanging up, "be ready to hit the ground running. The more settled we are in our new house before the wedding, the better."

In fact, during their last few phone calls, his mantra of "Buy a house and get set up" had bordered on annoying. Elle teased him about it, calling him 'The Repeater.' "Hear you loud and clear, Jeremiah."

Elle paused now, glancing around the cottage living room. Stirred up dust tangoed with southern sunbeams. The bookshelves running under the dining room windows were vacant, as were her desk and the linen closets. The furniture remained as part of the lease . . . what else?

Elle fanned herself with an old church bulletin she'd found among the books. The cottage air was hot and stale. She'd opened the windows in the morning to let in the cool, fresh air blowing off the creek, but the breeze had settled and the sun streaming through the windows was hot.

She'd just decided to close up and click on the air conditioner when Julianne came through the front door with Rio in tow.

"Wow, it's hot."

"The air is cranking." Elle stooped down to embrace her niece. "Hey there, pretty girl." To Julianne she asked, "You're taking me to the airport tomorrow morning, right?"

"Yes, and Mama is picking you up when you come home. We've worked it out." Julianne collapsed on the couch. "It's an oven in here."

"Looky, Auntie Elle." Rio stuck her little behind up so Elle could see her pink backpack. "We went to Wals-Mart."

"Wals-Mart? I'm jealous." Elle turned Rio toward the hallway. "Run to your room. I have a surprise for you."

Rio didn't need to be told twice. At Auntie Elle's, she had her own room. With her mama, she shared. And for the hundredth time, Elle thought Rio was possibly the most beautiful child she'd ever seen.

"What'd you get her?" Julianne propped her feet on Elle's tired but sturdy coffee table.

"Just new a coloring book and crayons."

"Can you keep Rio for me tonight?"

"Where are you going?" Elle shuffled through a pile of linens she'd pulled from the hall closet. She'd pack her new towels and washcloths, left the rest for the renter.

"Out." Julianne shoved off the couch and headed for the kitchen. "We just ate at McDonald's. Got any fruit in here?"

"To relieve your fast-food guilt?" Elle heard the fridge open, followed by the hiss of a Coke can.

"Naturally."

Rio ran to the living room with her new coloring book and a box of crayons.

"Color on the coffee table, Rio." Watching her made Elle's heart ache. In a few weeks, these impromptu visits would cease.

Julianne came in from the kitchen with a Diet Coke and a bowl of grapes. "Eat these, Rio, please." She set the bowl on the table next to the coloring book, then plopped onto the leather couch just inside the shade. "So, can she stay?"

Elle leaned over the back of the couch propped on her elbows. "If you tell me where you're going."

"I told you. Out."

"With whom? And to where?"

"Really, Elle, you ask too many questions." Julianne popped a grape into her mouth. "Rio, good job on the picture. I love a solid purple cat."

"Seems I remember someone asking me a lot of questions the other day," Elle said. "Rio, remember to color between the lines like I showed you."

"Maybe she doesn't want to color between the lines." Julianne tossed a grape at her sister.

"Maybe if she learned to color between the lines first, then she'd be an expert at coloring *outside* the lines." Elle arched her brow at her sister and tossed the grape back.

"I'm not telling you where I'm going. It's my business."

"Let's see, wasn't it you prying into my life just a few days ago? Now I can't ask where you're going if I keep your daughter overnight?" If Jules really needed an overnight sitter, she'd have no choice but to go to Mama or one of their other sisters. And if she hated Elle asking questions . . . ?

"I have a date." Julianne seemed to think these four words sufficed as an answer.

"An overnight date?" Elle suspended "date" for emphasis.

"No, but we're going to Charleston for a play. I'll be home late. Besides, I have to pick you up at the crack-o-seven anyway. It just seemed easier."

"Who is he?"

"A man."

"Do we know him?" Elle motioned toward Rio with her eyes. "You can't go around with just anyone."

"If you don't want to watch her, just say so." Julianne fired off the couch for the kitchen. "Finish up, Rio, we've got to get going."

Elle caved. "Jules, I'll watch her, but what's the harm in knowing where you're going to be and with whom? Do I know this *date?*"

Julianne picked up her handbag from the coffee table. It rattled with keys and who knew what else. "Call my cell if you need me." She stooped to kiss Rio. "Be good for Auntie Elle."

Elle followed her out to the front porch. "Do not be late to pick me up for the airport."

Julianne stopped at the bottom step. "You don't have to marry him, Elle."

"Stop hinting, Jules. What are you trying to say? You don't like him, do you?"

"Yes, I like him. A lot. I don't like him taking you away, and I'm sure you don't either."

Elle shook her head, turning for the house. "Good night, Jules. See you at seven, and don't be late."

# Four

DALLAS

Thunderstorms rolled over the plains and delayed Elle's fight to Dallas by three hours. When the wheels finally barked against the tarmac, she exhaled tension and subtly stretched the knots from her shoulders and legs.

The only thing that made this horrid day and dreadful flight worthwhile was the anticipation of seeing Jeremiah at the end of the Jetway. She'd covered all of her apprehension and worry with daydreams of the week.

House hunting, kissing, planning their future, kissing, meeting her new church family, kissing, watching old movies and eating pizza, kissing . . .

Given the all-clear by the flight attendant to use electronic devices, Elle fished her cell phone from her bag and dialed Jeremiah. As it rang, she gazed out the plane's rain-splattered window. She couldn't see much of Dallas from the airport's gate, but just beyond the gray horizon a patch of blue was breaking through.

Jeremiah's voicemail popped on. "You've reached Jeremiah Franklin, I'm unavailable at this time . . ."

Elle listened, rising from her seat, hunched forward under the overhead bin, waiting for the passengers in the forward rows to deplane.

"Hey, babe, it's me. I'm here. Finally. I cannot wait to see you. This trip has been an ordeal." She smiled "thanks" to the man who reached in the overhead and tugged down her bag. "Starting with Julianne being late to pick me up. Then some kid spilled chocolate milk down my back in Atlanta . . . You know what? I'm sorry, this can wait. See you in a few minutes."

Elle tucked her phone into her bag as she strode down the Jetway. Just before stepping into the gate area, she paused to fluff her hair, adjust her top and jeans, inhale, exhale, and prepare to see Jeremiah's handsome face searching for hers.

But when she emerged, he wasn't there. *Hmm.* She checked the gate next to hers. No Jeremiah. Ah, of course, he'd need a ticket to get past security. Elle joined the rest of the annoyed and testy passengers moving toward baggage claim.

Jeremiah wasn't in baggage claim either. By the time the carousel's warning beep sounded and the conveyor began its slow, squeaky rotation, he'd not called or appeared.

Elle scanned the waiting passengers, then glanced out the exit doors to see if he was waiting in his car, but there was no sign of him.

All right, Jeremiah, where are you? Her stomach ached, anticipation mingling with frustration.

As her overstuffed brown suitcase appeared on the carousel, she reached for it. Her two smaller bags followed. She'd definitely overpacked. But she'd never been to Dallas before and she wasn't sure of all she'd need. Would the days be warm and the evenings cold? Did they dress up for church or go casual with jeans and nice tops? Did Jeremiah have dinner plans for them? If so, should she dress for Texas BBQ or fine dining?

So far, she'd only heard plans for a Sunday-night potluck dinner and days upon days of house hunting. She hoped to find an old Texas ranch house rich with ambiance and cowboy heritage.

Dragging her luggage off to the side, she dialed Jeremiah again. Listening as his phone rang, she imagined a quiet evening, ordering pizza, watching a movie, and stealing kisses.

His phone bounced to voicemail again. "Hey, it's me. I'm at the airport waiting. Call me."

Elle carted her suitcases out to the curb and perched on top of the big bag to wait. Other passengers from her flight hopped into waiting cars or climbed aboard shuttle buses. The first few minutes, she watched folks come and go, but as time passed and the dew of the rainy day seeped into her skin, Elle grew angry and impatient.

Shivering, she dialed Jeremiah, clamping her sweater closed with her chilled fingers. Voicemail. She clapped her phone closed as a Texas-sized blue word slipped off the end of her tongue.

Jeremiah pulled into DFW forty minutes late. Elle was cold, tired, and hungry. And angry. Her first night in Dallas and they fought—from the moment he put her luggage in the trunk to the moment he pulled into Steak n Shake for a quick bite.

"What'll you have?" The waitress glanced between them, hands on her waist.

"I'll have a burger and fries with a large chocolate shake." Elle's bracelets clattered against the table when she snapped her menu closed.

"I'll have the same," Jeremiah said, calm and collected, making Elle feel like a loon for being upset.

"I still don't understand why you didn't call or text." Elle tore at the edge of her napkin. If she looked at Jeremiah, she'd burst into tears. And frankly, she didn't have the energy for it.

"Babe, what do you want me to do? I was late. I'm sorry. We have a Wednesday-night leaders meeting and it went long. My phone was supposed to be set on vibrate, but I'd turned it off somehow."

"Fine, Jer, I understand long meetings and phones turned off, but didn't you even think to check the time. It makes me feel like you weren't anticipating my visit at all. I thought of you all day."

"Of course I anticipated you coming. I've thought of you being here since we decided on the dates. Don't make it sound like I dissed you on purpose. But as the leader, I can't just get up and walk out in the middle of an important discussion."

"I see, so if you're in a meeting and I call to say, 'Honey, my water just broke, the baby's coming,' I can only hope you're not leading an important meeting?"

"Elle, that's not fair. I can't believe—"

"No, it's not fair. Neither is you letting me sit there alone without even thinking to call. Why did you even go to the meeting? If I'd arrived on time, what were your plans for me?" The debate exhausted her.

"Your host family, the Farmers, were going to take you to dinner." Jeremiah slipped from his side of the booth into Elle's. "Babe, come on, let's not fight. Sets a bad tone for the week."

His kiss cooled her ire. "Please, Jeremiah, don't make me feel like an afterthought. Ministry is important, yes. Any career takes a certain level of commitment. But not at the expense of our relationship."

He wrapped his fingers with hers. "You are far from an afterthought, Elle."

She rested her head on his shoulder. "I guess it feels like it tonight."

"Let's forget tonight, then. Start fresh in the morning. We'll go out to a nice brunch, see a little of Dallas."

Elle lifted her eyes to his, kissing him. "Best news I've heard all day."

Seven days of house hunting. Seven days of headache. Elle walked the length of this brand-new home's living room listening to the sound of her heels click against the hardwood and bounce from the beige wall to the sculptured ceiling.

At what point had all of her expectations started falling apart? Could she rewind to where they were intact and start over? To the day before she arrived?

Jeremiah's voice resonated from the foyer where he talked with their Realtor, Lyle Dubois, between answering phone calls.

Today, of course, his phone is not accidentally turned off. Elle grimaced at her silent sarcasm. Did she not expect bumps in the road, especially with a man like Jeremiah whose high energy inspired everyone around him to move and shake?

Three months on the job and from what Elle observed and heard during the Sunday-night potluck dinner, Dr. Jeremiah Franklin had 3:16 Metro Church on the move.

While she loved his success, Elle struggled to see how she fit in the big picture.

Jeremiah's cell rang for the fifth time that hour. "Maurice, what do you have for me?" Maurice Winters was Jeremiah's assistant and longtime friend and the reason Jeremiah first heard of the senior pastor job.

Elle walked the length of the living room again and peered into the grassless backyard. Beyond the spattering of trees, the Texas sky darkened with more rain.

"Elle." Jeremiah angled his head into the room from the foyer, phone to his ear, the mouthpiece even with his jaw. "Lyle said the developer plans to lay the sod before we close." Back to his phone without waiting for her response.

"Thanks," she said. Lyle nodded a "You're welcome."

This week had been a whirlwind week of discovery. Meeting the congregation—all of whom Elle found warm and charming. Jeremiah had announced he'd been asked to host a weekly television show with the intent to start local and go national by the end of next year. After consulting his leaders, he'd agreed to start the pre-production process as early as April.

Two days later, while walking through the house Elle loved the most—a farmhouse outside the city limits with a big yard, trees, and a small, trickling stream—Jeremiah took a phone call, talked briefly, then announced to Elle he'd agreed to write a book to go along with the theme of the television show. Now he constantly jotted notes on napkins and the back of receipts.

Was she feeling overwhelmed? Big fat yes. Life was happening to her, not with her.

"Well, babe, what do you think?" Jeremiah clicked his phone closed and walked toward her.

"It's big. Lovely." Too new, too cold. "The yard is the size of a saltine. And there's not a tree in my line of sight."

Jeremiah circled the room's perimeter, commenting on the crown molding and the unique use of the floating staircase. "I love it. Lyle, what's the price on this one?"

Elle's temples tightened. Of course he loved the house. It was the image of him. Haute couture. Stylish, modern, pristine, and structured with intricate details not easily duplicated.

But she longed for vintage. An older home with creaking floors, odd-shaped rooms, hidden nooks, and a history of love and laughter.

"The price is in your range, Dr. Franklin." Lyle walked toward the center of the barren living room. "And in this buyer's market, we can offer several thousand less than the asking price."

The skinny Realtor under a cowboy hat shoved back his bright orange jacket, set his hands on his belt, and glanced between the two of them. Poor Lyle, caught between their tug-of-war of wants.

"Elle, what do you think?" Jeremiah nodded slightly. "Yes?"

She hated to sound like a worn, scratched record, but for the moment, the kind of house she moved into after her wedding and honeymoon was the only thing she had control over in her pre-Dallas existence.

"I don't know, Jeremiah. Isn't it a bit expensive?"

"Excuse us, Lyle." Jeremiah shuffled Elle out the back of the living room into the dining room. "I guess we haven't been able to talk in-depth about money."

And whose fault is that, Cell Phone Man? "It's been crazy, I know."

"Money is not an issue, Elle. I had the good sense not to squander my endorsement money from my football days."

"Oh, gr-great." His good sense tackled her last argument. "I'd never considered your football career."

"Elle, I make a good salary, but the board knows I have investments. Other than buying a nice house, I don't intend to flash money around. I'm keeping the Honda, not going to drive anything fancy. But I don't want to come home from a long day and hear you tell me the plumbing needs fixing or the attic is leaking."

Listen to his heart, Elle. How could she not agree? If Mama sat on her shoulder right now, she'd say, "Just go along, Elle. Do this for your man. You'll make it a home in no time."

"Your hesitation tells me you don't like it."

Did he hear her at all, read her language, understand her protests? "I'd feel like I was living in a hotel all the time. It's big and drafty. Everything is stainless steel and brass. The farmhouse we looked at is out of the question? I know the first house I liked needed too much work, but there has to be more like it around this great big city."

His eyes narrowed, but only for a second. He planted a quick kiss on her forehead. "Okay, Lyle, the woman of the house isn't feeling it. What else you got? Can you show us something with a little more character."

Elle slipped her hand into his and followed him to the foyer. "Thank you."

Five

At Jeremiah's small, bachelorlike kitchen table, he reviewed the house situation. Elle munched on a piece of toast and listened.

"You leave tomorrow and I think we're close. Do you like this one?" Jeremiah held up a picture of the Victorian home they'd toured yesterday.

"It was nice, Jeremiah, except for being in a crowded neighborhood amid twin and triplet Victorian replicas. No yard." She met his gaze. "Are you sure we can't go back to the mid home Lyle showed us the day before yesterday? It's not a fixer-upper, but warm and homey with a yard and a big maple in the front. And it's near I-35. The drive to the art district would be about twenty minutes."

Jeremiah gathered the printouts, then picked up his coffee cup, leaving the table. "About the gallery, Elle . . ." He filled his coffee cup.

His tone made her scalp tingle. "What about it?"

"Elle, seriously, when are you going to have time to run a gallery?" Jeremiah straddled the chair, sipping his coffee.

"What else am I going to do? If you're worried about it burdening our new marriage, I'll start slow and small. Open a few days a week, on special weekends."

He stopped her with a low laugh. "Being senior pastor of a large, growing church comes with a lot of responsibilities, expectations, and duties, Elle. I need you with me. I'm already on several ecumenical boards, praying at city council meetings, leading a study on culture and race in the church, never mind the church's calendar. Are you saying you don't want to minister with me? There's travel on my horizon. The television people want to develop segments with you, too, over the next year. You do want to minister with me, don't you?"

The man had just described a world she'd never imagined. "Of course, Jeremiah, but I don't want to abandon my work. Putting a ring on my finger doesn't negate the gifts and calling God has given me. At least that's not what I was raised to believe. I'm not Elle Garvey, art advocate and gallery owner, until some man gives me his name and then I'm a mini-him, his shadow."

His countenance darkened.

"Mini-me? A shadow? Is that what you think this is all about? Elle, I'm not asking you to be my shadow. I'm asking you to be my partner in ministry."

Elle shoved away from the table, carrying her plate to the dishwasher. How did he turn her arguments around so she felt selfish and silly?

"I understand, Jeremiah, but right now all I hear is me, me, me. And I don't mean Elle, Elle, Elle. This whole week has been about you. What you're doing, where you're going, what you want, who you know. Jeremiah, other than buying the house, you haven't asked me once about how I feel about any of this ministry stuff. Not one 'Pray about it with me' or 'What do you think of me doing television or writing a book?'"

"Babe, I-I would. It's just that, well, you're new, not in the loop, caught up with the details."

"And whose fault is that? Look, I don't want to sit in meetings or share every phone call, but I'd like an invitation to talk it over. All I get is the latest news flash."

"Fine, and I'd like to be in on your decisions. I don't feel good about your opening a gallery. At least not yet. Besides, there are hundreds of art galleries in the greater Dallas area. It'll take a long time and a lot of work to get established."

Elle crossed her arms and leaned against the kitchen counter. "And there are not ten times the number of pastors and charismatic preachers hocking the gospel on TV?" Her words snapped like the sharp end of a wet towel.

"I can't believe you." Jeremiah met her in the kitchen, his six-foot-three frame towering over her. "The more ministers of the gospel, the more we win to Christ. Babe, let's not blow this out of proportion. I'm just saying maybe the gallery is not a good idea. At least not right now." Jeremiah stopped, glancing at his watch. "Come on, it's time to meet Lyle."

"Jeremiah, you sat in Candace's office and promised."

He stopped at the edge of his living room, easing his wallet into his pocket. "I did, didn't I?"

"Yes."

"All right. Then let's talk after the wedding. Can you give me until then?" His smile radiated little warmth.

Elle appreciated his compromise but felt the echo of his first hollow promise. "All right, if that's what you want." She picked her purse off the table and followed him out the door.

"Elle, what do you think?" Jeremiah leaned against the kitchen island. "The location is good. Lyle says we can close next week."

Elle's bracelets made a tinkling sound as she brushed her hands though her hair, stretching the tenseness out of her back and neck. "I like the house if you do."

He shook his head, exhaling a hot breath. "If we move in and six months later you hate it . . ." He walked to the breakfast nook, arms akimbo. "Are you doing this because of what I said about the gallery?"

Elle's insides burned. "Is that what you think of me?"

He looked over at her. "No, but I had to ask."

If they failed at finding a house this trip, they failed even greater at communicating, each blinded in some way by their own expectations.

"Jeremiah, I won't hate it. Let's buy it."

"I'm not putting hundreds of thousands down on 'I won't hate it.' I don't understand why we can't find a house we both love."

His cell rang, and when he answered, he walked out the French doors.

Elle picked at the edge of the counter, batting away tears. *Horrible* was the only word she had for this visit.

Lyle entered the kitchen, his cell phone in hand. "Just talked with the seller . . . Oh, hey, Elle, you in here by yourself? Let me flip on the light. Guess this kitchen is kind of dark, I do admit. Maybe we can see to putting in some sky lights." He opened the door to the deck. "Get on in here, Jeremiah."

Lyle restarted his spiel when Jeremiah came inside.

"They'll take five grand less than asking, and"—Lyle wiggled his eyebrows. Elle hid a smile—"pay closing."

Jeremiah glanced at Elle, and she longed for the warmth she always felt from him. "It's up to you, Elle. Decide. I guess we can hole up in my apartment if we can't find a place."

"Don't you dare blame me." She didn't care if Lyle listened in; she'd not have Jeremiah dump their failure on her.

He sighed. "I'm not blaming anything on anyone."

Dallas had revealed a new side of both of them. Elle, the unrelenting artist. Jeremiah, the conquering achiever. She refused to be bulldozed, especially by the man she was marrying. But for the moment she embraced compromise.

"Let's buy it, Jeremiah." She smiled with all the confidence she could muster.

"Lyle, looks like you made the sale. Well deserved." Jeremiah came around the island to kiss Elle's cheek. His lips were wet and cool.

BEAUFORT

The quiet dark of the Sea Island Parkway—also known as Hwy 21, he'd discovered after finally consulting a map—spooked Heath. *Turn on a light, somebody.*

He'd passed the turn onto Fripp Point Road three times and was about to pass it again when, *Wait, was that it?* Mashing the brake, he whipped the van around in a U-turn.

"A-are we t-there, D-daddy?" After two long days on the road, Tracey-Love was ready to be *home.*

"Just about, sweetie."

"M-my t-tummy hu-hurts."

Heath angled around to see her, though she was barely visible in the dash lights. Four-year-old Tracey-Love had been sick since they left IHOP this morning.

"Hold on, we're almost"—the van nosed down with a hard bounce as the pavement ended in dirt and gravel—"there."

Turn right on Coffin Point . . . If that street name wasn't loaded with irony. Heath scanned the e-mailed directions in the dome light as Tracey-Love moaned quietly. Buckled into a car seat, Heath figured he'd do more than moan.

Lights glowed from the cottage at the end of the drive. Is this it? When the van lights landed on the side of the house, he caught the numbers. He parked on the red brick drive and cut the van's motor.

"Da-daddy."

"We're here, Tracey-Love." But not in time to keep her from retching all over the side of the seat. He unsnapped his seatbelt while shoving open his door. "I'm coming around."

Before leaving New York, Tracey-Love's nanny had handed over a list of instructions for her care and diet, but he'd tossed the list aside once they started traveling, figuring TL deserved a little carefree fun. Now . . . perhaps not such a wise idea.

The nanny followed his wife's health-food diet while Heath had followed the easy-going fast-food diet during this trip. Her stomach chose this moment to revolt.

The sweet, marsh-scented air mingled with the sour odor of vomit as Heath slid open the van door. Tracey-Love cried softly as he removed her from the seat.

"It's okay. Daddy let you eat too much junk. How about a nice warm bath?"

It wasn't supposed to be like this, Ava.

He hugged her to his chest, not caring if he soiled his last clean Ralph Lauren. "How do you like our new house, TL? Can you hear the frogs singing from the creek? The air is warm and thick. Tomorrow we'll go exploring."

Heath fished the house key from his pocket, the lowcountry perfume and night song confirming his decision to leave New York. He propped open the screen door with his foot and inserted the key. "Looks like our Realtor came by and clicked on the lights for us. Isn't that nice?"

"D-daddy . . ." Tracey-Love gagged, spilling the last of her Happy Meal down his back before dissolving into tears.

"Don't cry now. Come on, it's going to be fine." Heath fumbled with the lock, finally unlatching the door. "Once you're clean and in a soft bed, you'll feel better. Here we go. Look, isn't this pretty?"

After two long days, they were finally home.

Elle came out of the bathroom tying her robe around her waist, reliving Dallas for the hundredth time.

If being driven and an overachiever was Jeremiah's weakness, rehashing things in her head was one of hers. But she needed to understand, figure things out, find her bearings.

After saying yes to the house, Jeremiah had taken Elle and her host family out to a lovely dinner, and the next morning he kissed her good-bye at airport security and promised to call soon.

They exchanged an "I love you" and lingered in an embrace, but the entire flight home Elle ping-ponged between empty and bothered, elated and content.

She'd heard marriage was hard, but she didn't expect so much friction over opposite goals and desires. Over a house. Over expectations.

Sara Beth had ridden with Mama to pick Elle up from the airport. "Tell me, how'd it go? I want to hear all about the house."

"Do you know your daddy and I were married ten years before we bought our first home?"

"We argued a lot, Mama." She gritted her teeth when her eyes flooded. "We don't seem to like many of the same things."

Hadn't they liked the same things at one time? Food, movies, music? So far, nothing translated into the bigger areas of their life.

Elle gave the abbreviated version of her week with Jeremiah, careful not to paint him in too bad a light.

Mama was undaunted by the story of disagreements and differences. "Sara Beth here came home from her honeymoon ready for divorce court."

"Really, Sara Beth?"

"Yeah, we had a pretty horrible time." Elle's oldest sister had thick brown hair like Mama and wide-set brown eyes on a broad-boned face. "Parker and I had dated for over a year and never fought once. Went on the honeymoon and fought nonstop."

"Yeah, you unlocked all the sexual tension," Mama said with all authority.

"Mama," Elle squealed, heat prickling over her cheeks.

Sara Beth waved her off. "She's right. All the issues we'd ignored while dancing around unsatisfied passion started rearing their ugly heads."

Great, what did all this arguing and discontentedness say about

Elle and Jeremiah? Sexual tension? Hardly. Elle pressed her hand to her middle, remembering how she tightened and shivered every time his warm breath breezed her cheek or ear. Until this past week . . .

"Elle, don't worry. This will work itself out." Mama always said not to worry, as if, *poof*, just like that all worry vanished. "Oh, and good news. The invitations came while you were in Dallas. Your sisters and I spent an evening addressing them. I dropped them by the post office yesterday." She turned around in the passenger seat with a fake frown as if to lecture Elle. "So, young lady, you're getting married no matter what."

Well, in that case, what's a girl to do?

Elle remembered feeling better after that, kissing Mama's cheek and asking to pull into a drive-thru. She felt half starved.

At home now a little over a day, Elle had taken time to reflect and adjust her perspective. She'd hoped Jeremiah had done the same. What time was it? Nine ten. She'd wait another hour and give him a call before she went to bed.

"Hello, anyone here? Marsha?"

Elle stopped on the edge of the hallway leading into the living room. A tall, dark-haired man with a winter complexion stood by the front door with a tiny bit of a girl draped over his shoulder.

"Marsha?" His eyes fell on her face, then slipped down her neck to her robe . . .

"Who are you?" Elle gripped the loose edges of her robe and took a slow step backward. Her softball bat was in the hall closet, right-hand side.

"Heath McCord. Who are you?" he asked.

"Elle Garvey." She jerked open the door, fumbled for the bat, knocking boxes to the floor with a thump. She cocked the bat over her shoulder. "Don't take another step."

His eyes roamed the length of the bat. "Isn't this 21 Coffin Creek Point?"

"Back it up, bubba. Outside." Elle shifted the bat off her shoulder, circling it in the air as she stepped into the living room. Most robbers were cowards at heart. "What's with the girl?"

"My daughter."

When he was on the other side of the screen, Elle slammed the door and locked it, addressing him through the window. "Okay, who are you and how'd you get into my house?"

"Key. I've rented this place." He shifted the girl to sit on the crook of his arm, exposing a long, wet stain running down the front of his shirt. Her golden curls were tangled and frizzing around her pale face and hollow blue eyes. "My lease started today."

"Impossible. I'm the owner, and as you can see . . . still here." Elle lowered the bat. The name Heath McCord did have a familiar pitch. Was that the one Marsha had given her? "Doesn't your lease start in April?"

He shifted the girl again and Elle could see their weariness. "I asked for March fifteenth and Marsha Downey said fine and dandy."

Crud. Elle slumped, lowering the bat, recognizing the woman's catchphrase. Darn her. "I don't know what to tell you. I'm not moving out for another month."

"Is that my problem?" Heath cocked his head to one side, studying her through the window. "I've paid in full. Have the proof in my van."

Elle gripped her robe tighter. "You can have an extra month at the end of the lease."

"Thanks just the same, but I'd like my lease to start right now. It's been a hard year and a long trip." The girl lifted her head, muttered something, then shivered and buckled, covering herself and her daddy with bile.

Elle swung open the door. "Bathroom is down the hall. Towels are in the closet."

"He's here now, Marsha." Elle paced the length of her front-porch verandah, passing under the yellow door lamp, then into the dark corners and back to the light again. The summer material of her robe was too thin to protect against the chill clinging to the night.

"Sugar, what do you want me to do? The man's paid his money. Signed a lease."

Elle pressed the heel of her hand to her forehead. "Why did you tell him March fifteenth?"

"As I live and breathe, you said he could move in mid-March. I remember the night I called you."

"The night you were out . . . eating Mexican . . ." *And drinking Coronas.*

Silence. Then Marsha's wrinkled chuckle. "George tells me I forget details lately, but I could've sworn on my mama's grave you said March fifteenth. Goodness, I can hear your voice in my head now. *March.* You were going to set up house in Dallas before the wedding, as I recall."

Elle let her hip fall against the porch post. "Have a good night, Marsha." She glanced into the living room, through the window's sheers. Now what? A stranger was inside her cottage caring for his sick daughter expecting to be *home* after a long journey.

But Elle had been looking forward to her final days at home, prepping for the wedding, finalizing her packing and shipping boxes to her new home in Dallas. Taking a nap or two.

She turned to go inside as Heath crossed the living room carrying a towel-wrapped little girl. Slipping inside, Elle let the door click behind her. "Is she all right?"

"Too much junk food. Her mom was into healthy eating and I don't think her stomach found chicken nuggets friendly." Heath glanced at Elle. "Thanks for letting us in." Then to his girl, "Tracey-Love, wait here while I get your jammies?"

The girl shook her head and slung her arms around his neck. "S-stay w-w-with m-me."

"I will, but Daddy needs to get your suitcase from the van. Do you want to wear your new princess pajamas?"

Elle eased across the floor to the couch. This strange man in her living room, comforting his daughter in tender tones seemed so . . . lost.

"What's her name?"

"Tracey-Love."

"Hey, Tracey-Love, my little niece Rio is about your age and she left a pair of pajamas in the back room." She stooped to see her clear blues. "Do you like ponies?"

The girl stared, hands tight around Heath's.

"Yes, she does," Heath answered, locking his gaze with Elle's. *Thank you.*

"I'll run get them."

When Elle retuned with pony pajamas, she nodded toward the hall. "You can put her in there." The girl was already half asleep.

"Thank you." Heath slipped the gown over her head before unwrapping the towel. He picked her up. "Back this way? Which room?"

"There's only one. Can't miss it. The master bedroom is here, off the living room. And if she wants a drink of water, there're paper cups in the bathroom."

Heath stopped, turning to her with an easy smile. "I noticed. Thanks. Do you have children?"

"My niece is here a lot."

While Heath tucked in his daughter, Elle unloaded the dishwasher, meditating over the situation. *What's your tale, Heath McCord? Lonely-looking man with a four-year-old girl. And please don't be a parental kidnapping case.* Hadn't Marsha said he was a big-shot New York lawyer?

"Thank you again." He stood between the living room and kitchen. "This place is nicer than Marsha described. She said you're an artist."

"Gallery owner. Former artist who realized her limited talent."

Health regarded her for a second as if trying to understand. "I guess it's good to be self-aware." He held his stained shirt away from his body. "Mind if I grab a shower? Your name's Elle, right?"

"E-l-l-e. 'L' like the letter."

"Okay, 'L' like the letter, good to know."

"You're welcome to shower, but you're going to have to find another place to sleep." Elle shoved the dishwasher closed with her foot while reaching to close the bottom cupboard.

"I understand this is an awkward situation, Elle, but Tracey-Love has had a devastating year, the last of which was our trip down. I'm not leaving her alone in a strange place only to have her wake up with me beyond crying distance. I'll sleep in the room with her. The floor suits me just fine."

Elle draped the wet dish towel over the stove's handle. "How would you feel if your wife or daughter let a stranger spend the night? Even a seemingly nice guy like yourself?"

"I don't know, but I'm not leaving her." Heath hesitated, then turned for the hall. "Thanks for your hospitality. I'll find a hotel."

Elle breathed in, checking her emotions with her thoughts before trailing after him. "Wait, Heath, don't wake her."

He gazed down at her, the hall light filtering through the ends of his winter-blond hair. "Look, I'm exhausted. I don't want to debate this. I'll find a place tonight until I can work this out with Marsha."

"I called Marsha. She already confirmed your lease starts now." Elle pointed up and to the left. "I have a studio over my garage. It used to be a guesthouse. I'll sleep up there. You take my room. I suppose we can make do for a few weeks until my wedding."

His hands slipped to his side. "Now I feel guilty. I can find a hotel for the night."

"And then what? We still have tomorrow and the day after and the day after. You've paid fair and square. It's not your fault we're in this mess."

"Yours either." His low laugh brought the situation into true light.

"Give me Marsha Downey's address. I can go knock on her door, see if she has a spare room for the next month."

Elle motioned to her room. "I'll get my stuff together."

Heath looked dubious. "Are you sure?"

"Yeah, I'm sure."

In her bathroom, Elle packed up her toiletries. Heath's surprise arrival had jerked her out of her mental swirl.

When she came out from the bedroom, he was waiting on the couch, barely awake. "I left you a couple of good towels and put clean sheets on the bed. Tomorrow, I'll clear out more clothes."

He rose. "I feel like a heel, putting you out."

"Heath, you've actually done me a huge favor. Given me perspective. Sleep well. Hope your girl feels better in the morning."

Elle jogged across the backyard, autodialing Jeremiah. Better let him know what's up in case he called the house phone. But his voicemail answered and last week's reality washed over Elle again as she clicked her phone closed and entered the stale, hot studio.

Six

With the TV on but muted, Heath tapped his fingers over the keys of his laptop, his legs stretched to the coffee table. An overexposed brunette belted out a song on *American Idol*. The contest was down to the wire. Final twelve.

He rarely watched TV, but Ava had TiVoed *Idol* and he'd adopted her habit. Somehow watching people go for their dreams as he curled up on the couch with his wife hooked him.

Muted TV was fun TV. Effervescent Paula encouraged the singer by rocking back and forth, circling her hands as she spoke. The camera moved to Simon. Uh-oh. His expression told Heath the truth about the contestant.

Ava had wanted to be a singer or actress growing up, but when she went to college and joined the newspaper staff, a new ambition coursed through her veins. *"I wanted to star with Brad Pitt and kiss him like crazy. Then I discovered Tom Brokaw."*

Her still-familiar laugh echoed up from the overgrown valleys of his heart. He didn't bother to swish away the water in his eyes.

The opposite of Ava, Heath had never aspired to Hollywood-like fame. He wanted to live in the city, became a prosperous lawyer, bank his large annual bonus, take vacations and maybe drive a Maserati. And, of course, he also wanted to marry the gorgeous girl in his three-hundred-level poly-sci class.

Shoving the hot laptop off his leg, Heath slouched against the couch. How did all his aspiration now seem meaningless, if not cliché? Money purchased items like loneliness and heartache and packaged them in fancy cars and oversized bonuses.

What would he do differently?

Say no to Ava's broadcast career? Network News had really been starting to promote her, give her the spotlight.

Tell her no, she couldn't travel to dangerous, war-torn places? As if he could stop her.

Say no to the romantic, sexy evening when Ava had suggested they break their no-children policy "just to see" if they could make a baby? Nine months later, the blue-eyed cherub named Tracey-Love came whimpering into Heath's world and rained on the barren places of his heart.

What would he do differently so he wouldn't be sitting here now, alone and widowed, in a dimly lit lowcountry cottage owned by a baseball-bat-wielding strawberry blonde?

Nothing.

An image of Elle Garvey sashayed across his mind's eye, her hair falling over her shoulder, framing the sides of her slender face. Fiery green eyes watched him. Wonder who'd snagged her? Lucky man. Or so he thought. Hard to judge rightly based on their brief encounter. But he'd been right about Ava the first time he laid eyes on her as she walked across Yale's campus.

"D-daddy?"

Heath cocked his ear toward the small voice coming down the hall. "In here."

A rosy-faced Tracey-Love with large, sleepy eyes padded across the hardwood to him, crawling onto the couch, her thumb resting in her mouth.

"Does your tummy hurt?" Heath slipped his feet to the floor and hunched forward to see her face. Since moving into the cottage, he'd avoided fast food as much as possible.

"No," she muffled through her thumb, already drifting off.

Heath smoothed her hair, tight with tangles. He needed to work on keeping it combed, pinned back, or ponytailed, something. But it was so coarse and thick, downright exasperating.

TL's thumb slipped from her mouth as her breathing grew easy and even. Heath gently nudged his forefinger through her cupped little hand, thinking how soft and small it was. Not just her hand, but Tracey-Love.

The committee of "everyone" had told him to be firm with her, force her to sleep in her own bed, keep a strict routine. But she cried and begged to stay up with him, all at once afraid of the city's night sounds and every shifting shadow.

So sue him, he loved his daughter and didn't think chaining her to her bed, half terrified, at the age of four, constituted tough love. Time would heal her wounds and abate her fears.

Shoot, he didn't like sleeping in his bed either, and the city's night sounds terrified him too.

Six nights out of seven, Heath woke up in the wee hours of the morning stretched out on the couch with Tracey-Love sleeping on his chest.

Raising a daughter alone was never a part of the plan. *Lord, if You knew, why didn't You give me a son?*

Heath upped the TV volume a little. The contestant up now was his favorite, if he could claim a favorite. Looking back down at TL, the blue reflection of the TV screen covering her hair, he couldn't imagine one day she'd be grown, leaving him for her own adventures. Another man, even.

A month ago, he'd carefully Googled "girl stuff" like puberty, periods, and the potential number of hours he could expect a pre-teen to spend on the phone. One of the women's health sites listed stats that almost gave him a coronary. *Menstruation may start as young as ten.* Heath had clicked out of the Internet, stumbled to the kitchen, and wolfed down a pint of Ben & Jerry's.

Ten? That was less than six years from now. Ten?

And she may show signs of breasts as early as eight.

He'd dumped another glob of Hershey's chocolate into the carton. *Ava, I can't do this alone.*

Heath and his brother had a completely testosterone upbringing. Raised by their father after their mother abandoned the family for a string of deadbeat husbands she thought would take her on an adventure, he knew next to nothing about women until he fell in love with Ava their sophomore year at Yale.

His education had consisted of Dad's advice—"Never trust a dame"—and locker-room fables.

Many of his best friends were women, but he couldn't bring himself to ask any of them, "So, when did you get your period?" Or "How old were you when you started getting breasts?" Or "Do I worry about the little breasts or wait until Tracey-Love is, you know, *endowed?*"

Recalling his train of thought made him queasy all over again. He tipped his head against the sofa and raised his hands over his head. "Jesus, I know You and I are working out things between us since You took Ava, so I'm expecting You to help me out here on raising our daughter."

His cell phone rang and Heath stretch toward the coffee table, trying to answer before the ringing woke Tracey-Love.

"Yeah?" he answered with a rough whisper. "McCord."

"What's wrong?"

"Nothing. Tracey-Love is sleeping."

"Still not in her own bed?"

Heath frowned. Like Nate Collins was a model father. *He's not* even *a father.* "This isn't why you called, is it? To check up on my parenting skills?" As his agent and friend, Heath valued his counsel, except on how to raise his girl.

"Okay, just thought I'd chitchat before launching into business. How's your house?"

"Great, by a creek, nice side-screen porch, back deck, deep water dock. The owner is still here . . . some kind of moving mix-up. But she decided to live in her studio over the garage."

"And how's the book coming?"

"I just got here, Nate. Just started writing." Heath checked the laptop's screen. Yeah, just as he thought, no words had magically appeared. "But I'm mulling over some good ideas."

"Any chance those ideas are forming a bestseller? Heath, buddy, I've been talking you up all over New York, reminding editors of your legal work as well as your last novel they almost bought. Got a few salivating for the next John Grisham. You've got to give me something."

"Only John Grisham can produce the next John Grisham. However, you might have the next Heath McCord."

"My keen literary sense tells me the iron is hot, let's strike. A few chapters will whet the proper appetites. The publishing industry is hungry for something new and fresh. Do you have a rough draft?"

"What constitutes a rough draft?" Half a page of ideas? If New York wanted something fresh and new, count him out. He felt old and definitely dull.

Nate moaned. "You're giving me heart palpitations."

"You started this by talking me up too soon. I thought you were a good agent."

"I'm a great agent. Heath, if you're stuck—and please don't tell me you are—go with stories from your career. You've tried some pretty hefty cases. Or go with something political—intrigue in Washington. Shoot, you were married to one of the most—"

"I know who I was married to, Nate."

"Can I have something soon? Don't want the editors to think I was just leading them on."

"A few weeks." Months. He meant to say months.

"You're killing me," Nate said, but the tension in his voice ebbed. "So, are you and Tracey-Love settling into the slow southern life?"

Heath gazed down at the tiny person curled next to him. She kept his heart beating. "We're getting by, getting by."

Elle struggled. Since returning home, her communica-tion with Jeremiah had been on the run—on his way to a meeting, returning from a meeting, too exhausted to talk long. However, the plans to buy the house were progressing.

She spent several mornings Googling the Dallas art scene, calling gallery owners, making connections, cheered by the robust community. Once she and Jeremiah were married and settled, she'd prove to him she had time to work at a gallery. Then open one of her own.

This morning he'd texted her. "Look for something in the mail from me. Call you later."

Elle replied with a smiley face, encouraged that in the midst of transition, love would prevail. Mama was right, nothing to worry over.

Fixing a breakfast of instant coffee (never again) and a Pop-Tart (also never again), Elle rehearsed how she would address the issue of communication with Jeremiah when he called. They needed to figure out an effective way of dealing with their differences. Pastor O'Neal might be able to help when they met with him before the wedding.

But for now, she needed to clean out this studio and throw away stuff she didn't need, want, or plan to box for the movers to Dallas.

Little-girl screams drifted up from the yard below. Elle stepped over to check out the action. Rio appeared to be teaching Tracey-Love how to burp a naked baby.

Yesterday, Elle had spotted Tracey-Love playing in the yard alone and decided to introduce her to Rio. In the course of an evening, they'd become best friends.

Heath didn't seem to have many toys for Tracey-Love—had they left New York in a hurry?—so Elle dug through the boxes in the garage until she produced Rio's doll and baby stroller.

The grateful gaze in Heath's eyes lingered with her. Curious about his story, Elle didn't figure she'd earned the right to pry into his business and ask why Tracey-Love didn't have a mama.

"I left a lot of her toys in New York," he'd confessed as he stood with her in the yard.

Elle held up her fingers. "Two words, Heath: Wal-Mart. Cheap. Buy your daughter some toys."

"That's three words."

"Wal-Mart is hyphenated."

"And I call myself the writer."

"Writer? Didn't Marsha tell me you're a lawyer? Hey, Rio, baby, don't be so bossy."

"Yes, I'm a writer dressed as a lawyer. I work for a boutique Manhattan law firm, focus on criminal law, but I took a break, thought I'd write a little."

"What's your book about?"

"I have no idea. Got any good ideas?"

Smiling, Elle stepped away from the window. *Back to work. What is the gunk in this drawer?* She pulled out the work table drawer and dumped its contents down the mouth of a trash bag.

At the sound of a big growl, Elle looked out the window again. A bearlike Heath popped out from behind a tree and sent the girls scrambling and screaming to the deck, Rio's dark head bobbing up while Tracey-Love's blonde one bobbed down.

TL's grin could brighten the darkest sea. And Heath would be Rio's hero by the end of the day if he wasn't already.

"Do it again," Rio shouted to him.

"Okay, close your eyes." Heath rose up from his hands and knees. Something caught his attention. Elle pressed her face into the screen to see.

The FedEx man. "Hey, Chuck," Elle hollered.

The man squinted toward her voice. "What are you doing up there, Elle? Playing Rapunzel?"

"Except for the long hair and Prince Charming, yes."

"Got something for you. From Texas."

Elle rocketed toward the door, barely avoiding a face plant as her toe caught the edge of a wooden crate. She flew down the studio stairs, meeting Chuck where he stood.

"It's from Jeremiah."

"Trying to get a few brownie points, huh?" Chuck flipped Elle his box cutter. "Want to open it?"

She hesitated. What if it was personal? "Okay, but no peeking over my shoulder until I say it's safe." Elle took the box cutter. Kneeling in Heath and Chuck's shade, with a sliver of sun falling across the box, she sliced the tape and peered inside.

"Well, what'd he send?" Chuck's barrel frame blocked her light, but he kept his promise not to peek.

Heath waited on the other side of Chuck.

A bundle of CDs tied with the same ribbon she'd used when she gave him the recordings as a gift. The neckties she'd give him for Christmas. The pictures she'd had framed for his apartment in Dallas. The shells they'd gathered during their first walk on the beach. Movie stubs. The napkin she'd given him after blotting her lipstick because he said, "It smells like you."

Among the items, she found no note of explanation. Her skin prickled with heat. *Why would Jeremiah do this?*

Chuck cleared his throat. "Well, best get going. See you, Elle."

"See you." She couldn't look around at him. Had he seen the contents of the box? If so, did he understand?

Chuck and Heath's voices faded as they walked toward the

FedEx truck. In the next minute, the engine fired up, reverse whining as Chuck backed out the drive.

Elle stood, cradling the box in her arms, trembling. *Is he breaking up with me?* The thought made her queasy.

Heath called the girls. "How about ice cream?"

Yelling their agreement, they darted across the yard. Elle heard the doors open, then close.

I don't get it? Why . . . Her thoughts raced over the last few days. They'd agreed on a house, putting in for the loan. Jeremiah asked for her financials, which Daddy, her accountant, was gathering.

Heath's shadow fell over hers. "I have the feeling Chuck didn't bring something pleasant."

She shook her head.

"I'm sorry. Can I help in any way?"

"No, but thank you."

"I'm taking Rio with me." Heath waited, then backed away. "Be back soon."

It was hard to speak. Elle felt like any breath, any word or movement would be the thread that unraveled her. She felt numb and on fire at the same time.

Hearing Heath pull away, she started for the studio steps, her emotions beginning to boil. She burst inside, threw the box to the table, and yanked her cell phone from the top of her bag.

Jeremiah Franklin better answer this call.

Seven

On the loft floor of what used to be GG Gallery, Elle sat with her knees to her chest, her arms wrapped around her calves. The men working on Angela Dooley's remodel had stood aside when Elle barged in like a wounded animal and bounded up to the second level.

"Don't mind me," she'd told them, her voice hollow to her own ears.

"Hey, you can't come in here. This is a construction site."

"Leave her alone, Frank. Elle, you okay?"

"Fine, Gilly. Just peachy." Why she wanted to be at the gallery—or what used to be her gallery—Elle didn't know, but she climbed to the loft and huddled on the floor, the darkness comforting her.

Jeremiah didn't answer her initial call, nor the two dozen after. *God, what is going on?* Hopelessness locked on and Elle let her tears slip free. "What did I ever do to him?"

Wiping her cheeks with the back of her hand, feeling the grit of the construction mess grinding her skin, she'd dialed Jeremiah again and was rewarded for the twentieth time with his stupid, tired, recorded message. "You've reached Jeremiah Franklin, senior pastor at 3:16 Metro Church. I'm not available . . ."

Elle pressed End, her jaw tight. "You're never available."

Waiting for him to call in between all of her autodialing, Elle tried to fathom her relationship with Jeremiah coming to this. The enticing, electric sensations he'd created in her belly when he kissed her and slipped his fingers along the edge of temptation were distant and cold.

Drawing in a big gulp of warm, dusty loft air, Elle tried to make sense of it all. Was it Dallas and the big church? Was it her? Him? Did they not know each other as well as they pretended?

Why won't you call me back? She resisted the urge to smash her phone against the wall.

The last glow of daylight had slipped away from the store's pane window, leaving Elle completely in the dark when her phone finally rang.

"I'm in a meeting and my phone won't stop vibrating," he said without hello, without saying her name.

A string of blue words, many of which Elle had never uttered before in her life, flowed from her soul. "Then get out of the meeting."

"I told you I'd call later."

"The box came." Flat, honest confession.

Silence, followed by a heavy blast of air. "It wasn't supposed to arrive until tomorrow or later."

"Darn the efficiency of those FedEx boys." Her wounds dripped sarcasm.

Silence again. "It's not going to work, Elle."

Her tense muscles kept her from shattering into a million pieces. "What is not going to work, Jeremiah?" She'd given him way too much lead in their relationship. If he wanted to say something, he'd best speak plainly.

"You. Me. Marriage." She heard a door click closed and the echo of Jeremiah's footsteps in a hollow hall.

"Only because you're sabotaging it. You're physically and emotionally unavailable. I can't win."

"I can't win with you either. I told you, Elle, the ministry would consume me at first."

"When have I ever interrupted your ministry?" Now that it was going down, she couldn't stop shaking.

"Face it, Elle. You don't want to be married to a pastor."

"Jeremiah, I love you. I want to be married to you, not your job. I feel like you want me to simply fit into your life without bringing any part of myself. It's like I'm the right size, so give me the suit."

"I don't know how you can say that, but yes, I need a woman who can stand strong in ministry. Elle, if you want to do your own thing, chase your own God dreams, then go for it, but I can't let it get in the way of what He's called me to do." His confession sliced through her heart, painfully cutting. "I'm sorry. Those are hard words, but I felt you needed to hear them."

"You are so unfair and selfish, Jeremiah. How could you say that to me? I've never let my dreams get in the way of yours. I agreed to the house, agreed to move to Dallas *after* you proposed, agreed to wait on the gallery."

"Look, let's not cloud the issue."

"Cloud the issue? I think it's fairly clear, Jer—you don't want to marry me."

"Elle, I'm just not ready."

"You're thirty-five. When will you be ready?" His lame excuse angered her.

"It's not age, it's the work. I'm not in a place to take on marriage. I'm sorry. If I'd have known this when I took the job, I would've never proposed."

"Then quit." A sharp but logical resolution.

"Quit? The church?"

"Yes, the church. Quit for us."

"I can't quit the church, Elle," Jeremiah said. "I've made a commitment to these people. They've invested time and money in me and my vision."

"You made a commitment to me. Are you going stand before

God and hear, 'Kudos, son, for dumping the artist gal to pastor a church'? God, family, job, remember? You're not their savior, bubba. Last I looked Jesus earned that job."

"Can I deny God's calling on my life? Did Paul? Did Peter? We have to leave everything to follow Him. Even fiancées, if necessary."

If necessary? Sitting cross-legged, Elle buckled over until her forehead met the sawdust-covered floor. "You're asking me to give up everything to watch you soar, but won't budge one inch toward me."

"That's not my intention, Elle. I'm trying to be focused here. I don't know, maybe the timing is all off. I do love you." Elle felt his hesitation: *I think . . .*

"What happened to 'Love bears all things, endures and hopes'?"

"I can love you, Elle, even if I'm not married to you."

She resented his soft explanation. "But I want to marry you. I love you here, now."

"Are you saying you want to marry a man who's not ready?"

"Mama mailed the invitations, Jeremiah."

"I'm sorry. I know this is awkward and untimely."

The shaking faded as the sad tears began. "Daddy spent a lot of money; friends and family have made plans."

"We can't get married because people spent money and made plans." His patience sounded thin. "I've spent hours thinking and considering the consequences to our actions. Either way, it's difficult. But I want to do the right thing."

"Which is?" She wanted to hear him say, "It's over."

"Call off the wedding."

"All right."

Unbidden, peace began to slip over her. The pain shooting over her scalp ceased, and the tension in her jaw vanished. She was done. With the conversation. With Jeremiah. With the idea of Happily Ever After. Staring into the darkness, Elle clicked her phone shut.

In her room, Tracey-Love slept. At least Heath hoped she did. The day of running with Rio had exhausted her. If he had any remaining doubts about uprooting her from New York, today wiped them out.

She seemed like a new kid to him. During the simple dinner of grilled chicken and salad, she'd chatted almost nonstop, her stutter more pronounced with her excitement, but barely slowing her down.

After dinner, he'd plopped her in the tub with a bag of toys he'd snatched up at the Wal-Mart checkout line. (Elle's admonition stuck with him. *Wal-Mart. Cheap.*) The dirt from her feet and hands instantly browned the water, and under her sweat-stained face Heath discovered a pink sunburn on her cheeks.

"Daddy's going to have to buy a shotgun," he'd told her as he stuck the rinse cup under the faucet and poured it over her thick hair.

TL covered her eyes with taut little hands. "H-h-how's come, D-daddy? B-bur-r-rglars?"

"Yes, sort of." Heath wiped the rest of the water from her face with a washcloth. Burglars dressed as teen boys wanting to steal his daughter's affections.

Tracey-Love's wide eyes glistened. "Bad burglars?"

"TL, Daddy's just kidding. There are no burglars. We're all safe and snug. You're my girl, aren't you? Me and you, all the way, right?" He held out his palm.

"R-r-right." Tracey-Love slapped her hand over his, sending a splat of water across his shirt.

After the bath, two bedtime stories, and a song Ava used to sing (Tracey-Love made him stop. *"Y-you sound funny."*), Heath tucked her into bed. So far, she hadn't come searching for him.

With the house quiet and the porch beckoning him, Heath slipped out of his wet shirt, kicked off his shoes, and sat outside, lighting Elle's porch lamps, angling the wrought-iron rocker to face the creek.

In his hand, he gripped an unopened letter.

The edges of the handwritten, blue-ink address fanned across the crumpled white envelope. Months of being carried in his laptop case and jacket pocket had smeared the letters. Finally, he'd buried it in his top dresser drawer to pretend it didn't exist until he was ready to read it.

The move to Beaufort resurrected its presence.

Ava's letter.

Courage, man. Flipping it over, he gripped the small tear started on the back flap—enough to know he'd been there before, but not enough to expose the pages inside.

"Can't do it." Heath collapsed against the back of the chair, releasing the letter to the wrought-iron table. *Ava, it wasn't supposed to be like this.*

"Evening."

Heath jerked around to see a robust man with a broad chest and a Panther's ball cap stepping onto the porch through the screen door. "Truman Garvey, Elle's daddy."

"Heath McCord."

Their hands clapped together.

"She tells me you're from New York?"

"Yes, sir." He glanced around for his shoes and shirt. Right, he'd left them inside.

"Nice to meet you." Truman shoved his hat back.

"Please, have a seat." Heath reached for the letter, slipping it in his hip pocket. "Let me get a shirt."

"Have you seen Elle?" Truman asked, easing into an old Adirondack chair opposite Heath with an *oomph*.

"Not since this afternoon." Heath slipped into the kitchen, grabbed his shirt from the back of the chair, still wet from bath time. Before heading out, he leaned to listen for Tracey-Love. All was quiet.

Heath sat in the rocker. "What can do I for you?"

"That boy broke it off with Elle tonight."

"Her fiancé?" He couldn't think of any other boy who might break things off.

"Got a cola or something cold in the house? I'm a bit parched. Yeah, her fiancé called of the wedding. Just mailed off three hundred invitations too."

"Man . . . rough." Heath pushed out of his seat. "Got a few sodas inside."

"As long as it fizzes, it's good with me."

"Yes, sir."

Heath liked this man. Reminded him of his granddaddy. Simple, straightforward, told it like it was, no messing around. He pulled two cans from the fridge. One Sprite, one root beer. "Here you go, sir. Sprite or root beer."

"Most of my friends call me Truman." He took the Sprite and popped it open, motioning through the screen. "I saw the baby buggy outside on my way in. You got a girl?"

"Yes, Tracey-Love. Same age as your granddaughter, Rio."

"Tracey-Love?" Truman chuckled. "Now how'd you muster that name? Wife swindle you into it?"

Heath grinned with a swig of his root beer. "No, it happened by accident."

"Most of the unusual ones do."

"Her mom wanted to name her Tracey with Love as her middle name, after her great-grandma. Once we agreed, somehow we started calling her Tracey-Love and in the hoopla of her birth, Tracey-hyphen-Love was written on her birth certificate. We liked it and kept it."

Truman nodded, seemingly satisfied. "You raising her alone?"

"Apparently."

"Not your choice?"

"No, and no again."

"I raised five girls. Not alone, of course. Their mama did most of the work. I just handed over my paycheck and hoped to get a turn with the remote."

Heath whistled. "Five? And I was worried about raising one."

"Girls come with all sorts of accessories. Fits of Emotion, Bathroom Clutter, Boy-Called-Me Voice, Boy-Dumped-Me Wail, I'm-On-A-Diet Grump, I'm-Going-Shopping Scream, Sleepy Christmas Morning Stare . . ."

"I'm a dead man."

"Finest thing I ever produced was those girls. Wouldn't trade them for five sons, and I mean it. Had a good buddy with three boys. One caught the curtains on fire when he was twelve and should've had sense to know better. The older boy wrecked the family car in one of those illegal street-racing deals and spent a year in juvenile detention. And if that weren't bad enough, the youngest got two girls pregnant at the same time. Two. Neither one would speak to him, and my friend has two grandbabies he's never held."

Heath shook his head. "You make me feel lucky."

"You are. Even when you don't fee like it. But listen"—Truman tapped his chest—"you call me any time. I'll see you through."

Heath smiled, moved by the surety of the man's pledge. "I suppose you have some daughter worries tonight, though."

"Elle . . ." Truman tipped up his can. "She'll land on her feet after being mad, crying it out, fuming for a few days. She gave up a lot for that boy."

"How'd you hear about this if Elle is AWOL?"

"He called me. Go figure that, but I got to respect him for it. Figured he'd asked permission to marry her, he'd best do the manly thing and tell me he'd called it off. He felt like his new job took too much of his time and affection. Didn't figure it fair to Elle."

"He sent her a box of stuff today," Heath said. "She didn't look happy."

"I reckon not."

Heath tried to imagine what was going on in the man's life to give up a woman like the one he'd observed the past few days, church or no church. He'd witnessed the mistress of ministry destroy a man once so he made sure he kept his gaze steady on the only One who died for him.

However, when God required such a big sacrifice—Ava, his heart, his love—Heath struggled with God's perfect will.

"You like the cottage?" Truman asked, motioning to the pale-yellow board sides. "Elle bought it for like fifty cents on the dollar. We helped her fix it up."

"Yeah, I do—"

Truman's phone went off. He retrieved it from his shorts pocket. "Yep?" He finished his drink, *hmming* a lot. After a minute, he snapped the phone shut and clipped it to his holster. "She's at the house, weak and broken, but she'll live. Lady, my wife, actually said Elle seemed quite peaceful, considering. Full of questions, as you can imagine, asking why and how, though none of us know the answer."

"Certainly." Heath wondered how this man felt so free to share his family's intimate details with . . . well, a stranger.

Truman handed Heath his empty can. "Better go see what I can do. Thanks for the drink. See you in the funny pages."

Heath grinned. His granddad used to say that to him and his brother Mark, adding nicknames like "squirt" or "sport." *"See you in the funny pages, squirt."*

"See you in the funny pages, Truman."

Heath watched until the headlights disappeared into the darkness, wondering if he'd prefer to be in Elle's shoes rather than his own.

But brokenhearted is brokenhearted. Never embraced. Never treasured. Never easy. Heath figured every human being had a certain amount of God-ordained grace to endure their own unique brand of loss and pain.

He'd had seven months to get used to his. Elle? Maybe seven hours?

"Don't let your love grow cold, Elle Garvey."

He'd let his love chill. And now, as he began to emerge from his season of pain, he regretted it. At the end of all truth was Jesus. He'd never let Heath down, no matter what song his circumstances sang. Funny how when he needed God's love and peace the most, he'd given Him the stiff arm.

With the crickets harmonizing in a Coffin Creek chorus, Heath figured the place and timing was right for his own good-bye dirge to sadness and doubt.

God, Heath had learned, had a profound sense of irony. Imagine moving a man recovering from grief into a charming cottage next to a place called Coffin Creek. Sometimes it was only in dying one found life.

So, yeah, he got the irony, God. Bury the past, discover the future.

Maybe Elle had the same journey, for whatever reason.

Heath pulled Ava's letter from his pocket. He wasn't ready to read it, but he was ready to heal and move on. He dipped his head and confessed, "Jesus, I'm sorry for my cold heart. When I said I'd love You and follow You, I understood it didn't guarantee me a perfect life. You took Ava—or allowed her to be taken, I don't know which—but I just want to say to You it is well with my soul."

Tears flushed his eyes. Heat swelled in his torso. It was well with his soul. And where it wasn't, he longed for it to be.

Heath lingered until he felt his business with God had concluded. Rising to go inside, he turned off the porch lamps and retrieved Ava's letter. Back in the kitchen, he anchored it on the windowsill behind the lock.

By the end of summer, he'd read it. Surely the courage resided in him somewhere. If not, he'd burn it and forget it ever existed.

Eight

In the lowcountry, the sun didn't ask permission to burn through the glass and wake a girl up even at two in the afternoon—and remind her to sweep up the scattered pieces of her heart.

Lying belly down on the futon, cheek against her pillow, Elle saw the blue-and-white day march past her window. Mr. Miller's hounds bayed. A mower hummed over someone's yard of spring grass.

Six days ago, her future had been set—marry Jeremiah, move to Dallas. But a simple "I can't marry you now, Elle" had wrecked her plans, her hopes, a little of her identity.

Tossing off the sheet and thin summer quilt, Elle walked the sun-drenched floor to shove open the windows and flipped on the fans. The window air conditioner had frozen up in the night, leaving the loft hot and stuffy.

A scented breeze slipped through the screen. One thing Elle counted on: each new day bringing its own brand of anesthesia—hope. Elle leaned against the windowsill and inhaled, the day sweet and warm.

Mama and Daddy had been great, taking care of all the cancellation details, bringing her food, pretending she might be hungry.

What she hated the most? Feeling trapped by Jeremiah's actions and her own emotions. She had to stir herself up.

The sound of a chainsaw nabbed her attention. Across the yard, down the slope to the creek, a shirtless Heath stood before an oak stump, protective gear on his head, chainsaw gripped in his hand.

The lawyer was a wood carver? She'd watched wood-carving artists at shows, enthralled.

His taunt, broad back was reddish brown from recent days in the sun, and his winter blond was gradually becoming a summer gold. The ends of his hair stood on end from where he must have jumbled it with his hands.

Finally, he revved the motor again and bit into the wood. Sawdust flew around him like a gazillion blond gnats. The fragrance of warm wood filtered through the studio screen.

Elle's stomach rumbled. And she needed a shower. Leaving the window, half thinking she should do something with the rest of her day, take a step into the rest of her life, she booted up her laptop.

When she launched the Internet, her home page routed to a default. Just another reminder. She's taken down GG Gallery's Web page.

Surfing over to e-mail, she saw her Inbox contained over a hundred messages with subject lines like, "Sorry to hear" and "Praying for you." She read a few, but found them too depressing, so she skimmed the names until she found one that made her smile.

Caroline Sweeney. Today she needed her friend, even if she lived thousands of miles across the Atlantic.

To: Elle Garvey
From: CSweeney
Subject: I'm with you in spirit

Your dad e-mailed me about you and Jeremiah. Elle, I am so sorry! If I was there, I'd beat him up for you. What is he thinking? He'll never find anyone as beautiful, talented, and kind as you. He just won't.

This morning I read a notice in the online *Gazette* about the wedding being canceled. Canceled? Isn't that a strange thing to say of two people's lives and relationship? Baseball games are canceled. Cable television is canceled. Not a marriage.

Elle, I'm grieving with you, wishing I had ten-thousand-mile-long arms to reach you for a hug.

Daddy ran a notice in the Gazette? *What was he—Oh, forget it, Elle.*

It must seem like the world is ending, but wait and see what God will do. He must have something wonderful in mind.

Listen to me talk, the baby in God. Yet I've learned so much about trust and faith living in Barcelona. God has enabled me to do a job for which I had no training or qualifications. When I see my reflection in the mirror, it is the only part of me that looks and feels the same. If you'd have told me a well of confidence dwelt under the soil of my soul, I'd have never believed you.

The leap of faith I took to come here showed me who He created me to be.

I'm so convinced, even on the hardest days, He loves me, He's for me, and is intimately acquainted with every detail of my life.

I look forward to what God has for you, Elle. I know, I sound like I'm speaking Christianese. But can I help it all the good truths of God got labeled? He does love you. He does have good for you. I believe it.

In your dad's e-mail, he indicated it was Jeremiah's doing, but I believe it was God's. Don't be mad at me for saying it. If we were sitting with you in Luther's or the Frogmore Café, I'd say this to your face, I'm that sure.

I'm praying for you. If Jeremiah is yours, he'll return. And you'll welcome him. If he's not, you wouldn't want to be married to him. Trust God, Elle. After all, He IS love.

Since this new development, I changed my trip home to be later in the summer. There's so much going on here. Please consider coming to Barcelona for a visit. I'd love it and you can go to the beach every day, relax, read, pray, whatever. Paint. Elle, there's so many wonderful scenes and places to inspire you.

Mitch is coming next week. I really miss him. I don't know how much longer we can wait to be together. We're praying about what's next for us.

I love you, my dear friend. You're a jewel in my heart.

Always, Caroline

Elle wiped the tears from the edge of her jaw. *I love you too, Caroline.*

Julianne burst into the studio without a knock or "Woo-hoo, are you decent?" Elle was dozing on the futon, her pajama bottoms twisted and a sock on one foot. So far, her decision to venture out had ended at the computer.

"You look like crap."

Elle opened one eye. Julianne hovered over her, hands on her narrow waist. "Don't let the door slam on your way out."

"Get up." She tugged on Elle's arm. "We're going out to eat, get something greasy and fattening." Julianne picked a pair of jeans and a top off the floor, sniffing them. "Are these clean?"

"Being as I've only worn what I have on for the last week, I'd say yes."

"Good. Get in the shower." Julianne tossed the clothes to the futon. "Don't you have a closet in here? A chest of drawers?"

"No, I wasn't planning on being here that long. Jules, I don't want to go out"—Elle managed to sit up—"where people *know*. Did you see Dad ran an ad? In the paper? People will frown and bend their heads together, whispering, 'Poor Elle, couldn't hold on to her man.'"

"Who cares? You need to get out of this place, Elle. It smells and I'm concerned for you health. Besides, Rio wants to see you."

Elle arched her brow. "Really? Where is she?"

"Down in the yard with Tracey-Love. She's a sweet girl." Julianne peered out the window. "I saw him without a shirt." She glanced at Elle with an arched brow. "Somebody visits the gym."

"Don't arch your brows at me. If you like him, go for it. I think he's divorced or something."

"Are you going to let him stay in the cottage now that you're not moving?" Julianne waved Elle's jeans in her face. "Into the shower. Go."

Her feet hit the floor in a slow start. The earlier rumble in her stomach had morphed into hunger pangs. "He paid his rent in advance. And I don't know why I should mess up his life because of mine. If he was alone, maybe, but I can't do it to Tracey-Love." Elle stood without moving, clutching her jeans to her chest. "Besides, I have no visible means of support. Might as well have my mortgage covered until I figure where to open a new gallery. Oh, Jules, Angela Dooley is in my prime spot."

"You shouldn't have sold."

"She said after the fact. Not helping, Jules."

Julianne placed her hands on Elle's shoulder and turned her toward the small bathroom. "You can always stay at Mama and Daddy's, have the upstairs all to yourself."

Elle peeked over her shoulder. "And you don't live there be-cause . . ."

"All right, it was just an idea. If I lived there, you know Mama would take over Rio. What about living with Sara Beth? She and Parker have that large spare room."

"It's for Parker's mother when she comes. Besides, it smells like menthol and moth balls."

Instead of walking for the shower, Elle sat on the futon, her legs feeling weak.

Julianne sat next to her. "Does it hurt real bad?"

"Only when I'm awake. Thankfully, that hasn't been much lately."
She collapsed against Julianne. "The pain comes and goes. The night
Jer called things off, this giant peace came over me. I've been searching for that same security ever since, asking God to help me." But on
days like today, when she was tired and weak, it was hard. "C-can
you pray for me, Julianne?"

"Me?" Julianne's shoulder stiffened under Elle's cheek. "You're
asking the wrong sister. Sara Beth or Mary Jo, even Candace, but
me? No, no, no. I'm sure God doesn't want to hear from me."

Elle sighed and lifted off the futon. "I'll go shower."

"Wait, Elle." Julianne grabbed Elle's arm. "I'll do it. For you."
Elle sat, closing her eyes, molding her hand with Jules's.

"God, um," Julianne breathed in, then out. "Wait, Elle, come
on, I can't . . ."

"You can." Elle squeezed her hand.

"I feel so . . . silly."

"Maybe this isn't about you. Please, Jules, a short prayer, for me."

God, *a-hem,* Julianne here on behalf of my sister. Could You
please be with her, fill the hole in her heart, remind her that You
love—"

As Elle listened to her sister's halting but heartfelt words, peace
began to swirl in and around her. She felt light and free, as if she
were melting. She pressed her toes against the studio floor to keep
from sliding right off the futon. Julianne might not believe in the
power of her prayers, but Elle certainly did.

When Julianne said, "Amen," Elle lifted her head but kept her
eyes closed.

A Presence hovered in the room. Elle felt a cool breeze whisper
past her feet. Next to her, Julianne breathed deep and steady.

"Elle?"

"Yeah?" The studio atmosphere was like dipping in a cool blue
pool of water on a hot summer day. Elle wanted to soak as long as
she could.

"Do you feel something?" Julianne shivered.

"Peace."

"More than peace?"

"Maybe." A hot gust of wind hit the window's screen. Elle peeked from under her lowered eyelids. Papers rustled across the work table. A cone of sunlight formed a circle on the dull hardwood.

Elle saw it first, then Julianne. A small white feather appeared out of nowhere, riding the studio's breeze, drifting through the golden light.

"Elle."

"I see it." Elle let go and slipped off the futon, picking the soft white plume off the floor.

"Where'd it come from?"

Elle glanced up Julianne, who leaned away from the mysterious feather, looking this side of freaked. "I have no idea."

"I'm out of here." Jules went for the door. "I'll be in the car. Hurry up."

The breeze settled and the studio air returned to normal. Elle set the curious feather on the worktable, knowing in a weird, unique way, God had stopped by.

To: CSweeney

From: Elle Garvey

Subject: I'm doing well

Caroline,

I'm alive, hurting, but healing. Takes more than being dumped by my fiancé to kill me. Ha. In all your born days did you ever imagine this happening to any of us? To me?

I didn't.

My heart is heavy, wondering where it all went wrong. But I'm pulling myself together, slowly. Right now, sleeping and watching movies at Mama and Daddy's is my prescription.

I haven't had this much time on my hands since the summer before seventh grade.

There's a Yankee comeya with a four-year-old daughter renting the cottage. His grandpap was a benya so he's returning to his roots. He's a widower, not sure how or why or when.

Enough about me. Tell me about you and Mitch, and Barcelona. And hey, tell buddy-o-pal Hazel I said hey and she owes me an e-mail.

Much love, Elle

Under the low glow of the living room lamp, Heath set-tled down in the club chair with his laptop and propped his legs on the ottoman.

Nights were best for writing, away from the distractions of the day. Already he wondered if he could ever go back to his hectic schedule at Calloway & Gardner.

Four-year-olds made for great company. Today he and Tracey-Love had taken a long walk, colored, talked about learning to fish, and picnicked by the creek. Her stutter had not yet softened and he could tell it frustrated her. But as she healed from Ava's death, Heath believed the stutter would too.

He glanced at the sofa. At seven o'clock, the little girl slept in an S shape on the cushions, the tip of her wrinkled thumb touching her lips.

Shifting his gaze from TL to the laptop screen, Heath tried to focus on his story. As much as he liked to pretend, books didn't write themselves. Nate had texted him twice during the day: "How's it going?" followed by "I could use a few chapters."

It's been, what, a few weeks? Absently, Heath drummed his fingers against the keys, mulling over an opening line. Hemmingway said all he had to do was write one true sentence, then go from there. Easier said than done.

His arms were sore from wielding the chainsaw, carving out his angel. He hadn't carved since his last visit to the lowcountry the year before Granddad died. He wasn't sure where the unction had come from to take it up again, but Heath loved the release of physical work. Somehow, carving skimmed away another layer of the dull pain around his heart and found the fresh surface of hope. Day by day, he was starting to believe he could be happy again.

Tracey-Love shivered and moaned. Heath arched forward and snatched the afghan from the back of the couch and draped it over her. The early spring evenings were damp and cool.

Back to his blank page, Heath searched for the story brewing beneath. Closing his eyes, he let his thoughts wander. A picture of Granddad, a man of many adventures and stories, floated past his mind's eye. Stationed in the Aleutian Islands during the war, he'd flown P-36s and P-40s for the Army's 11th Air Force.

He'd been a tall, athletic, good-looking flyer with lots of charisma. When Heath was about fifteen, Granddad came to New York for an 11th Air Force reunion and invited Heath to tag along. That evening, Heath learned his granddad's exploits extended beyond taming the wild brush of Edisto Island.

Into his college years, Heath made a hobby of collecting and reading World War II books.

The first hint of a story settled in Heath's mind based on two of his loves, Granddad and history.

The Alaskan day was cloaked in its usual darkness and the few hours of light that dawned midday barely disturbed the hovering canvas of night. Captain Chet McCord of the 18th Pursuit Squadron entered the mess hall on Elmendorf Air Base, grabbed a dark mug of joe, and straddled a chair at one of the card tables.

"Tired, Captain?" asked First Sgt. Lipton in charge of the ground crew. He winced at his cards and tossed them to the table. "I got nothing."

Yes, Chet was tired.

"They keep you boys flying, don't they?" Lipton again.

"Can't let the Japs catch us on the ground." Chet sipped the coffee, then made a face. It had to be three days old. He'd give a month's pay for his mama's coffee.

Since the Japanese had bombed Pearl, "Yellow Peril" rocked the northwest, including Alaska and the Aleutians Islands. Bogus wave radio reports about a U.S. invasion kept citizens on edge and the Army Air Corps flying.

(Note to self: do more research on the army's position tactics in the Northwest.)

Across the mess hut, a boyish, carefree flyer from Oklahoma stood on a chair, pounding his palm. "All right, who has news from home? Come on, somebody, something, anything."

"Sit down, Wilkins. Stop tormenting the boys with your ugly mug. You know nobody has a recent letter from home."

Lieutenant Wilkins wasn't easily deterred. "Then who has old news from home? Stone, didn't you have a girl writing you regular? Alice whatshername, right? Long legs, Betty Grable figure."

Sgt. Stone shuffled cards. "Found herself an officer at the USO."

A few of the boys patted his shoulder. "Sorry, Stone."

"What about you, Captain McCord?" Stone shifted the attention away from himself. "Someone's always writing you."

"Yeah." Wilkins jumped off the chair. "Aunt Bess. Did she send you any cake lately?"

The men erupted with laughter. Aunt Bess was a camp legend. But not for her cake—for her face.

Wilkins circled the table, bringing the new recruits up to speed. "Boys, Aunt Bess ain't like my Aunt Bess." He formed an hourglass in the air with his hands. "Not a sweet little old lady, stooped over with a few teeth missing. No sir, McCord's Aunt Bess is a smart, good-looking doll with perfect teeth and hair like the rays of sun over the wheat fields. But she's the worst cook this side of the Mississippi. Sent us a cake once and we all ended up calling for the medic. Chet, I heard CINPAC is thinking of commissioning her cookies to fire at the enemy."

"What do you say, McCord? Any news from Aunt Bess?" called a private across the room. "I'd kill for one of her cookies."

More laughter. Chet surveyed the boys, leaning back in his chair. "Not a word, not even a crumb of rotten cake."

A debate started. Who would go back home and win Bess's heart, overlooking her lack of cooking skills? "I'd marry her. Don't care if she can't cook," determined a flyer from the back of the hut.

"You'll have to get in line behind me, Downs." This from Wilkins.

As an icy blast shook the hall, Chet hunkered down over his coffee, listening to the men argue over marrying a girl they'd never meet.

Heath reviewed his prose. Not bad. Maybe passable. He liked the escape of writing about another place and time, incorporating his love of history and heroes like his granddad.

Talk to me, Chet McCord. What's it like up there in the cold, frozen Aleutians?

A small, distant crash snapped Heath's attention. Looking up, he listened. Another crash. Louder this time. Shoving his laptop to the ottoman, he stood with a glance at Tracey-Love. She slept undisturbed. *Crash,* again. Who was breaking glass? Heath eased in the direction of the sound.

Crash. A high-pitched yell. Heath peered out the sink window, where Ava's letter still waited, and through the blueish-orange twilight caught Elle firing objects at the garage wall just under the studio's stairs. Something white and glistening exploded like porcelain fireworks and fell into the tall grass.

She bent to a box for another item. Heath squinted. A gravy boat? She lunged it, but this time the piece barely broke in two. He stepped outside and hollered from the deck.

"You throw like a girl."

Without breaking rhythm, Elle whipped another piece through the air. "In case you haven't noticed, I am a girl."

Yeah, he'd noticed. Too much. First time since Ava's death he'd *noticed* a woman. He eased her way, carefully, in case she got a wild hair and decided to lob something at him. A white-and-rose teapot popped against the block wall, cracked in two, and thudded to the ground.

"Put more shoulder into it," he offered.

"Of all the possible renters in the world, I get Roger Clemens?" Elle picked up a round platter and flipped it like a Frisbee, smashing it into pieces. "Satisfied?"

"Better, Garvey. Much better." He angled over to see her face. "What are you doing?"

"What's it look like?" She Frisbeed another plate.

Heath smiled when it hit. She was getting a rhythm. "Breaking dishes? But why?"

Stopping to catch her breath, Elle stared up at him, then pitched a petite vase.

Heath stood aside, gaining understanding. He'd been in the same place, grief iced with anger. He'd wanted to smash a few things, but in the end couldn't bring himself to do it. He'd given up too much to waste the things he and Ava had shared together. In many ways, *things* were all he had left to help him remember.

Elle side-armed a teacup. Good smash, nice tinkling resonance. "Remind me not to let Tracey-Love run around here barefoot."

"I'll shop vac later."

"Is this making you feel better?" he asked. The exercise didn't appear to be relieving her of anything, only fueling her anger.

"No, actually, it isn't."

"Are you destroying wedding gifts?"

"Sort of." She kicked the box. "Things I've collected over the years. Stupid things . . ." Her voice faded into a watery quiver.

"I'm sorry, Elle." Heath slipped his hands into his jeans pocket and just waited for her to go on. Throw another stupid thing or walk away.

"Why do girls want to be married so badly? Stupid, isn't it?" She wiped a light sheen of sweat from her forehead.

"No. And don't fool yourself; men want to be married just as much, if not more. Love and commitment are wonderful things."

Elle eyed him through blowing strands of her hair. "Is there a pile of broken china in your past? Lying on some New York lawn?"

Beautiful *and* perceptive. He was *noticing* her more every time they talked. "I can relate to your pain and frustration, Elle."

"You know what bites me most? I'm literally left with nothing while Jeremiah sits in his fancy Dallas pastor's office." She shoved the box again with her foot. "No husband, no gallery, no cottage, no life."

"Say the word and we'll move, Elle."

"I can't do that to you and Tracey-Love. Besides, you're paying my mortgage. Thank you very much."

"So maybe this whole breakup scene is a great opportunity instead of a horrible problem."

"Oh, crud, you're one of those glass-half-full guys." Elle fluttered her fingers at him. "Well, move on, there's nothing to see here. All the glasses are emp-tee."

He regarded her for a second, then, "Ever watch your soul mate sleeping in a casket? Ever watch the person who caused your heart to skip a beat be lowered into the ground with the preacher declaring, 'Ashes to ashes'?"

Elle's green gaze faded from impatience to concern and lingered on his face. "No, I haven't."

"Ever wake up feeling helpless and frightened, reaching for someone who's not there but should be. Ever wake up racked with guilt because you wonder if you'd just said no, or been more assertive, the one you love would be alive?"

Understanding blossomed across her face. "Heath, I'm so sorry. Here I am whining and complaining over a short-lived engagement. How long has she been gone?"

"Almost eight months."

"So you came here for more than writing a book."

"Yes. Needed a change, a break, a way to jump-start our lives and heal."

Elle slipped her arms around his waist, hugging him softly. "May you find it at Coffin Creek."

Caught off guard, Heath's arms hung at his side for a long second. It'd been so long since he hugged another woman. But when he felt she was about to step away, he slipped his arms around her shoulders.

"Same to you, Elle. Same to you."

Nine

MAY

The first Sunday in May Elle woke up with a craving to sing and decided she'd avoided church long enough. After showering and dressing in jeans and a wrinkled blouse, she stood in the middle of the studio.

One step forward, she'd be tracking for the door. One step back, she'd be on the futon sleeping the day away.

Nine forty-five. Decision time. Go or stay? She tried to press the wrinkles from her shirt with her moist palm. If she left now, she'd only be a few minutes late. But where was her handbag? Couldn't drive without her keys.

Bible? She had one of those, somewhere. Searching the boxes from the cottage bedroom, she found the Good Book under a pile of stuff from her bedroom.

Car keys in hand, she hesitated. How could she face all those people? Her church family? A congregation of folks who had expected to attend her wedding next Saturday? Folks who had adored and loved Jeremiah Franklin.

Elle jiggled the keys. Maybe she wasn't ready for church just yet. As the "loser" in this wedding-day disaster, she could only imagine all the speculations.

What did Elle do to make him dump her?

She must be crazy. If I had a man like Jeremiah . . .

Stop, Elle, and get moving. Grabbing her bag from the table, tucking her Bible under her arm, she started for the door. Then she saw it, just like the first one.

A feather, surfing the morning sunbeams, its twin lying on the worktable. Catching it in mid-float, Elle felt a wave of awe.

God, what are You doing?

Slipping into the back pew, Elle tried to focus on Jesus rather than the fact she was at Beaufort Community Church without Jeremiah.

Were people staring and whispering? With a quick gaze, she knew. The congregation was not preoccupied with her love life and marital status.

Burley, kind Andy Castleton, the Frogmore Café's owner, caught her eye and jutted out his chin. *Be strong, gal.*

All right, Andy.

She closed her eyes, ready to join the singing, when a small voice asked, "Is there room for me here?"

Elle looked down to see tiny Miss Anna standing in the aisle.

"Certainly, yes, please join me." Elle slid down to let her in.

"I've been praying for you," she whispered, her pulpy cool hand soft on Elle's arm.

Her declaration generated peace in Elle and when Spicy Brown got up in her frog-green suit to give the announcements, Elle sincerely exhaled.

In the pew by the sanctuary doors, she spied Heath with his eyes closed, the tip of Tracey-Love's blonde head barely peeking above the pew.

She admired his courage in starting over. And it was good to see him in the sanctuary.

Pastor O'Neal took the pulpit, his sermon lovely and lyrical, but wasted on Elle, who struggled with missing Jeremiah. For the first time, she understood how people succumbed to bitterness.

When the pastor concluded the service with an "Amen," Miss Anna turned to Elle. "I could use some company in the mornings at the prayer chapel. One puts a thousand to flight. Two, ten thousand."

Elle faced her pew companion. "What? The prayer chapel?" Damaged in Category 1 Hurricane Howard last year, the church had yet to raise funds to fix the ancient, original sanctuary. Boards still covered several of the windows. The last time Elle had gone in there with Daddy to box up the hymnals for safekeeping, she felt claustrophobic.

"How's 7:00 a.m.?" Miss Anna slipped her pocketbook down her arm, cradling her worn Bible.

"I don't know, Miss Anna . . . don't you have a regular prayer group?"

She plopped her blue hat on her head. Elle grinned as it slipped sideways. "Thursdays at ten. I'm talking about something different."

"Different? Prayer is prayer." Elle stood in the aisle with her.

"No, there's intercession, then there's face-to-face with the One who loves you intimately. That's what you're a-needing, Elle. And God has given you a unique gift—free time."

Face-to-face? Had anyone seen God face-to-face and lived? Even Moses had to hide in the rock when God passed by. But free time? Yeah, Elle had plenty. "Why the old chapel?"

"Been praying there for forty years. It's a special place, no distractions. Besides, it'll get you out of your house. This is your season, Elle." Miss Anna tapped her heart. "The Lord's been speaking to me about you. Seek Him now when nothing is demanding your attention. No schedule, no expectations. Then, when demand comes, you'll be ready."

God talked to Miss Anna about her? In church her whole life, Elle confessed she always found Miss Anna somewhat odd, but this morning her exhortation carried authority. "Seven a.m.?"

"Elle . . ." Miss Anna laughed. "You have too many faulty ideas. Now, come let the Lord set you straight."

Faulty ideas. Really? Pretty bold of Miss Anna, if not rude.

"All righty now." Miss Anna wagged her finger at Elle, stepping out of the row. "Seven a.m. See you there. Edna, are you free for lunch? My treat."

Watching her shuffle away, Elle wondered how she could break it to the kind, gentle old lady that she probably wouldn't be at 7:00 a.m. prayer. In fact, she probably wouldn't even be awake.

Dang it. Had that odd little lady hexed her? Not only was Elle awake, but she was wide awake. At 6:00 a.m. to boot.

After an I've-been-dumped-and-want-to-sleep-my-life-away effort, Elle untangled herself from the sheets and headed for the shower. Might as well see what was going on at the dank, smelly prayer chapel.

Soon after, grabbing a packet of stale crackers, she headed toward Mossy Oak in the predawn light. Thinking as she drove, she decided she had a few questions for God. Like why He'd let Jeremiah propose if he was going to dump her. Why He'd let her sell her gallery when two weeks later she'd be without a future.

Maybe a couple of mornings in the prayer chapel would help her reckon with her circumstances.

Turning into the gravel-and-shell parking lot, Elle cut the engine and slipped her keys into her purse. The chapel looked wounded and forlorn sitting on sandy soil, nestled between a half dozen thick live oak branches.

Grabbing her Bible, thinking she'd give this routine three, maybe four days, then resort to sleeping in again, Elle went inside. Yes, she needed to seek direction, but praying at four in the afternoon while driving down Ribaut was as good as 7:00 a.m. in the chapel.

The chapel was dark other than the stage lights and the array of pale color created by the only undamaged stained-glass window. Already up front kneeling at the altar, Miss Anna's face tilted toward the ceiling, her lips smiling. Music played from a small boom box and Elle tiptoed down the aisle to the second-row pew, right side. The hardwood under the bunching carpet complained.

"I knew you'd come," Miss Anna said without looking around.

Elle flipped the pages of her Bible. "Did you pray me awake?"

Miss Anna shook her head. "Once I do what the Lord asks of me, I leave it be, figure He's big enough to fulfill His own desires." The woman gazed right into Elle's soul. "You have a wonderful future and it begins right here in this dingy chapel, communing with God. Elle, it's from the wilderness places that God often promotes us."

Miss Anna fell silent after that, seemingly lost in her own world. Elle stared at the back of her fluffy head, the woman's comments echoing in her mind. *Wonderful future. Begins right here in this dingy chapel. Wilderness places where God promotes.*

Elle had spent most of her charmed life avoiding the hard, wilderness places.

For the first thirty minutes of prayer, Elle's mind wandered. She talked to herself, carried on a one-sided mental parry with Jeremiah, then wondered where she might open a new art gallery.

Toward the end of the hour, she settled down and actually talked to Jesus about her heart issues and read the first chapter of John.

When Miss Anna rose to leave, she stopped by row two, right side. "See you in the morning, Elle."

Elle snatched up her Bible and handbag. "Do you need a ride?"

"I enjoy the walk, thank you."

Driving down Bay Street, Elle slowed her car as workers hung a new sign over her old gallery. Dooley's Emporium.

Emporium? Angela was calling her gallery an Emporium?

Huckleberry Johns darted across Bay carrying his tank of environmental art, disappearing inside Angela's new place. *Good luck, bubba.* If Elle hated his smelly environmental art, the pristine, well-coiffed Emporium owner would loathe it.

Elle needed to sit that boy down for a long talk.

Passing Common Ground, she decided to stop in for a latte. Parking along Bay, she went inside the coffee shop.

"Hey, Molly." Elle had known the red-headed coffee barista since the two-year-old's Sunday school class when Elle was the teacher. Now Molly was old enough to serve cappuccinos and lattes. "Large mocha latte, please."

"One grande coming up."

Grande, large, whatever. Elle picked a table by the window and meditated on her morning. The prayer chapel wasn't as claustrophobic as she'd anticipated. But staying focused was harder than she imagined. Once she'd settled down, she enjoyed her prayers. Maybe even sensed God's presence a little. She realized now it had been awhile since she'd really felt connected to Him.

When had she drifted into social Christianity—God as Savior but not as friend? Elle couldn't pinpoint the season, but it was long before Jeremiah Franklin had come along and broken her heart.

Molly brought her latte around. "Sorry to hear about your wedding, Elle."

She shrugged. "It happens. Never thought it'd happen to me, but—"

"I'd die, simply die, if it happened to me. I mean, what's the point in going on? Life as you know it is over. All your dreams and plans. Love left you high and—"

Thank goodness for cell phones. Elle answered hers with abandon. "Hello."

"Where are you?" Julianne.

"Common Ground. Getting depressed."

"What? Why?"

"Molly. Can't believe I got dumped. Thinks she'd downright die if it happened to her."

"What does she know? I for one can't believe you're up before 8:00 a.m."

What a sarcastic sister. "Best be nice because if you're calling me this early, you want something." Her mama didn't raised no dummy.

"Can you watch Rio today?"

"Why? What are you doing? Can't you take her to the babysitter?" Elle spied a young couple in the corner of the shop. The man rubbed the woman's hands and arms, stretching over the table to kiss her. Elle shifted her back to them.

"It's only for a few hours, Elle. Shirley won't take her because she's getting over a runny nose. She's paranoid lately 'cause her kids keep getting sick. Rio asked to play with Tracey-Love."

Elle couldn't think of an excuse. She didn't have any stellar plans. Maybe organize the studio, but she didn't have a lot of zeal about it. "Why don't I just go with you? Hey, that'd be fun. Girl's day out. What are you doing?"

"You and your questions. Please, watch her for me."

"Me with questions? What about you with secrets? Are you hanging out with an ax murderer? Running drugs on the side? Stealing time with your mystery date?"

"Do you have to make everything so hard?"

"Do you?"

Silence.

"Will you watch Rio for me?"

"See you in twenty."

Ten

"Heath? Anybody home?"

The smack of the kitchen's screen door resonated through the house.

"Door's open." Heath read his last sentence for the fifth time. Something about it didn't flow. The rhythm was off.

"How do you know I'm not a gun-toting burglar?"

He glanced up. Elle stood in the doorway. *Prettiest gun-toting burglar . . . never mind.* "They don't usually knock and holler, 'Anybody home?'"

"Guess not." She smiled. Her best feature. And her hair. Very shiny hair.

"What are you up to?" It dawned on him she'd passed through the kitchen where he'd let a few days worth of dishes pile up in the sink. He told himself he didn't have time to clean up, he had a book to write, a kid to raise. But at the moment, he was a tad embarrassed about it.

"Waiting for Julianne to drop off Rio." She entered the rest of the way, sitting on the edge of a low rocking chair. "How long have you been going to Beaufort Community?"

"Few weeks. Your dad called and invited me."

"My daddy? Big guy with hats? When did you meet him?"

"He came by looking for you once."

"Ah, right, on Doomsday. Yeah, well"—she brushed at her shorts—"good for him to invite you to church."

"How are you these days? Any china-smashing urges?"

She set the rocker in motion. "No, but this morning it occurred to me having a relationship with God requires more than showing up Sunday, singing loudly, amening the preaching, volunteering for Harvest Festival, and joining the Christmas choir." She grimaced, giving Heath a theatrical thumbs-up. "Look at me, God. No hands."

He laughed. She seemed to have fun being honest with herself.

"I was in a bit of a God desert myself."

"Your wife died, Heath."

"No reason to box out God." He scooted his laptop aside. "Why is it when things go wrong, we run from Him instead of to Him?"

She rested her head on the back of the rocker that once belonged to Aunt Rose. "If I knew, I'd be writing the book and living on Fripp Island off the royalties."

He breathed out a short laugh. "Well, the first one who finds out, tell the other, okay?"

"Deal."

"Elle, you here?"

She angled back, gazing toward the kitchen door. "Jules, in the living room." She peeked at Heath. "Rio wondered if Tracey-Love could play."

"Absolutely. She's in her room." Heath clapped his hands against his legs and stood, calling down the hall. "TL, want to go with Miss Elle and Rio?'

A second later, the girl popped into the room, settling against her daddy, staring at Elle. Heath smoothed her hair, so coarse under his palm. "What do you say?"

Tracey-Love melted a little piece of him every time she fastened her blue gaze with his. "C-can you come t-too?"

Heath checked with Elle. "What did you have in mind? Can an old dad tag along?"

"I have nothing in mind. Come if you dare."

He dared all right, even though Nate waited for pages. He'd spent most of last night and today researching and outlining his book. But he'd be crazy to pass up a morning with his new friend. Especially with her delicate features and spunky wit.

"You talked me into it. TL, get your shoes."

A day out would help his muse uncover the rest of Chet McCord's story. In the back of his mind, a female protagonist had started to speak. There. Call today research. Heath figured he needed to spend a day with a woman to get the groundwork for his character. Maybe instead of being the next Grisham, he could be the next Nicholas Sparks.

He wondered how guilty he'd feel over Nate's coronary. *A relationship story? Love story?* Gasp, choke, *call 911.*

Heath walked out the back door with Julianne and Elle, talking about the whatevers of the day like the weather and price of gas as Rio and Tracey-Love ran-skipped hand in hand to the van.

"Hey, girls, let's drive in my car." Elle waved them over. "We'll put the top down."

Okay, seemed like fun. They watched wide-eyed as the top motored open. Heath helped Elle buckle them into the backseat, then slipped into the passenger side. "Where to on this lovely day?"

The crisp lowcountry morning was already warm as the sun rose, burning away the last of the predawn dew. Elle slipped on her sunglasses and turned the key. "Seems like a day for boating to me."

"I'm in," Heath said, turning to the girls. "Boating?"

Tracey-Love joined in with Rio's, "Yeah," though she'd never boated in her little life. This was good for her—new experiences, new memories.

Driving through Lady's Island neighborhoods toward Elle's parents' home where her daddy docked a small boat, Heath surfed the wind with his hand. The girls chattered as the wind whipped their hair about, but Elle drove in silence.

Let her be; she's working through more than a busted relationship.

Slowing, she turned into a wide, paved driveway and maneuvered a thin dirt road around to the back of her parents' house, a sprawling two-story with a wraparound porch, thick green lawn, and a deep-water dock.

Elle parked in the shade and led them to the dock.

"Heath, put these on the girls, please." She tossed over life jackets. On the boat, she checked the gas and other security thingies, Heath guessed, while he fixed up the girls and himself.

Finally, she motioned for them to climb aboard. "Girls, you stay seated once I get you in the boat, okay?" They nodded dutifully, grinning from ear to ear. "I don't want to feed the fish little-girl toes."

Tracey-Love's eyes widened, and she shot a fearful gaze at Heath.

"She's just teasing, baby." He cocked an eyebrow at her. *Want to knock out the fish-food chatter?*

She winced. *Sorry.*

"We're going to see dolphin and fish and birds." Elle tugged the tie from her hair and, angling TL around, finger-combed her hair into a ponytail.

TL stood still, facing the far shore, chatting with Rio. But Heath? He stepped close to watch and learn.

Elle concluded her boating instructions with a whip-twist of her hands and the tie. "If you want something, girls, just ask me or Tracey-Love's daddy, okay? There, ready to go?"

Just like that a neat ponytail. A miracle, a regular Houdini feat. Seemed easy enough. *Ha-ha.* He'd practice on TL later.

Elle fired up the motor. "Heath, untie us."

He jumped to the dock, loosened the rope, tossing it into the boat, hollering, "Ship, ahoy."

One day he'd look back and wonder what possessed him. Surely he knew better. But instead of jumping from the dock into the boat, Heath jumped straight down into a thick, deep mound of chocolate-looking pluff mud. It slurped him like a straw.

"Heath." Elle dashed to the side of the idling the boat. "Are you okay?"

"Yeah, I'm great." Laughing, he molded a pluff mud ball and lobbed it at her. She ducked even though it didn't come close.

"You know you're stuck, don't you?"

"What? No. I'm going to swim right out." Heath moved to demonstrate . . . except he couldn't move. His legs and chest were cemented into a pluff mud grave. "Um, Elle?"

She popped her hands together as she started to laugh. "Are you stuck, Superman? Do not tell me you purposefully jumped."

"It beckoned me." His expression pleaded with her. "Want to help a guy out? Laugh later."

Or now. Elle collapsed against the boat, her lilting laugh bouncing off the water and catching a ride on the breeze.

Meanwhile, Tracey-Love glared down at him with an enormous frown.

"Hey, Tracey-Love, isn't Daddy having fun? Elle? Still sinking."

Still laughing, she tossed him the rope, then nudged the boat forward, easing him gently out of the mud into the sleek water of Factory Creek. It'd been awhile since Granddad had warned him and Mark about the deep pluff mud: *"Fall in and I'll likely never find you to dig you out."* Heath had thought it was a Granddad scare tactic.

Now, some thirty-odd years later, apparently not. Swimming to the side of the boat, he did his best to wash off, then hoisted himself aboard. His finger- and toenails were darkened with mud he'd have to scrub out later, and his hundred-dollar deck shoes would never be seen again.

"Thanks," he said to Elle, who hovered over the steering wheel, shoulders shaking. "So happy I could amuse you."

Her cackle filled the air as she pounded her palm against the top of the windshield.

Heath sat on the cushioned bench between TL and Rio, who pinched her nose. "You stink."

"You don't say?" Muddy water dripped from his shorts and shirt.

Elle finally composed herself enough to putt-putt down Factory Creek and blast the air horn at a passing sailboat. "Hey, Mr. Crowley."

"Hey there, Elle. Sorry to hear about your wedding."

"Old news, Mr. Crowley. Look for me to open a new gallery."

"Never visited the old one."

"Then it's time to start a new tradition." She gave the engine another rev and an air-horn good-bye blast.

Sitting in the sun, Heath's wet clothes would be dry soon, though he'd have to live with the smell. Making sure the girls were seated securely, he moved forward next to Elle. "Done laughing?"

She snorted, once. "Sigh. All good things must come to an end." She handed him a bottle of sunscreen. "I'm sorry, you just looked so funny."

Heath popped open the lotion. "Think nothing of it, Elle. I'm so happy to oblige your funny bone. Laughter is the best medicine."

"You know it." Elle blasted the air horn over her head. "Hey, new day and Elle GARVEY is here to stay."

"Heath McCORD too." Yelling felt good. Released some much needed endorphins. "Okay, what am I doing with this lotion."

"Put it on the girls."

"Right, right." Heath slathered Rio and Tracey-Love with white cream, feeling a bit lucky to be sailing with his three favorite girls, and that Elle's last name wasn't Franklin.

When he handed the bottle back to Elle, she raised her sunglasses and arched her face to him. "Put some on my nose, will you?"

Okay, a nose. Nothing sexy about a nose. He squirted a dot to his finger, then touched the tip of her slender nose. His heartbeat echoed in his ears *love-ly nose, love-ly nose.*

"There." He swallowed, dropping the lotion into the crate anchored to the side of the boat.

She settled her sunglasses back in place. "How do I look?"

"Lovely." He watched her for a second, inhaling her fresh-flowers scent. If he didn't know firsthand, he'd never guess a broken heart beat inside her chest.

"How are the girls doing?" Elle peeked over her shoulder. "Y'all stay seated now."

"I don't think Tracey-Love could be more wide-eyed with wonder if she was shaking hands with Cinderella."

"When you go back to New York, she'll go kicking and screaming."

"Probably." He propped his arms on top of the short windshield, taking in the blue sky, the bank of palmettos and scrub oaks, the eagle drifting on the current. "This is beautiful."

Heath tried to imagine Ava standing next to him, but couldn't conjure up her image as clearly as he could a month ago. Lately, he'd crossed a major hurdle where life had become *his*, not *theirs*.

"Why writing and the law?" Elle ventured, watching the opposite bank. "Rio, Tracey-Love, look over there. Dolphin."

"Why art?" Heath dashed to the back of the boat as the girls arched over to the side. "Want to warn me next time, Elle?"

Dolphin were rushing fish to the shore and eating them out of the water.

"What yummy dinner, girls. Live bait." Elle rubbed her tummy, making *ummm* sounds. Rio wrinkled her nose with an "Ooo, yuck, Auntie Elle."

A single dolphin swam alongside the boat. Heath barely hung on to Rio as she dove to "pet the fish." The sleek-backed gray dolphin kept speed with the boat, surfacing, then diving, surfacing again.

"H-he's got a hole in his head." Tracey-Love wiggled her hand trying to touch it.

"He 'posed to." Rio, the expert.

"It's his air hole, how he breaths." Heath pulled the girls back to the bench seat. "Come on, settle back. You're leaning too far."

Elle upped the throttle, lifting her chin to the light, the air raking through her unbound hair. Yeah, Heath was definitely entering in a new phase. It'd been a lot of years since another woman fascinated him.

"What's next for you?" he asked as she slowed the engine, nearing an unanchored fishing skiff.

"Open another gallery," she said over her shoulder. "And forget I was almost married."

Heath moved next to her. "You never answered. Why art?"

Elle pushed her blowing hair away from her face. "My first memories are of drawing on bulletins in church, racing for the colored pencils and pictures in Sunday school. I decorated the hallways at home, the kitchen counters, even water-colored over all Mama and Daddy's wedding pictures."

Heath laughed. "How old were you?"

"Old enough to know better, but seriously, I had these new watercolors and I thought, *These black-and-white's need some help.*"

"Well, it's hard to argue with that logic." He squinted toward the shore thinking he needed to pick up sunglasses for himself and Tracey-Love on his next Wal-Mart run.

"I became very acquainted with my room over the years. If you know what I mean. Spent a lot of time sitting on the bed 'thinking about what I'd done.'"

"That would've never worked for me. I'd have planned how to perfect it for the next time."

"This is why Daddy says all children should be girls."

"Well, if there were only girls . . ."

Elle laughed, "No biology lesson necessary here, Heath."

"Ava and I weren't going to have children. We were thirty-four when TL came along."

"What changed your mind?"

"My wife's feet."

"This I got to hear."

"Yeah, weird, right. But she had these really long, gorgeous feet just like her mom. We started talking about the lineage of the long, lean feet and next thing you know, we're into a serious philosophical discussion about how our decision to not procreate is ruining our families' heritages. Eleven months later . . ."

Elle looked at him through dark Ray-Bans. "Why didn't you want children?"

"We wanted fast-track careers. Foolish. But then, it was all we knew. So what about you? When did you have the big revelation that art was your life?"

"I went on a field trip with my art class to the New York Met and encountered a Childe Hassam painting. I was sixteen, loved art, but had never been moved before. His work brought tears to my eyes. Until then, I didn't know art could speak. I was hooked on the idea of being a painter and communicating through colors, images, brush strokes."

"Do you paint? Why the gallery? I've been around enough galleries to know it's time consuming."

She steered the boat along the curves of the creek. "After four years of college and a year in Florence, *not* shaking or rattling the art world, I decided I wasn't good enough to make a living as a painter, so I funneled my love for art into a gallery. My friends swear it's all I talked about in high school anyway."

"Verbalizing your back-up plan in case the real deal didn't work out?"

She lifted her glasses and looked at him. "Yeah, maybe. Anyway, I took my Aunt Rose's inheritance to open the gallery. Might as well help artists who were good enough but just needed opportunity. I liked educating the public too, helping them experience what I did when I saw the Hassam paintings."

Elle powered up the engine and entered the Intracoastal Waterway. Heath stepped back to the girls. Rio's wide grin was sure to be a nice gnat catcher.

"I think Rio has the need for speed."

Elle glanced back. "More?"

"More." Rio yelled, clinging to the top rail while Tracey-Love clung to Heath.

Elle steered the speeding boat across the water. Rio giggled. Tracey-Love gripped the sides of Heath's shirt tighter. He had some work to do with her in the confidence arena.

A strange sensation swirled in his middle. *Carefree.* He settled back, squinting in the sunlight reflecting off the water, thinking of Ava without pain, musing over his book, liking the idea of creating memories with Tracey-Love. And discovering Elle.

Eleven

May tenth. Black Saturday. It should've been white and pink with beautiful lilies and stringed music.

And Elle wearing a white gown.

"We're going shopping." Julianne stopped by mid-morning, tugged away Elle's covers. "Then the entire family is meeting at Sara Beth's for a barbecue. Let's go."

"A family barbecue? Are we roasting my failure? Come on, Julianne, I can't stand the pity looks." After a great week of prayer with Miss Anna, and the carefree day of boating with Heath, Elle woke under a cloud.

"Get up, Elle. Celebrate today. Live it. Don't let disappointment win."

"Bye, Jules." Elle had already planned her day. Sleep for a while on her right side, then turn over and sleep on her left. Tomorrow, she'd get out there and start living.

"Elle, get up."

Shoot fire, Julianne had brought the big gun: Sara Beth.

Elle peeked over the edge of her quilt. "Hey, SB."

"In the shower, little sister. Mary Jo and Candace are waiting."

"I suppose there's no chance of y'all just turning and leaving, closing the door behind you?"

SB and Jules stared at her with their arms crossed, lips pressed into lines of disgust.

"I guess not." Elle shoved off the covers and headed for the

shower. Afterward, she came out dressed completely in black—
black bra, black panties, black jeans, black top, and if she could find
them, her black flip-flops.

Sara Beth rolled her eyes, sighing. "Lovely, Elle."

Julianne laughed. "Come on, Black Bart, let's go."

By nine o'clock that night, Elle had had enough of enduring the
day and yearned for the quiet solitude of her studio. She wanted to
fall asleep and wake up with everything Jeremiah behind her.

Her sisters had done a wonderful job of keeping her distracted
and laughing. She'd love them forever for it.

At Sara Beth's house, Daddy and SB's husband, Parker, barbe-
cued up some tangy ribs. The aroma made Elle's mouth water, but
her stomach posted a No Trespassing sign.

The family was overly cheery, avoiding all talk of love, relation-
ships, weddings, and Jeremiah. Even Elle, for that matter. No one
ventured, "What's next?" Or "Do you have any plans." And she was
sort of ready to answer those questions.

Mama passed by once in a while as Elle sat in the deck chair and
squeezed her arm. "You're being so brave."

Is there any other option?

Elle suffered more from feeling unanchored than abandoned.

When Parker organized a backyard volleyball game under the
lights, beyond the bright-blue eye of the pool, Elle slipped out and
drove home with her windows down, the warm velvety night clearing the heat from her mind.

She allowed herself one Jeremiah thought. *Are you thinking of
me?*

In the almost-plan, the photographer would be packing up as the
Beaufort Inn reception died down. She'd have danced in Jeremiah's
thick arms as the new and only Mrs. Jeremiah Franklin.

The thought made Elle shiver.

Pulling up to the cottage, she parked inside the garage with a
quick glance across the yard before hitting the stairs. The porch was

lit and she heard the faint hint of music. Strolling across the grass, Elle stooped at the porch door and peeked through the screen. "Having a party?"

Heath leaned around the back of the iron rocker. "Hey, Elle."

She open the door and stepped inside, motioning to her old boom box, folding into the rickety Adirondack chair. "Where'd you find that old thing?"

"Over in the corner, hiding under a thick layer of dust."

Elle laughed as she slid closer to Heath, aligning her chair with his. "I'll bet. I'm surprised it even works." Through the trees and Spanish moss, she saw the moondrops floating along the water's surface. "Sometimes I still picture you jumping in the pluff mud and—"

"Come on now, give a guy a break." He kicked the air around her leg, then stretching for his new cooler, producing a cold Pepsi. "Twelve packs were on sale at Wal-Mart."

"Can't beat that, now." The cold can felt good in her warm hand.

"I took Tracey-Love to the beach." She heard his smile. "It's incredible to watch her discover the world. I was so busy before—"

"Today was my wedding day," Elle confessed without much consideration or preamble. All day long she'd waited for someone in the family to ask her about it, let her talk for a few minutes, but no one had dared.

"Has it been a good day or bad?"

"Family day, trying to distract me. Sisters took me shopping. Then we had a barbecue."

"Dd-daddy?" A sweet voice pressed through the kitchen door.

Heath lifted up from his chair. "TL, what are you doing awake?"

"I-I-I had a sc-scary dream."

He held out his arm, beckoning her. Tracey-Love ran out, her little-girl feet barely making a sound against the porch boards.

"What'd you dream?" He cradled her in his lap.

Elle curled into her chair, watching. Listening.

"A-a-a big sh-sh-shark got me. Right he-he-here." She jammed her foot into the air, pointing to her heel.

"There?" Heath grabbed her foot and kissed her heel. Tracey-Love laughed. "No shark can bite my girl. Did you know when a daddy kisses his girl's foot, no shark can get her?"

Tracey-Love lifted her other foot. Heath gingerly kissed away his daughter's fears. "All better?"

"Kiss Miss E-Elle s-so no sh-shark can get her."

Heath gazed at Elle. "I bet Miss Elle's daddy already kissed her feet."

"Yes, after a lifetime of training, my daddy has kissed all his girl's feet." She wagged her finger at him. "It's true, bubba. The wrapping around her finger began the day she was born."

"Help," he gasped like a drowning man.

"However," Elle said, reaching over the side of her chair to tug on Tracey-Love's toes. "I'm all safe from sharks, but I would like an inoculation against dating shallow men. What do you got?"

TL shrugged, palms up. "I don't know."

Elle laughed. "Yeah, me neither."

"All right, it's back to bed." Heath kissed her forehead, then set her on her feet. "Run get in Daddy's bed. Don't turn on the TV."

"'Kay." She threw herself against Elle's legs, her arms hugging her at the knees. "S-see you, M-miss Elle."

The screen door creaked and slammed. Tracey-Love's running feet thudded through the house.

"She's gorgeous, Heath."

"My heart."

"Can I ask what happened to her mama?" After rescuing the man from pluff mud, Elle felt bold enough to inquire.

He scooted his chair closer to hers. "It's a long story and I believe you were saying this was your wedding day?"

She set her Pepsi on the porch floor. The cold beverage gave her the shivers. "I'd be dancing at my reception about now. We'd hired this great cover band and picked out a bunch of favorites and oldies for them to play."

How'd he make it so easy for her to expose her heart?

"Tell me, do you grieve the day or the man?" Heath sat with his head against the back of the chair, his face toward hers, softened by the light of porch lamps. An oldie drifted from the radio speakers.

"Maybe both. I did love him." She leaned on the chair's arm. "What is it about smart women choosing the completely wrong men?"

Heath's laughter purchased a piece of her melancholy. "You've got me. But men aren't immune. In fact, they're probably worse."

"Did you choose well?"

"By the grace of God, yes." For a moment, they were silent except for the tune on the radio.

Finally, "My friends Caroline, Jess, and I hauled that old boom box to the beach every weekend, every summer for three years. I'm surprised it isn't spewing sand." Elle dug at the peeling paint on the chair's wide, flat arm with the tip of her thumbnail, missing those carefree days.

"My friends and I set things on fire, blew up gas cans, ran from the police. Then I went to a youth rally at fifteen, met Jesus, and it didn't seem as fun to toilet paper trees and let air out of car tires."

"Really?" So, he was a friend of Jesus. Not just a seeker. "I walked the aisle at eight. Mrs. Gilmore sang 'Just As I Am' and I couldn't stop crying." Elle exhaled a bit of doubt. "It's good he dumped me, isn't it?"

"It was good for him to be honest, yes."

"Why does honesty hurt so much?"

"I don't know, but I suppose it's why we have a lot of liars in the world."

Elle laughed. Heath was good medicine.

"So, shopping, you said, with your sisters? What'd you buy?"

"Nothing."

"Nothing?" He whistled. "Is that allowed? Shopping on your ex-wedding day and coming home empty-handed?"

Elle pulled her feet up, anchoring her heels on the edge of her chair. "It's all about breaking the rules, McCord." The breeze from the creek carried a damp chill.

"At least you haven't resorted to greasy hair and army fatigues."

"Give me another week." She peeked over at him. Was he always this easy to be around, or was it just for her in this moment?

When their eyes met, he seemed to relax, stretching his long legs in front of him. "Way yonder in Texas, there's a man wondering if he made the right decision."

"I doubt it. Jeremiah is focused and driven. I don't see him wondering if he did the right thing."

The conversation drifted to silence as another oldie played, the frog choir chiming in with a little background vocal. "This porch and the creek is why I bought this place," Elle said softly. "It's lyrical and peaceful."

"Is it hard with me living here? I mean, when a person faces trial they usually like the comfort of their own home."

"Some days I miss the space, but the studio is home for now. It has no memories of him."

"I understand. But if at any time you—"

"I know . . ." She flopped her arm over the side of her chair, letting her fingers graze his arm. "So, Heath McCord, do you have a wedding anniversary?"

He crushed his empty Pepsi can and tucked it into a plastic bag. "December seventh."

"A Christmas wedding?"

"Yes, and I let her have her way until she asked me to wear a Santa suit at the reception." Heath waved his hand toward Elle. "I put my foot down. And no red cummerbund either."

She scoffed in feigned disgust. "Red? At a Christmas wedding. Gag, how tacky."

Heath laughed. "Ava didn't have much family growing up, so she really hyped up birthdays and holidays. Wanted all the traditions. Funny how two lonely, family-starved people found each other. Must be a familiar aura or something. After my mom left, Dad couldn't find the energy or heart to recreate any of the traditions."

"Is the letter in the kitchen window from her? I . . . saw it . . . the other day."

"Wait, how did we get back to talking about me?"

"Guess we both have things to put behind us." Elle tucked her legs tighter to her body, rubbing her chilled legs with her hand. The damp wet air soaked clean through her skin to her bones.

As the song ended, the DJ came on telling Beaufort and Jasper County it was ten o'clock, sixty-two degrees, and next up was a classic from Gladys Knight and the Pips. In two hours, Elle's life with Jeremiah would be completely behind her.

"My mom loved Gladys Knight," Heath reminisced aloud. "She'd play her albums all the time when I was about seven or eight."

"My uncle played the best of the sixties and seventies in the bays of his auto shop. Every time I hear Creedence Clearwater Revival, I get a hankering to play in a grease pit and tinker with old car parts."

His laugh was becoming familiar. "Bet that's exactly how Creedence envision their music inspiring people."

The barrage of commercials ended and the first bars of a slow, melancholy tune drifted across the porch.

Heath stood, extending his broad palm. "I'm not Jeremiah and this day didn't turn out like you'd hoped, but can I have this dance?"

The porch lamp captured the side of his face where a day's-end beard shadowed his high cheek and angular jaw. His eyes never shifted from her face.

"Please?"

Elle uncurled her legs, and when she rose out of the chair, Heath lightly circled her in his arms. He began to move slowly, swaying with each gliding step. The gap between them eased closed until his cheek rested against the top of her head and her cheek found the cradle of his chest.

Was it her heart thundering or his?

"Neither one of us wants to be the first to say good-bye . . ."

"This is a weird song to be—"

"Shh, Elle, let it be."

She closed her eyes, releasing the last of the day's sorrows as she danced on her wedding night in another man's arms.

Twelve

Miss Anna scooted into the pew next to Elle, bringing the homey fragrance of liniment and Miss Clairol. Her white hair billowed above her piquant face like a summer cloud.

"Well, here you are again. Second week. How do you feel?"

"Sleepy." The warm, low light of the chapel didn't help.

Miss Anna chortled as she squeezed Elle's hand. "What's the Lord been saying to you?"

"Get more sleep." A spontaneous yawn punctuated her point.

Miss Anna regarded Elle. "Well, you could always go to bed earlier. What are you doing with your time?"

"Squandering it." There, she'd said it—a bold-faced confession. But two months after selling her gallery, one month after being dumped, Elle remained unmotivated. She felt beige. Uninspired.

Other than venturing out for prayer, Elle had been camped at her folks since last Monday watching Lifetime movies and eating barbecue chips and drinking Diet Coke until she had caffeine shakes.

Mama, bless her heart, finally kicked her out last Friday night. "Elle, sweetie, I know it's hard, but you've got to pull yourself together. Figure out what you're going to do with yourself. You know you're always welcome here. Is that barbecue-chip crumbs on my new carpet?"

Elle had followed Mama's gaze. Hmm, oops. She'd picked them up as best she could, then hopped off the couch. "See you, Mama. Thanks for everything." Quick kiss on Mama's cheek and she'd skedaddled.

On Sunday night, Elle flipped on the oldie station Heath had tuned into the other night and curled up on the futon to make a list.

One, find a gallery location. Two, notify her client and artist list of said change. Three, call Huckleberry for a come-into-your-sound-mind meeting. Four, stock up on barbecue chips. Five . . . find a purpose.

This morning Elle brought the list with her to prayer.

"I suppose it seems odd, doesn't it?" Miss Anna folded her hands in her lap.

"What seems odd?" Elle doodled on an old bulletin she'd found tucked in her Bible. Out of nowhere, she'd had an idea for a painting during the prayer process.

"Prayer. Talking to a God you can't see, listening for a voice you can't hear, clinging to whatever faith exists in your soul."

"Sort of like running on ice."

"At times, yes." Miss Anna wagged her finger. "But don't mistake prayer for inactivity."

"Right, because sitting here is wildly active."

"Mercy a-mighty, we may be sitting, but the heavens are moving by the power of our words." Miss Anne flicked the air with her wrist. "Don't you forget that, missy."

Elle smiled, scooping her hair behind her ears. "All right, I won't."

Miss Anne clung to the back of the first pew and pulled herself up. "I'll see you in the morning."

"Enjoy your walk home."

Wednesday morning after prayer, Elle drove to Leslie Harper's real estate office to find a property for her new gallery.

The money she'd set aside from the first gallery's sale should get her a decent place with some left over for minor remodeling. She could be open by late summer. Tops.

"You couldn't have picked a better time to find a new gallery." Leslie was an *über*pro Realtor with intense exuberance. Elle had gone with her once to show an old broken-down double-wide to a young couple. Leslie patted the rotting aluminum side as she stood strategically in front of a gapping hole. "I tell you, a little paint and curtains in the windows . . . Good as new." *You won't even notice how the entire thing is listing starboard, about to fall off the blocks.*

The woman could sell water to a drowning man, and Elle knew she could make deals in the county like no one else.

For a while, they talked needs and price, then Leslie dangled a listing in front of Elle, looking quite pleased. "What do you say to the second story of the Bay Street Trading Company? Hmm? It's only for rent, but I believe we can talk them into a lease with an option to buy."

"Leslie, the Bay Street Trading Company? It's a perfect location."

"It's your lucky day." Leslie came around her desk. Tall and waifish, she seemed to sail instead of walk. "I'm really sorry about you and Jeremiah. If ever there was a match made in heaven, I thought y'all were it."

Elle kept focused on the listing. "It wasn't meant to be."

"Suppose not. Well, want to check out the Trading Company?"

They drove in Leslie's Lexus down Bay Street as she called to let the owners know she had a serious prospect. But first, a stop in Common Grounds because Leslie wanted a double espresso. Like she needed a jolt of caffeine.

"All right, let's go see your new gallery." Leslie said "new" with two syllables.

Down the sidewalk and up the outside stairs to the second floor of the Bay Street Trading Company. Elle wanted the space from the first glance. "Leslie, it's beautiful."

Bright, spacious, with polished hardwood and clean white walls. Even a bit of track lighting in place.

Leslie walked the perimeter, her heels thudding. "With a little modification for a gallery, I believe you can move right in, Elle."

Elle gazed down on Bay Street from the wall of windows. This was it. Home. "How much?"

Flipping through her listings, Leslie looked up with a done-deal grin. "In your price range. Best hire the workers because I do believe you've found a new gallery."

Kelly Carrington surveyed her appearance in the hallway mirror before heading down to breakfast, checking the patched seam in the back of her stockings, pulling her sweater tight around her middle.

Chet was out there fighting with all the other boys, facing danger or hunger, and all she could think of while getting dressed was how she wanted a new pair of stockings.

"Kelly, breakfast is getting cold. Come on, sugar." Mama's face appeared over the banister. "Are you wearing a sweater? Kelly, it'll be a hundred degrees today."

"Be right there, Mama." A hundred degrees? Not this early in June. But it would be hot. She'd wear the sweater anyway, at least until she got to work at the Gazette.

Before going down, she pulled out last night's letter to Chet. It was short and full of all the news going on around Beaufort, but not with her. She promised herself she'd tell him the next time she wrote. Or the next.

Are you well, Chet darling? Warm and dry, well fed and comforted? Do you have time to laugh or even cry?

She certainly did.

Heath looked up from the story, picturing Kelly, a mixture of imagination and Elle Garvey. His initial boating-day research had turned Elle into his muse. She had all the qualities of a great heroine—beauty and angst.

But did he want to write a love story? Set in Beaufort? In his head, it made no sense, but when he started writing Kelly's point of view, his heart shifted to her. She had a story to tell.

Nate's definitely going to have a coronary.

It was late and Heath decided to call it a night. Shutting down his laptop, he lay in bed on top of the sheets. Tracey-Love slept on the other side, curled and hidden under the covers.

For a long time, he chased sleep as words and ideas rattled around his head, every once in a while bumping into the vision of a strawberry blonde with green eyes and an armful of bracelets.

He couldn't forget the feel of her back under his hand as they danced, nor the fragrance of her hair. Something like a meadow, warm and earthy.

Since their dance, however, his dreams of Ava had returned, and often he woke up restless, feeling guilty.

He punched the pillow behind his head and clicked on the beside lamp. A yellow glow illuminated his corner. Checking on Tracey-Love, he peeled back the sheet, pressing his palm to her golden but strawlike hair.

You're missing her, Ava. She's beautiful.

In the last eight months, he'd experienced a lifetime of emotions, ending with him uprooting his career and child, returning to a place of his childhood innocence. Even though his new life without Ava took him farther away from the life they'd shared, in the quiet moments he missed her and wished he could hold her one more time.

In the expanded dining room of the Frogmore Café, Beaufort's little dining treasure on the corner of Harrington and

Bay, Penny Collins sang from the middle of the fresh lumber stage as Elle slid into the booth in the back with Julianne, Rio, and her friend Jessica Cimowsky for a girls' night out.

Elle liked the homey familiarity of the Frogmore. When Caroline owned the place, she'd spent weekday afternoons in the quiet dining room, talking with her friend, eating from Andy Castleton's yummy menu.

"Jess, where was it Stu Green dumped the ladies' room toilet when he was fixing the plumbing?" Elle asked.

Jess laughed, pointing. "Somewhere along the back wall. Oh, that was funny. And when he could spell *renaissance?*"

"Never judge a book by its cover," Elle said, reaching for a menu.

Caroline had insisted Elle add Stu to her Operation Wedding Day list. "Sure," Elle had agreed. "But he has to be able to spell *renaissance.*"

Stu Green not only spelled *renaissance,* he spouted its history.

"The question now," Julianne said, peering over her menu, "is if Heath McCord can spell *renaissance.*"

"What?" Elle balked. "You're crazy. One, I'm sure he can. He's a lawyer and a writer. Two, I'm not asking him, *hint, hint.* He's a friend. Period."

"Heath McCord?" Jess echoed. "The man renting your cottage?"

Julianne nodded with pinched expression. "Have you seen him? Dang handsome." She arched her brows. "Sexy."

Elle stopped her with a hard glare. "He's a friend." She'd kept her wedding night dance with Heath a secret. What would Jules do with that information?

"Good-looking how?" Jess wondered. "In a classic Hollywood way? Or more like Matthew McConaughy?"

"More like former jock turned single father with a touch of sophistication." Elle stopped, shifting her gaze between her sister and friend.

Jules made an "Oh my" face. "Someone has thought a lot about this."

Elle studied the menu she already knew by heart. "I have a lot of time on my hands."

Just in time, Mercy Bea, the Frogmore's senior waitress, set down a basket of Bubba's Buttery Biscuits, cracking her gum. "Y'all ready to order? Elle, darling, I sure am sorry about the wedding."

She closed her menu, putting it back in the holder. "Sometimes things don't turn out like we plan, Mercy Bea."

The blonde-bombshellish waitress pointed to herself with an exaggerated movement. "You're looking at the queen of things not turning out. The pot roast is really good tonight. Andy outdone himself."

Elle's stomach rumbled, but she wasn't quite ready for pot roast casserole. "I'll have a salad and grilled chicken."

"All righty." Mercy Bea scribbled their order while chatting about her young sons and how much teen boys cost. On her way to the kitchen, she greeted a new customer.

"Danny Simmons, sit. Take a load off. Good to see you. What'll you have to drink?"

"Tea sounds good, Mercy Bea." Danny started for the table adjacent to the back booth. "Hey, Elle, Julianne, didn't see y'all there."

"Evening, Danny," Elle said. In his mid-forties, Danny Simmons was a Beaufort County businessman, philanthropist, and golfing buddy of Daddy's. His blue eyes crinkled beneath Ralph Lauren-like silver hair. "Are you by yourself? Care to join us."

He stood stiffly, like a little boy unsure if he wanted to sit at the adult table, gazing at Julianne—who seemed intent on jellying up a biscuit for Rio—then at Jess. "Looks like you're full up here."

"I don't mind scooting around." Elle shoved against Jess.

Jess shoved against Julianne. Who did not budge. Instead she spread jelly on another biscuit. Rio had three on her plate already.

"Thanks, but I've got some work to do." Danny backed away. "So I'll just sit over here at this table here. Nice to see y'all. Sorry to hear how things went with Jeremiah, Elle."

"Thank you, Danny. I'm healing."

Elle pinched Julianne's arm when the man moved out of ear-shot. "What's the matter with you?"

"Ow, Elle." Jules jerked her arm away with enough force to swing her dangling earrings against her neck and hair. "What did you want me to do, jump up and down?"

Elle looked at Jess, whose expression reflected her own. "Do you have a problem with Danny Simmons?"

"Now why would I have a problem with the man?" Julianne broke open another biscuit.

Elle snatched it from her. "Rio has three already, Jules, and you have one. Are you seriously going to eat five jellied biscuits?"

Julianne wiped her hands on her napkin. "Scoot around, Rio. Mama needs to go to the little girl's room."

"Something's bugging her," Jess said as Jules disappeared around the stone fireplace toward the restrooms.

"A lot's been bugging her. She's more secretive than ever."

"Won't say what's up?" Jess searched the biscuit basket. Empty. She angled over the table for one of Rio's biscuits. "Can Aunt Jess have one?"

Rio nodded. Her lips were ringed with purple jelly.

Mercy Bea came around to refill their teas. "Gracious, y'all need more biscuits?" She snatched up the basket, then stopped by Danny's table. "What'll you have, Danny?"

He was mid-I'll-have-the-Frogmore-Stew when his cell went off. When he answered, he faced the wall and talked in a low tone.

"Did you find a new gallery location?" Jess scooped most of the jelly from the biscuit, then took a bite.

Elle broke from observing Danny. "Yes, second floor of the Bay Street Trading Company."

Jess's eyes grew round. "Elle, really? How perfect. Look, sweetie, I know Jeremiah broke your heart, but I'm so glad you didn't move away." She winced. "Beaufort is not Beaufort without you. When you were gone for a year, studying in Florence, then in New York, Caroline and I sat around Saturday nights asking, 'What would Elle do?'"

"I hardly feel like that girl any more." Elle gave Jess a weak smile. "But I'll find her again. Remember when *Forrest Gump* was filming here, and we tried out as extras?

Jess choked on her biscuit. "Caroline kept sneaking into the scenes with Tom Hanks?"

In many ways, Caroline was the most courageous of them, though she'd never ventured farther than Florida until she moved to Barcelona. Now she flew to places like Thailand and Belgium. She handled life with grace instead of fighting it.

Behind them, Danny was in motion, rising, clapping his phone closed. "Elle, please tell Mercy Bea I can't stay. Need to take care of something." He dropped a twenty on the table. "Have her box up my dinner. One of y'all can take it home."

"Is everything all right?"

His smile lacked light. "Could be better. Night, ladies. Good night, Rio."

"Night, Mr. Danny."

Thirty seconds later, Julianne reappeared. "The ladies' room had no toilet paper or towels. I had to hunt down Russell in the kitchen before I could pee."

"What's up with Danny Simmons?" Elle asked.

"How should I know? Ask him if you want to know what's going on in his life." Julianne checked out his table. "Oh, he left." Her shoulder's visibly relaxed.

"Here you ladies go." Mercy Bea set down their supper, and Elle's window of opportunity with Julianne was closed and locked.

Rio pointed, jumping up on the booth seat. "Hey, Tracey-Love." She waved her tiny hand in the air. "Tracey-Love!"

"Shh, Rio, sit down. Stop hollering across the café." Julianne jerked her bottom to the seat.

Elle gazed around Jess to see a dapper-looking Heath holding Tracey-Love's hand.

"Who is that?" Jess asked with too much pitch in her voice.

"Elle's new renaissance man," Julianne said, clearly glad to move the focus off of her.

Jess turned to Elle. "And you used to accuse Caroline of getting all the good-looking men. First Jeremiah, now him. Go for it."

"First of all, there's nothing to go for. Second of all, he's a widower and in the healing process himself." Elle picked out a biscuit. "Besides, he's too old for me, like thirty-eight. So, leave it be, y'all."

"Too old?" Jess echoed. "If Jules here can date a married forty-somethin'—"

"Jessica Cimowsky. Bite your tongue. I am most certainly not." Every ear in the café heard Julianne's rebuke. "Take it back."

Jess's eyes darkened. "Then what was with the shifting in your seat, suddenly running to the ladies' room when Danny appeared?"

"It's nothing, Jess. Drop it."

Jess's shoulders surrendered. "Jules, you're right. I'm sorry. Guess I read into things."

No, she read the situation right, as far as Elle could see. The trouble was getting her sister to admit it.

Julianne shoved her plate forward, her casserole untouched. "It's okay, Jess. I'm tired and edgy."

Jess ducked her head. "No, my bad, Jules."

"Forget it, I'm fine."

But something was eating her. Elle talked when things bugged her. Julianne closed up shop and hid.

Mercy Bea was leading Heath toward them. "Y'all got room here? Seems Rio knows this little gal."

Heath glanced around the table. "Evening, Elle, Julianne."

"Tracey-Love, sit by me." Rio pounded the seat with her palm.

Heath checked with Jules. "Is it okay?"

"Yes, Heath, please sit." Julianne shoved against Jess, who slid over.

Heath swung Tracey-Love into the booth next to Rio, glancing at Elle. "How are you?"

"I'm good." She hadn't seen him since the night of their dance, and now suddenly the booth's atmosphere changed with his presence. Her molecules seemed to be morphing and blipping. *Settle down in there.*

"You look good."

"You too." Elle glanced away when his gaze lasted longer than the ring of his compliment.

"By the way"—Jess offered her hand—"I'm the friend, Jessica Cimowsky."

"Nice to meet you."

"Hey, girls, where'd Danny go?" Mercy Bea paused at their table with a loaded dish of Frogmore Stew.

"He had to go." Elle pointed to the twenty. "He said to box it up—or, Heath, you want a plate of Frogmore Stew?"

"The reason I'm here."

"Well, hallelujah." Mercy Bea set down Danny's plate. "What can I get you to drink?"

"Sweet tea sounds good, and for this little beauty"—he touched Tracey-Love's head with his palm—"a salad and fries with a glass of milk."

"Can do. Mercy Bea Hart." She shook Heath's hand.

"Heath McCord."

"Pleasure is all mine. Now if these gals get too rowdy, you just let me know." Mercy winked and wiggled away.

"Jess, look at the time. We're going to be late for the meeting," Julianne said, shoving out of the booth, clutching her purse.

"Huh?"

"Yeah, huh? What meeting?" Elle asked. They'd planned to watch movies at Jess's house.

Julianne kept shoving and sliding until Elle was on her feet and

Jess nearly fell off the end of the booth. "We forgot about the down-town commission thingy."

"You are such a bad liar, Jules," Elle whispered in her ear.

"Ladies," Heath started, "was it something I said?"

"No, no, of course not. Really, we need to go." Julianne linked her arm through Jess's. "Elle, thanks for watching Rio."

Thirteen

Waterfront Park, nestled next to the Beaufort River, was sleepy with the aftereffects of the setting sun. Elle strolled along the Beaufort River with Heath, her left hand holding on to Rio, her right, Tracey-Love.

She apologized for the tenth time. "I'm sorry about Julianne and Jess. They're horrible liars."

"It seems they thought we should be alone."

Elle caught the tip of his grin. "More like my baby sister wanting to retreat and hide from her own secrets."

"She has secrets?"

Elle nodded toward Rio. "Several."

"I suppose we all have secrets." Heath's loafer heels scraped the cement in a soft, even gait.

"We have things we don't want shouted out in the town square, but lately Julianne is very secretive. Hidden."

Heath rested against a cement pylon, hands in his pockets, ankles crossed, his manner matching the drift of a passing sailboat. "When I was twelve, some friends convinced me to steal the bike from a kid down the street. A big dorky guy with Coke-bottle glasses who had never done anything to us but give us someone to pick on." He shook his head at the memory. "When he discovered the missing bike, he cried. And I don't mean boo-hoo, but a gut-level wail as if . . . I heard him all the way in our basement while I was watching TV. I ran out to see what had happened, for the first time feeling someone else's pain. I thought he'd gotten hit by a car or something."

"Oh, Heath . . . why are kids so mean?" Elle motioned for him to move on toward the bench swings where the girls could sit.

"I hid in the front bushes spying. Freddy's mom came out to see what was going on. He managed to tell her between sobs that his bike had been stolen. And you know what she did?"

Elle winced. "Do I want to know? If you tell me she boxed his ears . . ."

"She grabbed him by the shirt and yanked him inside. 'Do you think I have time to worry about your bike? As if we don't have enough going on without you belly-aching. You probably lost it and made up this story.'"

"Heath, you're kidding." Elle's heart pinged with compassion.

"I sat in the bushes, cold tears and snot running down my face, trying to figure out how to give back Freddy's bike without my friends finding out—because, you know, those guys were going to be my friends forever and what they thought of me mattered."

Elle related. "When you're twelve, you believe your friends are forever and ever. And there's no opinion but theirs. We can't imagine being old and decrepit at thirty, having new-old friends."

"In my mind, I'm still twelve. Well, maybe eighteen. Not this decrepit thirty-eight-year-old widow." At the cedar wood bench swings, Heath hoisted up Tracey-Love, then Rio.

"In my mind I am a thirty-year-old spinster."

Heath gave her an exaggerated up and down. "Spinster? Hardly."

His gaze ignited a heat flash. Elle shoved the swing forward. "Okay, maybe not yet, but thirty turns to thirty-three, which turns to forty really quickly."

A sixty-something woman jogged by, her arms pumping, her legs moving. "Evening, Elle, sorry to her about your wedding. I was looking forward to attending."

Elle waved off her sentiment. "Thanks, Mrs. Winters, but I'm moving on."

The older woman jogged in place, glimpsing at Heath. "I see. Good for you."

"Oh no." Elle patted Heath's arm. "This is my neighbor, Heath."

"Nice to meet you." Mrs. Winters bobbed her head, arms still pumping, legs marching.

"I meant I'm moving on with my life, opening a new gallery. I'll e-mail you the details."

"Oh, just the gallery. Too bad. But I'll look forward to it." She jogged off.

Heath laughed. "She's a trip."

"Yes, ever since I've known her, which is my whole life." Elle gave the swing a big push. Rio hollered higher. Tracey-Love gripped the bench arm with white knuckles. "Okay, how'd you manage to give Freddy his bike back?"

"How do you know I did?"

Elle caught his shifting gaze. "Just do."

"Freddy's bike was in my basement so I came up with a plan," Heath began. "Rat myself out to my dad and tell the guys he discovered it in the basement, recognized it as Freddy's, and took it over to him."

Elle approved. "Clever and quite honest, McCord. How'd it go?"

"Dad grounded me, which eased my guilt and kept me away from the guys for two weeks. Then walked with me over to Freddy's to return the bike and apologize, not just to him, but in front of the whole family."

"Your dad was a character-matters man, I take it."

"Still is. Not only did I learn a lesson about stealing and hurting others, but I saw firsthand how it robs people of their dignity. Even kids like Freddy. When he got the bike back, it was like his soul returned. He was somebody again, free to explore the world on two wheels. I think he rode that bike until our sophomore year. Later he told me how he'd saved his own money for years to buy that bike. And, when I apologized in front of his family, it humbled me. Cool Heath screwed up, and dorky Freddy was vindicated, even to his family. They looked at him differently. Am I explaining this right?"

"Yeah." Elle gave the swing another push. "It's how I felt when Jeremiah dumped me. The handsome preacher leaving the unemployed, unfocused artist."

"More like the beautiful, compassionate artist got rid of a selfish man."

Elle liked his point of view. "I'll keep telling myself your version. So, what happened to Freddy?"

"We became good friends in high school. He trimmed down but bulked up, played football, got contacts and braces, turned out to be this stellar student athlete with an Adonis-like face and build. Our senior year, he escorted the homecoming queen to the dance. Married her six years later. Several times he told me how much returning his bike was a pivotal moment in his life."

Elle lingered in the mood of the story for a moment. "Never know, do you?"

Tracey-Love reached up for Heath. She'd had enough of Rio's wild swing ride. "Never know what?" he asked.

Elle helped Rio off the swing. "When a miracle might show up on your doorstep. When some desperate situation becomes the most amazing opportunity."

"No, you never do." His response felt personal. Intimate.

She swallowed the goofy rise of emotion in her chest and reached for Rio's hand. "So, who wants ice cream?"

At 1:00 a.m., Elle lay on the futon staring into the darkness, her evening with Heath and the resonance of Freddy's story replaying in her mind.

If there could be a silver lining to her breakup with Jeremiah, maybe it was Heath. One moment he had her laughing so hard her sides almost split, the next had her eyes watering over the wounds of a boy she'd never met.

Heath had a way of making Elle feel like she could do whatever she wanted. It unnerved her that she wanted to know him more. After a foiled Operation Wedding Day scheme followed by the huge debacle of Dr. Franklin, she needed a break from romance.

Heath had driven Elle and Rio home after eating cones from Southern Sweets. When Julianne came by later, Elle gave her the dickens for rushing out of the Frogmore Café with Jess to attend a faux meeting. "What were you thinking?"

"Hey, just giving you a fresh chance at love."

"Fresh chance? Forget it, the kitchen is closed."

Julianne tried to argue with her, but Elle shoved her out the door so she could shower and slipped into her pajamas. Curling up on the futon, she formulated a new romantic motto based on the carefree song "Que Sera, Sera." *"Whatever will be, will be." Sing it, Doris Day.*

Next she worked on a gallery business plan so when Leslie called with a lease agreement, she'd be ready to go. Elle decided to run it by Candace for review.

At eleven, she clicked off the light and dozed for few minutes, but between the gallery possibility and the evening with Heath, she couldn't sleep.

One fifteen a.m. Elle kicked off the covers, realizing the quiet, hot studio was missing the hum of the window AC unit. Probably frozen again. Clicking on the light, she shoved open the windows and clicked on the fans.

Wandering around the studio, Elle thought if she lived in the cottage, she'd grab the remote and click on the TV. Back on the futon, she lay on top of the quilt and tried to sleep again to the hum of the fan. Her thoughts quieted and wandered like a slow ride on the river . . .

The banging studio door jolted her awake and sent her heart careening. She tried to stumble out of bed, but her foot was caught in the sheets.

"Elle, it's me, Heath." Panic.

"Just a minute." *Thump, thud. Let go of my foot . . .* She felt disoriented and weak.

"Elle . . ." His voice commanded her to open the door.

"Coming, coming." Free from the linens, she stumbled across the dark studio, reaching for the lamp by the work table. At the door, she dropped the security chain.

"What's wrong?" Her heart banged in her chest as Heath entered. She tugged at her baggy pajamas bottoms hanging low on her hips.

"It's my girl." Heath wrung his hands. "She's sick." His sandy-blond hair went every which way. "Throwing up, diarrhea—"

"Does she have a fever?"

Heath's skin appeared ghostly in the yellow light. "Yes. I think so. Yes."

"How long has she been sick?" Elle went back for her jeans and T-shirt.

"After we got home. Almost four hours now." Heath rocked back and forth with his fists tucked under his armpits. So unsure, this man.

"Let's get her to the hospital, Heath. Go get her ready. I'll be down in two seconds." But he remained dazed and frozen. Elle turned him toward the door and gently shoved him forward. "Heath, go."

The entire studio rattled as he bolted down the stairs.

"Jesus, he looks pretty upset . . . ," Elle prayed as she slipped on her jeans and searched for her shoes. Dang studio ate her flip-flops. Living in the cramped quarters had its drawbacks. Mainly, lack of closet space. Her clothes were everywhere, piled on the dresser, hanging off her easels, from the bathroom door, over back of the futon.

Ah, there they were. How had her shoes gotten wedged behind

the blank canvases Julianne brought over from the gallery? No time to ponder. Elle grabbed her purse and headed down to the yard, where she found Heath waiting by his van.

"You drive. I'm going to ride in the back holding her." Heath tossed her his keys. "Elle, please hurry."

Heath exited the exam room, his joints aching, tension gripping his jaw and temples. He found Elle alone in the ER waiting room sitting under an ominous dark window. She had a solid too-much-caffeine jiggle going on with her right leg.

When she saw him, she jerked to her feet. "What'd they say? Is she all right?"

"She's sleeping." He sat on the blue vinyl chair next to her, but only for a second. It hurt to stay still. "They hooked her up to an IV, drew blood." He walked to the edge of the room. "She screamed bloody murder."

"Do they know what's wrong? Virus? The flu?" The heat of her hand resting on his back comforted him.

"The doctor is *guessing* meningitis. Guessing. 'Hello, Mr. McCord, your daughter is dying and I'm *guessing* it's meningitis.' How do you even get meningitis?"

"Heath, she's not dying. Didn't you say she was sleeping? And after they run the test, the doctor will *know* what's going on. A kid can get meningitis any number of ways."

He stood with his feet apart, hands hooked over his crossed arms. "I'm horrible, Elle. A horrible father."

"Because your daughter is sick? Every one of my nieces and nephews spent a night or two in the hospital. Rio must have gone three times to the ER as a baby."

"Babies, yes. Tracey-Love, if you haven't noticed, is a little girl."

For a split second, Heath let himself be fiery mad at Ava. Justifying the heat in his chest by the idea she'd be cussing him right now if the situation were reversed. *I never signed up to do this alone, God.*

Elle moved in front of him. "I'm not going to let you be the martyr. You're tired and frustrated, I get that, but children of all ages get sick. It doesn't make you or anyone else a bad father unless you did it on purpose. Did you do it on purpose?"

He stared at some vague point beyond the reception desk. "No."

"I rest my case." She pressed her hand on his arm. "Heath, I've watched you, you're a wonderful father."

"No, I'm not." His posture softened with his tone as he gazed at Elle. "When we moved down here, I knew practically nothing about her. I can recite case studies, list a hundred client names and their case numbers, if we won in or out of court. Worse, I can give you stats on athletes dating back to their college days. Height, weight, averages per game, the names of their celebrity girlfriends. But my kid?" The look in her eyes contradicted his tirade. "The nanny sent me down here with a ten-page instruction manual, typed, single spaced. What Tracey-Love wore, what she ate and when. Bed and bath time . . . I didn't even know that Dora the Explorer was a cartoon."

"Heath, you're yelling."

"Maybe I want to yell." Heath stepped into the corridor. "Hey, everyone. I. Am. A. Bad. Father. That's right, you heard me. Bad father, right here."

Elle jerked him back to the chairs. "You want them calling social services? Crazy-acting single dads don't sit well with some folks." She stared at him, hands on her hips. "I didn't take you for the self-pity type. Listen to me, Tracey-Love is going to be fine."

He dropped down to the padded chair with a thump. "And what if she's not fine?"

"Heath." Elle knelt in front of him, her hands resting on his knees, and for the first time he realized he'd shown up in public wearing his sleeping pants. "Can we just take it one step at a time? Wait to hear what the doctor says."

"This is why we agreed to never have children. Ava and I were career people. What do I know about raising a kid?" He ran his hands over his face, laughing without merriment. "And guess what? Tracey-Love inherited my Fred Flintstones. We *still* didn't preserve the legacy of Ava's feet."

Elle slipped into the chair next to him. "Are you saying you wish she'd never been born? Heath, please . . . ," she whispered.

"No, no. I don't know what I'm saying. I'm mad at myself, mad at Ava . . ." He reached for Elle's hand and wrapped his fingers around hers. "Just keep saying TL's going to be fine, okay?"

"She's going to be fine. I mean it; I'm not just trying to make you feel better."

His eyes burned. "He wouldn't take her, would He?"

"Who?" Elle bent to see his face. The tip of her hair brushed his knee.

"God." He looked at Elle for hope, for assurance that a loving God would extend him mercy.

"Heath, no. I mean, He's God and He can do what He wants, but remember He is good and He is love. Even when we don't understand our circumstances. But right here, right now, I get the feeling He's not going to allow anything to happen to Tracey-Love."

Lord, help my weak faith.

Maybe this was a wake-up call. Get his head out of the clouds, forget novel writing, call Rock and return to the law. Rehire Tracey-Love's nanny, enroll her in a preschool where PhDs in child development could raise her, watch her, warn him if she was coming down with something.

Elle squeezed his hand. "What are you thinking?"

"Nothing." He squeezed her hand back.

"Mr. McCord?"

"Dr. Morgan." Heath jumped up, dragging Elle with him. "Is she all right?"

The doctor slipped his hands into the large pockets of his white coat. "We're almost certain it's viral meningitis, but we won't know until the labs come back in about an hour. We put her on a low dose of steroids. I want to admit her for twenty-four hours."

"Okay, fine, whatever. Where is she? I'm staying with her." The idea of his girl waking up in the hospital alone, crying . . . it physically pained him.

"Why don't you go home, get some sleep? A few hours. She'll be asleep at least that long, I assure you." Dr. Morgan placed a firm hand on Heath's shoulder. "Tracey-Love is in good hands. You'll be more value to her if you're rested and stable, Mr. McCord."

The good doctor was crazy. "I'm not leaving her alone. She is afraid of the dark and strange places."

"Heath," Elle said softly but firmly. "Go home, shower. Change your clothes. I'll stay with TL. You can bring back one of her toys, clothes for tomorrow. What do you say?"

Heath looked down at his old T-shirt and pajama bottoms. They were soiled from caring for Tracey-Love. "No, you go, Elle. Stop by Wal-Mart, get her a doll or a stuffed animal. But no bears. She doesn't like bears."

"Heath, you have a long day ahead of you. Go shower and change." Elle leaned in with a sniff. "You smell, friend, and you're going to embarrass your daughter."

He growled. "She's four."

Dr. Morgan turned to go. "I'll leave you two to duke it out."

Elle shoved Heath toward the exit. "Go. I promise I will not leave her."

He paused as the doors slid open. "I can't lose her, Elle. I can't."

"You won't. Have faith."

Faith? He'd poured out his last ounce the day they lowered Ava into the ground.

As Tracey-Love slept in the quiet hospital room, Elle ran her thumb over the pulpy spot around the girl's thumb.

Keep her, God. Give Heath strength.

TL's skin felt dry. In the yellow light haloing the bed, Elle found her handbag and searched for a compact bottle of lotion.

Cotton blossom. Elle poured a drop into her palm and massaged the lotion into Tracey-Love's hand.

"If your mama were here, I think she'd do this for you. Don't you? The doctor says you're going to be fine, up and playing in a few weeks."

The room door creaked open and Heath slipped inside, clean and combed, wearing a fresh button-down and jeans. "How is she?" He leaned over to kiss his daughter, dropping a Wal-Mart bag onto the foot of the bed.

Elle capped the lotion and dropped it into her purse. "Fever broke. The doctor came by . . . said it's viral meningitis."

"Yeah, he called my cell." Heath opened the bag and produced a pink-faced, cherubic doll with shiny, short blonde curls. "She wanted this doll the other day when we were shopping. I told her no, wait for her birthday."

"Very pretty. But you buy her gifts when she's sick and she might like being sick," Elle said with a wink.

"She better not. My heart can't take it." Heath broke the doll out of the box and set it under the covers with Tracey-Love. "It's cold in here. Is it cold to you?"

"No, worry wart." Elle stretched and yawned. The moment he walked into the room, her weariness took over. "What time is it?"

"Five thirty." He came around the edge of the bed and drew her into his arms. His clean breath brushed her hair. "Thank you."

"What are friends for?" It felt good to rest against him, but she smelled ripe and day-old. She needed a shower and sleep. "If you don't need me . . ."

Health stepped back to the bag on the bed. "You'll need a way home." He tossed over the van keys.

Right. "Call me if you need anything. I'll be back in the afternoon." Elle rested her hand on the door. "I told you, she's going to be fine."

"So you said." He smiled. "You are my voice of reason."

She slung her bag to her shoulder. "Have you seen my life, Heath? I don't think you want my voice whispering anything in your ear. I'll let you call a mulligan on that one."

"All right, how about when I'm a panicked, out-of-my-mind father with a sick girl, you are my voice of reason."

"Deal."

Walking down the corridor, Elle felt right about Heath being her friend, an intangible knowing that bypassed the mind and settled in her spirit. As she approached his van, she absently sniffed the sleeve of her shirt where his fragrance lingered.

Fourteen

After a shower, Elle burrowed under the futon blankets with a long sigh. It felt so good to stretch out and squish down into the mattress and pillows.

The AC had run all night without freezing up so the studio was cool and crisp. Perfect for sleeping. As she drifted off, she thought of Miss Anna praying alone in the chapel this morning . . .

The ring of her phone jerked her from a deep sleep. Curled comfortably in bed, she half decided not to answer it until she realized Heath might be calling.

But it was Mama.

"I heard about Heath's girl. Is everything all right? What's her name again? Something Love?"

"Tracey-Love." Elle needed water. "How'd you hear?"

"Sissy Doolittle works at the hospital. She called."

Eleven o'clock. The AC had finally broken down and the white lines of sun streaking through the gaps in the blinds heated the studio.

"Mama, can you organize some hospitality and prayer?" Elle popped open the minifridge with her foot. Empty. One of these days she'd have to grocery shop, seriously.

"Already called the hospitality coordinator at church and the ladies' Bible study."

"Thank you." Elle turned on the water and ducked her mouth under the cold stream.

"How are you? Sissy said you looked like an antique prom queen left out in the rain."

She wiped water from her chin. *Antique prom queen? Lovely.* "I'm fine, mostly tired."

"Well then, get on back to sleep."

Mama clicked off, and Elle fell face-first onto the futon. But her thoughts were starting to wake up. She'd wanted to call Daddy today to get a recommendation on a contractor for the gallery work.

Rolling onto her back, Elle peered through weary eye slits at her phone and autodialed her dad.

"Give ole Chaz Berkus a call," he said. "Tell him I sent you and to remember sixty-eight."

"Remember sixty-eight? What does that mean?"

"He'll know. You just tell him."

"Does this mean I get the work for free?"

Daddy laughed. "No, but pretty darn close."

When Elle's phone jarred her awake again, the windows were dark and the studio temperature had risen from cool to boiling. Dang AC.

She answered without looking at the number. "Heath?"

"No, Candace. Where are you?"

"Home, the studio." Water, she needed more water. She sat up, feeling eerie and foggy from the day's weird sleep.

"I'll be there in five minutes," Candace said.

"Why, what's wrong?"

"Not much. Just a little thing of Angela Dooley wanting to sue you."

"What?" Water ran down Elle's chin, dripping to her foot. "What are you talking about."

"I'll tell you when I get there."

Muttering to herself, Elle opened all the blinds, shoved open the windows, and clicked on the fan. By the pitch of the studio's shadow in the grass, she figured it to be late afternoon.

Angela Dooley suing her? What was wrong with that woman?

By the time Candace arrived, Elle was somewhere between freaked out and ticked off. "Candy, what is her problem?"

"You." Candace checked the table for paint stains before dropping her black leather bag down. "I could kill for a Diet Coke. You got one? Elle, it's roasting in here."

"The AC is on the fritz. And all I have is tap water."

Candace made a face. "Then let's do this quickly." She pulled papers out of her case and sat on the stool, pausing to fan herself. "Mama called about Heath's daughter. What a scare for him."

"Yeah, he was pretty upset, but she's doing well. Or at least she was when I left at five thirty."

"I was thinking on my way over here you should call Julianne, let her know since Heath's girl played with Rio." Candace pointed to the spot by her stool. "Stand here."

Elle stood where she was told—Candace had that kind of effect on her—and scooped her hair away from her face. She'd slept with it wet and now the ends were tangled. "All right, what has Angela Dooley's panties in a wad?"

"You mean, what are you doing to put her panties in a wad? She's friends with the owners of Bay Street Trading Company. Last night they told her they were renting the second story to someone who will be opening an art gallery."

"So, yeah, Leslie Harper and I looked at it. Candace, it's perfect." Elle stooped over, propping her elbows on the table, too tired to stand. "I couldn't believe it was available."

Candace flashed a set of documents. "Hang on to your hat, sister, because you can't open an art gallery in this county. Elle, when you sold to Angela, you signed a noncompete. Are you collecting feathers?" Candace stretched to pick up one of the two white feathers.

Elle slapped her hand over Candace's. "What's this about a non-compete?"

"These are gorgeous. Where did you find them?" Candace held the white plume up in the light. "It's perfect."

Elle ran her hands over her eyes. "They just appeared. One when Julianne prayed for me after the Jeremiah ordeal and the other before I went to church one Sunday."

"You're serious? Out of nowhere? What do you think it means?"

"God watching over me? Angels hanging around? People suing me?" Elle shook her sister's shoulder. "Talk to me, Goose."

Candace ran her finger along the tip of the thick plume. "Gives me chills." She looked at Elle. "Can I have this?"

Elle hesitated. Could she give away a God feather? "I don't know. I mean . . ." She reached for the second feather. God was generous, Jesus being His prime example. What was a feather among sisters? "Take it."

"Thank you." Candace tucked the feather in her attaché like a kid who'd just found candy. "Okay, to the business at hand. Elle, when you sold the gallery, Angela asked you to sign a noncompete."

"I vaguely remember." Those first months of being engaged were frantic and, in retrospect, a blur.

"And in doing so, you promised not to open another gallery for three years." Candace held up a document for Elle to read.

. . . agrees will not directly or indirectly engage in any business that competes with Angela Dooley in regard to art, the acquiring of, selling, or distribution for a period of three years.

The sun drifted behind a cloud and the studio faded to gray. "I can't open another gallery for three years?"

"You told me you read the addendum."

"I did, I did." Sort of. "But I was so busy . . . why didn't you tell me?"

"I asked you. I said, 'Elle, did you read the addendum?' You said, 'Yes, Candy, I'm not stupid.' And I said, 'Okay, just checking.'"

Moaning, Elle draped herself over the table. "I meant to read it thoroughly, but I was so distracted with wedding plans, closing the gallery . . ."

"The best you can do in this county is create and sell your own work."

"But I'm not supposed to be in this county. I'm supposed to be married, living in Dallas." She hammered the table with her fist.

"I'd never say this to anyone else, but, Elle, if you wanted to be married to Jeremiah, wouldn't you be?"

"Um, he dumped me." For a lawyer, Candace could be dense at times.

"Really? You didn't do a little sabotage work? Who draws a line in the sand over a haute couture home and a vintage?"

"Me, that's who," she said, face still pressed to the table. "Besides, it was more about opposing purposes. The day we sold the gallery, he sat in your office and promised me I could open one in Dallas. A week later, he reneged."

"And that was it? 'I can't open a gallery so I quit.'"

"I never quit, he did." Elle shoved her hair out of her face and leaned against the table. Heat prickled over her skin, more from the conversation than the temperature of the studio.

"Whether it was on some subconscious level or not, Elle, you sent him the message you weren't ready for marriage."

"Candy, you're crazy. Why would I sabotage my own life? I run around Beaufort for a year executing Operation Wedding Day against everyone's sound advice, humiliating myself, kissing a few toads, *blech*. Then, when someone finally invites me to the dance, I back out? He's the one who said he didn't have time for marriage. Not me."

Candace slipped the sale addendum into her case. "You said it first without words. You're an amazing woman, Elle, but I don't see you married to a pastor. Growing up, you hated the label "Deacon

Garvey's daughter." You always defended Mitch O'Neal, the rogue preacher's kid, because you felt the congregation placed unrealistic expectations on him. Now apply that to yourself as an independent, grown woman being married to a minister. Some women make great pastor's wives, but it'd drive you crazy."

"I loved Jeremiah, Candace. Isn't that enough?"

"Apparently not, because here you sit." She looked around the studio. "To be honest, I think you like this bohemian existence."

Elle's stared at her feet. After a night in the hospital and a day on her futon, she didn't know what she believed or wanted. "Maybe you're right."

Candace zipped her attaché. "Elle, if anyone can make lemonade out of lemons, it's you."

"Do you think Wild Wally has room for me on his lawn crew?"

Candace walked to the door. "Be serious."

"I am. If I can't open a gallery, what am I going to do?" Elle brushed the rebel tears from her cheek. She was tired of crying about herself, her past.

"You're not joining Wally's crew, Elle. I'll hire you at the firm first. Your job? Paint. And I don't mean with Sherman Williams. Get your courage back. Forget what your hardnosed, bitter professor said. Elle, trust me, somewhere in this rubble is a lovely silver lining."

"When you find it, give me a call."

"Will do. Listen, I've got to go. You okay?"

"If not, I will be."

It'd been years since she'd run, but this evening the stretch of her legs, the ache of her weak lungs straining for air, felt good.

Breath in. Breath out. Elle stretched further and faster, running

Rachel Hauck

in the sandy soil and grass along Hwy 21, the pine-perfumed wind in her face. Her ponytail swished from side to side with each stride.

When she returned to the studio, she showered, ate a bowl of dry cereal, and checked e-mail for the first time in days. Out-of-touch artists and clients still e-mailed about GG Gallery business. The inbox also contained more "so sorry" messages. And a new one from Caroline.

To: Elle Garvey
From: CSweeney
Subject: You have to be sitting down for this one

Elle,

Unplanned and not what we intended, but so romantic and perfect, Mitch and I were married last Saturday on the beach.

Elle jerked back with a shock of tears. Her best friend? Married?

When he came to visit, it just felt right. He called Daddy and Posey to make sure they wouldn't be hurt if we decided to get married without all the family and trimmings.

They blessed us over and over and promised a big reception when we came home.

Mitch's daddy had always wanted to officiate our ceremony, if and when, but he said, "Son, if you know it's right, marry her. We've been waiting a long time."

Isn't he the best?

Oh, Elle, it feels so good and right to be his wife. The timing was perfect. God knew. I can't believe I wasted so many years and countless hours sitting in the old live oak tree talking to No One when I could've been talking to the True One.

My boss, good ole Carlos, gave us a nice wedding gift—money

and two weeks off. Mitch has to go back to Nashville, but we can manage our marriage long distance for the next few months.

Hazel and a few friends from SRG International were witnesses. I'm sorry you were not one of them. We always promised we'd be each other's maid-of-honor, didn't we?

But if marriage is about the relationship, not the ceremony, then Mitch and I did exactly the right thing. We'll celebrate together when I come home.

I love you, Elle, and hope this news isn't sad for you in light of everything. But I wanted you to know. Praying for you.

Caroline Sweeney O'Neal
(O'Neal, did you see? My name is O'Neal!)

Elle read the e-mail twice more. *Way to go, Caroline.*

To: CSweeney
From: Elle Garvey
Subject: Congratulations!

Caroline,

Married? Ahhhhh . . . can you hear me screaming all the way from St. Helena? I'm so happy for you and Mitch. We've all waited a long time for this day. Remember when we were seventeen and Mitch started the pluff mud fight during the Water Festival? Then that night he kissed you in the back booth at the Frogmore Café. You've waited twelve years for that kiss to come to fruition. (smile)

I am doing well other than being sad I missed your wedding. I feel thickheaded and dazed sometimes, but with each hurdle, my inner strength grows. Recent news: can't open a new gallery. Sale addendum to GG Gallery prohibits.

Your comment, "God knew," challenged me. I've known Him my whole life, Caroline. Grew up in church. But I'm no more confident or aware of Him than when I was a girl. Only now, in the midst of pain and failure, do I find myself running to Him. I can speak to Him, but my ear is not tuned to hearing. That realization frightens me.

Is my life in shambles because He wanted me to stop and face Him, not dialog with my back to Him as I went about my day with half-hearted faith? Maybe. Either way, He gets to see my mug every weekday morning, seven a.m., Beaufort Community Church's prayer chapel. We have a standing date.

Candace actually thinks I sabotaged my relationship with Jer because at some deep level I didn't want to be married to him and living in Dallas. She claims I'd hate being a pastor's wife. Sheez, does that make me sound shallow or what?

Can't wait to see you. Send pics if you have any.
Love you most dearly, Elle

Without rereading, Elle sent her e-mail into cyber space, suspicious she'd written to herself as much as Caroline.

By now, late evening approached and Elle wondered when Heath would call. She fished her phone from her bag. Shoot, dead battery.

Plugging it in, she powered it up to find five messages from Heath. The last one thirty minutes ago. She dialed his phone.

"Heath, it's Elle."

"Where have you been?" Sharp, curt, a tad testy.

"My battery died and I just noticed. I'm sorry." She gazed around for her flip-flops. What was with this studio eating her shoes?

"Did you think to check? They were ready to release TL two hours ago. Can you please come and get us? If it's not too much of a bother."

Heath certainly wore lack of sleep like an ugly sweater. In a calm, low tone, she answered, "I'll be right there."

Rain drummed against the windows as Heath stretched out on the floor in front of the fire. He locked his hand behind his head, settling back against the pile of pillows, smiling when her footsteps resounded down the hall.

"Is she sleeping?" he asked.

"Like a baby." Ava smiled and lowered herself to the floor, pillowing her head on his chest. Absently Heath wrapped his arm around her.

"She's beautiful, isn't she?"

"Yes. And perfect. You do nice work, Mr. McCord."

"So do you, Mrs. McCord."

She raised up, propping on her elbow. "You're glad, aren't you? We made the decision so fast."

He brushed her hair away from her oval face. "If I were any happier, my heart would burst."

Ava nestled against his chest again. "Sometimes I hold her and cry. I can't believe she's ours."

"Want to try for another one?" He pressed her close.

Ava laughed gently, swatting his belly. "She's only two months old. I'm not ready for another one."

"Then you don't get my drift."

She responded to him with a lingering kiss. "I believe I do."

Heath rolled her onto her back, eyes to eyes, nose to nose, lips to lips. The fire wood crackled and popped. Ava's expression grew serious.

"If something happens to me, Heath, will you fall in love again?"

"What? Why are you talking about dying? Besides, there's only you for me, Ava."

"Because having Tracey-Love makes me think of things I never considered

before." She brushed her hands down the side of his face, caressing his lips with her thumb.

He sat back on his knees. This talk was nonsense. "If something happened to me, would you marry again?"

"If I fell in love, yes. She'd need a father."

"I'm her father."

"I know, but baby, if one of us dies, Tracey-Love would need another man or woman in her life."

Heath got up and walked over to the fire and stirred the coals. "Can we stop all this talk about dying? No one is dying."

"We need to be ready for whatever life hands us. Of course, we aren't dying before our time, but, Heath, we have to prepare for every scenario. If not for ourselves, for our daughter. I want you to promise me." She met him by the fireplace and wrapped her arms around his waist, pressing her face into his back. "Promise me you'll fall in love again. Marry a woman who loves you and Tracey-Love."

He hated this discussion. "No, I'm not promising anything related to your death, or mine."

"Heath, you must. Promise me. Promise me. Promise me."

Heath woke, gasping. Sweat gathered on his forehead, and in the dark room he couldn't get his bearings. What time was it? By the manmade light slipping through the drawn window slats, he guessed it to be the middle of the night.

The intensity of the dream clung to him as he clicked on the bedside lamp. So very real. When did he and Ava ever have such a conversation?

Invincible Ava never considered death, even when she danced with danger. Heath was the cautious one, making out the will, setting up disaster funds, trust funds, buying insurance.

Tracey-Love stirred on her side of the bed. Heath leaned over to check on her, sweeping her hair from her face. Home two days from the hospital, she was doing well, but he still worried, still carried the effects of his sleepless ER night.

The cottage was hot, and as Heath made his way to the thermostat, the old floor creaked under his feet.

It'd been a little while since he'd dreamt of Ava, and he didn't like it now anymore than he did then. In the weeks after her funeral, Heath dreamed of her screams and cries for help, exhausting himself in fruitless rescue efforts. He'd wake up drenched, legs kicking, the bed linens toppled onto the floor.

In the living room, Heath bumped the thermostat down a degree, and in a few seconds, fresh air circulated.

He walked to the kitchen and flipped on the light. Two a.m. Opening the fridge for a bottle of water, he caught the white and blue of Ava's letter waiting for him on the windowsill.

"We were lucky, Ava. The doc said it was a mild case of viral meningitis." He twisted open the water, taking a long swig. "She'll be weak for a few weeks, but should be running and playing like any healthy girl by the end of June."

Another deep swig.

"I was scared, babe. I can't lose her. And for the first time, I let myself be really mad at you."

Without consideration, Heath fired the half-full water bottle against the far wall. It hit the tile and puddled.

He banged out the kitchen door onto the porch. The gentle humid night rebuked his anger. He dropped to the edge of the iron rocker, whispering his emotions to God. First about Ava, then Tracey-Love being sick, and finally his behavior toward Elle.

Man, he'd been a bear to her when she'd arrived at the hospital. He groused and grumbled because she wasn't ready at his beck and call. But who'd gotten up at 1:00 a.m. to drive him to the ER, without one word of complaint? Not one hint of "You owe me."

She never defended herself when he suggested, rather rudely, she should remember to charge her phone battery. Instead she apologized again and drove them home in comforting silence, stopping by the pharmacy to fill a prescription and waited as he ran into Publix for Gatorade and juice. And when Tracey-Love asked for her new dolly, Elle hunted high and low. Discovering Heath had left it at the hospital, she drove back to get it.

Living in her house, imposing on her hospitality, he'd acted like a world-class jerk. He'd make it up to her. Figure out a way and make it up to her.

Fifteen

Between Caroline's e-mail, Candace's ridiculous accusation of sabotage, and Pastor O'Neal's Sunday morning reminder that Jesus said, "My sheep hear my voice," Elle needed to do some come-to-Jesus soul searching.

At thirty-one, raised in church, she could not confess she confidently knew the voice of her Lord.

Sitting in the chapel, second pew, right side, Elle felt like a blank slate. She had nothing going on in her life but Him, and for the first time, she felt completely surrendered.

And she liked it.

At the altar, Miss Anna remained vigilant, pacing back and forth this morning instead of kneeling.

How many years had the older woman been coming here, keeping watch? Forty? Elle's respect for her deepened. Don't mistake prayer for inactivity.

Closing her eyes, she offered her thoughts as a sacrifice to the Lord, gave Him her affection. But when a foreign thought flipped across her mind—"What do you want?"—her eyes popped open to a quickened pulse.

Me? What do I want?

"What do you want?"

Elle sat forward, peeking around. *Are you talking to me?*

"What do you want?"

Open a gallery and—

"What do you want?"

I just said, open a gallery— Arguing with herself, fine existential moment.

"No, tell Me what you want."

Her heart raced. The challenge was not from her mind but from Him.

Miss Anna stopped pacing and stood quietly with her head bowed.

Okay, what do I want? Elle settled down, shoved aside expectations and preconceived ideas, and lowered an empty bucket of desire through her soul.

I want to paint. I want to get over my fears, forget what my professor said to me and paint. There, she admitted it.

She waited, listening, sensing the life on her confession. Yeah, she wanted to paint. After six years of denying her heart, she wanted to paint. God knew, just like Caroline said. Elle wondered how long His question had hovered in the heavens, waiting for her to be still.

Forget Dr. Petit. "*I recommend a day job, Elle. You won't make a living as a painter.*" God wanted her to paint.

When she glanced over to Miss Anna, the woman was eyeing her.

"I think God is telling me to paint."

"Then do it."

"But how do I know when God is speaking and not my own—"

A white feather fluttered in the space between her and Miss Anna.

"Another one," Elle breathed.

Miss Anna snatched the feather from the air. "Been a long time since I've seen one of these."

Elle stood by her prayer mentor. "I have another one in my studio. What do you think they mean?"

Miss Anna handed Elle the feather. "God reveals Himself to us in creative ways. We've gotten so used to just the preaching and singing, I bet He feels a little boxed in sometimes."

Elle had certainly put Him in a box and on the shelf.

"Well, an hour or so of prayer and one white feather, I'd say we had a good morning." Miss Anna ambled up the aisle with her Bible tucked close. "Going home to tend my garden before the sun beats down on me."

"Can I give you a ride?"

Miss Anna laughed as she shoved open the chapel door.

Brooks and Dunn blasted from iTunes. The ceiling fans whirred. And Elle painted. Digging in her paint box for a tube of titanium white, she squeezed a dab onto her palette.

After her confession and encounter with God during prayer, she'd left the chapel with a surge of creative energy and decided not to let it pass. If she only painted for God and herself, so be it.

"Elle, hey, it's me." The knock on the door resounded with the bass drum of the music.

"Heath?" She jerked open the door. "Come in? How's Tracey-Love?"

"Fine, watching a DVD. We went to the doctor this morning and he's pleased with her recovery. What are you doing?"

"I," she said with a tip of her head, "am painting."

"Good for you." He came around to see the canvas. "Feathers?"

"You don't like it, do you?" She lowered the music.

"Insecure, are we?"

Elle showed him the two feathers she'd arranged on blue silk and set in a stream of sunlight. "These . . . just appeared."

"Appeared? Out of nowhere?" Heath reached for one. "May I?"

"Yeah, I had another one but gave it to Candace." Elle recounted the feather story while mixing burnt umber, cobalt blue, and the white with her pallet knife. "Weird, isn't it?"

"Why not feathers? Isn't there a Bible verse about the shadow of His wing?"

Elle brushed a bit of the blue on the canvas. Too light. "Read that verse yesterday."

Heath returned the feather to Elle's arrangement. "I'm sorry about my attitude the day we brought TL home."

She flicked the tip of the brush at him. "Forget it, I understand. I'm sure my attitude would've been worse."

"Don't excuse me. It was wrong." He walked over to the paintings leaning against the wall. "These yours?"

"Yeah, from college and my year in Florence. A few from studying at the student's Art League."

He pulled the unfinished *Girls in the Grass* from the pile. "This is incredible, Elle."

"Heath, it's not even finished."

"Yet I feel like kicking off my shoes and running in the grass."

Elle dropped her chin to her chest, curling her shoulders forward. "Don't patronize me, McCord."

She'd started *Girls in the Grass* during a hard summer between graduating college and growing up, during her term at the Student's Art League when all her doubts solidified.

Heath leaned the painting against the wall and picked up the one next to it. "Would you go to dinner with me?"

She looked around at him. He studied her painting of Coffin Creek under fog. "Dinner?" *Like on a date?*

"Dinner. I want to make it up to you for the other night." He glanced at her, raising the painting. "Can I buy this?"

"Buy it? You can have it. And you don't have to make up anything to me, Heath. You'd have done the same for me."

"I know, but I want to . . . please. Can I give you a hundred for it?"

"What? No, take it, please."

He came over to her, leaning so close her eyes could only see his. His scent filled her senses. Her skin rippled. "A hundred dollars. An artist is worth her hire. And you wouldn't have chewed me out for a dead phone battery. Dinner?"

Swallow. "F-fine."

"Tomorrow night at six?"

"Tomorrow at six."

Chet McCord propelled the Hawk P-36 into the blustery headwind. The aircraft shimmied with each frigid blast and his arms already ached from holding her steady. A picture of Kelly lodged in the instrument panel fell beneath his feet.

Nothing but soup up here today. What's the use of dawn patrol when there ain't no dawn? For a moment, Chet fought a slight panic, the grip of claustrophobia. If he lost his instrument panel . . .

The radio crackled. "Chet. Do you read me? Over."

A voice. Pike from Signal Corp calling to wish him good morning and remind Chet he wasn't alone in the world. He picked up the radio mike. "Did you figure out you owed me more money?" Chet had taken him in poker last night and Pike was none too happy about it.

"The opposite—you owe me money. There was a miscalculation." His laugh crackled over the radio. "What are you doing taking off on a morning like this?"

"Knitting Grandma a sweater. What do you think I'm doing?"

"Get down, McCord. You're flying right into a big squall with fifty-mile-an-hour gusts. Don't fool around with this. The boys at the weather station say it's a humdinger."

That explained all the turbulence. "Am I ordered down?"

"Why do you flyboys insist you can outfly the weather? Bring 'er home."

"If I waited for ideal conditions, I'd never take off. Short patrol, under the soup, then I'll be down."

Chet struggled to pilot against the icy winds. But at fifty feet, an unexpected cloud break revealed disturbed white-capped waters below. Seeing an opening like this in the dense fog was the equivalent of seeing the wide-open plains of Oklahoma.

Descending for a closer look at the water, Chet scouted for enemy subs or a wayward destroyer, then rolled the Hawk toward the northeast coast line and home.

At first, the greenish gray sub tottering on the surface escaped his eye. It blended with the fog and dreariness. But once he had a visual, he knew it was a Jap I-class sub. His heart thundered as he banked around for a strafing run.

When Heath's cell went off, it knocked him out of his growing manuscript. For a moment, he was Chet McCord, heart racing, about to fire at an enemy sub.

"Yeah," he answered.

"Blue Cooper here. Heath, how are you?"

He shifted his laptop toward the coffee table. "Blue, long time."

"You're a hard man to track down. Calloway & Gardner doesn't release information easily. I've had better luck with the Pentagon. Did you get my e-mails?"

"Yeah, sorry, guess I never responded. I moved south for a few months." Heath walked to the bedroom to check on Tracey-Love. She slept peacefully with her arm hooked around her doll, Lola. Best purchase he'd made in a long time.

"What do you think? Can you make it to the city in a few weeks for the Network News Awards? We'd like you to accept a lifetime achievement award on Ava's behalf."

He wandered the living room in circles. "Right, right. Tell me the date again." Only skimming Blue's e-mail, Heath had never registered the dates.

"June thirteenth. A Friday evening. She'd want you there, Heath." In his broadcaster's voice, Blue spoke as if he'd heard from Heath's wife a few minutes ago.

So moving on didn't mean leaving everything about her behind. "Yes, I'll be there, Blue. Thanks for calling."

It'd be a fast trip. Three days, maybe. He'd get with Rock, check up on Callaway & Gardner. But Tracey-Love wouldn't be strong enough to tag along.

Returning to the club chair and taking up his laptop, Heath wondered if he could ask Elle to watch TL and owe her another dinner of gratitude. Also, pay her five hundred for the painting. What was he thinking offering only a hundred? Cheap.

The awards would be black-tie, probably at the Grand Hyatt or uptown at Radio City. Where'd he stored his tux?

Reaching for his phone again, he dialed Rock. "I'm going to be in town for the Network News Awards. Want to meet for dinner?"

"Perfect timing. I need to talk to you about coming back, son. The inmates are running the asylum."

Rock, always exaggerating. "What's going on now?"

"Doc and Tom are pushing me out, trying to take over. I need a strong ally."

Heath tried to imagine any man, or two, outsmarting his old boss. "And you think I can help?"

"Absolutely. We'll talk when you're here."

"Rock, before you go, I've got a friend down here who's helped me out more than I can repay. She's an artist. You think we could stop in and see your old friend Mitzy Canon? See if she'd check out my friend's work, give her a boost in the biz?"

"Don't see why not. If anyone can launch an artist's career, it's Mitzy Canon, the artist maker. I'll give her a call."

"I owe you."

"Serious? Then when can I expect you back at the firm?"

"Night, Rock." Heath hung up and headed to the kitchen to clean up dinner.

Note to self: Check girl-stuff sites to see what age to start assigning household chores.

Sixteen

At two o'clock, Huckleberry John lumbered into Common Ground, his dark bangs draping over his right eye, titanium rings stretching holes in his earlobes. His slightly crooked grin seemed unsure when he spotted Elle.

"You beckoned, O great Elle Garvey?" He slumped into the chair across from her.

"Do you want something to drink?" She eyed him, dumping sweetener into her latte.

"Naw, I'm good." He flicked his hand through his hair. "What's on your mind, chicky?"

"You. How's your environmental art coming?"

"Good," he said, gazing lazily around the shop, dangling one arm over the back of his chair, drumming his fingers on the table.

"Did Angela Dooley accept any of your work?"

"She's a snob, Elle. I tried to tell her about the Coffin Creek crisis—"

"Come on, Huck. Be honest. What crisis?"

"See?" He tapped his forefinger against the table. "This is exactly how we go wrong in this country. We don't pay attention until it's too late." Passion fortified his response.

"Good point. I hear you, but you've got to learn how to present yourself and your projects. And maybe actually learn a little about art. Art may be garbage to some people, Huck, but garbage is hardly ever art. Especially if it smells."

"But I bet people will never forget my work." He was cocky, but cute.

Elle sipped her latte. Too hot. "Huck, you're ineffective."

"Do tell."

"Going around town with a fish tank of pluff mud and dead fish isn't going to help your cause. You're letting your message get in the way of the messenger. What are you trying to accomplish?"

"Art that focuses on the environment."

"Got anything up your sleeve besides fish tanks?"

"A few paintings, a couple of mixed-medium pieces," he confessed.

"Are they odorless?"

"Fairly. But"—his grin made her laugh—"they do stay in my apartment."

"Huckleberry, I have a long way to go in my own art, but one thing I've learned: first be an artist, good or bad, weak or strong, and let your message come out of the work of your heart. You're letting your passion ruin your art. Instead, let your passion fuel your art. Do you understand?"

"Kind of like put the gas in the tank, not all over the outside of the car."

"Exactly. You have to be patient. Art takes time."

Heed your own advice, Elle.

"Is that your nice way of saying I got a lot of work to do?" Huckleberry fussed, shaking his legs, stretching his neck, his arms. The man was incapable of sitting still.

"Not just you. Me too. I'm starting over with painting myself." A second sip from her latte burned the same spot on her tongue as the first sip.

"We should get together sometime. Hang out, paint or something."

Elle paused. Could she help him? While she'd been trained, she didn't feel much farther along than Huckleberry craft-wise. "All right, let's meet at my place since yours, um, smells."

"Elle?"

She angled around to see her friend J. D. Rand. "Hey."

A sheriff's deputy, he was one of her old gang from high school. Last year he dated Caroline Sweeney until she caught him cheating.

She introduced Huck to J. D., who said, "The man with the fish tank." Without knowing it, J. D. fueled Huck's cause. Elle knew then Beaufort had not seen, or smelled, the last of his eco art.

"Did you hear about Caroline and Mitch?" Elle asked J. D.

"Yeah, through the grapevine. About time, eh?"

"I'll say . . ."

Molly called J. D.'s order, but on his way out, he stopped back at the table, slipping on his Foster Grants.

"Bodean's having a summer kick-off party tonight. Branan Morgan is playing with his band. Lots of good company, good food, and cold beverages. Love to see you there, Elle. Huckleberry, if you can shower and find clean clothes, come on out."

Huckleberry glanced down at his shirt, smoothing his hand over a big chocolate-looking stain.

"I'll see. Thanks, J. D."

Elle hadn't been to one of Bodean's Mars versus Venus parties since Operation Wedding Day was in full swing. Tonight she had dinner with Heath. Maybe she could talk her New York lawyer friend into an evening with some good ole boys.

"Chet, are you out there? Come in."

Still banking around for a strafing run, Chet didn't answer Pike's call, maintaining radio silence. If the submarine located him, he'd be in the drink before he could fire one round.

"Come in, Chet. The mother is gaining. Get home."

Descending from the fog, Captain Chet McCord strafed the first enemy vessel he'd seen. Six months in the Aleutians and his greatest enemy was the cold, snow, and fog. His greatest victory: arriving home alive, not plowing into the side of a mountain.

Buzzing the con tower of the Jap sub, he peppered it with bullets, then rose into the fog before the enemy could man their guns. His fuel gauge told him to turn toward home.

"Pike, I'm coming home."

As Chet banked east, he caught sight of the sub as it submerged beneath the freezing surface. He'd only infuriated the gray beast.

His P-36 engine sputtered.

"No you don't." Chet tapped the fuel gauge. He had enough to return home. What was going on? The engine sputtered again, nearly stalling.

Chet pushed toward Kiska, gripping the stick, willing his bird to stay alive and warm. Another sputter and he knew. She was freezing up.

Heath paced beside his van, waiting for Elle. She'd called to say she'd lost track of time while painting—he liked the excitement in her voice—and was running a few minutes behind. She'd meet him by his van.

His *van*. He kicked the front tire. What he need was some cool, secondhand car like a convertible Corvair or a Triumph Spitfire.

After he dropped off Tracey-Love at Julianne's to spend the evening with Rio, he'd felt kind of lost.

First-date-like flutters ran down his ribs. *Just a casual dinner, McCord. With a friend.* It'd been eighteen years since he'd been alone with a woman not his girlfriend, wife, or colleague.

To distract himself, he walked over to inspect his angel carving. The core sculpture rose out of the wood, but the details needed to be carved out, sanded, and polished. He'd finish it someday. Before returning to New York.

Her fragrance arrived first. Like wild flowers in a spring meadow. When he looked around, he simply felt glad she was in the world. Proud and lucky to be with her. Even if just for one *friendly* night.

Her hair fluttered over her shoulders, her long brown legs kicked the hem of a flowing blue skirt. A trio of bracelets sparkled from the end of her arm.

He understood why men painted—to preserve images like Elle, real or imagined.

"You look beautiful," he said, his steady voice masking the rumba going on beneath his shirt.

"So do you. Mighty dapper in khakis and pullover. Very summer-in-the-Hamptons-darling."

Her breezy tone reminded him tonight was about one friend thanking another. No more, no less. His heart simmered down, slowing from a rumba to a boring ole waltz.

"A friend of mine is having one of his big parties tonight," Elle said as he held open her door. "Want to swing by after dinner?"

Absolutely. "I am at your command."

"Really, 'cause I have some studio windows that need washing."

"Windows?" Heath held his arms out to his sides, giving himself the once-over, grinning. "You got all this and you want windows washed?"

Maybe it was the soft music hovering over Panini's guests or the flicker of candlelight on the white linen tablecloth, but Elle's insides felt battered by butterflies.

Handsome Heath wore a blue shirt that matched his eyes, and his bold flirting as he helped her into the van downright messed with her.

"You got all this and you want windows washed?"

But as delectable as he was, her heart wanted to remain in a soft, safe place until the last fragrance of Jeremiah Franklin had faded away.

"Give me the scoop," he started, sitting back as their server brought a basket of warm bread and appetizer plates. "How often can I expect to get caught in the drawbridge traffic?"

"Daily, if you're out and about."

"I was thinking of putting Tracey-Love in school half days, give her something to do while I work."

"Leave early if you're concerned about time, but getting caught in bridge traffic is a legitimate excuse around here."

"Good to know."

Elle grinned, passing him the bread. On the way downtown, they'd been caught in bridge traffic, and for fifteen minutes New Yorker Heath drummed the wheel impatiently but listened as she talked about a painting she'd started.

He asked about the inspiration behind her idea—*drum, drum, drum*—offered a suggestion—"What is taking so long?"—talked about colors and the message of her work—"We're stopped for that one itty-bitty sail boat?"

"Yep."

He'd glared at her. "New Yorkers would riot."

The server returned for their order. Elle ordered a brick-oven pizza and Heath the pork roast.

"How's the book?" Elle leaned to one side, chin in her hand.

"Good, good." Heath spread his napkin over his lap, reaching for a slice of warm bread. "It's a World War II love story, which is giving my agent a heart attack, but it's what came out when I started writing."

"We're a slave to the muse, no? Why doesn't he like the story?"

"If one of your clients was a noted Manhattan criminal lawyer, would you want a love story set in wartime Beaufort and the Aleutian Islands?"

Elle laughed. "No, I guess not. I'd want a legal thriller or political intrigue."

"Exactly."

She brushed her hand over the linen. "When do I get to read this masterpiece?"

"When it's published."

Ha.

He didn't even crack a smile.

"Not even a peek?"

Heath tried to hide his grin with a bite of bread. "Maybe, we'll see."

"Okay, no more busting my chops about my confidence or sneaking peeks at my work."

"Yeah, let's talk about your confidence." His steady gaze made her butterflies beat their wings. "What happened to the girl who drew on bulletins and water-colored her parents wedding pictures?"

"Gave in to doubt. Let my confidence leak like air from an old bike tire. It became too hard to paint and believe I was any good."

"Doubt usually has a source."

Their server refilled their iced teas. Elle waited until she left to go on.

"I had a mentor at New York's Student Art League the summer after I came home from Florence. I was discouraged and thought if I could find someone who saw beyond my weaknesses, maybe I'd develop my craft."

"Elle, it's art. Very subjective."

"Sure but who wants their professors implying, 'Should've majored in basket weaving'?" Elle placed a slice of bread on her plate and reached for the butter.

"You're exaggerating."

"No, I'm not. I had an instructor in Florence as well as colleague who gave me the what-are-you-doing-here eye." Her first bite of bread was buttery warm. It had been awhile since she'd had much more than dry cereal, stale crackers, and barbecue chips. "I felt like a brown pony running in a pack of psychedelic ones and finding a way to stand out was impossible. People would ask, 'What's that spec of dirt doing on this gorgeous, mosaic masterpiece?'"

Heath laughed, covering his full mouth with his fist. "Elle, come on, you're not a brown pony. Besides, do you really believe every successful artist or writer had someone telling them, 'Go for it, Van Gogh. You da bomb'?" He arched his brows. "If there are vacancies in your Never Never Land, I want to move in."

She burst out laughing. "Okay, no, but somewhere, somehow, a voice has to tell the artist, 'Keep going. You have what it takes.'"

Their server stopped by. "Your order will be right out."

"What happened that summer? At the Student League?"

Elle leaned forward with her hands in her lap. "I wanted to study impressionism." She shook her head. "Way harder than it looks."

"Most *simple* things are."

"I met a visiting professor at the Student League, Dr. Petit, who gave private instruction. Paid a lot of money, painted a lot of hours, lived in a closet someone rented to me as an apartment . . . only to be told I'd better marry well or find a good-paying day job."

"Really, that harsh?" He wrinkled his face.

"By the time I left New York in September, I never wanted to pick up a brush again."

"Elle, he's one man."

"Sometimes one man is all it takes. I came home and started planning the gallery. Time was a commodity I didn't want to waste. So many people dedicate their lives to the wrong thing. I didn't want that to be me."

Heath reached for his tea. "Yeah, I know the feeling."

The server brought out their dinner, offering ground pepper and cheese toppings. "Can I get y'all anything else?"

Heath glanced at Elle. *Good?* "We're fine, thanks."

The conversation stalled as they ate the first few hot bites of dinner. Elle had been craving brick-oven pizza for a while. She closed her eyes as she chewed. "This was worth you yelling at me for a dead phone battery."

Heath cut a bit of his meat. "Glad to oblige. Okay, so you were so shut down by this rude professor. What inspired you to paint again?"

Elle wiped her mouth with the edge of her napkin. "A few days ago I was praying at the chapel and"—she tried to pass it off casually with a flip of her wrist—"God kind of asked me what I wanted. The desire to paint came back, so I thought I'd try. Not that I'm going to go showing my work or anything, but I'm taking it one day at a time."

"I believe God is wiser than Dr. Petit. How about you?"

Elle grinned, shook her head, and bit into her pizza. "Smart aleck."

Seventeen

A scratchy electric guitar lick-zapped the humid evening air as Heath walked a path of tiki lights to this Bodean guy's party.

"He's a friend of yours?" he asked Elle, spotting a circle of men, half of them wearing deputy uniforms, the other half in T-shirts and jeans. "Some party if the cops arrive before the fighting begins."

Elle laughed, bumping into him as she walked. She could do that all night and he'd not complain. "Bo's a deputy sheriff and so are most of his friends."

"Ah-ha." Way on the other side of the wide party lot, the band's lead singer belted out Sarah Buxton's "Stupid Boy."

Heath walked with his hand lightly touching her back, fascinated by the lively, good-time atmosphere. It reminded him of his Yale frat days before the kegs were tapped and the men drank freely. So far, he'd been there two minutes and no one had run by him beer drenched and naked.

The path to the party split under two signs: This way to Mars. This way to Venus.

"Mars and Venus?" He glanced at Elle.

"It started as a joke one year when Bodean was on and off again with his wife, Marley. Now it's party tradition."

"Is there a neutral planet where we can hang out together?" He scanned the landscape.

"Sure. Switzerland." Elle walked straight ahead, off the path, cutting across the grass and through the trees.

"Switzerland. Man, all this time I was thinking it was a country."

On the edge of the planetary lights, Elle found a picnic table situated between two oak trees. Heath sat next to her, his feet flat on the bench, arms resting on his knees. Through another set of trees, between the tiki flames and the ground luminaries, he could see the bandstand, a plywood dance floor, and patches of white moonlight.

"You know these people your whole life?" Heath asked.

"Most of them. If I didn't go to school with them, one of my sisters did. Or, shoot, see Edgar Forest over there?" Her bracelets tangoed when she raised her hand to point out Edgar. "Retired deputy. Went to school with Mama."

Heath liked the music of her bracelets. Ava had embraced the fashion of a New York journalist. Little makeup, except when on air, and a mostly black wardrobe. If she ever owned bracelets, Heath had never seen them.

Elle fascinated him with her green eye shadow, Cleopatra eyeliner, and a wardrobe color that didn't start with *B* and end with *K*. Ava wore pantsuits and pumps. Elle wore flowered skirts and shorts. Jeans and T-shirts. And Heath wasn't sure he'd ever seen her wear the same pair of shoes.

"Elle, the prettiest girl in the county. Finally, my party has class." A skinny man with cropped blond hair and wide shoulders strolled between the trees.

Elle slid off the table. "Bo, now I know you've said that to all the girls tonight."

He pressed his finger to his lips. "Shh, but with you it's true." The man held his beer away as he leaned in to kiss her cheek. "Sorry about the whole wedding thing, Elle. The boys decided the man must be crazy for letting you go."

Elle sat back next to Heath, dismissing Bo's comment with a *pffffbt*. "Wasn't meant to be."

"Just so you know, we broke our No Girls rule at the Wednesday-afternoon club and voted you an honorary member. Anytime you want to come over, hang out, shoot pool, throw back a few beers, you're welcome."

"Bo," Elle gasped, hand pressed to her chest, "I don't know what to say. I'm honored." She sniffled.

Heath grinned at Elle's expression. He liked seeing this part of her, confident and comfortable among her friends, out from the dark shadow of rejection.

"Bodean, this is my friend and neighbor, Heath McCord."

He shook Heath's hand. "Welcome, welcome. Stop on by Mars; we got a good beanbag game going."

"If I get bored here, I will."

The comment caused Bo to shift his gaze to Elle. "Well then, see you around." The man wandered off toward Venus and Heath heard, "Susanna, the prettiest girl in the county. Now my party has class."

Heath nudged Elle. "He's a piece of work."

"Sure is, but he'd give you the shirt off his back and the last dollar in his pocket."

"A lot of people in this town love you, Elle. And don't tell me it's because you grew up here."

"Well, it's true."

He touched her chin. "There's something very beautiful and tender about you. I bet half the men at the party would take a punch in the gut if someone threatened you."

She moved away. "Don't say things like that, Heath."

"It's true."

She shook her head. "I thought tonight was about friends."

He lowered his hand and stared toward the dance floor. "Right, right, friends." Without pausing to consider his emotions, Heath knew he wanted more. But she'd stationed the No Detour signs. Maybe she was right. He'd be going back to New York by the end of summer. Why start what he couldn't finish?

"Hey, you two, come on, hit the dance floor." Bo popped Heath on the back as he bustled past. "You can moon over each other later."

The music was loud and the heels of the dancers smacked against the plywood. If he didn't have two left feet and no rhythm, Heath might have led her to the dance floor, but he'd rather wait for a slow, swaying dance tune.

"You want to dance?" Elle asked.

"Only if you want."

"I'm good here."

"Me too."

She hollered over to Venus for her friend Jess to bring a couple of brownies and Diet Cokes. When Jess came over a minute later, Heath marveled. He couldn't think of one friend in New York who would respond nicely to such a request. *Get your own bleeping brownie. Who do I look like to you?*

"So, can I ask you a question?" Elle asked, breaking off the tip of her brownie.

"Absolutely." Heath took a big brownie bite. Man, when was the last time he'd eaten any homemade desert? He was going to have to learn how to make these.

"How long were you married to Ava?"

"Sixteen years. We met in a political science class our sophomore year at Yale. Got married two years later." Heath stuffed the last half of the brownie in his mouth, wondering if a Martian could venture over to Venus for a second piece.

"Was it love at first sight?"

"For me, yes." He waded up his napkin. "But Ava was this beautiful, smart, classy woman every sophomore man wanted. I was just another goofy guy with too much ego in a line of goofy guys with too much ego."

"Tough times in the Ivy League." Elle broke her brownie in two and gave half to him.

"If the entrance examines don't kill you, the competition among geeks and supergeeks will."

"Come on, isn't Yale the land of Chip and Babs, lots of money and perfect gene pools?"

"Things have changed. As it turned out, though, I was the only geek who believed in Jesus, so guess who moved to the front of Ava's class?"

"Jeremiah claimed he was enamored the first time he saw me. But my heart didn't get wrapped around the love axel until he kissed me. Then it was all over but the singing."

"Must have been some kiss." *Note to self.* He wasn't planning on kissing her, but if he did, accidentally or something, this tidbit was nice to know.

"Was it the kiss or just this really gorgeous man giving me his attention, coming along when I really wanted to get married?"

"Fine line sometimes between love and infatuation."

"How did she die, Heath? Can you tell me?"

"Tragically." He brushed his finger lightly down her nose to its soft tip. "I promise to tell you. I'm just having a good time tonight and—"

"I understand." Elle crumpled her napkin, holding out her hand for his trash. "Is her light too large to stand under?"

He dipped his head to see her eyes. "No, it's not."

"You don't compare every woman you meet to her?"

"I did at one time. I'll always love Ava, Elle. But if God blesses me with another love, she won't have to stand in Ava's light or shadow. Why do you ask?"

Elle shrugged. "Just wondered what life looked like from your chair."

"How about you? Do you compare men to Jeremiah?"

"You mean, 'Oh, here, take my heart and see if you can stomp on it harder than my ex? Oh no, sorry, didn't hurt me enough. Bye-bye.'"

Heath slipped his arm around her and pulled her to him, kissing the top of her head. "Come on, he had some great qualities or you wouldn't have fallen for him."

"True. Some days I wonder if maybe . . . I don't know, if things will settle out there in Dallas and things could work out."

"Perhaps." The news disappointed him, but it wasn't a total surprise coming from her heart. All the more reason for him to cool his own infatuation.

"My sister Candace thinks I sabotaged the relationship, but I didn't know . . ."

The band slowed down the music and the plywood-floor dancers moved together. Heath slipped off the picnic table. "Enough talk. Would you like to dance?"

"I'm beginning to see a pattern here." She put her hand in his without hesitation.

"Shh, don't spoil the moment."

When they reached the floor, Heath spun her into his arms, holding her to his chest.

"Elle, I have to go to New York in a few weeks to accept an award for Ava." She listened, her hips swaying with his. "Can you watch Tracey-Love for me? I'll pay you."

She lifted her face. "Pay me? Heath, you're in the South, dear heart. We take care of our friends, no debt incurred."

"This is the first time I've left her overnight since Ava died."

"I'll get Rio to sleep over and she won't have time to miss you. Funny, isn't it?" She rested her face against his chest. "Just because someone dies it doesn't always mean their life is over."

Heath pressed his hand against the silk of her hair. Forget the walls and borders, the No Detour signs. Maybe he'd start falling in love with her when he got back from New York, or after he read Ava's letter, perhaps even tomorrow. Or maybe he'd start falling a little bit right now.

Monday afternoon Julianne barged into the studio. "Come with me." She ran back out the door calling, "Hurry."

"To where?" Elle hollered out the window, the two o'clock sun reflecting off Julianne's windshield. "I have a brush full of paint."

"Well, clean it up, but hurry."

Ripping paper towels, Elle wiped her brushes, good enough for the moment since she'd be back to finish. *Dang Julianne.* Elle was just getting into this painting from a lowcountry photo.

She scurried around for her shoes as Julianne hollered, "Come on." *Beep, beep.*

Finally, wearing two different flip-flops, Elle ran down the stairs and jumped into Julianne's car. As she barreled down Lady's Island Road with the top down on her '85 Rabbit, Elle hung white-knuckled on to the passenger-door handle. Keith Urban sang from the stereo about needing a faster car.

"Do you have a hair tie?" Elle popped open Julianne's glove box. About a hundred McDonald's ketchup packets fell to her feet. But no hair tie.

So Elle held her hair with her hands, the ends tangling about her face, as Julianne jerked the Rabbit into the east-bound lane to pass the car ahead of her.

"Jules——" Elle pressed her foot against the floorboard.

The Rabbit's engine wound down. "Sorry, I'm just excited."

At the Meridian Road intersection, Julianne mashed the break and swung into a short, gravel parking lot attached to what used to be a beauty salon—its heyday in the era of the frosted beehives.

Lady's Island Beauty.

"Jules," Elle said, climbing out of the car, raking the wind from her hair. "I hate to be the one to tell you, but this place is closed."

"Remember how we used to make up stories about this place when we passed it?" Julianne hurried to the porch, which was broken down on one side.

"When did we love this place and make up stories?" Elle hitched up her baggy, paint-stained shorts.

"I thought it was you. Maybe it was Candace and me." Julianne jumped to the center of the porch and flung her arms wide. "Elle, ta-da! Welcome to Julianne's, Beaufort's newest and hippest salon." The clouds moved away from the sun and light fell over Julianne's feet.

"You bought this place?" Elle joined her on the porch, scarred and beat up with the rugged wheel marks of skateboarders. "When? How?"

"Today." Julianne held up a single key connected to a red twisty tie. "I finally have my own shop. No more working for *the man*." She scrunched up her shoulders and wrinkled her nose. "Even though Charlie is a woman."

"Is this why you've been so secretive?" Elle followed Julianne inside, breathing a dense, musty odor.

"Elle, open the window over there, will you?"

"Jules . . ." Elle tugged at the lower pane. "This place needs a *lot* of work." The window was painted shut.

"Most great things do, Elle." Julianne's hips wiggled as she tried to raise her window, but it was also sealed shut. In fact, none of the windows opened and when Julianne flipped the switch for the ceiling fans, the paddles moved once, then stopped.

Julianne gazed up, hands on her hips. "Looks like I'll have to get Buster out here first thing." Elle noted her relaxed attitude. "Now I know how you felt when you bought the gallery. Elle, let's spend the night here."

"We'd have to sleep with the front door open, Julianne. What'd you pay for this place?"

"I got it at a fair price, Elle." Julianne opened the cupboard doors, wincing as she pulled out a dead rat by the tail. "Ew."

"What's a fair price? You bought that piece-o-junk car for a thousand more than it was worth new in '85. Did you at least talk to Daddy or Candy?"

"I had all the expert advice I needed." Julianne dumped the rat in the solitary trash can. Her tone chilled the air between them. "In case you haven't noticed, I'm a big girl, all grown up with a daughter of my own."

"Whose advice? Money is not your strong suit, Jules." Elle walked past the out-of-date stylist stations.

"Really, Elle, you ask too many questions."

"You have too many secrets. Where are you going to get the money to remodel? Every one of the sinks needs to be replaced. The stations are old, the vinyl ripped." Elle kicked loose plywood dangling from the bottom drawer of one of the cabinets. "Did you get a termite inspection?"

"You know, Elle, you're a snob."

She spun around. "Snob?"

"You heard me. You think you're the only one who can run a business, do her own thing? Look at you, couldn't even compromise on a house with Jeremiah. You had to have it your way."

The accusation cut and Elle started to strike back, but when she saw the timidity behind her sister's eyes, she knew Julianne needed her kindness, not justification.

"I'm sorry, Jules."

"Elle, I know I can do this. I've loved doing hair as long as you've loved art. I've worked six years at Charlie's." Julianne slapped her hand to her heart. "It's in here. I'm ready."

"Jules, I don't doubt your heart or ability. I'm just concerned about the money." Elle glanced around the square room with a row of tall windows on each side. Beneath the dirt and grim, she imagined the salon's former charm.

Yet cracks slithered along the plaster from the ceiling to the floor. The dry hardwood needed sanding and polishing. When Elle twisted the knob on one of the old hair dryers, it broke off in her hand. "It's going to take money to fix all of this, get new equipment."

Julianne jammed the knob back on the dryer. "If you must know,

I used the last of my Aunt Rose inheritance, and I have a personal investor."

"Personal investor?"

"Your enthusiasm is wearing me out, Elle. Let's go. I need to pick up Rio." She halted when the front door opened with a soprano squeak and Danny Simmons breezed in, tan and smiling, wearing golf shorts and an over-sized pullover.

"Is this Julianne's Place—" His expression darkened the moment his gaze fell on Elle. "Hey, Elle."

"Hey, Danny." Did he expect her to believe he thought this place was open?

"I saw the cars . . . thought we had a new salon in town." Danny roamed the room, arms akimbo, pretending to inspect the place. He stopped by the sinks and the three of them—Elle, Julianne, and Danny—stood in a triangle of silence.

"Guess this place is not quite ready for business." His chuckle sounded hollow. "I'll run by Charlie's for my trim."

Julianne gripped her hands together. "Yes, Mr. Simmons, set up an appointment at Charlie's." She attempted to walk him to the door, but her feet seemed glued to the floor.

"Tell your daddy we need to hit the links soon." Danny hesitated as if he wanted to say more, then nodded at Elle and left.

"Jules, what's going on?" Elle asked.

"Nothing. You heard him; he thought we were open for business." Retrieving her handbag from where she'd dropped it by the painted-closed window, Julianne smacked the dust from its bottom.

"He's married," Elle said softly.

"Was married." Julianne stopped pounding her purse. "She left him for another man two years ago and they were separated long before."

"And you know that because . . ."

Roaming the length of the stylist stations, Julianne tried to tug open the top drawers, but the handle snapped off. She whimpered and threw it to the floor. "Why can't you just be happy for me?"

"I am happy for you, honey. I am. I'm also curious and a little scared. More for your heart than anything else."

"My heart is safe, Elle, trust me. I know all about walls and boundaries." A crimson hue crept along the edge of her face and neck.

"I'm not so sure Danny Simmons is—"

Julianne's stiff posture broke. "I love him." The confession hung between them.

"Jules, really? How? When?"

Julianne stared out the window, arms crossed. "I ran into him one night during last summer's Water Festival. We were both on our way to the shuttles, but we started talking and walking, next thing I knew it was three in the morning and we'd circled the city a hundred times."

"He's twenty years older than you, Julianne. What do you have in common?"

"Lots of things, actually." She smiled. "Sara Beth always said I had an old soul. Danny and I like the same movies and sitcoms, music and books, same political and religious views. We're both single parents."

"Is he your investor?"

She nodded.

"Is he cosigning a loan? Giving you money?" Elle kept her voice low and even, not wanting to be the combatant.

Julianne flicked a tear from her cheek with her finger. "He's helping me, Elle. Isn't that enough or do you have to know all the details?" She stuffed her purse under her arm. "I need to go."

"I'm sorry I rained on your parade." Elle stopped her with an embrace. "Sweetie, I'm happy for you. More for the salon than him, but if he makes you happy—"

"He does, Elle." Julianne broke free from Elle's arms. "But please, please, what happened here today is between me and you."

Julianne held up her pinky finger. "Pinky swear. No one outside this room right now will ever hear of this."

"What? You're in love. Most people want to tell the whole world."

"Elle, pinky swear." Julianne's voice left no room for debate. "If you don't, I'll make up a lie so horrible about you—"

"Your own sister?" Elle slowly raised her pinky, challenged by the hard glint in Julianne's eyes.

"Not a word, Elle."

She wrapped her pinky with Julianne's. "Pinky swear. Not a word."

Eighteen

MANHATTAN

Mitzy Canon's art gallery, *821*, was a converted Chelsea warehouse with high ceilings, exposed steel beams, a thousand carefully aimed lights, and a definite chill in the air. At least to Heath, though he liked the paint on the cement floor—fiery red. Nice touch. Made him feel like he walked on the cover of hell.

A stringed quartet played Brahms in the far corner while gallery guests and patrons viewed colorful images of headless bodies painted by new artist Geraldine V.

Heath considered himself to be opened-minded about artistic expression, but this Geraldine V. baffled him. If he looked too long at her images, a darkness weighted his soul. The opposite of how he felt holding Elle's Coffin Creek painting—which he'd hung in the cottage living room (over her protests).

A black-tie server handed him a glass of white wine without asking if he wanted it. When the next tray passed by, Heath returned the favor.

Where was Rock? He'd gone off to find Mitzy fifteen minutes ago. Heath walked the perimeter of the gallery, recapping last night's awards ceremony and tonight's dinner with Rock.

The ceremony was lovely and honoring of Ava. But even as he accepted the gold and crystal award on her behalf, the gesture felt vain.

She's not here, he wanted to say. *The place where she now lives outshines the sun.* Yet spending an evening reminiscing and laughing did his heart good, and put some distance between his growing feelings for Elle.

He wondered what she and Tracey-Love were doing. He'd called in the morning to check on TL, who cried the entire call. But Elle seemed to have things under command.

"She's afraid you're not coming back, Heath. But I'm assuring her you will, so nothing stupid, McCord."

"Promise. Nothing stupid."

So the tremors from Ava's death still shook his little girl.

This evening he'd dined with Rock. Heath decided if the man ever left the law, he could go into acupuncture. He knew all of Heath's pressure points and how to massage them. Until they arrived at the gallery, Heath had all but decided to fly back to St. Helena, pack up, and return to Calloway & Gardner next week.

Yes, they had some critical and interesting cases coming up, but Rock needed him to help balance the power. And Heath expertly played that game.

"Heath . . ." Rock waved as he made his way across the gallery with a slender woman draped with a silver gown and lots of diamonds. *The* voice of the American art scene, Mitzy Canon.

"Heath McCord." She stretched her hand for him to kiss, not shake. Very Morticia Addams. "So sorry to hear of your wife's tragic demise."

He cast a glance at Rock, who shrugged; he hadn't told her.

"Thank you, but I'm confident she's in a better place."

"One can only hope." The reflective gallery lighting made Mitzy's eyes appear hollow in her attenuated face. "Rock tells me you have an artist friend. Don't we all?"

"Her name is Elle Garvey."

"And what's her story?"

"She owned a gallery. Sold it to move away, but things didn't work out. She's down on her luck, trying to sort out life. She's been a good friend to me . . . after my wife's tragic demise." Behind him, Rock snorted. "And I'd appreciate it if you could look at her work. Help her out."

Mitzy sipped her wine, flirting, winking at a passing gallery guest. If Heath hadn't been standing two feet from her, he'd wonder if she heard a word he said.

"Is she tortured?"

Heath arched his brow. "Tortured?" Rock nudged him in the back. "Yes, very tortured."

"The good ones always are." Mitzy motioned to a man on the other side of the gallery. "I'll be happy to review her work. I'm always looking for new stars." When the man appeared at her side, Mitzy asked Heath to write down Elle's information. "If we like her, we'll ask her to show in our spring opening."

Heath gave Mitzy's assistant Elle's information—e-mail and cell— then backed toward the door. "Rock, it's been fun."

"You'll be in touch?"

"I'll be in touch." Heath shoved the door open and stepped into the crisp Manhattan night. People hurried along the sidewalk and the street was a sea of red taillights. In the distance, a horn blew. A taxi stopped at the corner to pick up a fare and from the open doors of a nearby café, music played.

But all he wanted to hear was the sound of the wind in live oaks and the cicada's river song.

"All right, ladies, these are the rules."

Elle knelt down in front of Rio and Tracey-Love. Twins with different mothers, the two of them—both with round blue eyes, button noses, and pink cheeks. One with blonde hair, the other with brown.

"Dip your feet in the paint, then hit the canvas, running, walking, or twirling, whatever you like. Fall down, roll around." Elle held up her finger and tried to sound firm. "But you must have fun. Ready?"

"Ready," they said in unison with bent-knees bouncing.

Elle raced with them to the bowls of tempera paint, steering each girl to the right canvas board on the studio floor. "This one is for Rio's mama, and—yeah, over there, TL—that one is for your daddy."

Squeaking like puppy-dog chew toys, the four-year-olds skated, slipped, and slithered around the canvas, mixing body and paint. Elle had bundled their curls with do-rags and dressed them in Rio's old shorts and T-shirts, but they managed to cover every inch of themselves with paint.

"Tracey-Love, here's a spot you missed." Elle pointed to a small corner of the white canvas. TL stomped her reddish-blue foot on the spot, very pleased with herself.

"Look it, Auntie Elle." Rio pointed to a red face print.

"Rio, very creative." A glob of paint dripped from her chin.

When the entire canvas was covered without a square of white, Elle threw the girls into the shower with a large bar of soap.

"Rio, your mama's coming to get you. And, TL, your daddy's coming home tomorrow."

"I w-w-wanna st-stay with you." It'd taken until this moment for the girl to exhale and find security within herself.

"Me too." Rio, the mimic.

"Tell you what, we'll have a sleepover real soon."

She peeked in the shower. The girls were trying, but remained covered with paint. Elle would have to get wet if she wanted to return them to their parents clean. Clothes and all, she stepped in.

"Aunt Elle forgot to take off her clothes." The girls covered their mouths and giggled.

Once she toweled them off and dressed them in clean clothes, she dashed in the shower for her own quick clean up and change, setting the girls to work with coloring books on the futon.

"Knock, knock." The studio door eased open. A male voice asked, "Everyone decent?"

Elle came out of the bathroom with an armload of wet towels as Danny Simmons stepped inside.

"Danny."

"Evening, Elle." His eyes roamed over to where the girls colored. "Julianne had a meeting with the contractor for the work on her new shop. She asked me to pick up Rio."

"You won't mind if I call her to check, will you?" Elle glanced around for her phone.

Danny flipped his forward. "Use mine."

Elle hesitated, reaching slowly. "What's her speed dial?"

He cleared his throat, fist to his lips. "One."

Elle pressed One, then Talk. "Hey, Julianne, it's me, Elle. Did you send Danny to get Rio? Well, I was just checking . . . right . . . I do trust you . . . okay, fine."

Elle shut the phone and handed it back to Danny. "Rio, get your things. Mr. Danny is taking you home."

Rio chattered on with Tracey-Love about something as she slipped on her backpack. Elle stepped toward Danny. "Are you serious about my sister?"

"Yes." Simple, but without explanation. The Beaufort businessman and philanthropist moved away from Elle. "Rio, you ready?"

The little girl was flopped over the futon, showing Tracey-Love her doll, not disturbed at all by Danny's presence.

"Is Julianne your mid-life crisis? Last grab at your fleeting youth?"

"When my wife left, I canceled my mid-life crisis. I'd had enough drama." He leaned toward Elle. "This may be hard to believe, but I love your sister. Age has nothing to do with it. Rio, you ready?"

"She leads with her heart, Danny. And there's more at stake here than you and Jules." Elle motioned to Rio with her chin.

He reached for Rio's hand and led her to the door. "I'm fully aware of all that's at stake, Elle."

A light burned in the front cottage window as Heath parked on the brick drive, finally home. The digital dash clock clicked to 12:00. Midnight.

He pulled his keys from the ignition and reached to the passenger seat for his bag. The delayed flight from JFK had aggravated him, reminding him of the things he didn't like about the city—the pace, the congestion, the traffic and flight delays, not to mention high prices and taxes.

The moment he'd exited the Charleston airport, he'd powered down the windows and all but hung his head out like an eager dog lapping up the wind.

Inside the cottage, a single lamp lit the living room from a front corner and Elle slept on the couch with her arm draped over a curled-up Tracey-Love.

Heath dropped his bag to the floor by the coffee table and lowered down in front of them, kissing Tracey-Love on the forehead. "Baby, I'm home."

Elle jerked awake, struggling to sit up, her eyes locked in a sleepy squint. "Heath, hey."

"Hey." She was too cute with a frizz of orange-tinged blonde hair falling over one eye.

"Let me put her in bed." Heath scooped up the zonked Tracey-Love and carried her to her room. "Wait for me, okay?"

"I'm not sure I can even move."

When he came out, he plopped next to Elle on the couch. "What'd you do? I've never seen her so worn out."

"We played a lot." She yawned. "Did you have a good trip?"

"Interesting and reminiscent. When I took a leave from the firm, the partners gave me a six-month limit or lose my position. The senior partner wants me back. Claims he's losing the firm and needs me to keep the power balanced."

Elle leaned forward to see him, her hair falling over her shoulders, the last hint of her perfume wafting around her. Her eyelids still at half-mast. "What do you want to do?"

"Talk to God, think. But pretty sure I'm not leaving before September."

"How did the award ceremony go?"

"Very nice, but it seemed sort of empty, after the fact."

"Was it good for you to be there?"

"Yes, and I was honored to accept the award on her behalf."

Elle tapped his chest, over his heart. "Bubba, how're you doing in here?"

My heart? In here? "Difficult, if you must know. Brought back a lot of memories, but at the same time closed windows and left doors ajar."

She shoved her hair out of her eyes. "See, that wasn't too hard."

Heath regarded Elle for a moment. "She died in Iraq. Went embedded with an army unit to do a story on the plight of the Iraqi women."

Elle eased back against the couch. "Iraq? Heath, I had no idea."

"Last May she went over to do a story for the Network News on the Iraqi medical conditions. She found it deplorable for women. We're in the twenty-first century, but their conditions were more like the first century. Women regularly dying in childbirth, without everyday medical and sanitary supplies. Things we take for granted."

"I can't imagine."

"When she came home she couldn't get the story out her mind. She begged for an assignment to do a full-fledged documentary. I didn't know about the request until she was leaving."

"Did she think you'd say no?" Elle turned sideways, tucking her feet underneath her.

"I don't know."

"Would you have?"

"Probably. We had a three-year-old girl. She was gone a month the first time. I adjusted my caseload then, but I planned to make it up when she got back. We had this idea we could both be full-time, Mach-10 career people and full-time, outstanding parents." Heath kicked his shoes off under the coffee table.

"The concept is way easier than the execution."

"By the time I found out, Ava was all but on the plane. That's what adds to the sadness of her death. We were at odds when she died. From the moment she left, to our last conversation."

Elle rested her head against the top of the couch. "But she knew you loved her, right? You knew she loved you."

"Yeah, in the I-made-a-commitment-and-I'm-not-backing-out sort of way. But we needed to be together to hash out some issues."

She combed her hair back, slipping her fingers through the long strands. Heath felt her movement in his gut and averted his gaze.

"This is where Jeremiah and I fell off the wagon," she said. "We didn't want to duke it out in a forever commitment. We wanted to fall in love, get married, and both have our way, a hundred percent."

Heath pictured Elle standing up to the all-pro wide receiver. "I'd buy a ticket to that show."

"You would, would you? Very unentertaining. A lot of nonverbal speaking." Elle poked his arm. "But tonight is about you. Go on with your story."

"Turning the tables on me from your supposed wedding night, eh?" Actually, it felt good to talk about Ava outside the demand of grief.

"Yes, so go on."

"Her second trip went well, as only an Ava trip can go. She'd filmed a lot of great stories and was excited about the women she'd interviewed. A week from coming home, she heard of a village in the southern region where a lot of insurgent fighting kept the people locked in terror. The medical conditions were very poor and she wanted to go down. The army granted her request to go embedded, and on a hot August day . . . the vehicle she rode in was shelled. The report said everyone died instantly."

In the sparse light from the lamp, he saw the sheen in Elle's eyes. "I'm so sorry."

"The news literally shocked me. These, like, electric impulses fired all over my body. My mind couldn't compute the news for a long time. I try to remember Ava died doing something she loved, not caring about her own life to make a difference for others. If I could have her alive and not pursuing her passion?" He shook his head. "I wouldn't change a thing. So few people have a passion. And if they do, they don't pursue it. Bravo for her. She died for what she believed in."

"You make me wish I could've known her." Elle slipped the afghan from the back of the couch to cover her legs.

"You would've liked her, become friends and terrorized me, I'm sure."

"Someone has to do it."

"I was sleeping when they called. We'd been e-mail arguing intensely for a week about this embedded trip. Too dangerous. She accused me of not trusting her instincts. And I didn't. Passion can blind reason sometimes. Plus, the firm was in the middle of a capital case and I couldn't focus on TL like I needed to." Heath sat forward. "Do you want something to drink?"

"Water sounds good."

"We argued the night before she headed south, got cut off, and couldn't reconnect." Heath got up for the kitchen, opened the fridge, then walked back to the living room with two waters, running his stocking feet lazily over the floor. "Fourteen hours later, she was dead."

"Listening to you now, it seems so impossible, like, 'No, it can't be. Bring her back.'"

"I felt that way for about three months, wrestling with the permanence. Ava wasn't coming back." He sat down, closer to Elle than he'd been before, and passed over a water. "It meant a lot to me to know Tracey-Love was safe with you while I was gone. Since Ava died, I haven't left her with anyone overnight. So, did she do okay after I called?"

"She missed you, Heath, but she finally settled down last night. I let TL and Rio paint with their whole bodies. They're quite a pair."

"Bookends. One without a daddy. The other without a mama."

"I never thought of it, but yeah . . ." Elle twisted the cap off her water. "Here's some gossip you missed."

Heath swigged his water, cooling his parched throat. "Do tell."

"Julianne is opening her own salon, and it appears she's dating one of Daddy's friends, Danny Simmons." Elle gave him a how-do-you-like-them-apples expression and took a shot of water.

"Do I know Danny Simmons? Is this a bad thing?"

Elle laughed, tossing the afghan off. "He's twenty years older than she is, Heath." She took another gulp of water, then wiggled her toes into her shoes.

"Right, right, I forgot love came with age boundaries."

Elle made a face at him. "Whose side are you on?"

"No one's. What's wrong with this guy other than being ancient? You know, I have a good mind to accuse you of ageism."

"Oh, please. Save me your New York lawyer speak." Elle headed toward the kitchen. Heath rose to follow. "There's nothing wrong with Danny. He's a good man, successful, kind, but twenty years older than Jules. Just feels creepy." She shoved open the screen door. "Thank you for telling me about Ava. I'm sorry you lost such a treasure."

"Thanks for listening." He flipped on the outside lights. "Look at me, walking you out your own door."

She gazed toward the studio. A lone light shown from the window. "It doesn't feel weird to me. My sister Candace accused me of being a bohemian."

Rachel Hauck

"I suppose there's a little bohemian in all of us." Heath tucked his hands in his pockets as Elle stepped off the deck. "Thanks again for everything."

She walked backward across the yard, her smile standing out in the darkness. "Anytime."

Nineteen

Prayer at the chapel became a crimson ribbon woven through the top of Elle's June days, tied neatly around afternoons of painting in her studio.

This particular morning she'd felt restless, unable to focus, prayer more difficult than usual. Miss Anna prayed out loud with her Bible open so Elle hitched to her spiritual wagon. The woman prayed a lot for faith, the ability to trust and give up her unbelief.

Elle considered her own loyalties. *Who do I trust most, God or Daddy?*

First response? Daddy, of course. He loved her, cared for her. He'd raised her. Worked his whole life to provide for her. But at the end of the day, he was still a weak, flawed man.

God, on the other hand, Elle thought, loved her beyond expression, beyond understanding. At least that's what the Good Book said. So, if she had to choose, even with her weak faith, she'd have to choose the unseen God.

The idea? Trust God over man. Trust Him over herself.

The notion lingered with her all day. Elle paused from working around the studio, preparing for Huckleberry to come by for an art lesson.

"Lord, give me the kind of faith that believes wholeheartedly."

"Elle, you here?" Footsteps resonated from the studio stairs.

She grabbed the hair tie lying by the sink and opened the door to Huckleberry. "Come on in, Huck."

Dang, if the boy didn't look like his namesake, Huckleberry Finn. Plaid shirt, buckle overalls, cuffed pant legs up to his shins, flip-flops. All he needed was a piece of straw dangling from between his teeth.

She motioned for him to enter. "Ready to paint?"

He popped his hands together. "Where's my easel?" Coming around the work table, he stood in front of the only white canvas Elle had set up.

"We're going to paint this together." She tapped the picture taped to a second easel. It was an old picture Granddaddy Garvey had taken of Factory Creek at sunset during the seventies. Granddaddy had captured orange and red rays bouncing off the dark water. And up in the top left corner, a small paddle boat sat alone in the marsh grass.

The image always evoked an emotion from Elle, as if she understood the boat drifting, waiting to fulfill its calling, even at sunset.

Huckleberry squinted at the picture. "An itsy boat? Can I add some trash, 'cause I can tell you, Elle, the creeks are becoming more and more polluted."

She cupped her hand over his mouth. "We are painting it exactly as we see it."

"No trash?" he asked through her fingers.

She dropped her hand, wiping it against her apron. "No trash. I'm trying to get you to expand your horizons."

"Why don't we paint in tandem, you know, then compare our expressions?" He picked up the palette knife.

Elle took it away from him. "Don't make me regret doing this."

"Testy." He dug his hands into his big pockets, trying to frown.

"Okay, let's mix some paint, then talk about how we want to approach the painting."

Trying to get Huckleberry to settle down and paint the original picture was like trying to bridle a fly and train it to fetch. But after an hour of forcing him to focus and start over (thank goodness for the fluidity of oils), she sat back and watched him recreate a beautiful scene, emotion and all. He had incredible talent, and if he applied himself, he could have the impact he so desperately wanted.

When his session ended, they set up a future date before he left, then Elle cleaned the brushes and palette, thinking she needed to run over to Mama and Daddy's to do laundry. The dirty clothes pile was beginning to merge with the clean. Her cell phone rang as she started sorting whites and colors.

"I hear you're painting." Darcy Campbell, owner of downtown's Wild Heart Gallery, was on the other end.

"A vicious rumor, Darcy."

"Huckleberry told me. He was in trying to peddle his smelly art. I tell you, Elle, I'd support his cause if he could present it in a socially ingratiating fashion. Last time he came in, the place reeked of dead fish for two days."

"When was he there? He just left my place."

"Yeah, he said you're helping him paint."

"Trying." Elle dumped her whites into a Wal-Mart bag. "He's really talented, Darcy, but so fascinated with garbage."

Darcy's chuckle spilled into Elle's ear. "No kidding. So, was he right? Are you painting?"

"Maybe."

"I'll take that as a yes. Great. I'm featuring you for the Summer Art Walk and don't go letting any of the other galleries talk you into showing with them. You're exclusive with me for September. Can you be ready?"

"Ready? No, I can't be ready." Darcy's Charles Street gallery was *the* best gallery in the lowcountry. Located in an 1886 home, it had elaborate cast-plaster moldings, ceiling medallions, stone fireplaces in every room, and jib doors opening to the verandahs. She maintained its rustic, cultured atmosphere and often showed work by New York and London artists. Names. Not wannabes.

"Then get ready. Nothing like a little pressure to motivate you creative types. I want to help launch your career, Elle."

"Darcy, I have no career. I'm dabbling, not painting-painting."

"Well, stop dabbling and get serious."

Sigh. The woman kidded not. Darcy took the business side of running a gallery extremely seriously and Elle had learned a lot from her. Darcy also had the marketing acumen and art-world connections to give an artist a leg up toward New York or London, Paris, or LA.

"Darcy, please hear me. I appreciate you, but I have nothing to show. I am barely painting. Most of this is just for me. Therapy. Worship, if you will. I'm not good enough to have people pay ten dollars, let alone hundreds."

A car door slammed on Darcy's side of the call. Keys jingled. "You forget I've seen some of your early work. I've always admired your use of color and ability to capture the emotion of a scene."

"You flatter me, but no." Elle snapped open a second Wal-Mart bag to start bagging her jeans and tops.

"I'm not flattering you. I'm tired of watching you *play* at art."

The AC unit kicked on, shoving aside the warm air for cool. The afternoon sun heated the studio through the glass.

"Darcy, I appreciate you, I do, but give me a year or two."

"Do you really want to waste another year? If you're pushing Huckleberry to be the artist and the man he's called to be, then I'm doing the same to you. Feel my finger in your back?"

Elle dropped the laundry-filled Wal-Mart bag and walked over to her paintings. She liked *Feathers.* And *Girls in the Grass.* There was the unfinished *Downtown Beaufort*, and oh, a painting from last fall when Hurricane Howard went over them and she hunkered down with Caroline at her place.

Then Heath's voice haunted her. *God is wiser than Dr. Petit . . .*

"Five paintings."

"Six."

"Maybe."

"Now I can tell you Sir Lloyd Parcel will be showing too."

"Darcy, Sir Lloyd Parcel? You can't hang my work in the same gallery as his, let alone the same county, the same state, the same country."

"Simmer down. Ruby Barnett is coming down to do the review. This will help her ease into your work. It's a brilliant plan. I'm featuring Lloyd and you in my *ArtNews* ad."

"Ruby Barnett? Dang, Darcy, are you trying to destroy me before I even get started? She's one of the toughest art critics."

"All the more to have her view your work now. Elle, I heard Angela boxed you out, and while I'm not a religious person, looking at what's happened to you the last few months makes me think the Divine is trying to get your attention."

A needlelike chill raced down Elle's arm. "Perhaps, maybe, we'll see. But Darcy, let this first show be the hometown girl with her homegrown paintings. Give me a chance to see if I'm any good. No press, please."

"Sure, whatever you say." Darcy didn't mean one hollow word. "You won't regret this."

Elle pressed End. She already regretted it.

In the den, Kelly paced, listening to NBC's "Saturday Night Dance Party" while her fourteen-year-old sister played Monopoly with their sixteen-year-old brother.

"Hal, you landed on my hotels." Christie held her palm under Hal's nose. "You owe me a million bucks."

Hal slapped her palm. "There."

"Cheater. Give me the money. Kelly, tell him to play fair."

"Hal. And Christie, he doesn't owe you a million bucks. Tell him how much he owes. Fair and square."

Another week without a letter from Chet. She felt ill just thinking about it. Was he hurt? Dead? In prison? No longer in love with her?

Surely his mama would call if he was missing in action or killed. Kelly pressed her hand against her growing middle. At times, fear dwelt there as much as their child. She feared the worst. Not death, but that he no longer loved her. By this time next month, their secret would be known. She'd let out her skirt waist as far as it could go.

"Kelly, I declare you're making me nervous with all that pacing," Mama said without looking up from her knitting. "Why don't you call Rose or Shirley, see if they want to go downtown. Get a malt or something."

"Sure, Mama."

Kelly phoned Rose, who was "dying to get out of the house" and promised to call Shirley. "Meet you at Harry's in fifteen."

Upstairs, Kelly changed her blouse and shoes, then combed her hair and found the Johnny Jeep hat she'd worn on her first date with Chet. When she turned to go, Mama stood in the doorway.

"Oh, you scared me." Kelly exhaled, thrusting her hand over her heart. "What are you doing sneaking around a girl's room?"

Mama eased the door closed, her eyes on Kelly's middle. "We should talk about it now before your daddy sees."

Heath scrubbed cereal from yesterday's bowls before loading them in the dishwasher, staring out the kitchen window toward the grove of oak and pine in the lot next to Elle's, pondering the lives of Kelly Carrington and Chet McCord.

Kelly being pregnant surprised him, but he knew it happened to a lot of women. Had Chet married her before they consummated their love or was it a night of passion before he shipped out? He'd have to decide, but he liked the complication the pregnancy created.

Especially since he'd left Chet flying over the artic North Pacific with his engine freezing up.

Last bowl in the dishwasher. Heath loaded the detergent and pressed Start. The machine's low hum was the only noise in the quiet house. He'd enrolled Tracey-Love in a day school this week, and he missed her little-girl sounds—singing softly, playing with her dolls—and the way she set her hand on his knee before asking, "C-can you put on a movie?"

But the interaction with other children seemed to be boosting her little confidence.

Meanwhile, he used the alone time—ten to three—to write and research. He'd spent today researching the Aleutian Islands, the Warhawk P-40, North Pacific war history, and war babies. The further he dug into history, the more he wrote, the more the story gripped him.

Leaning against the sink, he gazed at the heat waves rolling across the yard and found it hard to imagine Chet suffering in icy Alaska. He'd have to dig around his boyhood memories of New York winters, playing outside with Mark until they couldn't feel the tips of their toes, to write a true experience for the southern flyer.

Suddenly Elle emerged from the heat waves, dressed casually and free-looking in baggy brown shorts and a white tank top. She carried a metal box by its handle, striding for her car, her arms and legs moving in graceful synchronization.

Art in motion. More and more, his fictional heroine Kelly mirrored the real-life woman of Elle Garvey.

Watching her drive away, Heath thought of their little encounters the past two weeks—Elle wandering over as he sat out on the screened porch, or grabbing a quick dinner out with Tracey-Love.

A couple of times as he walked out to the van to go pick up Tracey-Love, Elle threw open her window and yelled down at him, "Afternoon, McCord."

"Afternoon, Garvey."

The other night she told him a story about her friend Caroline, a K-Mart blue light she'd wired to her old Mustang, a dark night, and a Beaufort County deputy. Had him doubled over.

He wondered where she was off to this afternoon?

The tip of Ava's waiting letter caught his eye. Making sure his hands were dry, Heath reached for the envelope. If he ever thought he'd want more than friendship with Elle, or anyone like her, he'd have to read this letter.

Turning it over, he flicked at the small tear, then returned the letter to its perch on the windowsill behind the lock. Not today. Leaving the kitchen, Heath flipped off the light.

Sitting on the tarp-covered floor of Julianne's salon, her wood palette next to her, Elle painted a marsh scene over fresh drywall. Despite initial doubts, she conceded Julianne's success. The shop remodel had gone quickly, though the subject of her boyfriend-investor remained taboo.

Concentrating on painting the last blade of grass in the shade, Elle jerked around when her cell beckoned with an out-of-area tone.

Oh, let it ring. Then an odd, pinging thought. *What if it's Jeremiah?* She reached back for the phone lying on the edge of the tarp. "Hell*oooo*."

Oops, she'd swiped the side of Julianne's new beige cabinets with paint. She *psssted* at Jules to wipe it off. Not surprisingly, Julianne muttered a few blue words before and after Elle's name.

"Is this Elle?" Crisp, pristine, foreign.

"Yes, it is."

"This is Mitzy Canon of 821 Gallery in Manhattan."

Elle held the phone away from he ear, reviewing the number, but the screen read PRIVATE. "Excuse me, I thought you said Mitzy Canon."

"Listen, I'm pressed for time, but a friend suggested I review your work."

Her heart pumped blood so fast her arms went limp. "Did Darcy Campbell call you?"

"I'm speaking of Heath McCord, married to the reporter who died, Ava. What a tragedy. She was beautiful. Can you send me a résumé and samples of your work? There's a possibility of featuring you as a debut artist in our spring show."

"T-this spring?"

Mitzy rattled off her personal e-mail so quickly Elle's only writing implement was her paint brush, her only writing surface Julianne's wall.

mcprivate@821gallery.com.

"How soon would you like—"

"Yesterday." End of conversation.

Elle closed her phone, trying to comprehend what had happened. Mitzy Canon? Heath knew the artist maker?

"Who was that?" Julianne gathered up the paint-stained paper towels, the cabinet wiped clean. "Elle, you look green. Is everything okay?"

"I just agreed to send Mitzy Canon—*the* Mitzy Canon—samples of my work. Oh my gosh." She rose off the floor. "And I harassed Darcy Campbell for inviting Ruby Barnett to write reviews during the Summer Art Walk."

Julianne mashed the dirty towels on top of the over-stuffed trash can. "Mitzy Canon? *The* artist maker woman?"

"Yes, *the* Mitzy Canon." Elle's voice echoed down the salon and back. "Somehow Heath knows her, and because of him or something, she called for samples of my work."

Julianne's eyes popped wide. "Go Heath."

"I don't know, Jules, why would I—"

"Uh-uh, no you don't, Elle. You're not backing out." Julianne gripped her shoulders. "You are strong and brave about everything, it seems, but this. Forget college and the cranky professor. Go for it."

Elle made a face. "She said with no risk to herself."

Julianne went back to unloading boxes. "It can't hurt to send them, right? You already think you stink. What's one more opinion?"

"What a comforting notion, Jules." Elle smacked back down to the floor, facing her mural. "It's enough to believe I stink, why not have the top voice in American art agree with me?"

Elle dipped her brush in the marsh grass paint. *Heath, what'd you do to me?* Leaning back for her phone, she autodialed him.

"Did you talk to Mitzy Canon? Why? Um-hmm . . . thank me? Heath, I was just being a good neighbor . . . like I'm not going to go with you to the ER . . . You took me to dinner." She chewed the tip of her thumbnail. "I'm not sure I want Mitzy . . . right . . . I know . . . got to start somewhere, sometime. But this is Mitzy Canon, top of the food chain . . . I do know my own work and talent, Heath. I live in my skin . . . um-hum . . . Okay, okay, don't get testy. I'll send her something. Dinner?" Elle checked the salon's new wall clock. "About an hour? Want to go to Luther's? Okay . . . bye."

Twenty

At five o'clock, Heath came out of the bedroom slipping his wallet into his jean's back pocket. Elle knocked on the kitchen door. "Heath, you ready?"

"I was just about to get you." He opened the door to let her in, raking back his damp hair from his eyes. She carried a large canvas board. "Another Elle Garvey masterpiece?"

"No, the first Tracey-Love McCord." Elle turned the canvas board for him to see. "Your daughter's handiwork."

Heath picked his watch off the coffee table, snapping it on. "Incredible. How'd you do this?" He took the board from her, studying the swirls of paint.

"Filled pans with tempura paints and told the girls to have fun. Julianne hung Rio's in the salon."

Heath ran his fingers lightly over the dried surface of red, blue, and green, and all the shades in between. "This is a true gift. Thank you. I'll hang it in my office." He set Tracey-Love's masterpiece against the wall, motioning to a check on the coffee table.

Elle read the number, then peered at him. He liked the surprise in her eyes. "Five hundred dollars. For what?"

"My first Elle Garvey. *Coffin Creek Fog.*"

"Heath, you said a hundred. I can't take this. You're raising TL alone and not working."

"You can and you will." He whispered, "Sadly, death comes with high dividends."

"Now I know I can't take it." Elle thrust the check at him.

"You will. I bought your work and this is the price I'm paying. Besides, Ava loved art and would be thrilled to discover a new artist and pay for an original piece." Heath angled to see down the hall. "Tracey-Love, did you get lost in there?"

Elle slipped the folded check into her bag. "Then I'm glad my first sale is to you, Heath McCord." She sat in front of his open laptop. "When do I get to read your first chapters?"

"It'll cost you." He pushed the laptop closed, afraid she'd see her reflection in the voice and movement of Kelly Carrington.

"Five hundred dollars?" Elle retrieved the check, waving it under his nose.

Heath laughed. "Keep your money, Garvey. You can read it when it's ready."

She captured his arm with her hand. "I owe you more than money, Heath. How can I replay you for speaking to Mitzy Canon? It'd take years, if not a lifetime, for me to get her attention."

"Elle, it was my pleasure. Besides, I didn't do much. Just asked my boss for an introduction." When he peered at her, his heart stirred. Pulling away, he called for TL again. "Let's go, Daddy and Miss Elle are hungry." He turned to Elle. "She's going to be a woman who is always late."

Elle sat back in the club chair, legs crossed, foot swinging. "My sister Mary Jo drove Daddy nuts. We actually left her behind several times. Daddy thought everyone was loaded up and off we'd go."

Tracey-Love bounced into the room. "It's about time, girly." Heath swung her up in his arms.

In the van, Heath snapped TL in to her car seat while Elle combed and tied back her hair.

"There, ready to go. Daddy strapped you in and Miss Elle fixed your hair."

Tracey-Love grinned, hugging her doll, crossing her ankles as if she'd been ready to go for hours and the grown-ups had kept her waiting.

Opening Elle's door, Heath said, "To Luther's for a burger."

A car turned onto Coffin Point. Heath leaned toward the sound. A blue Ford rental stopped next to the van.

"Who's that?" Elle stooped to see the man behind the wheel.

"You know him?" Heath stooped too.

"Oh my gosh." Elle snapped back her head. Heath glanced between her and the man stepping out of the car. Her cheeks paled under wide, unbelieving eyes.

"You know him?" But as she uttered, "Jeremiah," he'd recognized the former star athlete.

The man was large, commanding, absorbing pheromones. Heath puffed out his chest, lifted his chin.

"Hey, Elle," said the pheromone hog, surprisingly low and uncertain.

"What are you doing here?" Elle moved into the space between them.

Yep, drawing all the female molecules for himself. Heath knew the type. Hated them.

"Hey, babe." Jeremiah's smile was white, magnetic, a beacon.

Heath took a step into the space too. Couldn't send Elle to the sharks alone.

"Jeremiah, what are you doing here?"

"Came to see you, Elle. I've missed you." He peered at Heath. "Jeremiah Franklin."

"Heath McCord."

Their hands clasped with a *pop.*

"I'm not interrupting, am I?" Jeremiah motioned to Elle, then Heath, his confidence surging beyond his tentativeness.

"We're on our way to dinner," Heath said with another step toward Elle.

"I was wondering if we could talk." Jeremiah tipped his head to one side, eyes squinting, his tone solid but beckoning.

"We're on our way to dinner," Heath repeated.

Elle pressed her hand against his chest. "Give us a minute, Heath, please?"

Was no an option? He'd rather stand sentry to make sure this guy didn't hoodwink her. His vibe was snaky. If Heath walked into his church, he'd have left before the announcements.

"Heath, please."

"I'll wait inside with Tracey-Love."

Back in the cottage, Heath tucked behind the sheers and peeked out the window slats. Jeremiah chatted with Elle, all cool and breezy, as if he were asking her out on a first date.

With her back to him, he had no idea what was going on with her. She nodded her head. Jeremiah stroked his hand down her arm, then angled to kiss her forehead.

Ooh, she was coming to the house. Heath jerked away from the window.

"Heath?"

"In here." He met her at the door, struggling to tone down his attitude. "What does he want?"

"Heath, easy. He didn't break *your* heart."

"No, but this is a perfect play from the guys-with-big-egos book. Drop a girl, realize there's nothing better out there, and come running back."

"Heath, I need to hear him out. He came all this way."

"Are you serious?"

"Yes. Heath, what is your problem? I need to go with him, see what he wants."

"Of course, because it's the perfect play from the book—the dumped girl goes running back to the guy-with-big-ego because she's stupid and he gets what he wants."

"Stupid? Because I want to hear why he flew fifteen hundred

miles to talk to me? And stop calling him guy-with-big-ego. It's like the pot calling the kettle black."

"Me? No, don't put me in his brand of he-men. This is what's wrong with women." Heath gestured wildly, hands in the air, as if the entire female population was running amuck. "You forget your-selves, turn off your brains the moment a handsome man says pretty please. But we like the chase, Elle. Don't let him manipulate you."

"There's no chase, Heath. I'm not running. He's being nice and humble. Something's happened and he wants to talk about it."

"That's humble? He couldn't buy humble." He'd gone too far. He could tell by Elle's expression. "Elle, I'm sorry. This is none of my business. Go, have fun. I hope it turns out well for you."

"I'm sorry about dinner, Heath. We'll go later." She paused in the doorway. "You know I have to do this, right? And it doesn't make me a dumb dame."

"Elle, you are a million things, and dumb dame is not one of them."

"Don't worry, I know all about the guys-with-big-egos playbook."

"I won't. You're a grown woman and can take care of yourself."

She jutted out her chin. "Exactly. See you in the funny papers."

Yeah, right next to Charlie Brown.

Jeremiah stopped at the Shrimp Shack for a couple of shrimp burgers, then continued down Hwy 21 toward Huntington State Park.

Their conversation started out stiff and formal, but gradually the tension evaporated as Jeremiah asked what she was up to these days. *You know, everything that's happened since I broke your heart.*

Really, she'd worked the broken-heart angle long enough. Hated being trapped there. With her hands gripped in her lap, Elle gave him a breezy update.

"So, my days are about the two *Ps*—painting and prayer."

"Painting and prayer. Interesting."

"I meet with Miss Anna for prayer and that's how I started painting."

He glanced over at her as he steered down Hwy 21, a seriousness shrouding his almond-shaped eyes. "You're as beautiful as ever."

"So are you." She gazed out her window at the palmettos and pines, squinting at the glassy marsh.

Okay, she'd lied to Heath. The only thing she knew about the plays in the guys-with-big-egos book was that sometimes they worked.

Jeremiah turned into Huntington State Park, paid the fee, and chose a picnic area on the ocean side. So far, he spoke little of himself.

A brisk salty breeze combed through Elle's hair as she sat under the canopy of pines and faced the surf.

"Shrimp burger and fries." Jeremiah handed Elle her food, sitting next to her. She waited for him to say grace, but he bit into his shrimp sandwich without so much as a pause or glint of reflection.

"I've missed the Shrimp Shack," he mumbled, mouth full, wiping mayonnaise from the corner of his lips.

Elle took a small bite, chewing quickly and swallowing, smashing down the napkins when the wind whistled through the pines and whisked them across the table.

"Jeremiah, what is going on? You didn't come all the way here to have a shrimp burger with me in the park."

"No, I didn't." Jeremiah flicked crumbs from his finger. "I'm still in love with you, Elle. I've missed you and regretted how things ended between us."

"Not an e-mail or a call in three months. How much was I really on your mind?"

He scooted closer to her, and the heat from his skin caused her to tingle. "Out of sight, but not out of my mind or heart. I was a fool to let you go, and I want you back."

Elle shoved her food aside, hearing him but not comprehending. "Just like that? Here's a shrimp burger and my heart? What changed, Jeremiah?"

"Me. I've changed." His turned her face to his by the tip of her chin. "Do you still love me?"

"No." Even she didn't believe her answer. "I don't know." Sitting here, expressing his heart, wanting her, humble and handsome . . . she didn't know what she wanted. She'd spent the last four months letting go of everything, starting over, a clean, blank canvas before God.

"Candace thinks I sabotaged my Dallas trip because I didn't want to marry you."

"That theory only matters if it's what you think."

"Jeremiah," Elle started, "what changed you?"

He picked at the table's peeling paint. "I quit."

"W-what?" she whispered, grabbing his forearm. "You didn't."

"Taking on that church was the biggest mistake of my life. It cost me friends, time, desire—you. I let myself be blinded by delusions of television and big ministry. Move over, T. D. Jakes, Jeremiah Franklin has entered the building."

"What happened?" Her fingers squeezed his skin.

"Clash of power. Little did I know this small band of leaders only wanted a puppet." He peeked at her from under his brow. "And here I came, prideful, arrogant, thinking I was being promoted by God. After all, I deserved it. Look at all I can do for God's kingdom. I walked right into their trap, close-eyed and stupid."

The scenario sounded ludicrous. "Why would they want a puppet? Jeremiah, I wasn't around long, but I saw the church, visited with the people. They loved Jesus, wanted to impact the community for good."

"The congregation, yes. But the leaders are manipulators, a bunch of Jezebels. If the pastor opposes them, or executes his own plan without their expressed written consent, they go into action like a

Microsoft virus, poisoning the other leaders and key members of the congregation."

"And no one stops them?"

"Like who? If the pastor can't . . . I had two-thirds of the church believing these leaders—four couples in all—rode a chariot into God's throne room every night and returned with unspeakable oracles. The remaining third knew better but were either intimidated, naturally, or had been burned once and weren't going to go there again."

"Jeremiah, that's horrible."

"And I witnessed them in action." Jeremiah got up from the table. "Can we walk?"

Elle kicked off her shoes and joined him where sand met pine needles. His feet slipped in the sand as they walked into the head wind.

Jesus, what do I say to him?

After a long silence, he said, "Now I understand why the church went through senior pastors like melting ice on a hot August afternoon."

"What about your friends? The ones who recommended you?"

"They are a part of it." Jeremiah stopped as if his next step required too much energy. His gaze was lost out over the sea. "Maurice figured I'd go for the television thing and let him run everything else. The sad thing is, Elle, they don't understand what they are doing. They love Jesus, but are blinded by their own ambition."

"It's like a movie script; I can't believe it." Elle stood with him, arms crossed, sea salt coating her skin. "But I know you wouldn't be here otherwise." She looked up at him. "Are you okay?"

"Wrestling with God, bitter, but working through it. Why did it appear to be a great opportunity if it was all going to fall apart?" He touched her shoulder. "I'm glad you weren't there."

"I've asked myself a similar question all summer. If we weren't right for each other, why didn't God intervene sooner?"

But how else would I have rented the cottage and met Heath?

"And what did you conclude?" Hand in his pockets, he started walking again. Sadness shadowed his high cheekbones.

Elle stared at the back of his shirt, pressed against him by the wind, and filtered his question through her last thought . . . *"How else would I have met Heath?"* Her breath caught for a moment.

Jeremiah stopped in the sand, twisting sideways to look at her. "Elle? Did I lose you? Must have been some conclusion."

She flashed a smile, moving toward him. "Sorry, trapped by a random thought. No big conclusion, Jer. It's just I discovered that sometimes falling apart is the will of God, the opportunity to draw near, to grow in love."

He pinched his brow into a *V*. "Not sure I signed up for that version of Christianity."

"Me neither, but what if God meant for your Dallas church plan to fall apart? For my wedding and gallery aspirations to come up short? What if failing is really succeeding?"

"Unto what gain?" His tone mocked a little.

"Godly gain. He who loses his life for Christ will gain it."

Jeremiah regarded her, then shook his head. "I gave up football to answer the call. You sold your gallery, rented the cottage to follow Him with me."

"Maybe that was only the first part of the journey."

"I'm taking a job at FSU. Assistant athletic director. One of my old coaches is there. He opened the door."

"You're leaving the ministry?"

"Seems it left me." Jeremiah bent down midstride, picking up a shell, and flung it at the water. "Three years of divinity training, shot."

Elle hurried to walk in front of him, to see his face. "One bad experience and you quit? Jeremiah, where's the heart of a star athlete, the one who breaks tackles striding for the goal?"

"Quoting my own sermon to me won't change my mind."

Elle observed as he flung another shell. But they were too light for the breeze and dropped to the beach without flying.

"You accepted already?"

"Ministry either breaks a man or makes him, and I'm getting out before I'm broken."

"Maybe that's the point, Jeremiah. Brokenness."

Jeremiah lifted his hand toward her hair as it blew across her cheeks, but dropped it before touching her. "I can be broken in Tallahassee as much as any place."

"You know what I loved about you when I met you?"

"My dashing good looks?" He smiled, half teasing, half hunting.

"I loved your confidence. You knew your calling. You were strong where I was weak." The wind picked up, wrapping Elle's skirt around her knees.

"Just because I'm changing my career doesn't change who I am, Elle. I can be there for you, help you find what you're looking for."

"I'm praying my way there, Jer, and I like the journey, bumps and all."

The dipping sun unrolled an orange and red banner across the blue expanse, and in this place of beauty, Elle grieved for Jeremiah. Not only did the Dallas experience wreck his ministry, but it seemed to have looted his personal relationship with the one called Christ.

Jeremiah swept her to him with a single-arm embrace. "Elle, I love you and I need you. The night we broke up, you asked me to quit the church instead of you, and I refused. I made the wrong choice. But not once did I doubt proposing. You were the one for me from the first moment I saw you. Elle, you're the one for me now." He bent toward her, hesitating, then carefully dusted her lips with his. "Marry me."

Twenty-One

She didn't sit in her usual spot, second pew from the front, right side. Instead, Elle lay prostrate on the chapel floor before the altar, nose pressed into the worn carpet, dark spots forming where her tears landed.

Sleep had evaded her most of the night as she'd tossed and turned, tangled in the sheets. Finally, at five thirty, she'd showered and driven to the chapel.

Jeremiah's surprise return was one thing. But his surprise proposal jerked her back into a world she'd packed up and labeled "Over. Move On."

Did she want to marry him? While she'd spent the past three months healing, forgetting him, had she really? Just seeing him awakened dormant feelings, wants, and desires.

"Jesus, what do I do?"

Still face down on the worn carpet, Elle fumbled for the tissue box. It was there somewhere. Glancing up between tangled strands of hair, she found it just outside of reach. She crawled over, pulled one free, and blew her nose.

"What's troubling you, Elle?"

She turned. Miss Anna watched her from the second-row pew, all peace and prettiness in a faded blue dress with white flowers. "Seems we've traded places. You at the altar, me in the pew."

"Jeremiah showed up last night, Miss Anna." Elle walked on her knees over to her mentor, box of tissues in hand.

"What did he want?"

Elle blew her nose again. "To marry me."

"Goodness." Miss Anna patted the bench and moved over. "What did you say?"

"What could I say? I told him I need to think and pray. And in his usual confident way, he said he'd wait for me, no matter how long."

"My, my. That boy was always so determined."

"He's bitter, Miss Anna. His experience with the Dallas church was not good. He quit."

"I see."

But his overtures, the expression in his eyes, his tenderness of his touch lingered in her thoughts. "The things that drove us apart are no longer a factor. He is genuinely sorry about what happened, but I'm not sure I'm the one to walk him through his valley."

Did her confession sound unloving? Didn't love conquer all, keep no record of wrong? Never quit? Never fail?

"A bitter man only grows more bitter unless he surrenders everything—his pride, his reputation, his identity to God," Miss Anna said without a *hmm* of wonder.

"But aren't we supposed to love one another, help one another?"

"Jeremiah needs to figure this mess out the way you did, by speaking to Jesus."

"Were you ever in love, Miss Anna?" Elle dabbed the tears from her cheeks with a balled-up tissue, thinking she'd spent two months praying with this woman and knew nothing of her.

"Once upon a time."

"Miss Anna, you're smiling. Look at you." Elle bent forward to see her face, curious about the man who made her blush like a young woman all these years later.

She wondered if Jeremiah's name did the same to her cheeks.

"My father insisted I go on with my education after high school, so I went up to the College of Charleston. Oh, Elle, I had a ball. It was after the war and campus was so gay and lively. My roommates were very special gals. We became such dear friends—to the day each one passed. We attended all the dances and parties. Some of the young men wanted to court me special, but I was having too much fun to go with just one boy."

Elle gave her shoulder a sisterly nudge. "You go, Miss Anna."

"Naturally, that's when I met Lem. He was a looker, so strong and masculine. Earned medals for his courage on the battlefield. My girlfriends and I were standing at the refreshment table admiring him amongst ourselves when he walked right over, bold as you please." Miss Anna spread her hands beyond her shoulders. "Broad shouldered, dancing blue eyes, a thick mop of wavy black hair every one of us spent hours primping to get. We didn't have fancy curling irons like you girls today. Well, like I said, there he stood and us girls froze like four red-lipped popsicles." She popped her hands together.

Elle propped her chin in her hand. "Did you know he was coming to talk to you?"

"Oh my, no." Miss Anna gazed off as if seeing Lem on the horizon of her memory, absently fiddling with the edge of her collar. "My girlfriend Peggy was the pretty one among us. All the fellas wanted her."

"Except Lem."

"Except Lem." Love rooted her answer. "He was as kind and good on the inside as he was handsome on the outside."

"Miss Anna, don't keep me in suspense. Did he ask you out?" The magic of reminiscing was starting to sweep her away. How had Miss Anna ended up here keeping company with an old chapel instead of growing old with the man she loved?

"He asked me to dance and when he turned me onto the floor, I knew I'd never leave his arms."

She sighed.

Elle echoed.

"Six months later, he asked Daddy for my hand, but to tell you the truth, I think Daddy prompted him a little." Her little chortle came from a distant place in her heart. "Daddy loved him as much as I did."

"So you married him. Lem Jamison."

"Yes, ma'am, I did marry him. He was my world. Ten years later he died, and we never had any children."

Elle tore at the wadded tissue her hand. "Oh, Miss Anna, your heart must have broken."

"Into a million pieces. He was standing out in the yard, looking at our peach tree, calling for me to come out and join him. It was a lovely spring afternoon. But I wanted to finish up my dishes. I was rinsing the iron skillet when he collapsed right before my eyes. By the time I got to him, he'd gone on."

Elle brushed her hand lightly over Miss Anna's arm. How could she seem so peaceful and right about her life? "I'm so sorry."

"Last thing Lem ever said to me was, 'Anna, honey, come see this.'" When she glanced at Elle, she smiled. "Such a profound man, don't you think."

"Miss Anna, how can you joke? You're talking about the man you loved. What'd you do?"

"Lived my life. But Lem's breath had been my very own. I had to learn to breathe for myself. Daddy moved me home. Eventually I worked for him, then took over his business."

"You never wanted to remarry?"

"Not right away. I missed Lem so much. I was lost and confused. Out of plain ole desperation, I got down on my knees one night and begged the Lord to show me how to get rid of the pain and live for Him." She gripped her Bible tighter to her chest. "You're second generation, you know, Elle."

Elle glanced at her for a long second. "Of widows? Please say no, because I'm not even married yet."

"Goodness, no." Miss Anna patted Elle's leg. "Dorothy Morris prayed in this old chapel—of course it was the sanctuary back in them days. When Lem died, she approached me to come pray with her. I'd read about my namesake in the Bible, a woman named Anna praying in the temple. So I thought I'd give it a try, see what Dorothy had been doing every morning for years."

"I see." A sense of awe couldn't bypass her sense of terror. Elle wanted to be a woman of faith and prayer, but in her core being, she wasn't sure she was willing to pay the price. "So you chose me like Dorothy chose you?"

"I didn't; He did."

"So, what do I do about Jeremiah?"

"Pray. It's all you can do. Pray and move the heavens to answer."

Rain grayed the morning as Elle drove to Daddy's Port Royal office on the corner of Ribaut and Barnwell.

She parked in a visitor slot next to Daddy's Cadillac and reached over to the passenger seat for a bag of Bubba's Buttery Biscuits and homemade strawberry jam.

As a salesman, Daddy spent most of his office hours in the car and on the road, but since Elle could remember he spent the quiet morning hours in the office doing paperwork.

She tried the front door. It was unlocked, so she slipped into the reception area, careful about invading unannounced.

Last year Arlene Coulter had redecorated the offices for a huge discount as a favor to Elle, replacing the old seventies rust-colored shag carpet and dark-wood paneling with polished hardwood and drywall. She hauled off the plastic and wood-laminate office furniture and moved in real cherry desks with ergonomically correct chairs.

A soft rain began to *rat-a-tat* against the picture pane. Elle peeked down the hall from the reception area to see if Daddy's light burned.

"Daddy?" Why hadn't she bothered to phone first? This was his only time to work undisturbed. "Daddy?" Knocking lightly, she peered into his giant, square-shaped office with a wall of windows.

He was jamming with headphones on.

Smiling, she moved in front of his desk, jiggling the bag of biscuits. "Oh, Daddy . . ."

He snapped off the headphones. "Elle, what are you doing here?"

She sank down into the western-style leather chair he'd insisted Arlene buy for his office. *"Leave the frou-frou stuff in the reception area."*

"I brought biscuits."

"From the Frogmore?" Daddy's interest peaked.

"Of course from the Frogmore." When she opened the bag, butter-scented steam drifted out.

Daddy swiveled around, opened the bottom door of his credenza, and produced two plates. "All right, pass them over."

"Jeremiah is back, Daddy." She picked out a biscuit before handing the bag to him. She'd only bought three—one for her, two for him.

He rocked back in his desk chair, leaving the biscuit bag for now. "And?"

"He left the church in Dallas, which is a long, sad story, and now he wants to marry me." Repeating it out loud didn't bring any more clarification.

"I see."

Elle popped the top off the minitub of jam. "He accepted a job at FSU to be the assistant athletic director."

"Um-hum."

"You got anything to say besides 'I see' and 'um-hum'?"

"I suppose. Seems to be a trend with that boy, accepting a job, then asking you to marry him."

Elle set aside her biscuit, not really all that hungry. "I noticed."

Daddy rocked forward, propping his arms on his desk. "Do you love him?"

"If I do, does that make him the right choice for me?"

Daddy's face remolded into his "father" expression, the one with fleshy lines between his eyes and around his nose. "What about Heath?"

She jerked her head up. "Heath? What does he have to do with anything?"

"Just helping you sort things out."

"No, you're complicating the matter. What makes you think . . . Daddy, Heath is a friend. Period." *What time is it? Eight thirty?* The morning had barely started and she felt beat by the day.

"Elle, you've been praying, spending time with the Lord. You've changed. I see it in your eyes and countenance."

"Fine, Daddy, but how does that help me answer Jeremiah?" Elle needed to stand instead of sit. She walked to the window and twisted open the wood-slat blinds. The rain had thickened. "He could've left Dallas without ever coming here, gone straight to Tallahassee, and I'd have never known. But he didn't. He came back for me."

"Tell me, this church business, how has it affected Jeremiah?"

"He's bitter, confused."

"You want to marry a man struggling with his identity and faith? Elle, consider how blessed you were to have escaped the troubles in Dallas."

"I know, Daddy, believe me. But maybe it was just a timing issue. Maybe I let all my hopes go and now God is giving them back to me. Are hard times a reason to say no to the love of a good man?" The rain cleansed the city of the grime collected during the hot, dry July. Elle felt a part of the washing.

Daddy stood beside her. "If you have to decide in a rush or because some biological or romance alarm clock is going off, then you're probably going to make the wrong decision. But if over time you and Jeremiah still find it right, I'll support you."

She tipped her head against his shoulder. "Thank you, Daddy."

"But if I were you, I'd go home, look in the mirror, and figure out why every time I heard the name Heath McCord the light in my eyes could illuminate a stormy night."

"Captain McCord, you're looking well this morning."Colonel Norman Sillin grabbed a chair for himself and sat down, not bothering to unbundle his winter garb.

Chet struggled to sit upright in the company of his commanding officer. But the cast on his arm and leg rendered him practically immovable. "Colonel, sir, anxious to get back on duty."

"Not with those things." The colonel pointed to his casts. "Even a hotshot like you needs two good legs and arms. Guess you heard a band of Eskimos coming off a fishing excursion rescued you."

"It's what I hear, sir."

The duty nurse came around, pushing the mail cart. She was dark and petite, not at all like Kelly, who was tall with long waves of strawberry hair. But something in the nurse's smile made him crave his girl back home. "Letter for the captain."

"Thank you."

The return address was Kelly's. Chet tucked the envelope by his side, returning his attention to his commanding officer.

"The doc says you're going to be out for a few months."

"Not my prognosis."

"We can use you to train new recruits, but we'll get you back in the air as soon as possible."

"Thank you, sir."

"The medical staff claims you were mumbling about Japanese subs when they doctored your leg."

Maybe it was the crash, or his imagination, but Chet could've sworn a whiff of Kelly's perfume drifted under his nose. "Yes, sir, I fired on an I-Class sub in the Gulf of Alaska, about a hundred and fifty miles off shore."

Colonel Sillin jotted in a small notebook. "Looks like they're closer than we realized. Meanwhile, we're working on getting replacement squadrons up here. Jack Chennault and his neophyte flyboys, some with less than eight hours of flight time, left Washington yesterday." The colonel stood. "On the way here, his little lambs got lost and scattered all over God's white Alaska."

Chet grinned. The ore in the Alaskan soil rendered instruments useless half the time. "Do we know where they are?"

The colonel slipped his notebook into an inside pocket. "They don't even know where they are. Can't even begin to know where to launch search parties. It's Chennault's problem."

"You know what they say: never send a boy to do a man's job."

"Now you tell me." The colonel smiled, stowed his chair away, and turned for the door. "Get some rest. Read that perfumed letter from home."

"Yes, sir." Chet shifted against the featherless pillows, small blips of pain moving across his body——arm, leg, head.

He started the letter by savoring Kelly's handwriting. It's how he'd first met her. He worked at Lipsitz Department Store and she signed for packages her mama ordered. Chet brought the white envelope to his nose for a long inhale before tearing it open.

The fragrance stirred memories of their last night together. He didn't regret their passion, though he regretted the pain of compromising Kelly. But he'd told her if she wanted to stop, he would.

The preacher's daughter was one of the truly good girls. One who spoke of Jesus like a friend. She'd been crazy to take up with the likes of him. But he loved her in a way that made him ache. Enough to love her God if need be.

The letter brought its own healing balm, like a cool bath after a long day working his daddy's lowcountry fields. He flew for her, for the life he wanted with her.

In the heavy gray light barely passing through the hospital hut's dirty windows, Chet read his name, written by her beautiful hand.

Dear Chet,

Darling, I'm shaking as I write this to you, hoping this letter finds you well. It's been weeks since a letter from you arrived.

Chet heard her rebuke and smiled. The letter in his trunk totaled ten pages now, scarred with eraser gum and smudges of lead, but his emotions didn't spill onto the page as easily as Kelly's. Already her voice and heart lifted from the page and settled over his soul.

While patrolling the Alaskan coast, he'd written dozens of eloquent letters to the woman he loved, only to have them evaporate the moment he pressed his pencil to the rough paper.

Please write me soon so I can hear your voice and that you still love me. Darling, you're going to have to love me. We're having a baby. I'm about four months now. Mama saw my growing waist so she came to my room last night. She was upset and disappointed. I knew she would be. I'm sorry for what we did, but I'm not sorry about our baby. Can I feel both so strongly?

But now we have to figure out a way to tell Daddy. I reckon he'll be mad, but so what? I'm a grown woman. I suppose we got things turned around, and it'll be an awful embarrassment to the congregation, but what's done is done.

But, darling, a baby. You and me. I hope she looks like you.

All is swell here, otherwise. Christie and Hal are still fighting like the cat and dog they are. Rose is missing Ted Bell pretty bad, but he writes. (Can't you do the same, darling?)

My job at the paper keeps me busy and from going insane worrying over you. Old senior editor Cray Harris actually gave me an assignment the other day. I declare, he might as well have had his leg sawed off without anesthesia, giving a story to a woman. You know I'm a down-home girl who wants to raise a family and keep house, Chet, but that man makes me want to shout, "Suffragette!"

Guess I'd better close this so I can hand it to Mr. McKenney when he comes by for the mail. I love you, darling, very much.

Your girl,
Kelly

That was it. Heath closed his document. If he read one more word, he'd fire his laptop against the wall. Enough editing, rewriting. It'd taken him days to write that scene. How had his first two novels come so easily? Because they stunk, that's why. He wanted this one to work.

Just send it. Let Nate decide.

Heath launched his e-mail, attached the proposal, scribbled a semicoherent note, and clicked Send before he chickened out.

Beyond the windows, the South Carolina wind and sun beckoned him. He had a few hours before picking up Tracey-Love . . .

Peeling off his shirt, he changed into his old shorts, exchanged his flip-flops for work boots, and grabbed his gear for carving.

Outside, steam rose from the rain-soaked ground, and the heat revived him. Heath revved the chainsaw and settled into carving, the vibration shocking his sleepy, stagnant writer's blood.

When he stepped back to survey his work, he lifted his goggles, hooked his ear guards around his neck, and wiped away sweat with his sleeve. The look of the angel rising from the wood satisfied him.

A pointy finger tapped his shoulder. He turned.

"Elle."

"Hey." She shoved her hair from her face, motioning to the carving. "It's going to be beautiful." Stepping around him, she smoothed her hand over the angel's head, then jerked it away.

"Watch out for splinters."

"Now you tell me." Elle picked the small wood sliver from her palm. "How's the book?"

"Sent a formal proposal to my agent this morning." Had she come here for small talk? Heath raised his guard, watching her. He didn't want to be, but he was mad at her. For leaving him hanging the night they were supposed to go to Luther's, for being beautiful in every way and getting under his skin. Mad at himself for letting her in without caution.

"He asked me to marry him," she said.

Saved him asking the question. "Is that what you want?" Heath bent forward to blow sawdust from the angel's rough-hewn toes.

"I don't know. A lot has changed. He's at FSU now, the assistant athletic director."

"Well, there you go. You won't have to be a PW and live up to all the churchy expectations. I hear FSU has a great art department."

"I didn't say yes." She peeled a jagged piece of wood away from the angel's body.

"Elle, I swear——" He shook the chainsaw at her, then tossed it to the ground. A wet clump of grass stuck to the chain. "Where's the girl with the banging bracelets and the growing confidence? The one who lives in the tower, sees angel feathers, and drives a clueless single father to the ER? The one who put her fears and past behind her, who dared to dream again?"

Emotion swelled in her green eyes. "She's standing right here."

He picked up a sheet of heavy sandpaper. "I don't get women like you."

"Oh, really? I don't get men like you."

"What's to get? I'm easy, simple, straightforward." *Sand, sand, sand.* He worked the angel so hard his muscles ached under his skin.

"Ha! Simple, not. Straightforward, maybe. Why are you so ticked at Jeremiah, a man you don't even know?"

Sand, sand, sand. "Because I know his kind, Elle. Seen hundreds of them. Their inflated pride make them appear confident, but all they're looking for is someone to prop them up."

"You're wrong about him."

Heath paused with the sandpaper. "For your sake, I hope so. By the way, did you e-mail your work to Mitzy?"

Elle stuck out her tongue. "I did, about two weeks ago. Happy?"

Sand, sand, sand. "I sense big things, Elle."

When he glanced up at her, his hand slipped and he rammed his finger into the rough-hewn angel, driving a fat splinter right under the nail. Dropping the sand paper, he breathed a sour word.

"Heath, what'd you do?" Elle cupped her hand under his. "Let me see."

"Easy." On reflex, he tried to pull free when she tugged at the splinter.

Elle hung on. "Let me get it. Don't be a big six-foot baby."

"Two. Six two."

"I stand corrected." Elle tried to pinch the splinter free, but the sliver of wooden angel remained embedded. Heath squirmed and winced. Now he remembered why he'd quit carving years ago. It wasn't his Yale education or law degree, even lack of time. It was splinters. And the needles required to dig them out. "Elle, you're going to have to get a needle. It's the only way."

"Come up to the studio then. I just bought a sewing kit."

In the bare light of Elle's teeny, tiny bathroom, she sterilized a needle with alcohol, then glanced into Heath's eyes. "Ready?" She poised the instrument over his finger.

"I'm ready. Are you?" He'd dig it out himself, but his Florence Nightingale smelled like warm cotton. It reminded him of Tracey-Love's hospital room, when he came in and Elle was rubbing lotion on his girl's hands.

Elle drew a deep breath, aimed the needle, then stopped.

Heath shoved his hand toward her. "Believe me, it'll hurt me more than it'll hurt you. Just do it."

It took a few tries and a lot of Elle wincing, but she freed the splinter. "There, now, that wasn't so bad."

"For who—you or me?"

"Me." Still holding his hand, she rooted in the medicine cabinet for Bactine.

At once, it wasn't about the splinter anymore. He wanted to hold and kiss her. "I need to go."

She let his hand slide free. "Okay. Heath, I know what you're saying about Jeremiah. But I have to see this through, settle our relationship in my heart."

"Yeah, I know." Gently he pulled her to him, his arms locked around her. When her hands slipped about his waist, he almost exposed the tender, new emotion rooting in his soul.

Heath McCord was in love for the second time in his life.

Twenty-Two

PLEASE JOIN US FOR THE GRAND OPENING
OF
JULIANNE'S
MERIDIAN ROAD
JULY 7TH
7:00–9:00 P.M.

The shop flowed with well-wishers, each one with a paper cup of punch in their hands, waiting a turn for a five-minute neck massage, a manicure, or a free hair consultation.

Daddy dragged the mayor, who happened to be a boyhood friend, over to the manicure tables. A photographer from the *Gazette* snapped his picture while Lacy soaked his hands in sudsy water.

Julianne glowed like Venus on a clear night, as the queen of her universe and quite pleased about it.

Rio, dressed in a pink dress and white shoes, mimicked Julianne's every move, right down to her airy laugh. She dragged Tracey-Love—who wore an old pale-green dress Rio had outgrown and a pair of green Crocs—in tow.

On the half hour, Julianne drew for prizes—courtesy of Danny Simmons, Elle guessed—and the small shop never emptied. Prizes won so far were a free "spa" day at Julianne's; gift certificates to Luther's, Panini's, Plums, and the Frogmore Café; a night at the Beaufort Inn; and a starter kit from big sister Sara Beth's cosmetic line, SB Cosmetics.

At eight o'clock, Julianne stood by the refreshment tables and rang her old school bell. "This time around we're drawing for an iPod Nano."

Big excitement over this prize. "Draw my name," Elle called, but Julianne shushed her. "Sisters of the owner are not eligible."

A small rumble rose from the contingent of Garvey Girls. Fine, but as Elle stood shoulder to shoulder with Sara Beth, Mary Jo, and Candace, she was more curious about the absence of Danny Simmons than who would win the media player.

Closing her eyes, Julianne fished in the basket for the winning ticket. She smiled when she read the name. "Tracey-Love McCord."

The girl's eyes grew round and her mouth formed a little *O*. She gazed back at Elle.

"You won, baby. Go get it."

TL moved forward at a snail's pace, staring down at the dark polished tongue and groove floor, holding out her palm.

Julianne lay the square iPod in the center of her hand. "Congratulations, Tracey-Love."

"T-thank y-you." She ran to Elle. "I win, I win."

Elle dropped down. "Won't Daddy be surprised?" Heath was home rewriting his chapters. His agent still wasn't thrilled with a World War II love story, but he'd gamely given Heath feedback.

"Elle." Mama leaned over her shoulder. "The punch bowl is low, but it's after eight. Do you think we should mix up more?"

"No one's left yet and we have another hour." Elle lifted the bowl and headed to the back room as several of Julianne's high school friends arrived.

Julianne had turned the former mud room in the back into the break/storage room. As Elle kicked open the door, she heard a strained, tight-jaw conversation.

"Are you going to keep it a secret forever?"

"The grand opening is not the time and place, and you know it."

Elle discovered a cornered Danny and a fiery Julianne. Well, this answered her where's-Danny question. She motioned to the bowl. "Need more punch."

Opening the fridge for the ingredients to make Granny's famous Cherries Jubilee (soft on the Jubilee) recipe, Elle kept tuned to the whispers behind her, hating the way the conversation dimmed the joy in Julianne's eyes.

Danny had no right. Partner, investor, boyfriend, or whatever. How dare he barge in here and demand something of her during the salon's grand opening.

"Drop it." Julianne.

"Fine, but we're revisiting this." Danny, of course.

He brushed by Elle as she tore open the packets of gelatin and dumped them into the punch bowl. He closed the door with a quiet click, leaving the sisters to huddle under a weighty silence.

Elle twisted open the ginger ale, thinking, praying as her sister wept quietly. "Are you going to tell me?"

"Always with the questions, Elle." Julianne ripped two tissues from the box on the table.

"Always with the secrets, Jules."

She pressed the thin tissue under her eyes to soak up the water. "Everything is going so well. Why does he have to push me?"

"At the risk of asking another question, what issue is he pushing?"

Mama chose *this* moment to check on her refreshment committee (Elle). Her lovely round face peered into the utility room. "Is the punch ready? I declare, twenty more people showed up. Mary Jo is giving them the grand tour. Julianne, are you doing another prize drawing?"

"Yes." She kept her tear-stained face away from Mama by pretending to rearrange the hair coloring on the shelves. "Ask Daddy to do it, please. The prize is the Hilton Head weekend."

Instead of consenting and leaving, Mama stepped into the room and shut the door behind her. As if it wasn't hot and tense enough. Elle averted her gaze. If she looked, she'd crack. Every family had a squealer, stoolie, snitch. The Garvey Girls had Elle. Stool pigeon, first class. She couldn't help it. One look from Daddy and she always broke like cold glass in a hot oven.

"Everything all right in here?" Mama moved between Elle and Julianne with slow, metered steps.

Elle stirred the punch and watched the floor. The tips of Mama's perfectly painted red toenails peeked through peep-toe pumps. Mama stopped, pointing her toes in Julianne's direction.

"We're fine, Mama." Julianne shuffled boxes. "What are these doing here? Out of order?"

"Elle?" Mama's toes implicated her now. "Is this about Jeremiah? You girls seem very distracted." No malfunction of her Mama Radar.

"Not at all about Jeremiah, Mama." More punch stirring and a slight sloshing, but Elle held together. "The punch is ready. Can you open the door for me?"

The red-tipped toes hesitated, but did as Elle asked. "I'll have Daddy do the drawing. Come on out, Julianne. Save the straightening for business hours."

Mama exited and Julianne grabbed Elle's arm. Red punch rolled like the tide up the side of the bowl, nearly spilling over onto her white tank.

"Not a word, stoolie. You pinky promised."

Elle clinched her jaw. Maybe they were too adult for pinky promises. "All right, but whatever is going on with you two, fix it."

"It's not so easy."

"Then make it easy." Elle's leg started to cramp from stretching to hold open the door. "I've got to get this punch to the table, but we're not through with this conversation."

"Yes, we are."

"No, we're not."

Heath had fallen asleep at the kitchen table using his laptop as a pillow, snoozing comfortably until his cell phone broke into his slumber.

He jumped up, slamming his knee into the table leg, and stumbled to the living room.

"McCord." He fell to the couch, squinting against the afternoon light slinking through the southern windows.

"It's Nate."

"Nate who?" Heath propped his head against the couch arm and dropped his arm over his eyes, warding off the glare.

"Very funny. How it's going?"

"You tell me. Did you get my pages?" As his brain eased awake and started to function, Heath became aware of time and place.

"Didn't you get my e-mail?"

Heath glanced at his watch. Four? Crap. Tracey-Love's day school had let out a half hour ago. He shot off the couch, scrambling for his keys, stomping around for his new boat shoes.

"What e-mail?" *Forget shoes, go barefoot.*

"Yes, I e-mailed. Said I loved it. I'm getting attached to Chet. I sent a proposal to six publishers."

Heath burst out the kitchen door and jogged for the van. "Any word?" He cradled the phone on his shoulder as he buckled in and fired out of the driveway.

"It's only been a few weeks, Heath. Publishing is hard business. Marketing wants one thing, the editors something else." The meter of his voice was slow and casual, like he couldn't decide if he wanted to walk to the corner store for a soda or not.

"Give it to me straight, Nate."

"They passed."

"All of them?" The news hit hard.

"Yeah, I pressed them for an answer since I knew they'd set aside time for your proposal as soon as they got it. But right away, I heard no interest in a war piece. Legal thriller, New York City crime, suspense? Yes, but no wartime love stories."

"I see." Heath realized how *much* he wanted a book deal. Chet and Kelly deserved to have their story told and read. He paused at the Fripp Point stop sign, waiting for late-afternoon traffic to pick up before turning onto Hwy 21. If he got caught in drawbridge traffic, he'd really be late. The school should've called.

"They're salivating for another *The Firm*."

"What happened to fresh and original?"

Nate sighed. "Okay, a fresh and original *The Firm*. Heath, you've done your research, the writing is solid, great characters and setting, but marketing for war stories is tough right now."

"I'm sure you did your best."

"He said dubiously. Hey, old friend, I met editors, bought a lot of coffee and lunches on your behalf."

"Okay, advise me." Heath tapped his brake as the traffic over the bridge slowed. Shoot, he'd caught the bridge light. Way in the distance, two sailboats with towering masts drifted toward the bridge, unhurried, without a care.

Sure, they didn't have a little girl, waiting for her delinquent daddy.

"You can keep working on this book. I'll keep looking for a publisher. But it'll take time. Or you can get to work on another legal thriller. With your improved writing, I think we'll go to auction before the printer ink is dry. Based on your legal experience, you could pound out something in a month. Just remember to change the names to protect the innocent."

"What are my chances with another publisher and the war story?" Heath drummed his fingers against his steering wheel. Except for the anxiety of being late for Tracey-Love and Nate's news, he might have enjoyed the view from the crest of the bridge—a hazy pale sky, the sheen of light bouncing off a sun-kissed river, the peaceful drift of a sailboat toward home.

Elle had warned him about bridge traffic. *Leave early*.

"A friend of mine is a publisher over at a new house, Poplar Books. They're very small, but serious about publishing. I can send the manuscript over there. If they want it, the advance will be in the low five figures. And they lean toward literary works."

"Send it."

"I'll keep you posted."

"I guess if I have to set it aside to write something more popular and mainstream, I will."

"Just keep it in the back of your mind, Heath. And don't think you're selling out. There's more than one kind of book in that soul of yours. So, you write a legal thriller to get established, then you can write World War II novels."

Heath thanked him, then listened as Nate rambled on about something—a date he had last week? He kept saying "she" and "her." Heath peppered his side of the conversation with "um-hum" and "really." He was too distracted by the rejection news and being late to pick up Tracey-Love to listen like a good friend.

When Nate hung up, Heath tossed his phone into the passenger seat, drumming his hands on the wheel. *Let's go*.

No one wanted a war novel? Bump 'em. Heath thought the world could use a few more war novels. People forgot sacrifice so easily.

The bridge light flipped to green and Heath's foot hovered between the brake and gas, waiting for the line to move. *Come on*.

Tracey-Love's white-sided daycare came into view minutes later. Heath turned into the parking lot and shifted into Park. The late-day sun splashed the center of the yard with white gold. The place felt deserted. He popped open his door.

"Tracey-Love? Anybody?"

He started for the doors when he spotted Tracey-Love. She sat alone with her feet dangling from a bench, her ankles crossed and locked.

"Hey, baby."

She jerked her head up. Dirt streaked her cheeks and chin; her eyes were red rimmed.

"D-d-daddy." She launched herself from the bench, her pink sundress flapping around her knees as she ran. Her backpack swung from her narrow shoulders. Slamming into Heath's arms, TL gripped his neck so tightly he choked. She shivered with sobs.

"Shh, it's okay, it's okay. Daddy's here, Daddy's here. What happened?" Heath tried to see her face, but she kept it buried against his neck. She was hot and sticky.

Still cradling her and speaking in low tones, he walked toward the school door and pried it open. "Anybody here?"

A stern-lipped Miss Millie met him at the threshold. "Well, you made it."

"Mind telling me why my girl was sitting out on the bench alone, crying?"

"She wouldn't wait for you in here." Miss Millie walked around a low table, sliding pint-sized chairs underneath. "She was convinced you weren't coming."

"Why would she think such a thing? Tracey-Love, Daddy needs you to stop crying. Please." He lowered her to the floor, wiping her tears with his thumbs. But one tiny arm remained locked around his neck.

The long-haired, flowing-skirt preschool teacher moved to the next table. "Where's her mama, Mr. McCord?"

"Not here. And you should've called if she was so upset."

"We tried. The later the hour, the more she fretted. Is her mama deceased?"

"Died a year ago August."

Miss Millie's expression softened with understanding. "She thought you weren't coming because you'd gone to visit her mama in heaven. And once you go to heaven, you don't come back."

Heath recognized Tracey-Love's adaptation of his death explanation. "Did you assure her I was coming?"

Miss Millie paused from straightening chairs. "Mr. McCord,

death is a complicated issue for children. Because they don't fully understand, adults tend to think all is well, when perhaps—"

"Since we moved here, she's been doing well."

"Has Tracey-Love talked about being abandoned?"

"Not to me, no."

The woman knelt next to Tracey-Love and smoothed her hand over her tear-stained face. "It's going to be all right. See? Like I told you." She peered at Heath. "You might want to explain the difference between death and being late."

Why did she have to make him feel unfit? "I'll do that."

Scooping up Tracey-Love, Heath carried her to the van, making a promise he could only keep in theory. "Daddy won't leave you. I'm here for you. Going to harass your boyfriends, teach you to drive, send you to college, walk you down an aisle, one day, way, way off in the future, and give my best girl to another man."

Her grip eased as he opened the van door. "I-I wa-was scared." She crawled into her car seat, her light slowly returning.

"I know you were. Sometimes daddies are late; it doesn't mean we are never coming. Do you understand?"

She nodded, but he was dubious. He'd keep an eye and ear out for her fears of abandonment. "Hey, I finally put some songs on your iPod. Want to play it when we get home?"

"C-Can we get s-some ice cream?"

"Ice cream? Before dinner?"

"P-please?"

Ava, is that you rolling over in your grave? "All right, ice cream sounds good for brave little girls." He buckled her seatbelt, then grabbed her chin. "Tracey-Love, look at me. I will never leave you. Do you understand?"

She rested her head against the car seat. "Not like Mama, huh?"

"Sweetie, people die. We can't predict it or stop it, but to the best of my ability, I'll be here for a long, long time." He smoothed his hand over her knee, which bore a new scrape. "Mama loved you more than anything, TL. She's in heaven because she tried to help other mamas and little girls. And in fact, her old job gave her a big trophy for being brave. How about we put it in your room?"

"Did she get ice cream, too, for being brave, like me?"

"Yes." He smiled, smoothing his hand over her flyaway hair. "Or maybe she picked a big green salad with light dressing. Yum." Okay, so he'd ruined Ava's plan to raise TL a heath-food nut. Some things had to give. "Anytime you get scared or have questions, you come talk to me, okay?" He tickled her ribs. "Okay?"

She frowned and shoved his hand away. "C-can we get ice cream now?"

"Yes, ma'am."

Heath loved the sound of TL's singing and chattering as they drove to Publix, then home. With the drama over, she'd returned to her usual self.

These moments were the kind that made him miss Ava the most, when he wanted to turn to someone who knew exactly how he felt and brag about what a beautiful child they'd made.

A gritty, gray fog hung over the creek, unusual for a July day as Elle drove home from morning prayer where she spent recent days praying about Jeremiah.

Finally settled into his Tallahassee residence, he called daily, e-mailed nightly. Last night, moments before their good-bye, he'd told her he loved her. "Just say the word, Elle, marry me."

His confession reminded her of her original feelings for him and Elle wondered if she'd ever stopped loving him.

Daddy had pointed out to her the other day as she lay on his couch—watching Lifetime movies, thinking of her next painting during the commercials, and calling it work—that she needed to make some kind of decision about Jeremiah or cut him loose.

The whole situation frustrated her. He'd dumped her. The decision to take him back should be simple—no, double dog no with a cherry on top.

But her heart refused to agree. For some wild reason, she wanted to give him a fair chance. Ignore how he'd treated her in the past. And with an odd understanding, she felt Jesus wanted her to give him this consideration too.

Parking beside the garage, Elle jogged up the studio stairs, intending to do some cleaning, then actually work on those paintings she envisioned during Lifetime commercials.

So far, she had three halfway decent pieces for Darcy's show—ones she didn't deem closet-worthy. But, since Mitzy's invitation, Elle felt her confidence growing. Maybe Heath was right—big things were coming.

Darcy Campbell had gone bonkers with Summer Art Walk advertising. Magazine and newspaper ads, flyers listing Elle's name right in there with Sir Lloyd Parcel like she was a somebody.

The whole art community had to be scratching their head.

Darcy called yesterday confirming that her friend and noted art critic Ruby Barnett would just happen to be in town for the festivities.

Yeah, so much for her promises to keep it low key.

Dropping her keys and purse on the work table, Elle surveyed the studio, not sure what to do next or where to begin. Her Wal-Mart laundry bags lined the short wall by the bathroom. Clean clothes were gradually moving to a new dirty pile. Why she didn't break down and find the laundry baskets in the garage remained a mystery.

Snapping on the AC, Elle popped open the fridge for a bottle of water. The futon looked inviting. Maybe a morning nap was in order. Clearly this was going to be one of those what-to-do, end-up-doing-nothing days.

Elle peered out the window into the yard wishing she had a pool.

A quick dip later in the afternoon would be nice. Or she could drive over to Mama and Daddy's, or Sara Beth's. When she did, she ended up hanging out too long, staying for supper, watching TV, shooting the day all to pieces.

She'd become a full-blooded bohemian. *Clearly you have too much time if you're standing here dissecting an afternoon of swimming.*

Deciding to work instead of surrendering to laziness, she set out her palette and the *Memory Book* painting she'd started a few days ago. She'd read a verse in the Old Testament about God listening to conversations and writing things down. Terrifying? Yes, but fascinating. One morning in prayer, she had a flash image of words one might find in God's memory books so she decided to put it to canvas.

"Isn't God good?"

"Jesus loves you, friend."

"Here, have this cup of cold water."

"Please, take this twenty. It's not much, but I hope it helps."

"I forgive you."

With her palette knife, she began mixing colors, but when a car door sounded, she peered out the window. Heath?

Danny Simmons.

He caught her gazing and motioned for permission to come up. Opening the door, Elle waited.

"Morning, Elle." Danny's tan was accented by a stiff, white Ralph Lauren polo.

"How're you, Danny?" Elle motioned to the stool by the work table. A fight-or-flight decision flickered behind his eyes. Could he finish what he was about to start? "It's okay, I don't bite."

He perched on the stool. "You haven't heard why I'm here yet."

Crossing her arms, Elle leaned against the table. "Why are you here?"

"I want to marry your sister."

She gauged his sincerity. "Why are you telling me?"

"Because I want you to talk to her, convince her it's the right thing. She turns me down every time I ask her."

"Forget it, Danny. I'm not going to talk her into marrying you. If she's turning you down, she must have a reason. You might consider moving on."

The light in the room shifted as the sun moved behind a cloud. The AC hummed like a good AC unit.

"I've watched you, Elle. Julianne respects and listens to you."

Elle squinted at him. "She never listens to me."

"There's more to this story than Julianne and me." Danny held up a single finger.

Elle eased her arms down to her side. The resonance in his voice captured her attention. "And what would that one be?"

"Rio's mine, Elle." No hesitation, no door for questions.

"Rio is yours? As in—"

"I'm her father."

"You're Rio's daddy?" It seemed insane, ludicrous. Of all the possible Danny Simmons confessions Elle could've conjured up, being Rio's daddy was not one of them.

"I want to get this out in the open, marry Julianne, and be a family. Rio calls me Mr. Danny. My own daughter . . . Mr. Danny."

She stared. "I-I can't believe it. You?"

"Yes, me."

Elle walked around her easel, hand pressed to the back of her neck. She looked back at him. "This is unbelievable. Rio's daddy? How?"

"We met, connected, one thing led to another . . . Do you need more, or do you get the picture?"

"I get it."

"So, are you going to help me or not?" The desperation in his eyes leaked out in his voice.

"If she's yours, where have you been the past four years?"

"On the outside looking in. Julianne stiff-armed me until this year. I finally wore her down."

"Why don't you man up and talk to Daddy?"

He arched his back a little with a sarcastic nose-laugh. "She'd kill me. You don't think I've tried every possible angle. Sorry to tell you, but you're my last resort."

"Good to know."

Danny slid off the stool and paced a little. "Elle, I'm forty-eight and divorced. My ex hates me and sees to it my kids do too, except when they need money. I have a chance to right some wrongs, do something good for two people I love more than my own breath." He regarded Elle for a moment. "Do whatever you think is best, but I'd be forever indebted if you could help me."

"You overestimate my influence."

"I hear you're a praying woman. If you don't have the influence, perhaps He does."

He heard she was a praying woman? "Perhaps."

"Thanks, Elle." Danny exited the studio without looking back.

From her window, she watched him go, feeling for the first time the longing of his heart. *"My own daughter calls me Mr. Danny."*

Twenty-Three

Julianne's was busy when Elle entered the salon. The bell on the door announced her arrival. "What are you doing here?" Julianne clicked on the shears to shave the neck of the man sitting in her chair.

"Came to see you." Maybe she should've waited until the salon closed, but hanging around the studio thinking of Danny's confession had stoked a fire in Elle's belly. She tried to settle down and paint, but when she rehearsed confronting Julianne for the hundredth time, she decided to talk to her in person.

"Afternoon, Elle," Mrs. Pratt called over her shoulder from where Lacy polished her nails. "I hear Jeremiah's back in your life."

Julianne ducked her embarrassed cheeks behind her client's head.

Big mouth. Talk about your own life if you want to gossip. Maybe coming in during business hours to confront her wasn't such a good idea.

"He is, Mrs. Pratt." It's all the woman needed to know.

Julianne finished up with her customer, a young man dressed as a civilian but with the strut of a marine. She thanked him for coming by, then reached for the broom. "What's up, sister dear?"

"Can I talk to you? In private?" Elle motioned to the break/storage room.

"Sounds serious." Julianne swept brown hair into a dust pan. "Let me check on Miss Dora's set first." She walked over to the dryers, lifted the hood, felt the curlers, then told the woman five more minutes.

In the back room, Elle sniffed around the last of the morning donuts, but decided against eating one.

Jules yanked open the fridge. "Now that I have my own business, I can't imagine how you sold the gallery."

"Love is blind."

"Maybe, but it shouldn't make you stupid." Julianne pulled out a bottle of water, letting the door swing shut. "What's wrong? Is it Jeremiah?" She grabbed a basket of towels off the dryer. "I'm going to say this straight up, Elle. I know SB, MJ, and Candace agree—the man doesn't deserve you. Do you really want to be married to him after what he did?"

"People make mistakes, Jules."

"Fool me once, shame on you. Fool me twice, shame on me."

"Is that why you won't tell Mama and Daddy about Danny?"

Julianne didn't flinch, but folded a towel, tucking her red lips into a tight line. "I don't know why they have to know who I'm dating—"

"He told me."

"Told you what?" Julianne snapped another towel from the basket. "Danny Simmons is used to getting what he wants and it burns my hide to have him sneaking around to the family, talking about my business."

"He seems to think Rio is his business." Elle picked up a towel to fold, keeping her voice low. *I'm on your side.*

Julianne thrust a folded towel onto the pile with such force the stack toppled to the floor. She swore as she stooped to pick them up. "Now I have to wash them all over again."

"The floor looks clean to me. Isn't there a five-second rule?"

"No, there's not." Julianne shoved Elle aside and tossed the fallen towels into the machine.

"Is he Rio's daddy?"

"You with your questions." She measured out detergent and poured it in, slamming down the lid.

"The irony is killing me, Jules. You won't use a towel on a customer that hit a clean floor for two seconds, but you're willing to let your family and friends believe Rio came from a one-night stand?"

"Towels and my personal affairs do not equate." She trembled as she reached for the remainders in the basket.

"Jules." Elle grabbed her hands. "Is it true?"

A light knock against the door and Lacy called, "Julianne, your four o'clock arrived."

"Thanks, I'll be right out." Julianne eyed Elle, control replacing the tremors. "So what if he is?"

Why did she make everything so hard? "Then you can come clean, get married, move out of the dump you call home. Rio can have a daddy, Jules."

"It's not that simple."

Elle smacked her hand down on the washing machine. Her bracelets clanked against the metal. "Why not? Why is everything so complicated? Do you know how relieved Daddy and Mama would be? Maybe a little weird about the age thing and the fact that Danny is Daddy's friend and all, but, Jules, they'd be elated."

Steely brown eyes held on to Julianne's resolve. Elle knew her sister's cloaked confession did not mean one brick in her wall had come down. "I'm not telling anyone anything. And you're still under our pinky oath."

"I'm sorry, that's not good enough. Jules, you best give me a reason why you won't come clean on this. You have a wonderful man who loves you and longs to do the right thing."

"I have a customer." Julianne stepped around Elle.

"Do not go out that door, Jules."

With a desperate sigh, Julianne fell against the door, holding her head high, fixing her eyes on some point beyond Elle. "You want a reason? You think this is so cut and dried, black and white? Just confess, Jules, all your problems will be solved. No, they won't. Nothing can remove the shame. I'm ashamed, Elle, and it physically hurts to think about it." Her terse words flew like arrows.

"You're not the first woman to have a baby out of wedlock." Elle tread with a light step.

Julianne's eyes glistened as she absently bit her bottom lip. "He's been divorced three years. Rio is four."

Elle crossed her arms in an academic way, as if she'd just grasped the law of entropy. "Okay, a small complication—"

"Small complication? You think I'm going to waltz into Truman and Lady Garvey's house and confess their foolish and stupid daughter had an affair with a married man? I won't do it. It was bad enough telling them I was pregnant. Every time I'm with them, I feel their disappointment."

"Don't see them through your guilt, Jules. They love you; they're proud of you. They strutted around here like peacocks at your grand opening."

"Okay, maybe the ordeal of their daughter having a baby out of wedlock has passed. Besides, it's happened to half their friends. It's not so shameful anymore, but, Elle, if I start letting on that Danny Simmons is Rio's daddy . . ." She snatched a tissue from a nearby box and blotted under her eyes. "I won't do it, not to them. Danny can live with it."

"Do you love him? What if this isn't about you or Danny or Mama and Daddy. Could it be about Rio and what's best for her?"

"What's best for her is what I say. Danny isn't leaving me many options, Elle. If I'm with him, the truth has to come out. He won't have it any other way. He's tired of being in the background and frankly, I don't blame him. But, Elle, this is one valley our love can't cross."

"Not even for Rio?"

Julianne lowered her eyes, shaking her head. "It sounds simple, but—" A single tear dangled from her chin. She wiped it away with the back of her hand. "Imagining the look on their faces as they hear one of their adorable offspring willingly carried on with a married man, one of Daddy's friends, no less, is the stuff of nightmares."

Lacy knocked again. "Are you coming? He says he's in a hurry."

"Be right out, Lace."

How had Jules borne this alone for so long? Elle would've cracked under the pressure. "At the risk of sounding like a hundred-year-old hymn, I think I know someone who can take away your burden of guilt and shame."

"I've prayed, Elle, if that's what you mean." Julianne checked her makeup in the mirror before easing open the door. "Maybe some of us are just destined to be shackled by a heavy burden."

Twenty-Four

Since his conversation with Nate, Heath's novel determination suffered. He'd not touched his laptop today since checking e-mail before driving TL to school.

Should he continue to pen a book no one would ever read? A real artist would say yes. Art for art's sake. Elle seemed willing to create work no one would ever see. But her issues were different from his. She was insecure. He was efficient.

Maybe it was Heath's practical side. Or his ego. But if he worked his backside off preparing a case, writing a book, or carving an angel out of a tree stump, somebody had better benefit from it.

So maybe it was back to Manhattan and his Central Park apartment with a cleaning service and take out. He'd finish Chet and Kelly's story on the weekends, see if Nate could land it a home.

Lately, he missed waking up in the morning with a distinct sense of purpose, reviewing case details as he showered, reading briefs on his train ride downtown. And the other night he'd had a craving for the kabobs served by the Indian place on the corner of Lexington and 49th.

Plopping down on the couch, he reached for the remote, surfed a few channels, then clicked the TV off. He was restless. Ready to move on with his life.

When he'd moved down to St. Helena, he'd wanted to forget

himself, get lost in something that had no ties to Ava. But nearing the anniversary of her death, he was ready to be found.

Wandering out to the screen porch, he eased down into the iron rocker and listened to the melody of the creek.

Maybe writing a book didn't matter as much as healing and closing those final doors of grief. Looking back, he'd done well. Only one door remained. The letter.

Heath thought for a moment, mentally testing his tender spots, then went to the kitchen. Ava's envelope remained perched in the window, crisp and faded from months of southern sunshine.

Walking out the kitchen door and stepping off the porch, he took the slope of the yard toward the dock, crossing the pine needle garden where the angel-with-splinters waited. Taking a bench seat between two pylons, Heath considered his options while staring at the horizon where clusters of island trees appeared like rolling hills.

He could drop the letter in the water right now and forget she ever wrote it. Or he could read it and say good-bye forever to his first true love.

Or take the letter back inside and let it ride on the window's ledge for a few more weeks.

Coward. Just read it.

"Heath? You here?"

Heath lifted his head, listening.

"Heath?" A knocked echoed across the yard.

"Out by the creek."

A dark-suited man rounded the side of the cottage. *Rock?* What in the world? Heath slipped the letter into the pocket of his shorts, laughing as the man practically disrobed in the yard. Coat dangling off his fingers, tie undone, shirt opened with the tail out. "It was a nice sixty-two when I left the city. What is it, a hundred here?"

"Eighties. What are you doing here? Come inside, cool off."

Heath lead Rock to the kitchen and popped open a couple of cold Cokes.

"Bless you, my boy." Rock gulped down half the can. When he came up for air, a burp slipped through his teeth. "Pardon me, but that hit the spot."

Heath sat in the chair opposite his old boss and friend. It was good to see him. "So, you didn't come all the way down here to share a Coke with me and shoot the bull, did you?"

"You e-mailed me about the book being rejected, so I thought, *Strike while the iron is hot, Calloway.* Booked the earliest flight down."

"Taking advantage of a man when he's weak?"

Rock toasted Heath with his Coke. "Whatever it takes. The fight's getting pretty nasty up there. Old school versus the new, arguing over administering the PPP."

"The old PPP." *Profits per partner.* He'd earned more than his share over the years.

"I need you." Rock's message never changed. "They're turning my law practice into a competitive, bottom-line machine. First thing in the morning breakout meeting? Money, profits, billable hours. When I started the firm, I wanted to practice law. And so did everyone working for me. Now it's about making money through the law."

"I'm pretty sure I'm coming back in September."

"Make it a 'for sure' and I'll be a happy man. Doc has Olivia Hancock slotted to take your partnership if you don't return." Rock downed the last of his Coke. "A man works his whole life for something he believes in, makes a bad choice, and a couple of snot-nosed Harvard guys change everything."

"See, there's where you went wrong, Rock. Harvard grads." Heath glanced at his watch. "I need to pick up Tracey-Love. Want to ride along and grab some dinner after?"

"Did you notice airlines don't serve squat for food anymore?"

"I'll take that as a yes." Grabbing his keys, he ushered Rock out the back door and set Ava's letter back on the windowsill.

Out back on the deck of Luther's Rare and Well Done, five o'clock was still bright and warm.

From where Elle sat with Jeremiah, she could see the right half of Waterfront Park, the sparkling Beaufort river, and the sleeping boats docked at the marina.

"This job was tailor made for me, Elle." Jeremiah poured a tiny bit of dressing over his salad. "The staff is great; we click and flow, share common ideas and goals."

"I'm glad, Jer. I can hear it in your voice when you call. So, did you find a new apartment?"

"Yeah, I did, but"—he took a slow stab at his salad—"I'd rather wait for you this time. Our marriage license is still valid, and Pastor O'Neal could marry us tonight if we wanted." He caught her eye, communicating passionate things unsaid.

If he'd made the suggestion last night when he pulled into the cottage driveway and met her at the studio, she would've said yes. The futon had provided an inviting, soft place to say "hey" and continue to get reacquainted.

For the few weeks he'd been back in her life, Jeremiah had eased off the idea of marriage until last night when he whispered, "I love you, Elle. I want you."

Since stepping down from ministry, Jeremiah's passions burned hotter, more fierce. Last night Elle was the one who challenged the journey of his kisses along her neck and down the edge of her top.

Right? Wrong? Everything in her wanted to respond.

"Elle, what do you think?" Jeremiah bit the salad off the tip of his fork.

"I don't know, Jeremiah. It sounds exciting, but—" She stirred her salad. His confidence and excitement intoxicated her, but this new insistence on marriage made her bristle.

While she took months to pray and wade through her disappointments, Jeremiah had moved forward with rocket speed and intensity. Elle felt sluglike and dull compared to him.

He wiped the edge of his lips with his napkin. "Can't talk you into a quick wedding yet?"

"If we do this, Jer, we're doing it right. We disappointed a lot of people last time." *Mostly me.*

"All the more reason not to make a big fuss this go around. Get married quietly, hold a reception later. Save us and your parents the expense—"

"Miss Elle." A fuzzy little blonde head crashed against her lap.

"Tracey-Love, where'd you come from?" Elle wrapped the girl in her arms, kissing her forehead.

"M-my daddy." Tracey-Love pointed back at Heath, a very serious tone in her voice, as if Miss Elle should know better.

"Yes, you did." Elle glanced up at Heath, turning Tracey-Love around, pulling her crooked ponytail free. "What are y'all doing?"

"Elle, this is my boss, Rock Calloway." Heath motioned to a slender, silver-haired man who carried an aura of sophistication. "He's after a good burger."

Elle looked up at him as she combed TL's hair into place with her fingers. "You've come to the right place. How was school today, Tracey-Love?"

"We have ants."

"Do you?" Elle swished the girl's hair into a sleek ponytail.

"An ant *farm*, right?" Heath gazed down at her, a soft, pleasant look in his eye, fatherly pride around the edge of his face.

"Yep, farm, but they don't grow veg-ables." She bobbed her head, so serious.

"They don't? Goodness, but we love our vegetables."

"Except broccoli." TL curled her nose.

"So, Mr. Calloway, how do you like the lowcountry?"

"Hot. But beautiful."

"You'll get used to it." She glanced at Jeremiah and introduced him. The men gripped hands.

"Jeremiah used to play for the Dallas Cowboys, Rock," Heath said.

"Did you now? My old favorite team. I follow the Giants these days."

The comment sparked football talk until the waitress came out and asked if Heath's party wanted to join the table.

Elle stiffened. Jeremiah and Heath at the same table. She'd never get her dinner down.

"No, thanks," Heath said. "We'll take the vacant spot in the corner."

Jeremiah asked for the bill. When he'd signed the credit card receipt, he led her off the back steps toward Waterfront Park.

Elle glanced over at Heath. "See you."

"Night, Elle."

Rock gazed at the water. "The artist?"

"How'd you know?" Heath had settled it in his heart. Elle was with Jeremiah.

"The look on your face. She a threat to my plans for you coming back?"

Rock should turn off his people radar and enjoy the freaking view. "I thought you were hungry. Read your menu so we can order."

Rock chuckled, opening his menu. "Either way, congratulations, you've entered the land of the living. And it's a good thing I decided to come down, remind you there're a lot of beautiful women in New York. Artists too."

"They're not the same." Heath scanned the burger section, not really reading. "She's probably going to marry him."

"Probably? I know a lawyer who used to get acquittals on a probably. Reasonable doubt, my friend. Make your move. The Barbeque Burger looks good."

Heath peered at Rock. "If I make my move, it may ruin your plans."

"Bring her with you. A married Heath makes a happy lawyer."

Rock closed his menu. "But don't come to Calloway & Gardner pining for her. I'll have no sympathy."

Heath heard Rock loud and clear. In fact, he expected nothing less from the man.

"Any word from Mitzy Canon?"

"Nothing more than a request for samples." Heath picked up one of TL's crayons and started coloring her picture.

"Hey, this is mine." She shoved his hand away with an intense furrow between her eyebrows. "You color yours."

Rock laughed. "She can handle you just fine."

Heath put his hand on her hair. "Getting there."

The waitress came around for their drink order, and Rock picked out a couple of appetizers. "Make your move or live with the consequences."

Heath watched Tracey-Love color carefully between the lines. "It's nothing, Rock, a schoolboy crush."

"Do you love her?"

Heath hid his eyes behind a swig of tea. "I told you, a school boy crush."

Jeremiah swept her into his arms, kissing her temple. Elle smoothed her hand over the thick pump of his chest. The water and grass-scented wind also carried a hint of Jeremiah's sandalwood fragrance.

"Offer still stands," he said, dipping his head for a kiss. "I'll call Eli, and in an hour, you'll be my wife."

"Jeremiah, come on, you're not serious. What about our families and friends?"

"They'd understand. We're not young, starry-eyed kids who don't know the difference between the pageantry and reality."

"Even so, I want my family there, and my friends. Besides, I'm working a show for Darcy's Summer Art Walk. And who knows, maybe Mitzy Canon will want to show my work in her gallery. I can't just pick up and—"

"Paint in Tallahassee. Travel up here whenever you want."

A river-wet gust slipped along the edge of the park. Her excuses weren't buying her any time.

"It's not *doing*, Jeremiah. It's *being*. I can *do* all day long. The question is can I be with you? Can I trust you? Will something come along that causes you to choose yourself, your career, over me?"

"That's the old Jeremiah."

"Old? Already? It's only been four months since we broke up, only a few weeks since you quite the job."

They walked through a warm pocket of evening as they made their way to the marina parking lot. "I've changed, Elle. Look close enough and you'll see."

If she had to look close, had he really changed?

He walked beside her, graceful and casual. "So, who's this Mitzy Canon person you're talking about?"

"She's a gallery owner in Manhattan and based on her experience and networking, she's earned this reputation as an artist maker. If she says an artist is good, then they are good."

"And she thinks you're good?"

Elle shrugged. "From your lips to God's ears. So far, she's only *reviewing* my work for a *possible* place in her spring show."

He paused to watch a couple of jet skis, reaching for Elle, locking her between his arms. "Hmm, interesting."

Really? Could've fooled her. But he was trying. His breath and lips were hot on her cheek, then neck.

What if they called Pastor O'Neal? Would he even marry them? Jeremiah's hands moved around and up her waist. Elle caught her breath. "So, Jer—"

He backed away at the ring of his cell. "Alex, what's up?"

Elle fell against the concrete pylon as Jeremiah released her.

New rule: make no decision while in physical contact with Jeremiah. Brushing a mist of perspiration from her forehead, Elle steadied her pulse with deep breaths.

In the distance, Jeremiah's footsteps smacked against the pavement. "You're kidding . . . He signed a letter of intent? Excellent. I'm sure Coach was relieved . . . Yeah, Florida almost convinced him . . ."

As he circled back toward her, Elle grabbed his arm and steered Jeremiah toward the swings, where she'd come that night with Heath and the girls. She hadn't thought of it until now, but Heath's Freddy story still resonated in her heart.

She sat, setting the swing in motion, feeling her senses returned. Run off and get married. No, she would not do it.

Jeremiah walked back and forth, talking. He was all smiles when he snapped his phone shut.

"We've been in huge competition over this high school quarterback with the University of Florida."

"And you won?"

"We did. This is really going to rev up the team and the boosters." His cell rang again. More animated talk about football stars and who was going to beat the Gators next season.

The conversation lasted a few minutes and the moment Jeremiah hung up, Elle moved to recapture the conversation. "So, you wanted to know about Mitzy Canon? She asked for samples of my work and I e-mailed them off."

Jeremiah eyed her for a second. "Babe, am I wrong here or did you just send this artist maker mediocre work? Artists paint for years to get some kind of recognition. You, you know, owned a gallery. Just started painting a month ago. Are you sure you want this Mitzy looking at your paintings when you're not confident it's your best?"

Dread steals one's breath away at the oddest times.

"I sent some of my recent paintings, Jeremiah. Heath thought they were good."

"Heath? That guy's in love with you, Elle. What does he know? What does he do anyway?"

"He's a lawyer and a writer."

Jeremiah made a face. *See?*

"He wouldn't lie to me, Jer." They'd tangoed enough times for her to know he was an upfront, honest man.

"Not on purpose, but, hey, men have gone to war over a pretty face."

"Thanks a lot; you're no help." Her heart raced. *Don't panic, Elle. He's just yapping.*

"I'm sorry, but I'm in the business of perfection. If you can't show or do your best, wait until you can."

Go ahead, panic, Elle. He's right. Jeremiah's little speech resurrected every doubt and fear Elle thought she'd conquered during her summer of prayer and painting.

"What should I do, then, call her and say never mind?" *Help me, Jeremiah. Advise me.*

"That might not be a bad idea—" Cell phone again. "Franklin." Jeremiah listened, his slow, white smile forming. "Yeah, Pete, I heard. Alex called . . . Yes, it's great news . . ."

Why was it so hot? Elle lifted her hair off her neck. Was Jeremiah right about sending her work to Mitzy? When he finally hung up, she pressed him.

"What if she likes my work, Jer? Wouldn't that be incredible? I'd have my first New York show."

"It happens. But, Elle, come on, those kind of situations are rare. Making it as a writer, artist, even athlete takes years and—" Cell phone, again. He answered. *Why not? He wasn't doing anything important.*

"Yeah, can you believe it? This kid will bring the other recruits who are teetering . . ."

Anxious, a little angry, wanting to make a point, Elle snatched Jeremiah's silver nuisance from his hand and hurled it toward the murky marina water like it was a pulled-pin grenade.

"Elle, what're you doing? My new phone—" Jeremiah lunged for it, way too late, as it made an insignificant splash. Probably didn't even bother the hungry fish. "What's gotten into you?"

"I'm sick of competing with that thing. You're a cell-phone whore, Jeremiah."

"It's business."

"No, it's yuk-yuk-yuk, look who we stole from the Gators. Well, bubba, good for you. I'm no Gator fan, but I'm not going to compete for your attention. This"—she circled her hand between them—"is what I was talking about. We can do together, eat, go to church, walk, talk about you, but there's no room in your world for me, Jeremiah. Can't you see?"

"No, I don't. There's plenty of room for you in my world."

As if caught in some cosmic paradox, Elle's cell rang mid-diatribe. Jeremiah glared.

"It's the first time all night." Elle fished it from her bag. "Hello?"

"Elle Garvey? It's Mitzy Canon."

Twenty-Five

June 1, 1942, Umnak Island, Aleutians

The camp slept in an eerie silence as Chet stepped outside his tent into the dull, gray light of the Aleutian summer morning, zipping up his mackinaw. Ducking into the chilly and constant breeze, he trekked toward the tarmac where the new P-40s were tethered.

A group of new recruits to the 11th Pursuit Squadron slept huddled under the belly of the planes with no hope in sight for better quarters. Umnak was a new, ill-supplied post.

Coming to the end of the steel-mat runway, Chet scanned the barren, desolate horizon. Not a tree or shrub to engage his line of sight. Just gray.

The words of Kelly's latest letter surfaced in his thoughts. He'd memorized every word, every curlicue, dotted i and crossed t of her elegant script. He thought he was a hero until she wrote of her own bravery. Though she'd never call it courage. Only facing her fears.

The lover part of him wanted to climb atop a P-40 and shout it to the fog-laden mountains, "I'm the luckiest man alive."

Knowing he was bringing a kid into the world, knowing the strength of his future wife changed his heart and how he planned to fight the war.

He'd make it home alive. He'd see the sunrise over the ocean, watch the moon gliding over the marsh grass.

"Out for an early constitution, Captain?" Lieutenant Cimowsky nudged him with a cup of black coffee. "It tastes like cow pies smell back home, but it's hot and will give you a morning jolt."

Chet hooked his finger through the handle. "Just what I ordered."

Cimowsky tipped his face to the fog. "Do you think the sun's up there? Somewhere?"

"Sun? What's a sun?"

Cimowsky laughed, spewing a little spray of coffee. "The big yellow ball we used to wake up to back in the lower forty-eight."

Chet sighed. "It's been too long. Too long."

Cimowsky motioned with his mug. "Eerie, isn't it. Like something's not right. A silence deeper than the quiet."

Chet's gut churned. "Yep, something is up. Can't see it, but I feel it."

Cimowsky tapped Chet's arm. "Let's grab some chow."

"Be there in a second." Chet took Kelly's letter from his inside pocket. It was wrinkled from his constant refolding.

Darling,

I hope this letter finds you well. I miss you so much. With our baby growing every day, I cannot help but think of you and pray for God to keep you. Are your ears burning? I talk to Him about you a hundred times a day.

Mama and I spoke to Daddy about our situation. He was upset, disappointed, and I cried until my stomach ached. Then he came around to me, Chet, kissed me, prayed for me, for you and our baby.

I asked if I could speak to the congregation. Why let the gossips have one up on me. If I confess and repent, what can they do to me? I'll trust my reputation to my Savior.

Daddy refused, but I think Mama and Jesus convinced him. So this Sunday I stood up and said what I'd done.

Chet's belly lurched at the image of Kelly standing alone, expos-ing her sin. As if she were the only one among them.

"I'm pregnant," I said. "Yes, I sinned, let my passions take over, but I love my man, and he loves me. We'll make it right. But before God and you, I repent."

Oh, darling, I trembled like a pup during a storm. Judge Brown sat right on the front row with the most sour look of condemnation. Mrs. Parsons shamed me out loud and demanded Daddy put me out of fellowship.

Then, of all things, Carwood Nixon stood up in the back row and said, "I've been having an affair for the last six months." And his wife sat smack next to him.

Art Samson stood next. "I'm drinking away the family fortunes."

Ginger Levine got up saying she couldn't stop gossiping and knew she'd hurt so many people by spreading stories.

We had a revival meeting right then and there, folks weep-ing at the altar, asking God and each other for forgiveness. Everyone had forgotten what I'd confessed. Afterward, the love was so thick in the room I could taste it.

I think our child is going to do great things. Not even born and look what he started.

Chet folded the letter and tucked it away. Kelly Carrington, his brave girl. "God," he whispered, "if You can see fit to forgive Kelly and all those folks, maybe You can see fit to forgive me."

On the trailing breath of Chet's prayer, a private busted out the hanger along the tarmac.

"Japs! Japs!" He pulled on his gear and dove into a bunker.

Chet's gaze shot to the gray soup over head. He saw nothing, but heard the hum of the enemy. Tossing his coffee to the ground, he raced toward his aircraft as Rufe float planes cut through the clouds and descended over the base.

A car door slammed. Heath lifted his head, listening, half his brain stuck in the scene he'd just rewritten. Did he like the revival interlude? Too preachy? Maybe, but certainly authentic for the forties healing-and-revival era.

Rufe float planes. Did the Japanese fly them in the Aleutians? He'd dropped the term in from memory, so he'd better Google it.

A second car door slammed. Voices. Heath shoved his laptop to the club chair's ottoman and stood. Ten fifteen. The house had been quiet except for the *tap-tap-tapping* of his fingers on the keyboard.

Heath had tucked Tracey-Love into bed an hour ago, and so far she remained there. Rock retired to Heath's room a little before ten. His flight back to New York left Charleston at nine a.m., so he planned to rise early.

Muffled yelling.

The noise came from the kitchen side of the house so Heath strolled to the fridge without turning on extra lights.

He craved something cold and fizzy to drink, warm from writing with the laptop on his legs, but if he drank caffeine now he'd never go to sleep. He opted for water.

Chugging down half the bottle, Heath peered out the window, above the edge of Ava's letter. Elle? The studio's stairway light haloed her silhouette. A broader, darker shadow followed. Must be Jeremiah.

Their voices rose, then fell. She angled toward him, then turned away. He grabbed her arm.

Fight for yourself, Elle. Don't let him manipulate you. Heath had half a mind to open the door and cheer her on. But he knew . . . it was none of his business.

But if he were Jeremiah, he'd fight for Elle. She'd be worth every emotion, every act of love.

The silhouettes stood apart for a long moment, then Elle pressed her hand against Jeremiah's arm. She pointed to the studio and started up the stairs. It took a few seconds, but he trailed behind her.

Years of trial law had trained Heath in body language, but tonight, peering through the darkness wearing the spectacles of his own emotions, he was clueless.

Are they taking the argument inside? Making up?

When his cell rang, he jumped and darted for the living room, snatching the phone from the end table.

"McCord."

"Did I call too late?" Nate. Couldn't think to check the time before he dialed. Ambient noise filled the background—laughter, clicking glass, and clashing plates.

"You always call late." Heath straddled the ottoman, easing into the club chair.

"Yeah, that's because I'm out here stumping for you." The voices dimmed.

"Stumping for me? At a party?"

"Some swanky dinner where I met up with some old editor pals of mine."

"Yeah?" Heath gripped the water bottle. Face a difficult judge? No problem. Persuade a jury? Piece of cake. Hear his book was rejected? Nervous water-bottle crusher.

"Seems they're interested in war novels, think they'll make a comeback in a few years and are scouting for good manuscripts."

"No word from the small press, Poplar?"

A second, then two ticked off before Nate said, "They passed, Heath."

"I figured." Heath scooted to the edge of the chair.

"They loved the concept, so much they just bought a war book and are putting a lot behind it. But they loved your writing. So, while I shmoozed with my editor friends tonight, I dropped this little tidbit and got the conversation rolling. Heath, we'll find a place for this story. But if you want to work on a legal thriller—"

His posture slumped as he fell against the back of the chair. "Rock came down for a surprise visit this weekend, Nate."

"Can't live without you?"

"Something like that. Wanted to make sure I remembered my six-month deadline. I'll be back in the city by the middle of September." His decision came swift, without contemplation. "Guess I got this novelist thing worked out of my system."

"Heath, don't give up. We've gotten close. Your talent will make a way. Keep sending me what you've got, I'll pitch it. Shoot, I'm doing this as much for Ava as you."

Heath said good-bye, tossed his phone to the table, and shut down his laptop. Clicking off the lamp, he stretched out on the couch and tugged the afghan over him. For a long time, he stared into the darkness, praying, seeking the wisdom of heaven.

Light footfalls echoed down the hall and a warm little body shoved in next to him. Rolling over on his side, Heath smoothed her rough hair with his palm and kissed her moist cheek.

In the morning, he'd confirm with Rock—the September return date worked well for him.

The prayer chapel was hallowed and quiet when Elle entered Monday morning, sitting in her usual place, second row, right side.

Miss Anna knelt in front by the altar, her hands lifted in silent worship.

Opening her Bible, Elle tried to read the words written in red, but tears interfered.

She sniffled and prayed for a long while, struggling to find contentment in God despite the weekend's events.

"Want to tell me about it?" Miss Anna shoved Elle aside so she could sit.

Elle wiped her cheek with her fingers, wiped her nose with a very weary tissue. "Jeremiah and me . . . it's over."

"And you regret it?"

"No." Lifting her head, Elle stiffened against her rolling emotions. "Not really, but I sure as shootin' didn't want to go through it twice."

"Well, now you know. He's not the one for you."

Elle's laugh lightened her own sadness. "I wanted him to be, but when I looked close, Miss Anna, I saw the truth."

"One doesn't sit before the Lord long without learning to hear the unspoken."

"The New York gallery owner called too. The one Heath McCord put me in touch with and—"

"Heath McCord. Reminds me of my Lem. Now he's one to mourn losing."

Elle laughed over her tears. "Are you turning matchmaker on me?"

"No, no, just saying, you know, in case you wondered about my opinion."

"We're only friends." Great friends, if she thought about it.

"I suppose it's wise not to jump into another emotional dance just yet."

Elle grinned at Miss Anna's choice of words, suddenly warm with the memory of dancing with Heath.

"Tell me about this art woman."

"Mitzy Canon. She's a voice in the art world and called me to say clearly I was an amateur and to assure me of her opinion. She sent my work to other gallery owners and critics who agreed with her."

Miss Anna laughed. "I see. God is making it hard on Himself. Upping the ante so He can prove Himself to you."

"Doesn't feel like He's on my side at all right now."

"Oh, oh, my dear friend, how will you ever learn of His goodness and faithfulness if you never slay a Goliath? Nothing is impossible with Him."

Miss Anna grabbed the back of the pew, pulling herself to her feet, and gathered her Bible, pocketbook, and old sweater. "See you in the morning."

Elle decided to pray awhile longer. "I'll be here."

Miss Anna paused in the open doorway, her face sweet and cherubic, her eyes almost glowing. "Yes, I know, you will."

"Wally. Hey, it's Elle Garvey . . . I'm good. Listen, I was wondering . . ." She paced the studio, feeling silly now that she'd called him, but she wanted something to do with her days. Add a little cash to her flow, avoid draining all her savings until she earned a living in art again. "Do you have any openings on your lawn crews?"

He guffawed. Loud, in her ear, slapping his palm against the steering wheel, repeating her story to whoever sat next to him. "It's Elle Garvey, wanting a job . . ."

"Wally, I'm serious. I'm sort of in a setback here and thought I could use a job to get me out of the studio . . . I can't understand why you're . . . Wally, stop laughing . . ."

Elle pressed End. Okay, maybe it was a crazy idea, but, *aurgh,* couldn't she have control over some element of her life? She kicked a leg of her easel. It teetered and swayed. Her reaction was emotional, even after a night's sleep and a morning of prayer, but she'd decided to slay her Goliath by giving up on painting and men for a while.

The idea of sweating in the hot sun, challenging her muscles, letting the lowcountry sun brown her skin appealed to her. For now.

The studio stairs rattled and Elle looked toward the door. She recognized the distinct sound of someone taking two steps at a time. When he landed on the top step, she called, "Come in, Heath. The door's open."

He breezed in. "How'd you know it was me?"

"The rhythm of your step, running up, two at a time."

"So, you're on to me." He smiled, white against brownish red.

"Yeah, McCord, I'm on to you." Elle gathered the papers on her work table—bills, printed e-mails, notes she'd jotted during prayer, mostly painting ideas—and stacked them in a neat pile.

"Are you okay?"

Elle dusted the table with her hand. "Yeah, I'm fine. Why?"

"I heard you coming home the other night with Jeremiah."

Hmm, right. "I gave him his ring back. It's over."

"I'm sorry, Elle." He bent to see her face.

She swatted in the air in front of him. "No, you're not. Say it: you were right. He's a self-focused egomaniac. Should've known when he stumbled over how to spell *renaissance*."

Heath wrinkled his expression. "Renaissance?"

"Long story, but I used to say the man I married had to spell *renaissance*. Sort of my litmus test, after finding out if he loved Jesus, naturally."

Staring across the studio, Heath moved his lips, the letters tumbling off his breath. "R-e-n-a-i-s-s-a-n-c-e. *Renaissance*."

Elle rang an imaginary bell. "Ding-ding. We have a winner, Johnny. Tell the man what he's won. Okay, I'll tell you, Bob. A grand, fun-filled life married to Elle Garvey. Just say . . ."—she slowed— ". . . I do and . . ." She stopped. He was looking at her. Warm, she felt really warm. "Shew, what is up with this old AC?"

Heath billowed his T-shirt. "Is it on the fritz? It's roasting in here."

Rachel Hauck

Elle clicked the knob up one, then glanced back at Heath. "Better?"

"Much." He picked at a thick drop of paint on the table. "It's good you tried with Jeremiah, Elle. Really. Now you know."

Elle paced the studio, starting to feel the clutter.

"I didn't see Jer was wrong for me because I didn't want to see. Me, a college-educated woman, head in the sand."

"Don't put yourself down, Elle. It took a lot of courage to walk away from a successful, good-looking man offering you love, commitment, and marriage."

"Like you were his biggest fan."

"But I'm yours. And I didn't want to see you with a phony like him."

She snatched the broom from the corner. "I used to think women who stayed with cheating or abusive men were crazy and stupid. Now I understand a little bit why they do it." Her eyes watered. "What if I didn't have a good family, friends, a mentor like Miss Anna? What if I didn't know Jesus? How can they walk away from the one bit of security being offered, even if it meant enduring some pain?"

"You're right, Elle. Makes me grateful."

"Look at me whining. You lost your wife. I can't imagine, Heath." Elle pointed to him with the tip of the broom handle.

"Elle, I'm going back to New York in September."

She stopped with the broom. "I see."

"Rock needs me and Nate's not having much success with my book. Another publisher turned me down."

"Mitzy Canon turned me down."

His torso collapsed with disappointment. "What'd she say?"

"Blah, blah, immature, blah, blah, no good, blah, blah, second opinion of critics and gallery owners, blah, blah, you should do something else with your life, blah, blah."

"Forget her. She's a New York art scene snob."

262

"Then why'd you drag my name past her? She told me to go back to my hole in the wall."

"But you won't." Heath hopped off the stool and walked over to the wall of paintings. "Elle, every time I see your work, I feel something."

"Like you're going to be sick?"

"Stop, no. I feel hope, inspiration." He shrugged. "Makes me want to go write something, create with words what you create with colors."

"Then be my guest, take the paintings. Give them to friends and family for Christmas."

He exhaled. Elle almost felt his wind on her side of the studio. "You're showing these in the Summer Art Walk."

"I called Darcy today and canceled. She's ticked, but she'll get over it. Jeremiah was dead on about one thing: if your work isn't excellent, don't go trying out for the A-team."

"He's your number one fan, is he?" Heath set the feather painting down, picking up another one. Downtown Beaufort.

"I threw his phone in the river and——" Elle snorted, leaning on the broom.

Heath snapped his gaze to her. "You didn't."

"Called him a phone whore."

"Bold." He smirked.

"I thought so." Three days later, it was still funny.

"Why'd you throw his phone in the river?"

"Because I was trying to talk to him and he kept taking calls about football players and, yo, how cool was his team. It was stupid and I shouldn't have done it, but it brought our relationship to center stage."

Elle leaned the broom against the table and straightened the paintbrush carousel. Huckleberry was coming by for a lesson. "So, New York. Are you taking Tracey-Love?"

"I thought I might."

"Rio will bawl her eyes out."

"TL too. She loves Rio. And you."

"She's very special, Heath. Ava would be proud." Elle opened the turpentine jar, dipped in a paper towel, and wiped down her already cleaned palette. "Did you read the letter yet?"

"I've tried, keep getting interrupted. Visitors, phone calls. But I'll make my summer-end deadline. It's time, I know it."

"You'll get your book published, Heath."

"You'll show your paintings around the world."

"Ha, not if I don't paint them."

"If I promise to keep writing, will you promise to keep painting?"

She tossed the paper towels in the garbage, then knotted the white bag. "Maybe. Maybe."

When she walked around the table, the trash bag dangling from her fist, Heath reached out and molded her into his embrace, his cheek firm against her hair.

Dropping the trash, Elle gripped him, burying her face into the soapy fragrance of his shirt.

To: Elle Garvey
From: CSweeney
Subject: Coming home

Elle,

Mitch and I decided today to be in Beaufort for Christmas. I cannot wait. Let's take out my old boat and drift on the Coosaw.

I'd write more, but Carlos and I are off to Thailand for a meeting.

Love you, Caroline

Lights turned low. A quiet calm in the cottage. Heath roamed down to Tracey-Love's room, the bare floor cold against his bare Fred Flintstones.

It'd been several nights since he woke up with her curled against his back. He prayed the returned to New York wouldn't set her back but add to the strength of her lowcountry victory.

Sitting on the edge of the bed, careful not to wake her, Heath pondered his decision. Not that he could change his mind, but once a child was involved, the ramifications were greater.

"I've been meaning to tell you, we're going back to New York, TL," he whispered into the dark. "No, not right away, but in a few weeks, after Labor Day. I talked to Granddad. We'll spend Thanksgiving with him and Uncle Mark, Aunt Linda, and the cousins."

He shoved aside the emotion of missing Elle.

Straightening her covers, Heath wandered into the living room, then the kitchen. Without pausing to think about it, he reached for the letter, flipped it over, and tore open the envelope. Two pages fell out and he carried them to the living room.

Heath,

Babe, I'm in a hurry, but I have to write my thoughts before we move out. I hated getting cut off in the middle of our discussion. You were angry with me, and it's unsettling to be at odds. Especially when I'm thousands of miles away. Lately it seems we are trying to fight for control. And, Heath, I don't want that. Neither do you, I imagine.

Don't be angry with me for being on this assignment. It's just something I have to do, and I believe God is with me. Pray to Him for your peace and mine.

I wanted to tell you this news in person, but I can't wait. Besides, a man has a right to know he's going to become a father, doesn't he? How and when he hears the news isn't as important as the news itself, right?

I'm pregnant, Heath. I wasn't feeling well and just thought it was fatigue from the hectic summer schedule, but then I got to thinking . . .

A test confirmed it. I should've told you first thing when I called tonight. Maybe we wouldn't have argued. Maybe we would've argued more. I'm sorry, babe.

I'm about eight weeks now, give or take. The last few months have been so busy I've hardly noticed anything about myself.

Surprise, right? First we didn't want any and now we have two. Maybe this one will have my feet since our dear girl has your boxy ones.

I'll be home before the end of the first trimester. I know it's hard to believe, but this pregnancy only fuels my passion to raise awareness for the medical conditions for women here in Iraq. Their hospitals and clinics are raided. The villages are subject to attacks, abductions, and intimidations. We are so free, Heath, and they are still wanting and waiting.

I was thinking of a little brother for Tracey-Love? We could name him Ben-Love. Ha-ha, get it? Been love . . . okay, I know, too corny for a woman of my education and sophistication.

In three weeks, I'll be home and celebrating our new child with you. I hope he has your eyes, nose, and mouth—because they are so perfect—and your athletic ability. But my brains.

Kiss TL for me. Tell her I love her and miss her terribly. I'll call you the first moment I can.

I love you, as you know I do, so very much.

Your girl, Ava

The pages fluttered from his fingers to the floor.

Twenty-Six

Billowing clouds with rain-filled bottoms mounted in an azure sky as Elle drove to morning prayer, a slight yearning to sit in His presence swirled inside her.

The chapel came into view, and Elle tapped the brake, turning into the parking lot. The maintenance crew had finally fixed the front window and removed the plywood cover so the old building no longer looked like a set extra from *Pirates of the Caribbean*.

The chapel floor moaned under her footsteps as Elle walked down the aisle. Miss Anna's spot by the altar was vacant.

Elle set her Bible and notebook down, sitting where the woman normally knelt, drawing her knees to her chest.

Hey, God, it's me, Elle. For the first time in her life, she was beginning to understand why He was the Prince of Peace.

"Elle?"

She opened one eye. *Jesus?*

"Elle?"

Jesus sounded a lot like Julianne. Elle opened her eyes and looked over her shoulder. "Hey, what are you doing here?"

She stood at the end of the aisle, stiff yet trembling with a haunting stare. Her chestnut hair was scooped back in a loose, uneven ponytail, like she'd fix it on the run. A brown stain dotted her orange top.

"Jules?" Elle got up from the floor.

"I can't sleep, I can't eat." Her sister twisted her hands together, then raked them through her hair, pulling more strands from the blue scrunchy. "My heart pounds so hard I can't breathe. I'm nervous. I snap at Rio. Last night she tipped over her milk and I almost slapped her in the face."

Julianne raised her hand in demonstration, then broke into a deep moan, sobs melting her frozen posture.

"Shh, it's going to be okay." Elle held her shoulders with her arms and led her to the front row pew. "Tell me what's going on."

For a long while Julianne wept against Elle. Tears fell to her lap, leaving large, dark spots.

When she lifted her head, Elle's top was wet with sorrow. "Can you tell me what started all of this?" She snatched the box of tissues from the altar.

"You, that's who." Julianne ripped a couple of tissues from the box and wiped her naked cheeks.

"Me?" Elle thought back over the last few weeks. She'd barely seen Julianne.

"You just had to talk to me about Danny, about coming out with the truth." The pink ring around her eyes deepened to crimson. "Couldn't you tell him to mind his own business?"

"Julianne, did you want me to ignore him? 'Oh, hey, Danny, thanks for stopping by and telling me about you, Rio, and Jules. How 'bout them Clemson Tigers?' Sweetie, he wants to right a wrong. Give you and Rio his name."

Jules blew her nose. "I've told him a hundred times, I can't do it to Daddy and Mama."

"Is this really about Daddy and Mama? They love you, want the best for you and Rio."

Julianne lowered her head. "I'm such a disappointment to them."

"Where are you getting your information?"

"Come on, Elle. Mama didn't want another child after you."

Julianne tore at the wadded tissue in her hand. "I've heard her say it. Daddy wanted a son—"

"Jules, that's not fair. To you or them. Mama didn't want another child after Sara Beth came screaming into the world. And Daddy's never even so much as hinted at being disappointed in having girls."

"I know, I know, but it got stuck in my mind somewhere along the line, maybe when Mama ranted about not having a life of her own, or when Daddy ranted about too much estrogen in his house and where could a guy find a full roll of toilet paper?" Jules did a great imitation of Daddy searching for toilet paper.

"He's just a grumpy ole bear. You know he never meant it to sound like he'd rather have sons."

"He loves sports and none of us could care less. You, maybe, the only one remotely interested in listening to him talk about golf handicaps."

"Jules, Daddy loves you. I've always suspected you were his favorite since you look the most like Mama. And any one of us could've been a son. Don't throw yourself on that sword."

"I was the only one who didn't go to college. The only girl who didn't pledge Phi Mu."

"Okay, now you're playing the martyr."

The sobs cycled around again, and Julianne fell against Elle's shoulder, pressing a fresh tissue over her nose and mouth. Elle brushed her hair from her eyes and whispered under her breath, *God, I cannot, but You must deliver her. Please. Reveal Your love.*

Beautiful, elegant, commanding Julianne could no longer protect her Achilles' heel. Shame.

"I'll go with you," Elle finally said.

Julianne lifted her head and blew her nose again with a fresh tissue. "I know." Her voice was soft with tears. "But it won't change how I feel."

"Can I pray for you this time?"

Julianne tears pooled in the shallow crevasses of her face, around her nose and lips. "Do you think God will ever forgive me? I've done such a horrid thing." She cut a fast glance at Elle. "When we met, his wife was on the verge of coming back to him."

"Sin is sin, Jules. When and how much doesn't change God's ability or level of forgiveness. Only thing we deal with is the consequences. Your sin is not unforgivable. All you have to do is ask."

Julianne dropped to her knees with a thud, her weeping gentle at first, then nearly violent, her repentance vibrating through every word. "Oh, God, oh, God, oh, God, please, please, I'm so sorry, so sorry. F-f-forgive me, please. I can't, I can't take this shame any longer."

Tears rolled down Elle's cheeks as she stood in witness of her sister's redemption.

"Is this breaking and entering?"

"Maybe, but I *do* have a key." Elle had told Heath the first day that it unlocked her studio as well as the cottage. He stepped aside for Darcy Campbell to enter, reaching around for the light switch on the inside wall.

After Elle refused to give her paintings to Darcy, Heath had looked her up and asked if she was willing to do a little stealth work. Darcy cackled. "You've come to the right woman."

The plan? Wait for the right moment and steal the paintings. Okay, borrow them. This afternoon Heath stopped by the studio to say hi, see if he could figure out her coming and going.

Pay dirt. Dinner at her folks with Julianne. Tonight.

Darcy paused, taking in the studio, hands on her hips. "She lives here?"

"Temporarily." Heath tucked his key in his pocket. "Her paintings are over there."

For a long five minutes, Darcy studied each painting, shaking her head with an *um-um-um.* "You did right to call me, Heath." She picked up the *Feathers* painting. "This is fabulous."

"If you want them, let's go."

Darcy grabbed two of the six paintings she wanted and hurried to the door. "She's going to be mad, isn't she?"

"As a hornet." Heath carried the two largest paintings down the stairs to Darcy's waiting SUV. "But this is for her own good."

"Let's hope she sees it that way."

Heath slipped the paintings into the back, careful not to bump them. "I'll take the heat for this, Darcy. If she gets mad, blame me."

"What? And let you get all the glory?" Darcy's sandpaper laugh told him she liked a good fight.

"Have it your way."

"I like to think positive. Let's just call it delayed gratitude."

İn Mama's burgundy and oak dining room, the only sound was the clink of flatware against Pfaltzgraff dinner plates and the slurp of tea followed by, "This is good chicken, Mama" and "Can you pass the corn bread, please?"

Elle tried to think of a funny, distracting story to replace the suspecting silence, but her mind could conjure nothing. *Blank.*

On the drive over, she'd talked strategy with Julianne, who seemed oblivious to anything but her demise as a Garvey Girl.

"They are not going to disown you."

"I can hear Daddy now: 'You are dead to me.'"

"How many times have you actually seen *Fiddler on the Roof*?"

"Hundreds. Rio loves Tevye."

Elle took the opportunity to remind Jules that they lived in South Carolina and were in no way connected by faith or culture to nineteenth-century Russia and she should trust in the love of God if she couldn't trust in the love of her parents.

Halfway through his plate of dumplings, Daddy tossed his napkin to the table. "All right, what's going on? Elle, Julianne? I lived in a house full of women for forty years and it's never been this quiet. Only thing talking is the plates. Elle, is it Jeremiah? Is he still calling you?"

"No, Daddy. He's respecting my decision. We're over for good." Elle flipped her gaze to where Julianne shoveled a buttered wedge of corn bread into her mouth. The crumbling edges scattered in the corners of her mouth.

"You two haven't been this quiet since the womb. Lady, what do you think?"

"Tru, I'm just as curious as you." Mama reached back to the sideboard for the tea, refreshing everyone's drink though they didn't need it. When she set the pitcher down with a hard thunk, a burst of fear blipped in her blue eyes. "It's not Rio, is it?"

"No, Mama, no. It's not Rio," Julianne said with a dry, corn bread accent.

Gulping tea, Julianne tried again. "Daddy, Mama . . ." She stopped cold, like hitting a tree going a hundred miles an hour.

Daddy prodded. "Julianne?"

"I declare, you're scaring the good sense out of me." Mama resituated her chair, thumping the legs against the dining room carpet.

Julianne glance at Elle, who gave her a nod of courage. "I didn't bring Rio with me tonight because she's with her daddy."

Daddy stared. Mama's mouth dropped open, then clapped shut. Elle wanted to reach over and tip up Julianne's chin, knock off her veil of shame, but the confession was part of removing it forever.

"Who might that be?" Daddy asked, calm, gentle, not at all like a grumpy old bear.

"Julianne, that's wonderful." Mama added her special lilt to *wonderful*—an exaggerated tone meaning "What's going on?"

"I've always known who Rio's daddy was. I didn't tell because I didn't want anyone to know." Julianne stared at her hands in her lap.

"I see." Mama sounded exactly like a mama discovering one of her babies could not run to her in a time of trouble.

"Why are you bringing this to us now?" Daddy's voice balanced on the narrow line between compassion and command.

Julianne lifted her head, trying to smile. "Can you give me a minute?" She scooted away from the table and disappeared into the hall bathroom.

"What do you know about this, Elle?" Daddy asked, picking up his knife and fork, then putting them down again with a sigh.

"I just found out myself. Can you please be patient and understanding?"

"Is she afraid?" Daddy asked.

"A little. Mostly ashamed."

Mama cupped her forehead with her hand. "Land sakes, my heart is playing 'Seventy-six Trombones.' I never imagined she'd confess something like this. It's been over four years." Mama's face contorted as if she'd just figured something out. "Elle, is he a criminal, a murderer, married?"

"Mama, please, wait for Julianne."

Her little sister returned with her phone in her hand. "I called him. He's coming."

"Mind telling us who he is?" Daddy asked.

Julianne stood, hands resting on the back of her chair. "It's-it's Danny Simmons. He's Rio's daddy."

A silent and unseen *whoosh* dropped into the room. *All right, Julianne.*

The kitchen door slammed without a *Knock, knock, any-body home?* Heath glanced up. "Who's there?"

Elle's flip-flops slapped against the hardwood and she stood right over him, fists on her hips. "Where are they?"

Where are they? Heath took a moment to shift from nineteen forty-two to the present and think why Elle might be glaring at him with narrowed green eyes.

Ah, the paintings. "Where's what?"

"No, you stole them. My paintings." Her bracelets clattered as she flung her arm toward the studio.

No use trying to cover it up. "I called Darcy. She took them to her studio."

"How did she get in? Did you let her in?"

Heath stood to gain leverage in this argument. "You told me my key worked on the studio door, so—"

"Unbelievable." She swatted the air with her fists. Heath ducked, just in case. "You had no right, Heath. Who do you think you are?"

"A friend."

"No, a friend doesn't go sneaking around behind people's backs."

"But we do force each other to confront our fears."

She tapped her chest with her finger. "You take liberties with our friendship that aren't there. It's my work, my career, my decision. May I remind you that the last time you tried to push my work into a public forum, I was told to go sit at the kids' table and leave the real art to the adults?"

"I'm not letting you quit because of a snooty gallery owner."

"You beat all, you know it?"

"Elle, I see you driving to the chapel for prayer every morning. I see the peace riding on your countenance. And yet you have no faith that God is bigger than Mitzy Canon?"

She paused on the edge of the kitchen. "I would've never sent your book to an agent or editor, or even a friend to read, without your permission. Especially if you warned me about how insecure you felt. But that's exactly what you did to me."

Man, she was right. She was out the door before he could apologize. He chased her across the yard. "Elle, wait, stop." But she continued to her car in long, lean strides.

"Heath, you leave in a few weeks, right? A month? Let's just call a truce until then. You stay out of my way and I'll sure as shooting stay out of yours. I don't think I can afford your kind of friendship."

Twenty-Seven

The first night of the Summer Art Walk opened on a starless night the last weekend of August. The *Gazette* gave Elle's work a nice write up, but tonight Ruby Barnett would act as judge.

The morning after Heath and Darcy stole her paintings, Elle met the gallery owner on the historic homesite's front porch with a cup of coffee from Common Ground.

"I'm not giving you back your paintings. Keep the coffee."

"Then you leave me no choice. I'll call the law."

"Then you leave me no choice. I'll sue for breech of contract."

Check and mate.

So, for the better part of an hour, Elle loitered outside the gallery opening night just beyond the reach of the streetlights, watching Wild Heart Gallery visitors come and go.

So far, she hadn't heard anyone guffawing or grumbling.

"What are you doing out here?"

Startled, Elle jerked into the tree and scraped her arm on the bark. "Heath, what's the big idea sneaking up on people in the middle of the night?"

"Middle of the night? It's eight o'clock." He stood too close. "What are you doing out here?"

"What's it look like? *Not* going in."

"Are you seriously going to hide out here all night?"

"Yes."

He moved closer, violating her personal zone. "Still mad at me?"

Not really. "Of course."

His eyes lingered on her face before he walked off, down the street, disappearing in the brown shadows of evening fading to night.

Folding her arms, Elle propped against the tree, considering for a second Heath might, just might, have a point. Go inside, get it over with. Yesterday after prayer, she'd peered through Darcy's side window to glimpse her display.

The paintings didn't even look like hers—new frames, hanging on a burnt-yellow wall, the images vibrant and beautiful.

"I'm sorry."

Elle turned to see Heath with a single white rose. "Nice touch, McCord."

"Friends?"

She touched the slick pedals to her nose. "Yeah. Sorry I got so peeved."

"Sorry I borrowed your paintings." Heath grabbed her hand, gently tugging her up the main walk to the gallery's verandah. "I wouldn't miss your debut. Can I escort you inside?"

"Please."

Wild Heart Gallery shone, from the highly polished floor to the perfectly aimed lighting. The gallery fragrance was cinnamon with a subtle hint of drying oils.

Darcy preserved the home's original layout, using the formal dining room as her main showroom. And there she hung Elle's six paintings.

Candace's heels thunked and echoed in the dining room as she crossed over to meet Elle when she entered with Heath. "*Feathers* is a fantastic painting."

"It turned out."

Gallery guests moved in, then out. Mozart drifted over them from the mounted speakers.

Heath squeezed Elle's hand and she decided to stay in the comfort of his shadow. Sara Beth arrived a few minutes later with Parker, and after them Julianne and Danny.

The most beautiful thing in Darcy's gallery? A radiating, shameless Julianne. "Danny, didn't I tell you?" she said to her fiancé. "Elle's paintings are beautiful."

"Yes, you did. I might have to commission a few pieces for some of my buildings."

"Do it while you can, sweetie," Julianne said, "before she's famous and we can't afford her."

After Julianne's tense confession during dinner at Mama and Daddy's, Danny had arrived with Rio, bringing every raw emotion and question to the surface.

Daddy invited Danny into his study where they talked in loud, stoney tones. Mama entertained Rio with a book. Julianne stared out the French doors. Elle prayed in the kitchen.

But by the time she hugged the family good night, Julianne was in Danny's arms, Mama wiped tears from her cheeks, and Daddy agreed to his baby girl's November wedding.

"Julianne, there's Carl Yawn. Let's go say hi." Danny escorted his fiancée across the room.

Heath bent down to Elle's ear. "Is that Rio's father?"

"Yeah, she finally told Daddy and Mama. There I was doing a good deed for my sister while my friend robbed me blind."

Grinning, Heath rubbed his palms together. "What? We were also doing a good deed."

"Whatever." She bumped him with her hip.

Darcy entered with an elegant, poised black woman. "This is Elle Garvey's work, Ruby. Isn't it fascinating?"

Elle stepped from behind Heath. Might as well face the music.

"Only six? It's a good thing you're showing Sir Lloyd Parcel, Darcy, or I'd consider this a waste of time." Ruby dug in her low-slung black leather bag.

Only six? *She hates them already. Floor beneath me, open up.*

Darcy glanced toward Elle. "Ruby, this is the artist, Elle Garvey."

Elle approached, her hand extended. "It's lovely to meet you."

Ruby reluctantly gripped Elle's fingers. "So you say now, until you read my review."

Ruby Barnett walked slowly along Elle's display, observing each of the six paintings, taking notes. When she stopped in front of *Feathers*, she lowered her arms to her side, paper and pen gripped in her hand.

Candace and Sara Beth watched on the other side of Heath and Elle. Julianne returned, whispering, "Is that the reviewer? What's she doing?"

"Yes and I don't know."

Something about *Feathers* had her attention. Or disdain. For those who knew of the feathers apparition, the painting ministered. But if they didn't know, Elle wondered if her simple rendition of white feathers positioned against a midnight blue silk would evoke any emotion or interest at all.

After a moment, Ruby scribbled in her pad, then moved to the next painting. Elle watched the slow sag of her shoulders. She tried to write again, but stopped, putting her notepad in her bag.

"Darcy, where are the Sir Lloyd Parcels? I met him in London last year. A fascinating man."

Darcy didn't catch Elle's gaze. "His paintings are in the front room, Ruby. Are you sure you don't want to spend more—"

"The Parcels please."

"Through this door." Darcy motioned to her assistant, Christine. "Please bring Ms. Barnett some water."

Heath's broad hand slid along Elle's shoulder, a comforting gesture. "I'm sorry."

"How rude." Candace circled the small family gathering, "I'm going to go ask her what she—"

"Candace, don't you dare." Elle blocked her older sister. "You want to make it worse by insulting her? 'Elle Garvey's amateurish work was highlighted by her immature sister.'"

Candace conceded, frustration sharpening her expression. "Fine. For you, Elle. But she barely looked at them."

"She reviews hundreds of paintings a year, Candace. She doesn't have to look long to know what's good."

"Then I'm done here." Candy reached around Julianne to her husband, Alex. "Want to take your wife to dinner? Might as well take advantage of a night without the children. Jules, Danny, want to come? How about you two?" Candace regarded Elle and Heath.

"I think I'll stick around," Heath said.

"Me too." Elle recognized a familiar Presence in the ancient dining room and she wanted to stick around.

"Hey, Elle. Great stuff." Deputy J. D. Rand's booming voice broke the silence of the show room. A stunning, willowy brunette clung to his brawny arm. Nothing about J. D. was understated.

"Evening, J. D. You remember Heath McCord from Bodean's party."

"Yeah, bubba, good to see you." The men grasped hands. "This is Eloise Bell, new in town."

"Nice to meet you."

"Love your work."

Heath nudged Elle. Ruby had returned and stood in front of *Feathers*. J. D. moved on with Eloise.

"Ruby." Darcy joined her. "Are you all right?"

"Yes." Her answer faded between the *y* and the *s*.

Elle and Heath waited by the stairwell, watching. When Ruby lowered her chin to her chest and her shoulders collapsed, Darcy whispered to her.

Ruby sobbed, shaking her head, mumbling, slowly sinking to the floor.

Darcy disappeared in the powder room off the front left, returning with a tissue box, and knelt next to Ruby.

More gallery visitors entered, spotted Ruby on the floor, then exited.

"This is why you paint, Elle," Heath whispered. "You touch people in the hidden places."

Maybe it'd been five minutes, perhaps fifteen, but when Ruby lifted her head, she gazed back at Elle with glossy eyes.

"My father was a musician," she said, propping herself up with her hand flat on the floor. "Traveled all over the south with a blues band, sending home what money he didn't spend on food and women for my brother James and me. I was twelve years old, hiding five- and one-dollar bills from my mama in a cigar box under my bedroom floor board so she wouldn't spend it on bourbon."

"You never told me this story, Ruby," Darcy said.

Heath shoved Elle closer.

"I've pushed so much out of my mind, Darcy. We lived on the outskirts of Charleston, nothing much more than a shack. But James and I kept it clean, studied hard in school, looked after Mama."

"What is it about the feathers, Ruby?" Darcy asked.

"So many things," she muttered. "One hot summer afternoon, right after the war, Daddy was heading off to one of his gigs. Mama fought him like there was no tomorrow. I hid under my bed, the mattress springs snatching my plaits, tucking my head in my arms, crying, praying for Mama to leave him alone. Doors slammed. Mama cracked Daddy's cheek with her hand, begging and screaming for him to stay home, get a job shrimping or working construction. But music was Daddy's true love." Darcy ran her hands over Ruby's shoulders. "My mama warned me against a tuba player.

"Next thing I hear is '*Pssst*, Ruby, baby.' There was Daddy standing at my window with two perfect white feathers." Ruby gazed up at the painting. "Just like the ones in this painting."

"They fell out of nowhere," Elle offered. "One in a prayer chapel, two at my studio."

Ruby shoved off the floor and Heath steadied her with a touch to her elbow. She dusted off her navy linen suit. "Daddy claimed they were from our guardian angels, said they'd keep James and me safe.

But I wanted Daddy safe. "Don't worry about me none. If the Germans couldn't kill me . . . He was larger than life, my daddy."

"What happened to him?" Elle asked.

Ruby glanced back at her, then strode over to the painting. "Never came home. When his letters stopped, Mama tried to find him, but we never got to the truth. We heard he took up with a white girl in Mississippi and got lynched. Another rumor was the band's car went off the road in a bad storm. Mama lived for bourbon. James and I left home as soon as we could. I'd stored Daddy's feathers in a cedar box under the bedroom floorboard. During my college years, the house burned down, the fire destroying the feathers. All I had left of my daddy were those feathers. I grieved for them until now."

"Ms. Barnett, please, take the painting. My gift to you."

"Miss Garvey, I'm a reviewer. If I received art as gifts, I'd never be able to write an honest word. I buy the art I love." Ruby's gentle laugh dispelled the last ribbons of tension. "Darcy, I'd like to purchase this piece, please."

"Wise decision, Ruby." Darcy gave Elle the I-told-you glare.

"I haven't cried over my daddy in many years, but a debut artist brought the harsh reviewer to her knees."

"Perhaps I had help from the Divine."

Ruby retrieved her handbag, taking out her notepad and pen. "Of that, I have no doubt."

Truman and Lady had volunteered to keep Tracey-Love if Heath wanted to go to Elle's opening night. *Push, push, hint, hint.*

It'd been a long time since a girl's father observed Heath with a glint in his eye. On second thought, had any father looked at him with a glint in his eye?

Ava's pop had merely given him the once-over with a low grunt and said, "He'll do."

Heath liked having Truman's respect and cloaked blessing, but he was days away from leaving St. Helena and did not want to start what he couldn't finish.

Elle's good-bye to Jeremiah still echoed over the murky waters of Coffin Creek.

She turned into her parents' drive behind him and Heath met her at the front steps. "I can't shake Ruby's story."

"Every time I picture her sitting on the floor, sobbing, I tear up." Elle gripped his shirt sleeve. "It's humbling, Heath. To be used by God when my faith was so weak, after being so angry with you and Darcy."

He slipped his hand into hers. "This is only the beginning, Elle. You probably won't know how many people your work touches, but Ruby is a drop in the bucket."

She pressed her forehead to his chest and wept softly. He held her, letting the Spirit complete what He'd begun.

"I'm a mess," Elle said, finally stepping away, wiping her cheeks. "Good thing Sara Beth's makeup is waterproof."

"You're lovely, Elle, tears and all." Heath pinched her chin with his fingers and brushed under her eyes. "But you'd better tell Sara Beth her waterproof mascara formula isn't working."

Elle started for the house. "Um, no, you tell her. Last time I gave input . . . was the last time."

Just inside the Garvey door, Tracey-Love accosted Heath. "Daddy." Then Elle. "Miss Elle."

Rio smacked them with her dazzling wand. "We're princesses."

"I see. Very pretty."

Tracey-Love patted her satin play dress. "I'm Cinder-nella. Rio's S-snow White."

Heath scooped her up. "And I'm your handsome prince."

"No, no." TL laughed as though he'd lost his marbles. "You're my daddy. Zac Efron is my prince."

Heath set Tracey-Love down with a gaping glance at Elle. *What the heck?* "Who is Zac Efron?"

"*High School Musical* star. Rio's babysitter has a teenaged daughter." She shook her head.

Truman clapped him on the back. "Welcome to my world, son. Can I get you a root beer?"

"Please, and leave out the root."

Elle propped her elbows on the counter, grinning, munching on a couple of baby carrots.

Screaming and swooping, touching everything they passed with their sparkling wands, TL and Rio disappeared upstairs.

Elle kissed her mama's cheek as she carried empty ice-cream bowls to the dishwasher.

"Tell me, how was the big debut? Elle, we're going by the gallery tomorrow night with Doug and Esther."

"Better than I thought. People seemed to like the paintings."

Heath made a face. Ten minutes ago, she'd wept against him, moved by how the Lord used her. "Elle, tell them what happened."

"It's nothing, really, but . . ." She recounted Ruby Barnett's story with Heath interjecting the adjectives and details Elle was too shy or humble to add.

Truman and Lady listened. None of it seemed to surprised them.

"This is only the beginning, Elle," Truman said.

"Exactly what I told her."

"We'll see. Ruby Barnett is one woman."

Heath chugged his root beer and talked a minute of golf with Truman while Elle discussed Julianne and Danny's November wedding with Lady.

When Tracey-Love popped into the kitchen, Heath herded her toward the van. "It's past your bedtime, kiddo."

"See you back at the ranch," Elle said as she steered Rio toward her car.

One minute down the road, TL fell asleep. Heath glimpsed at her in the rearview mirror, slumped over in her car seat. Returning to New York was going to be way harder than he ever imagined.

At the cottage, Heath scooped up Tracey-Love. Hard to believe the dog-tired girl had been a fairy princess an hour ago.

With Elle, he tucked the sleeping beauties into bed and flipped off the light.

"Want to sit on the screen porch? It's a nice night." He wasn't ready to end his evening with her.

"Yes, I want to sit and think, let tonight sink all the way in."

A dewy scent perfumed the breeze as it brushed against the screen. "Rain," Heath said absently, moving his chair closer to Elle's.

"There's this . . ."—she pressed her hand over her stomach— ". . . feeling, as if I've just done something I was born to do. Isn't that weird?"

"No, I think we all have those special moments."

"What if y'all hadn't taken the paintings? What if Darcy had caved and returned them to me? What a blessing I would've missed."

"But you didn't. So don't think about it."

"This year . . ."—emotion slanted her words—". . . was so very hard. But God in His mercy and wisdom is redeeming it, redeeming me."

Heath put the iron rocker into motion with the heel of his foot. "One sleepless night after Ava died, I clicked on the TV, stopping for some unknown reason to watch a very dramatic preacher. Man, he was annoying, but he said one thing that hit me so hard it carried me through the next months. Jesus, he said, knew the splendor and glory of life after the Cross. It's why He hung there, died, and rose again, making all of heaven's beauty available to us. Everyone. I remember he said 'everyone' over and over. I understood he meant me—broken, hurting, angry Heath McCord. Made my trial seem bearable."

"It's true, just hard to comprehend."

"I read Ava's letter."

Elle turned to see his face. "When?"

"About a week ago."

"Can you tell me . . . I mean, was it a good letter?"

"It was odd reading her words, mentioning things as if they were yesterday, but knowing it'd been over a year. She apologized for our fight, but I couldn't even remember some of the things we said."

"Are you glad?"

"Glad I read it, glad she wrote it. I want to save it for Tracey-Love so she can read a little about her mother's passion for the job she was doing, see her handwriting. In this computer age, I'm not sure I have anything of hers handwritten. A few cards, maybe."

Elle sat back in her chair. "Doesn't seem fair that you can't respond."

"A response now would only be for me and my comfort. She's in a better place, doesn't need my apology. But there was a final part to her letter."

"Good or bad?"

"She was pregnant." The wind shoved the screen making the porch lights appear to sway.

Elle jerked around, her shock showing in her wide eyes. "Oh my gosh, you're kidding. You didn't know? At all? Did you want more children?"

"We'd changed up"—he cleared his throat—"some things, so it was a possibility, but we weren't trying. In the letter, she was very excited."

Slipping out of her chair, Elle knelt next to him, her hand easy on his knee, like the night in the ER. "Are you okay?"

He wrapped their fingers together. "I spent a few days thinking and processing, praying. I was a little mad, but I'm tired of being ruled by death, ruled by the past. I'm happy to know I'll see another child some day, but it's done." Heath peered into her eyes. "Does that make me sound harsh?"

"No, just human and that you're finally healing."

He traced the curve of her jaw. "I'm going to miss you."

"And what am I going to do without you, carving angels in my yard, teaching me to break china, kicking me in the pants when I want to quit?" She pressed her cheek against his palm.

"You are so much stronger than you know, Elle. Don't you know how much you've brought healing to me and Tracey-Love, caused me to open my heart again?" Brushing his hand over her sleek hair, he thought if his heart let go, he'd cradle her on his lap and kiss . . . "I just remembered something."

Elle slipped back into her chair as he went inside and returned with a CD, flashing it in front of Elle before popping it into the boom box.

"What is it? I didn't see the jacket."

"You'll see." He flicked the On switch, pushed a button, and the jazzy melody of "Neither One of Us" spilled from the speakers. "Dance with me."

As she stepped into him, Heath inhaled the scent of her skin, felt the curve of her hip beneath his palm, and led her in a slow sway to the melody of their beating hearts.

Twenty-Eight

After buckling Tracey-Love into her car seat, Heath jogged up the studio steps two at a time. "Elle, are you home?" The door rattled under his light knock.

She opened, sleepy-eyed and sexy. His hand tingled with the ghost feeling of holding her the other night. "What's up?"

"Got something to show you." He followed her halfway across the studio, but kept his distance. Their last dance had awakened a spark of love and he didn't want to fan any flames. "What'd you do last night, party?"

"Ha, yeah, me and Mama, helping Jules plan her wedding, woo, tying one on." She stooped to the mini-fridge, twisted open a Diet Coke. "I can't wake up today. After prayer, I came home and fell asleep."

He made a face. "You okay, planning your sister's wedding?"

"Oh my gosh, yes. Please, get the girl married." She raked her hand through her tousled hair. "I'm way over my own marriage fiasco. Besides, I haven't seen Jules this happy since before Rio was born." She offered him a cola.

He declined. "But can you spare an hour or two to go with me? I want to show you something."

"Sure, I was going to pick up Rio from the babysitter for Jules. Is Tracey-Love in school or with you?"

"She's in the van. Let's get Rio and go."

"Not so fast, now. Where to and is food involved?"

"It's a surprise and food most definitely can be involved."

"Can I have five minutes to shower?"

Heath's eyes widened. "Five minutes? Marry me."

"Okay," she said in a lazy, sleepy voice.

His pulse thumped. *You're messing with me, Garvey. And you don't even know it.*

"See you in the van. Five minutes."

At 7-Eleven, Heath gassed up and bought Elle a couple of sugary donut sticks at the check-out counter. He tossed them to her when he slipped behind the wheel. "I believe this fulfills the food requirement."

She tore them open. "What, no coffee to dunk them in? Cheapskate."

He grinned and turned the ignition. "Can't set the bar too high. Won't be able to live up to my stellar reputation. Which way to pick up Rio?"

"Yeah, got to protect that stellar rep. Turn left out of here, then the first right."

After picking up Rio from Shirley's, Heath drove out to St. Helena Island with the windows down, the radio blasting a Sara Evans's tune, and the wind filling the van. At Cusabo Road, he eased off the gas and drove up to a pale-yellow clapboard house nestled among pines and live oaks.

He cut the engine and popped open his door. "Well, what do you think?"

Elle stepped out as Heath unbuckled the girls. "Are you buying this?"

"Yep." Swinging TL up in his arms, he stood beside Elle, who gripped Rio's hand. "My own St. Helena cottage. Nothing fancy, but when Marsha Downey brought me out here, I fell in love with it."

Tracey-Love smacked her palms to the side of Heath's face. "Are we going to live here, Daddy?"

He touched his nose to hers. "Yes, when we visit. Want to see inside?"

"Yeah." She squirmed to join Rio and took Elle's other hand. The three of them walked under the canopy of shade toward the front steps.

The scene tugged at Heath. It felt too much like a family. He was leaving, moving back, joining Rock's battle. He'd already been reading case histories, gearing up for his first day while the novel languished.

But Elle, unlike Ava who charged his young-man lusts and challenged his ego, caused him to pioneer a new part of his soul, discovering an area of his heart reserved for her.

Was it possible to find first love a second time?

Heath conjured up images of them, aging and gray, sitting on the cottage porch chatting about the kids. She'd paint in a sunlit corner while he tapped out his next best seller. And when the moon rose to its phoenix above the circle of the earth, he'd take her in his arms and dance to the melody of their hearts.

"Heath. Hey, bubba, did you hear me? Are you going to add a porch?" Elle stood on the short board steps, smiling.

Sweat beaded on his brow. And he stood in the shade. "Um, yeah, add on. Sure. Hadn't thought much about it, but why not?"

"This side of the house will get the good evening shade. A porch would be perfect."

Beautiful, dude, you're fantasizing about your twilight years with a woman who's fantasizing about front porches and the evening shade.

Elle stepped aside as he unlocked the door.

Inside, she spun around to see every angle. "I know why you fell in love with it."

"The seller did the remodel."

The house was prettier to him this afternoon than when he'd toured it with Marsha. The pine floor shone like glass in the light falling through the windows. The pinkish-beige walls cast warm hues, and Elle stood in the middle of it all.

"It's so bright." She walked to the far corner and peered out the window. "I could paint in here."

"I'll leave you the key. Use it any time."

She swerved to face him, arms crossed. "It's sinking in now, you leaving."

"Yeah, I know." He jingled his keys. Did he hear longing in her voice? "Elle, I want to——"

Tracey-Love burst into the great room with Rio chasing her. "Which room is mine, Daddy?"

"Any one but the big one." Heath winked at Elle.

"Will you have time to visit?" she asked.

"Not at first. Maybe by spring."

"By spring?" she echoed in a whisper.

Heath agreed—spring was a long way away. "So, how about the fireplace? It was redone. And in here, they gutted the kitchen, knocked out a wall to create the great room."

"It's a lovely place, Heath." Elle leaned against the granite counter and for the first time since he'd met her, he felt the lingering heat of her gaze. "What were you going to say before, a few minutes ago?"

"I don't know. It's hard to formulate——"

Tracey-Love and Rio must have gone wild. From the back of the house, doors slammed and banged, screams echoed down the hall.

"Hey, TL, Rio, you're shaking the rafters. Come in here, we'll go outside."

A blonde and brunette torpedo-fired into the kitchen, bypassed Heath and Elle, and slam-bammed out the kitchen door to the backyard. "A swing!"

"Man, it's like watching the Road Runner chase Speedy Gonzales."

"She's a long way from the scared girl who stuttered," Elle said, walking to the back door, gazing out.

"You're part of that reason, Elle. She needed a woman in her life."

"She's easy to love, Heath. Ava would be proud."

"Somehow, I think she's watching, cheering us on." Heath pressed the screen-door handle. "Want to check out the backyard?"

Elle tipped her head. "Of course. I hear it has a swing."

Under an ancient live oak, Rio and Tracey-Love attempted to climb into the tire swing, without success. Heath picked up one, then the other, threaded them through the tire hole, and gave them a gentle push. The breeze carried a scent of fall.

"The falls are nice in New York," Elle said out of nowhere, reaching for the live oak's swinging tendrils of Spanish moss. "Football season, crisp days, and cool nights."

"And I'll be holed up in an office, leaving too late to see the day, riding a dark subway home."

"I could never do what you do."

"I could never do what *you* do."

"And what is that? I'm nothing special."

"You can't still believe that. What is it with beautiful, talented women and insecurity?"

"Comes with the territory?"

Heath laughed. "Run it out of town on a rail then. Elle, you spend five mornings a week sitting before the King of Kings. Worship is not a one-way street. As much as you want to give to Him, He longs to give to you. Stop resisting."

Elle stood silently. Heath gave the tire a big shove. Had he overstepped his bounds?

"You're right, Heath. I forget and focus on my weakness too much."

"Don't we all." He wanted to segue into the interrupted kitchen conversation, but Rio erupted, screaming, followed by Tracey-Love, squealing. One of them wanted out of the swing and did something to the other, and in a split second the backyard was filled with screaming.

"All right, you two, stop. Rio, TL didn't pull your hair on purpose." Heath slipped the girls from the swing. "Where're your dolls?"

"In my room." TL crossed her arms with a pout at Rio.

"Run get them so we can go. Who wants food?"

Everyone.

"What do you want to do for dinner?" He grabbed at the end of Elle's flying hair.

"I haven't grilled out at all this summer."

He raised a brow. "Burgers on the barbie?"

"Burgers on the barbie."

Every once in a while, Elle glanced up from her art book open on her lap to watch Heath sand the last pointy edge off the angel. About an hour of daylight remained and he boasted finishing the carving before he left next week.

They'd had a fun day, the four of them—Heath, Elle, Tracey-Love, and Rio—seeing Heath's new place, stopping by Publix for dinner fixings, refereeing spats between Tracey-Love and Rio.

With the aroma of grilled burgers still hanging in the air, Julianne and Danny stopped by. They ate the final two burger patties, finished up the barbeque chips, then called for Rio. "Time to go home."

Tonight was the first phase of easing Rio toward the truth about Mr. Danny.

As they pulled away, Heath tossed TL into the bath, then into bed while Elle cleaned the kitchen.

Not ready to call it a night, Elle decided to flip through art books while Heath carved.

"Watch for splinters, McCord," Elle hollered before going back to her book. Danny planned to commission a piece for his Hilton Head office and Elle wanted to get ideas about creating a piece with strong shadow and light.

"Ha, you just want to jab me with a needle again." Heath stood back, surveying his work.

Elle set her book aside and strolled across the lawn in her bare feet. "Are you taking the angel with you?"

Heath wiped the perspiration from his forehead. "Certainly don't want to haul it to Manhattan. I can leave it here or take it to my new place."

Elle smoothed her palm over the high arch of the angel's wing. "This may sound strange, but I believe there's an angel standing guard over the prayer chapel. Can we take it over there?"

"Absolutely."

Twenty-Nine

To: CSweeney
From: Elle Garvey
Subject: Love?

Have crush on my tenant, Heath. But he leaves in a few days. Can hang on to my heart until then. He's just so . . . real. I feel like he knows me better than I know myself. He's widowed but dealing with it, honest with himself, with me. Sigh.

How are you?
Love, Elle

August 1942

Chet entered the log-shaped Quonset briefing hut with the rest of the squadron leaders. The round-walled room contained a desk, four short rows of chairs, and Colonel Chennault standing by a map of the Aleutian Islands.

Taking a seat on the back row near the heater, Chet didn't like the swirl in his stomach. Something was up.

Lt. Jason Web sat next to him, the collar of his mackinaw flipped up and tucked around his neck. Winter temperatures iced the early

September days. *"Now I know how a popsicle feels, thanks to Uncle Sam."*

"Relax, Web, it's still summer," Chet said. *"Wait until fall."*

When the minute hand exactly hit the hour, Chennault launched into his briefing. "We're advancing."

Chet sat forward. Yeah, something was up. Just when Umnak started to feel like home. They had movies in the evenings, electricity, and decent chow.

Chennault slapped the map with his pointer. "Adak is two hundred and fifty miles from the enemy on Kiska. We're moving in next door, boys."

When the colonel finished the briefing, he tossed a small black box at Chet. "Captain McCord, I think these major clusters will look good on you."

Chet caught his promotion in midair. "Thank you, sir."

He'd write to Kelly tonight and tell her of his reward and advancement, though he'd rather tell her he was coming home.

Nine o'clock. Heath shoved his laptop aside, his legs burning. His shoulders were tight from concentrating so hard on the scene. This was his last night to work on the story before the business of Calloway & Gardner consumed him.

A little more than halfway through the book, he figured with some focused weekend evenings he could have it done in five or six months. If Rock didn't work him to death.

But he felt at odds with himself, as if he'd driven too far down the road after taking the wrong exit. It'd be hard to get back.

Just the anticipation of leaving.

Wandering down the hall, stepping over the boxes he'd packed—most of it Tracey-Love's new toys—he flipped on the hall light to peek in on his daughter. Her long legs and arms were sprawled across the bed, with tangled strands of hair flowing over her pillow.

Two days ago he'd dropped three hundred dollars updating her wardrobe when it seemed overnight her little jeans had turned into flood-waters and her shirts barely covered her belly.

She'd turn five in November and be another year closer to the dreaded puberty.

Gently he moved her legs under the blanket and tucked the edges around her shoulders. Sitting on the edge of her bed, he dropped his arms over his knees.

"What do you think, Tracey-Love? Should Daddy just grab Miss Elle, kiss her until she can't breathe, tell her there's more where that came from and walk away, hoping she'll chase me?" His confession sparked a laugh. "Daddy must think a lot of his kissing, huh?"

Her quiet breathing serenaded him. Good thing she slept. He reckoned a four-year-old didn't need to hear about her daddy's love life.

For a while, Heath prayed and listened, then wandered into the kitchen where he nuked a cup of day-old coffee and stepped around to the screened porch.

The moonless night was warm and cottony. But before he could sit, his phone went off. This late. Had to be Nate.

"How's the World War II masterpiece?"

Heath sipped his coffee. "Masterpiece? Kind of a big word for my small book."

"I sold it."

"Come again." The iron chair creaked when Heath dropped down.

"Bell Harbor Press loved it, Heath. Of course, the manuscript needs some work, but when I talked to their senior acquisitions editor, Wade Donovan, he said they'd been looking for a war book and yours is the one they want. He loves your writing and made a solid offer."

Heath might regret this confession, but, "Nate, the book isn't finished. Who is Bell Harbor Press?"

"Can you get it done in six months? I told them you could.

They're an elite Boston publisher with a few bestsellers on their roster. Welcome to your lucky day, Heath."

"I don't know what to say."

"Say yes and you'll buy me lunch when you get here. We can discuss the details."

"Okay, yes. Nate, thanks, man."

Heath checked to see if any lights glowed from the studio. When he saw the yellow square above the garage, he checked on TL, then darted out the door, across the yard, and up the studio steps, two at a time.

In the pre-dawn light, Elle walked across the wet morning grass toward Heath, who waited by the van with Tracey-Love. The little girl was dressed in pink with her hair combed into a funky Pebbles Flintstone sprout.

Heath wore a crisp, clean oxford shirt, giving the term *road trip* a new level of class. His eyes followed her.

What do you see, Heath?

Last night, Heath had been so excited about his book deal. But she'd slept restlessly, struggling to find ground for her emotions. In the darkness, she'd talked to Jesus, "He's just a friend, right? A really good friend. I mean, how could he be more? I just broke it off with Jer; he just closed the final door on his life with Ava. I can't go giving my heart to a man moving away. It's crazy. Besides, I have no idea how he truly feels, and . . ."

When she couldn't take the head-heart debate any longer, she snatched her iPod Shuffle from the clutter on her dresser, plugged her ears with a Justin Rizzo play list, and drowned out the voice in her head with his.

"All packed and ready?" she called, very cheery, not at all a reflection of her heart.

"Looks like it."

Elle lowered down to Tracey-Love's eye level. "I'm going to miss you."

The little girl's lip quivered. Her blue eyes swam. "I don't want to go to New York." Tracey-Love flung herself against Elle. "Who's going to fix my hair?"

"Oh, baby . . ." Elle bit her lip to keep from laughing. During her brief St. Helena stay, Tracey-Love had blossomed from little girl to big girl. "TL, you'll have your nanny, Junie, and teachers. And one day your daddy will figure out how to make a ponytail. Maybe. If not, you'll be in junior high and fix your own hair."

Heath shot her a look. "Did you just insult me?"

"Yes."

"But I don't want him, I want you." Tracey-Love tightened her grip.

Elle buried her face in TL's sweet fragrance, her eyes filling.

Heath knelt next to them. "Tracey-Love, we talked about this, remember? Mr. Rock needs Daddy for a little while."

But she simply cried, limp against Elle.

"Shh, Tracey-Love, it's going to be all right. We'll talk on the phone and computer, see each other in Daddy's camera."

"And we'll come back as soon as we can." Heath's eyes met Elle's.

"Spring is a long time away."

"Yeah, I know." Heath shook his head. "I thought about Christmas, but in the excitement of actually selling my first book, I didn't consider the time commitment. I'm going to be writing nights, weekends, and holidays for a while."

"When you're weary and frustrated, remember I'm praying for you."

"C-can y-you can come to New York and visit me?" Tracey-Love cheered up, wiping her wet checks with her hand.

"Maybe, yeah. Sounds like fun." *If your daddy asks.*

Heath stared at her. "Maybe?"

"Yeah, maybe."

He smiled. "I like the sound of maybe. Okay, TL, we have got to get this show on the road."

"Be good for Daddy. I'll talk to you on the phone soon." Elle gave Tracey-Love a kiss and squeeze before Heath buckled her into her seat and slid the door shut.

Heath faced her, saying nothing for a few moments. "I don't want to say good-bye."

"Then don't." She hunched up her shoulders, shivering though she wasn't cold.

"What are you saying?"

Elle kicked the toe of her shoe against the grass. "I don't know. I'm going to miss you. A lot."

"I'm in love with you, Elle." The confession exploded, blowing open all the unspoken emotion.

"I might—maybe—be in love with you. I couldn't sleep thinking about it."

Then he was kissing her, warm and heart meltingly, drawing her to him. When he lifted his head, she pressed her face to the familiar spot of his chest. "Now what, counselor?"

Heath covered her back with his arms and kissed her forehead. "I don't know. This wasn't my planned good-bye speech."

"Is this crazy?"

"A little." Heath kissed her again, holding her face in his hands. "Elle, love was the last thing on my mind when I came here. All I wanted was to get beyond grief. Maybe write a book. Get to know my daughter."

"I never, ever thought we'd be standing here like this. I'm supposed to be married, living in Dallas."

"No, Elle, you're supposed to be with me."

Tracey-Love knocked on the window with a muffled, "Daddy, let's *goooo*."

"Now she's ready." Heath opened the sliding door. "Just a second, Daddy's talking to Miss Elle."

Heath led her around to the driver's side, fell against the door, and pulled her to him. "The lawyer part of me says be practical, take time apart, be sure of your feelings. The man part of me says find Pastor O'Neal and gather the family."

Elle brushed her lips against his. "I think I knew the night Jeremiah came back."

"I knew the moment I walked into the cottage with a sick Tracey-Love. You faced me down with that bat and a steely green gaze." He breathed in another kiss. "Elle, you are the whole package for me. Two days of knowing you and I was envious of Jeremiah. I don't know what the future holds for us, but want to try?"

Little doubts creep in at the oddest times.

"Every part of me is screaming yes, except that small voice that tells me it won't work." Elle adjusted his collar and ran her hand down the even row of his shirt buttons.

"Tell that little voice to shut up and listen to me."

"Shut up and listen to Heath."

Her Minnie Mouse impression made him laugh. He hugged her, kissing her cheek. "Let's take it one phone call, one e-mail, one day at a time."

Elle looked up at him. "But I'm quite sure I'm in love with you, McCord."

"I'm positive I'm in love with you, Garvey."

To: Elle Garvey
From: CSOneal
Subject: Re: Love?

Love? Really? With your tenant? Elle, girl, love finds us when we least expect it. Look at Mitch and me. Don't worry about long distance. It can actually be a benefit if you're both committed. I'm happy for you. Are you happy? What's the status?

Got to run. So many last-minute details to tie up before I leave. More later.

Love, Caroline

OCTOBER

Sitting in an empty chair at Julianne's salon on a lazy morning, Elle winced as her sister prepared to read Ruby's *ArtNews* review of her work. Her bracelets gathered at her elbow as she held her hands lightly over her ears.

Julianne spread the magazine on her lap, looked at Elle, then began to read.

Wild Heart Gallery
Beaufort, South Carolina

Lowcountry artist Elle Garvey previewed six paintings during the Summer ArtWalk at Darcy Campbell's Wild Heart Gallery.

Lush paintings from Girls in the Grass *to* The Memory Book, *Garvey's oils on canvas are sentimental and thought provoking. Her style, an attempt at Childe Hassam impressionism, does not come up to par, yet her images capture the viewer without letting go.*

Garvey's work possesses a spiritual depth rarely seen in today's artists. There's a message of peace and hope. In a world searching for answers, longing for comfort, Garvey's work comforts without words.

She is a fresh voice on the art scene and I welcome her.

—Ruby Barnett

Julianne sighed. "'And I welcome her,'" she repeated. "Elle, your first review is fantastic."

Elle reached for the magazine. *Fresh voice. Spiritual depth.* Only in God could one do the impossible. Caroline had proved it first.

"You're going to be famous," Lacy said, cracking her gum, reaching for a broom to sweep over the floor.

"Hardly." But Elle sat for a minute in Lacy's confidence, rereading the review, thinking she'd buy a dozen or so *ArtNews* copies in case this was her first and last great write-up.

"Well, do you want me to do your hair or keep reading about yourself?" Julianne spun Elle's chair toward the mirror.

"Let me enjoy my success. It could be my last."

She read the review again, dissecting each sentence. What did Ruby really mean? Did it sound as good the third or fourth time through?

When her cell went off in her handbag, Julianne tossed it to her. "Let me know when you're ready for your hair, your highness."

The caller ID said Heath. "Hey."

"I just read *ArtNews.*"

Elle smoothed her hand over her review. "What? Counselor, you don't have time to fool with art magazines. Aren't you working on a big case?"

"The guy at the newsstand called me so I ran down to get one. Are you beaming?"

"What, no, come on, I knew all this. *Pbbfff.* I don't need Ruby Barnett to confirm my great talent. Heath, I tell you, my phone's been ringing off the hook."

"My BS meter is pegging."

Elle laughed. "Okay, yes, I'm beaming."

"I'm proud of you." His exhale tingled in her ear. "I hung *Coffin Creek Under Fog.* It's getting rave reviews from the associates."

Julianne passed by making kissy noises. Sure, get a little freedom from shame, gain a little confidence, and turn annoying. Elle shushed her.

"The cottage still smells like you, but you're not there."

"Smells like me? Elle, clean the place, break out the Lysol."

"Then I'll lose the last of you. If you can't be here in person, at least let me keep your fragrance as long as it lingers."

Julianne shoved Elle out of the chair. She had another customer. Elle sat under a dryer. "How's the book?"

"Slow but sure. I got brave and e-mailed you the first half this morning. No pressure, Elle. Read it if you want."

"Finally. I'll love it, Heath, I know I will."

"Elle, something else. I know we wanted to see each other at Christmas, but I took on a tough case. It's consuming my days and creeping into my nights. I'm going to need the holiday downtime to write."

Elle flipped the pages of the magazine with her fingers. "Oh, okay. I understand. Maybe I can fly up . . . sometime. I mean, if you want—"

"Want? If you only knew, Elle. But I have no free time to spend with you. I'm barely getting home to read to Tracey-Love and tuck her in."

"How are we supposed to move forward if we are never together? If you're changing your mind, Heath, just say so."

"My mind has not changed. This is a calendar issue, Elle. Be patient. Let me work this out."

"Then I have to tell you, this feels all too familiar, Heath. Jeremiah did the same thing to me."

"I am not Jeremiah."

"I won't let it be done to me again." Elle caught her reflection in the salon mirror.

"Can we talk about this later? I'm due in court."

"Just think about it, Heath. Maybe we're not meant to be. We just got caught up in the leaving. Perhaps neither one of us wants to be the first to say good-bye."

Nothing for a long moment. Then a weighty sigh. Elle pictured him standing at his desk, pressing his fingers to his brow. "How'd we go from 'I'm sure I love you' to a seventies R&B song?"

"We've had a month to think, pray, get into our own routines."

"Are you telling me you want out?

"No, but I'm trying to figure out where this relationship is going."

"Fine, then can we do this tonight?"

She sat up, shoulders back. "Yes. Have a good day in court."

"Yeah, okay. 'Bye."

Elle pressed End, staring at the review, the melody and lyrics of Gladys Knight streaming across her heart.

Thirty

Elle prayed alone in the chapel this morning, keeping vigil in Miss Anna's spot by the altar. Her mentor had missed prayer yesterday, but when Elle called to check on her, she insisted she was fine.

"My bones wanted to sleep in, is all. I'll be along tomorrow. I feel the Lord stirring in me."

Elle peered at the door. She might come late. There was time.

Meanwhile, focusing was hard for Elle this morning. Her thoughts wandered from the painting she was working on for Danny to the resonance of Heath's voice as they talked last night.

Maybe we do need to step back, reevaluate our relationship.

She'd cried herself to sleep. While they set nothing definite, Elle suspected Heath caved to her doubts. *God, I'm a saboteur. Why do I keep doing this?*

Because he was in New York and she was here? If the ache in her heart was any indication, she loved him more today than yesterday.

Lord, keep me from myself. I give my heart, Heath, our relationship, all my fears to You. Increase in me so I can decrease.

The chapel doors creaked. Elle rose up on her knees. "Miss Anna?"

"Morning, Elle."

"Good morning, Pastor O'Neal."

He sat on the front row pew and patted the bench next to him. "Join me."

"Is everything okay?"

"We got our first fall chill this morning." Pastor O'Neal puffed on his cupped hands.

"It was hard to get up. I slapped the snooze one too many times. Had to leave the cottage without a shower."

He chuckled. "The chapel used to have a fireplace, over there by the communion table. But when the place almost caught fire, the board closed it off."

"I have a feeling you didn't come here to reminisce about fireplaces. Is Mitch all right? Caroline?"

"They're fine. Still planning to be here for Christmas." He shifted, clearing his voice. "Guess there's no easy way to say this . . . Miss Anna died in her sleep, Elle."

No. Impossible. Tiny blips of electricity prickled over her skin. "Pastor O'Neal, no. I just spoke with her."

"Her sister found her peacefully lying in bed, smiling." His eyes shone as he stared ahead.

"Jesus Himself probably came for her," Elle whispered.

"Would she have it any other way?"

"Would He?" Tears slipped along the crevices of her cheek. Slipping her fingers in her hip pockets, she stood at the altar. "What will I do without her?"

Pastor O'Neal joined her, handing her a white note. "Anna gave me this for you about two months ago, instructing me not to give it to you until the right time. Said I'd know when."

Elle brushed her wet cheeks with the back of her hand and took the note.

"I'd like you to speak at her memorial."

"I'd be honored." A tear dripped from her chin.

Pastor O'Neal wrapped his arm around Elle's shoulder in a fatherly fashion, then lifted his hand to the Lord. His sweet baritone offered a sacrifice to God. "It is well . . . with my soul."

Elle's knees betrayed her. She slipped to the floor, weeping.

Yes, it is well. But, oh, Miss Anna. I have so much I want to talk to you about.

Eli O'Neal's song ended, but it drifted over them, echoing between the dark beams.

Elle cried, face first in the carpet, piling tissues beside her head. When her grief eased, she sat up and examined the note in her hand.

In her shaky handwriting, Miss Anna had written "For Elle." The blue ink from her pen smudged on the beginning of each letter. She unfolded the page.

"Carry on."

Elle smiled though fresh tears fell, and a small white feather landed on the note, slid to the edge, and dropped into Elle's lap.

To: Heath McCord
From: Elle Garvey
Subject: Miss Anna

Hey,

Pastor O'Neal visited me at the chapel this morning. Miss Anna died. How will I walk in her large, humble shoes, Heath? She spent forty years before the Lord. Forty. Doesn't it make life seem so simple? Like the Westminster catechism. "Glorify God and enjoy Him forever."

She left me a simple note that tapped deep emotions. "Carry on." I saw another feather. I cried most of the day but am getting under control. Am going to Daddy and Mama's tonight. Julianne's wedding is two weeks away.

Heath, all this has made me realize I'm worried too much about my life, about being in control. Yeah, I pretend to be surrendered, but I'm not. I'm sorry for my attitude the other day. Sorry for pushing, sorry for comparing you to Jeremiah. It's not fair and I know it. Please forgive me.

I gave my heart and fears, you, and our relationship to the Lord for the thousandth time. And I'll do it again until I get it right.

I love you. I do. No strings, no conditions, just you and me.

Kiss Tracey-Love for me. Maybe she can call me on Skype this weekend.

Hope you're not letting the law overshadow writing. Please, don't. I've been reading the book. I love it. I see a bit of myself in Kelly. Hmmm. I'm crushing on Chet, and am fascinated by the history.

You're a beautiful writer, Heath. I've never even seen the Aleutians, but I felt Chet's journey.

Talk soon.
Yours, Elle

To: Elle Garvey
From: Heath McCord
Subject: Re: Miss Anna

Elle, I'm so sorry to hear about Miss Anna. My heart is grieving. I wish I were there with you. I'll call you later tonight. Book is coming along. Finished chapter twenty. Your input helped a lot—especially with Kelly's character. You have an artist's eye, Elle, beyond painting . . .

There is a lot of you in Kelly. You were my muse.

I'm sorry too, Elle. We're both learning to be in a relationship all over again. Well, I am. Ava was more devoted to her career than me at times, so staying late, giving up personal time was okay with her. I understand it's not with you. Frankly, it's not with me either.

I miss you. More than you know. I've played the Gladys Knights and the Pips CD so much TL is singing, "Neither one of us wants to be the first to say . . . Ooo" (She adds the "ooo." Gets me laughing.)

Ah, I hear Rock coming down the hall.

I love you, Heath

DECEMBER

Staring out his twentieth-floor window, Heath watched snow fall from gray-bottomed clouds toward Lexington Avenue where miniscule people, all dressed in black, scurried from corner to corner, shop to shop.

Four more months of this gray and black Manhattan landscape, and he might be certifiable. The weather icon on his desktop told him Beaufort was fifty-two under a hazy blue sky.

"Bored? With your caseload?"

Rock's voice turned him from the window. "Thinking." Heath half smiled at his half truth. He was thinking, but not of his caseload.

He missed the lowcountry; he missed the scent of the marsh and spending his afternoons with Tracey-Love. He missed his mornings with Chet and Kelly. He missed stepping out to the screened porch with a cup of coffee and gazing toward Elle's yellow studio window. In those moments, just the knowledge of her straightened his crooked, broken lines.

Rock sat in the club chair that had once reminded Heath of Ava but now reminded him of a life to which he no longer felt connected.

"When I was a young associate at Bernstein and Barrows," Rock spoke with intent, measuring each word, "old man Bernstein would walk through the associates' office, listening, stopping to address a case, asking us details about our assignments. He asked us what we knew about the senior partners, what we knew about each other."

Heath listened. Rock had never told him this story before.

"I kept my eye out for him because I didn't like being surprised. If I looked up from my files and he stood there, I wanted to at least be ready."

"What was his purpose?"

"Find out which associates had the chops to make it. Who could remember details. Who paid attention to people."

"Are you trying to tell me something? Am I slipping?"

"Yes. Your spark is gone, Heath. It's not just Ava's death anymore. You don't want to be here."

Heath exhaled, rocking his chair from side to side, hating the sensation of letting Rock down. "It's only been a few months."

Rock leaned forward, pressing his palms together. "You're no good to me, Heath, if your heart's not in it."

He picked up the pen Ava had given him when he'd passed the bar. "The transition hasn't been easy."

The older man laughed. "Yeah, and the artist isn't helping. Nor the book deal."

"By the new year, I'll be settled into my old routine." He had to be if he wanted Elle to be in his life. Finding time for her had become a priority.

Rock walked to the door, pausing with his hand on the knob. "The talking heads are predicting a foot of snow. If you hurry, you might make a flight to Charleston before the airports shut down. I hear the South is lovely at Christmastime."

Heath eyed him. "What are you saying?"

"Heath, do you love her?"

He clicked his pen on, then off, on, then off. "Yes. I do."

"Then be with her. If there's any good in Ava's death it's that you understand life is fleeting. You have a second chance at love. What are you doing here?"

"Taking it slow."

"Slow? Heath, I know you're trying to be wise, keep your word and loyalty to me, but I really can't stand to see your long face around here anymore. I'll figure out a way to deal with Doc and Tom. Selling out and playing tennis all day looks better all the time. Now, get on the plane or you're fired." Rock pulled the door behind him as he left.

"Nice try, Rock," Heath called after him, looking again at the gray day, pieces of Elle's e-mail floating across his mind. *I love you. I do. No strings, no conditions, just you and me.*

Heath reached for his office phone. "Pam, get me two tickets to Charleston, nonstop. I don't care about the cost."

Then he dialed Junie. "Pack Tracey-Love for a week in South Carolina. Pick her up from school and meet me at JFK. I'll call you with more details.

Snatching his coat from the rack, he thought he'd have enough time to swing by Tiffany's.

Elle sat between Caroline and Jess under the lights of the Frogmore Café, listening to Wild Wally reminisce about Mitch O'Neal's first touchdown pass at Beaufort High's star quarterback. Wild Wally, of course, was his lead blocker.

"I looked around and the defensive end was in my face. Plowed me right into the turf, but not before Mitch threw a perfect spiral to Olinski."

They'd heard the story a gazillion times. And they listened for the gazillionth time. Tradition.

"Mitch." Andy Castleton, the Frogmore's Emmitt Smith-sized owner, leaned over the country singer's shoulder. "Some of the customers wonder if you could sing a song or two. It's not our normal music night, but what do you say?"

His wide smile offered Mitch no option to say no.

"Come on, Mitch," Elle urged. "I'd like to hear some of your new stuff."

He checked with Caroline. "What do you say, babe?"

"Go for it. Your music saved this café over a year ago."

Mitch stepped onto the stage and tapped the mike. "Well, Andy said some of you wanted a song, and since you're the hometown crowd, I'm more than happy to oblige." He strummed and tuned. "Like always, it's good to be back in Beaufort."

Elle sat back, at peace, at home. She'd kept her vigil of prayer and painting, missing Miss Anna. Missing Heath. But content.

"In case some of you didn't know," Mitch said as he perched on the stool, "Caroline did the honor of marrying me over the summer."

A light applause peppered the room. Elle ran her hand over Caroline's shoulders.

"This is a song I wrote for her."

Elle eased down in her chair as Mitch's elegant serenade billowed over the Frogmore, cushioning her soul. But when her backside vibrated, she jerked her bag to her lap and retrieved her phone from the clutter of things she called "what I need to carry around every day."

She had one text message. Tipping the phone toward the stage lights, Elle read the tiny screen. From Heath. She smiled and opened the text.

"Where r u?"

Elle hit Reply. "Fgmr with gang. C and M r here."

What a weird message. Why would he text her on a Friday night? Holding her phone in her lap, Elle propped her chin in her hand and listened to the last of Mitch's song. She was definitely going to get his new album.

Somewhere in the middle of his fourth song, chairs scooched around behind her, people were shifting, and Julianne was whispering too loudly to Jess, who reached around to tap Caroline's shoulder.

Elle slapped the table with her palm. "What are y'all fussing—"

Heath stood at the end of the table, looking like the last minute of a long day with his fading blond hair going every direction, his tie drooping, and his tan herringbone coat skewed across his shoulders. "Hey."

"Hey." Elle rose slowly, her pulse thickening. "What are you doing here?"

"Is there room at this party for one more?"

Julianne jumped up so fast she tripped over Danny. "Yes, please, take my seat. Hey, Heath, welcome."

"Hey, Julianne. Congratulations."

"Thank you."

"I dropped Tracey-Love off at your folks. Rio was still squealing when I left."

"She's been missing her."

"Julianne," Elle said, "did you know about this? Jess?"

"Not at all."

"How would I know anything?"

From the stage, Mitch continued to sing. Heath walked over to her. "Rock fired me. Said I belonged down here with you."

"He didn't."

Heath nodded. "Yeah, he did. And he's right."

She shimmied as a *swoosh* splashed her emotions. All her composure began to leak. "What are you saying?"

He stepped closer. "I love you. I want to be with you. If it's possible, you're the second first-love of my life and I'd be stupid to spend another moment away from you."

Okay. Yeah, that's a good reason to be here. Elle flew into his arms with a burst of tears. "I'll move to New York with you, Heath. Whatever, but I want to be with you."

He kissed her, firm and unyielding. "Marry me." His lips brushed her ears. "Marry us."

Mitch's song ended and his last strum rang out over the café.

Heath went to bended knee. "I spoke to Truman. He says I can have you if I want you."

"Way to sweep a girl off her feet."

The woman at the booth next to the party table leaned into Heath and Elle's private circle. "This is way better than that boy's singing."

Elle cut her a glance. Mrs. Paladino. Figures. Local gossip columnist. "Hush."

With his eyes fixed on Elle, Heath retrieved a blue box from his pocket. "Will you marry me?"

"My stars. Tiffany's," Mrs. Paladino burst out, apparently unclear about the meaning of *hush*. "If you don't marry him, I will."

"Marie," the man at her table protested, "you're married to me."

Mrs. Paladino beat the air in front of him. "Pipe down. Well, girl, are you going to say yes?"

Elle bent down to her knees, wanting to confess her love face to face, eye to eye, heart to heart. "For a summer, you were my friend, my sanity, the one who challenged me to believe when it felt impossible. I am so honored to know you and call you friend. I can't believe I can one day call you husband. Yes, Heath McCord, I'll marry you."

His lips touched hers, soft and tender at first, then hungry and passionate, finding the core of her heart.

Around them, above them, the café erupted with cheers. Mercy Bea shoved in between them, shouting, "Cake, on the house!"

Heath pulled Elle to her feet and whirled her in his arms. Folks congratulated them with shoulder pops and teary hugs.

Mama and Daddy breezed in with Rio and Tracey-Love, followed by a harried-looking Sara Beth and her brood.

"At the risk of my beauty reputation, I herded everyone to the car when Mama called. I did *not* want to miss this."

In the midst of the celebration, the rest of the Garvey Girls arrived as the Frogmore staff passed plates of Andy's fluffy white cake.

Heath never loosened his grip on Elle's hand.

It'd been a long year, but Miss Anna was right: promotion often comes from the wilderness. Elle had learned about herself, about love, and the hope of prayer.

"Elle, where's your cake?" Mercy Bea fussed. "Andy, I need a piece of cake for the bride-to-be."

Elle pressed her hand over her stomach. "I'm not sure I can eat, Mercy Bea."

When the cake arrived, Elle reached for it. One bite would be nice. But the bottle-blonde jerked the plate back.

"What in Sam Hill?" Mercy Bea squinted, pinching free a perfect white feather. "Good grief. Elle, don't worry, I'll get you another piece. Giving the bride a feathered slice of cake . . ."

Heath slipped his hand around Elle and squeezed her close. She peered up at him through a blur of tears. God knew. He always knew and in His unique way had blessed Elle with His signature touch. He'd always been with her—now and then—in the moments of darkness, in the times of light, when she doubted and when she believed.

Did she understand true love, soul mates, the perfect one? Not at all. But she understood God was blessing this moment, giving her Heath as a true gift.

"Mercy Bea, please, it's fine." Elle held out her hand. "I want that piece of cake, and the feather."

"What? It's contaminated. You don't know where that feather's been."

Heath laughed, taking the feather between his finger and thumb. "Yeah, actually, we do."

Acknowledgments

Scripture tells me to owe no one anything except a debt of love. Often during the journey of writing a book, I forget to pay, though I'm indebted to many. This is my feeble attempt to thank them.

Jesus, the God-man—real, eternal, everlasting, full of love and mercy. I'm undone to think that I know and love You because You first loved me. My debt of love to You can never be paid, but daily I give You my heart. I am Yours; You are mine.

My husband, who encourages and prays for me and keeps me on the right side of the yellow line. I absolutely could not do this without you. Joyfully I pay my debt of love to you. You are an amazing, true-blue, godly man.

Susie Warren, friend of my heart, brainstorming machine, fiction queen, and my sanity check. Thank you for being on the other side of the phone so many times while writing this book and for cheering with me in the good times. Your friendship is an incredible gift and blessing.

Christine Lynxwiler, for a really fun Sunday-after-conference of brainstorming, and for your friendship and constant encouragement.

My family. I'm so glad to be your daughter (in-law) and sister, niece, and cousin.

My friend Chelle, for praying, listening, and asking, "How's it going?"

The fabulous team at Thomas Nelson, for giving me a chance to live my dream. Y'all are the rock stars. Thanks for sharing your stage.

Rachel Hauck

Ami McConnell, editor extraordinaire. Thank you for believing in me, for your insight into this manuscript, and for encouraging me with words that still linger in my heart.

Leslie Peterson, another editor extraordinaire. Thank you to the power of ten for your time, insight, and ability to say, "Well done. Now, here's what you need to fix."

Karen Solemn, for your insight and encouragement, and for leading the way.

Katie Sulkowski, for becoming a fast friend and for challenging me to look and see farther down the road.

To the artists who shared their experiences: John Houghton, Elizabeth Brandon, Deana Bowdish of The Gallery in Beaufort. And Brett Stebbins, who put a brush in my hand.

My father-in-law, John Hauck, for "standing on the wall" in the Aleutians during WWII so we can be free. I will not forget your sacrifice. I love you.

Reading Group Guide

1. In the first chapter, we see Elle's love for art. Have you or someone you know ever pursued a career, relationship, or ministry because you felt your real desire was unobtainable?

2. Elle flies to Dallas to look for a house, but she and Jeremiah cannot agree on anything. Think of a time when you adamantly disagreed with someone. How did you resolve it?

3. Heath McCord moves to the lowcountry to heal and get to know his daughter. Was there a time in your life where a geographic change helped you move on emotionally?

4. Elle learns in a very bizarre way that she's not getting married. Discuss a time when you learned of bad news in a less than ideal way. What was your response?

5. When Heath first meets Elle, how does he react? What is happening in his heart? What is your response as an observer of the scene?

6. Elle hides in her studio for a month after Jeremiah breaks up with her. We all respond differently to pain. Discuss healthy and unhealthy ways to deal with grief.

7. Miss Anna is a composite of our grandmothers. What is unique about her? Could you do what she did for forty years?

8. In this life, Miss Anna didn't live out many of her dreams. But she had a revelation. What was it? How did this revelation buy her more in eternity than anything she could've achieved in this life?

When a Southern waitress inherits a
Lowcountry café, she suddenly has to balance
more than just her next food order.

An Excerpt from

Sweet Caroline

```
┌─────────────────────────────────────────────────┐
│                                                 │
│   Welcome to the Frogmore Café                  │
│   Home of Bubba's Buttery Biscuits              │
│                                                 │
│      Open: Mon–Thurs 6 a.m.–4 p.m.              │
│          Fri–Sat 6 a.m.–9 p.m.                  │
│             Closed Sunday                        │
│                                                 │
│          Jones Q. McDermott,                     │
│          Proprietor since 1957                   │
│                                                 │
└─────────────────────────────────────────────────┘
```

1

June 4
Beaufort, South Carolina

The sun rises in a pinkish-blue spring sky over the
Beaufort River as I exit the old drawbridge and turn left onto Bay Street.
My rusty red '68 Mustang jerks and shimmies, threatening to quit on
me—again—while from the radio, Tim McGraw sings when the stars
go blue.

The old girl's carburetor sputters and chokes. Mimicking Dad, I
bang the dash. "Don't die on me, Matilda. I'm late for work." I mash the
clutch and gun the gas, desperate to keep her alive. Matilda rattles and
clanks in defiance.

Last month, while waiting for the drawbridge to swing closed, Matilda
shot a plume of black smoke out her tailpipe and stalled with a *kerplunk*.
What followed was a lot of car-horn swearing, then being pushed across the
bridge by angry drivers who'd as soon shoot me as help me.

The car is giving me a rep.

But today I make it over the bridge in spite of Matilda's rattle trapping. Paul Mulroney of Mulroney's Bistro glances up from sweeping his walk as I rumble down Bay Street. He shakes his head, shouting something I can't quite make out. I smile and wave, doing my part to enhance community relations.

At seven thirty in the a.m., downtown Beaufort wakes up with a slow, sleepy feel. By midday, the streets will flow with tourists and tanned retirees looking to buy a slice of lowcountry life. If only people would make their way down to Jones McDermott's—may he rest in peace—little Frogmore Café on the corner of Bay and Harrington.

"A town treasure," the *Beaufort Gazette* called the Café in a story about Jones the day after his funeral. More like *forgotten* treasure. If it wasn't for the regulars—most of them senior citizens over sixty—the Café would be *sunken* treasure.

Making the light at Church Street, I swerve into the Café's gravel-and-crushed-shell parking lot. Stopping in the shade of a thick, ancient live oak, the Mustang's motor chokes and, at last, dies. "Ho, boy." When I try to restart, the engine refuses to fire.

"Fine, swell, great. Be that way."

Anointing the moment with a few soap-worthy words, I fish my cell phone from the bottom of my backpack and autodial Dad. While it rings on his end, I study the back of the Café. The paint is faded and peeling from a thousand afternoons of baking in the hot South Carolina sun. One side of the porch leans and slopes.

Since Jones's sudden death from a heart attack a few weeks ago, I've been managing the place with the rest of the crew—Andy, Mercy Bea, and Russell—trying to make a go of things. Business is slow. Money is almost nonexistent. Unfortunately, the heyday of the Frogmore Café echoes in the Valley of Time alongside beehive hairdos and eight-track cassettes.

Daddy's phone rings for the third time. *Come on, pick up.*

Rachel Hauck

Mercy Bea Hart, the Café's senior waitress, steps through the kitchen door, lighting a cigarette, indicating to me with a jab at her watchless wrist that I'm late.

Thirty-some years ago, Mercy Bea had her fifteen minutes of fame when she won a Jayne Mansfield look-alike contest. Got her picture in a Hollywood magazine and appeared on *The Mike Douglas Show*. Ever since, she's maintained her once-won image—dyed-blonde bombshell hair, curvy figure with just the right amount of cleavage, red lips, and long, lacquered fingernails.

"Yeah, Caroline, what's up?" Dad's crisp question is accompanied by the grind of heavy equipment.

"Matilda."

"Again? Caroline, it may just be time to get rid of that thing."

We've had this conversation. "Can you tow it to CARS? Please?" I glance at my watch. Seven thirty-five. While I take care of the Café books, I also wait tables, and my regulars arrive at 8:02.

"Where are you?" Dad asks.

"The Café parking lot." Hitching my backpack higher on my shoulder, I lean against the car door. The morning is muggy but breezy, fragrant with the sour scent of the dark, soft pluff mud of the river marsh.

"At least you made it to work this time." A chuckle softens his tone. *Kudos for Matilda.* "See, she isn't all bad."

"Keep telling yourself that, Caroline. I'll be along after this job. I'm down in Bluffton, and we're having trouble with the equipment."

"Thank you a thousand times over, Daddy."

"You're welcome a thousand times over."

Pressing End, I stuff my phone into the front pocket of my backpack and head for the Café's kitchen door. Mercy Bea snuffs out her cigarette in a stained-glass ashtray. "You're late."

"What are you, the time-clock gestapo? I was caught in bridge traffic."

"Can't be running in here late, Caroline." She settles the ashtray on the windowsill and follows me inside. "And you best get rid of that broken-down heap. Half the town's push-started you. Growing tired of it."

"How lucky I am to live in such a warm, friendly place. How's business this morning?" In the office, just off the kitchen, I flip on the light and unzip my backpack.

"Slow. I cleaned the bathrooms for you." Mercy Bea leans her shoulder against the doorjamb and picks at her brilliant-red fingernails. "Land sakes, I've got to get my nails done."

"You cleaned the bathrooms? For me." Tying on my apron, I gaze over at her.

"Don't act all surprised." She pops and cracks her gum. "You covered for me a few times when my young-sons got into trouble." Mercy Bea is a single mom of two teen boys she affectionately refers to as "young-sons."

"So . . . anything new from Jones's lawyer?"

Aha. This is why she cleaned the bathrooms—to butter me up for information. Not that I'm keeping secrets. "Not since he called last Wednesday. He's still tied up with an estate case in Charleston. Said he'd be down as soon as he was free."

"Well, you let me know if you hear from him, now."

"Don't I always?"

Even though I'm not the senior Café employee, Jones's lawyer, Kirk Harris, deals directly with me. My guess is because I've been handling the business side of the Café for two years. It's the reason Jones hired me.

"I could use your help around here, Caroline. Someone to teach the Café ropes," Jones said to me one afternoon when I stopped by for some Frogmore Stew.

Learning the Café ropes wasn't high on my list of life goals, but between Jones's aged puppy-dog eyes and a mental picture of my Granddaddy Sweeney looking down from heaven, whispering, "Be sweet, Caroline; help out my old friend," I couldn't say no.

Jones started me out waiting tables, then added on bookkeeping and ordering. Turns out everyone at the Frogmore Café wears multiple hats. Though I'm not allowed to cook. All on account of almost burning down Beaufort High when I took home ec. But that's another story.

Exchanging my flip-flops for my black work clogs, I glance at Mercy Bea. "So, how'd your date with Ralph Carter go last night?"

Mercy Bea responds with a Cruella Devill cackle. "Oh, dear girl. He was a loser with a capital L-O-O-S-E-R."

"You mean L-O-S-E-R."

"That's what I said."

"You added an extra *O*."

"Caroline, I can spell *loser*." Her exhale is edgy. "I've certainly acquainted myself with enough of them."

Whatever. "So, all your great hair dye and makeup went to waste?" I retrieve my pen and order pad from the desk, then stuff my backpack into the bottom drawer.

"On him, yes. Though I looked pretty darn hot, if I say so myself."

"Miss Mansfield would be proud."

"I had a little bit of a flirt with a Marine pilot when L-O-S-E-R went to the toilet. Turns out he was married. But"—she jabs the air with her finger—"in my defense, he wasn't wearing a ring, and the wife was outside on her phone."

I snap my fingers. "Those darn non-wedding-ring-wearing pilots."

Mercy Bea whirls away from me with a huff, stopping long enough to point at the clock. "Hurry on out. The breakfast-club boys will be along soon."

I return to the kitchen. "Morning, Andy." The exhaust fans over the oven compete with the soulful sounds coming from the mini boom box on top of the reach-in. All I can hear is the bass line. "What's today's special?" The Emmitt Smith–sized cook looks up from pulling a couple of green peppers from the lowboy. "Barbeque chicken with choice of three vegetable sides—greens, corn, fried okra, corn on the cob, fried tomatoes, peas, or mashed potatoes. Bubba's Buttery Biscuits, of course, and a drink. Choice of dessert. Pluff Mud Pie or vanilla layer cake."

"I ordered more produce and shrimp Friday. Should come today."

"What'd they say over at Fresh Earth Produce?" Andy chops peppers for one of the breakfast-club boys' country omelet. "Rice Dooley is wanting money, I bet."

"Well, he doesn't consider us a charity." I snatch a hot, fresh biscuit from a baking sheet. Steam rises from the fluffy white middle when I pull it apart.

Rice: *"We need some sort of payment, Caroline. Look, I know Jones didn't leave y'all in good shape, but can we see something?"*

Me: *"I understand, Mr. Dooley. I'll get a payment to you this week. But we need corn and shrimp or the Frogmore Café is without Frogmore Stew."*

"I know you're doing all you can to juggle things, Caroline." Andy whacks an onion in two.

The soft bite of my biscuit melts in my mouth. "Unfortunately, there's more debt to juggle than credit."

In the aftermath of kind and compassionate Jones McDermott's death, I discovered a hard truth: he was a horrible businessman. As a result, I've learned how to tap dance around due dates, how to stretch imaginary dollars.

"Any word from the lawyer?" Andy asks, turning to the stove, pouring eggs into a hot skillet.

I'm going to write "Nope" across my forehead and point to it when people ask, "Any word from the lawyer?"

"Nothing new."

"Are you thinking what I'm thinking?" Andy leans over the prep table toward me. "Mercy Bea is hoping Jones left the place to her?" He grabs a handful of diced veggies and sprinkles them on the cooking eggs.

"Why would she want this place?" I gesture to the dingy white kitchen walls and cheap linoleum floor. "It's a money pit, in need of some serious loving. The old girl needs an owner with deep, generous pockets."

"Mercy Bea or the Café?"

Brushing biscuit crumbs from the corner of my lips, I laugh softly and head for the dining room. "You're bad, Andy."

A guttural *um-um-um* vibrates from the cook's immense chest. "This money pit is putting food on my table, paying the bills. Gloria's been out of work for over a month now on account of her back. I need this job. I'm believing God has a plan."

The cook's confidence makes me pause at the kitchen door. "If there is such a thing as an all-knowing, all-seeing All Mighty, He *might* have a plan for the Café. But Jones? I'm not so sure."

Andy's large shoulders roll as he laughs. "Guess you're right about Jones. Yes sirree. But the wife and I are praying, Caroline."

"You do that. I'll wish upon a star."

"All my songs tell a story. But this one is special. It's about looking backward while moving forward. About chasing dreams. Endless country roads, and tender faith."

—Mutli-Platinum Recording Artist Sara Evans

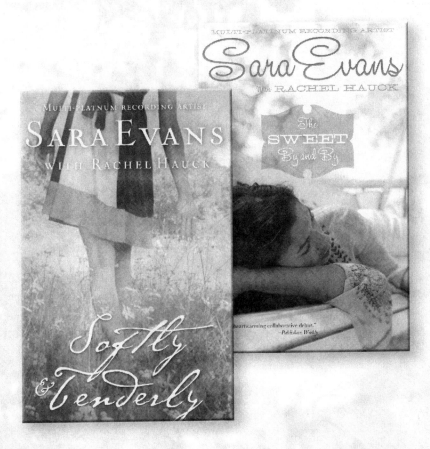

The Songbird Novels: An enchanting series of grace, redemption, and love by Sara Evans with Rachel Hauck.

About the Author

RITA-finalist Rachel Hauck lives in Florida with her husband, Tony. She is the author of *Dining with Joy*; *Sweet Caroline*; *Love Starts with Elle*; and *The Sweet By and By*, co-authored with Sara Evans.

CPSIA information can be obtained
at www.ICGtesting.com
Printed in the USA
LVOW07s1920231216
518607LV00004B/31/P